The Seer and the Scribe

Spear of Destiny

A Medieval Murder Mystery

G.M. Dyrek

LUMINIS BOOKS
Published by Luminis Books
1950 East Greyhound Pass, #18, PMB 280,
Carmel, Indiana, 46033, U.S.A.

Cover art design and interior illustrations for *Spear of Destiny* by G.M. Dyrek.
Cover art direction by G.M. Dyrek and Elynn Cohen.
Medieval border adapted from engraving by Master I. A. M. of Zwolle, The Netherlands, 1480-1490, entitled "Allegory of the Transience of Life."

ISBN-10: 1-935462-39-3

ISBN-13: 978-1-935462-39-2

Printed in the United States of America

10 9 8 7 6 5 4 3 2

To Jeff and David,
my encouragers, and to
Hildegard and Volmar, their
tremendous accomplishments,
my inspiration.

Acknowledgments

I'd like to credit all my brilliant teachers who have influenced me over the past years with their finely crafted murder mysteries: Agatha Christie, Sir Arthur Conan Doyle, P.D. James, Umberto Eco, Ken Follett, Ellis Peters, Peter Tremayne, Laurie R. King, Ariana Franklin, to name a few of my favorites. Reading murder mysteries has always been a secret indulgence of mine and like any artistic apprentice, I've learned so much from these talented authors and owe them all an enormous debt of gratitude. On a similar note, I'd like to thank those authors that have taught me about the 12th century and Hildegard's life and works, namely the works of Barbara Newman, Sabina Flanagan, Barbara Lachman, Anna Silvas, Priscilla Throop, Dr. Wighard Strehlow, Dr. Gottfried Hertzka, and Matthew Fox. It has been their meticulous research and translations which have fueled and enlightened my own research. We truly stand on the shoulders of giants.

On a more personal note, I'd like to express my deepest heartfelt appreciation to my son David, who from infancy on has shaped my passion for storytelling and has always been my most enthusiastic supporter. As my first critic on the earlier drafts, his insightful comments strengthened the story considerably. I also owe a special thanks to my niece, Melissa McIntosh, whose image appears on the cover as Hildegard and my son David who posed as Volmar for both the cover and the inside illustrations. I will always be indebted to my husband Jeff, who has endured with such loving patience the temperament of a dreamer and optimist, while tirelessly editing my works over the years.

None of this, however, would have been possible without the kind support, advice, and encouragement of my editor and publisher at Luminis Books, Chris Katsaropoulos, and the market director and president, Tracy Richardson.

STAUDERNHEIM
SPONHEIM
VINEYARDS
NAHE RIVER
YEW TREE
MONASTERY OF
DISIBODENBERG
ENTRANCE TO
OSSARIUM
GLAN RIVER
LODGE
BERMERSHEIM

Surrounding Region of Disibodenberg

ALSENZ RIVER

MAUSETURM

BINGEN

RHINE RIVER

CITY OF MAINZ

LEPER'S COLONY

SAINT JAMES MONASTERY

SAINT MARTIN'S CATHEDRAL

GMD

ADVANCE PRAISE FOR
THE SEER AND THE SCRIBE:

"The author strews her tale with generous measures of intrigue, sudden violence, poison, evidence to decipher, secrets waiting to be revealed, specters either holy (in Hildegard's case) or otherwise, and figures and incidents drawn from history . . . A study kickoff with a distinctly different duo of detectives."
—*Kirkus Reviews*

"Move over Brother Cadfael—there's a new sleuth in town, younger and just as smart. Throw in a medieval mystic who sees visions and talks to dead people, a couple of murders, a villain worthy of Darth Vader, lots of well-placed sensory details, and interesting secondary characters and *The Seer and the Scribe: Spear of Destiny* is a perfect book to launch a series."
—Brenda Rickman Vantrease, *New York Times* bestselling author of *The Illuminator* and *The Heretic's Wife*

"Dyrek draws readers into the world of medieval monastic life with a keen knowledge of the era and an eye for compelling characters. Opening the book will feel like stepping back into a long ago world of mystery, murder, and faith."
—A. LaFaye, Scott O'Dell Award-winning author of *Worth*

The Seer and the Scribe

Spear of Destiny

A Medieval Murder Mystery

The Monastery of Disibodenberg
Paulus' Herbal Gardens
Infirmary & Guest's Quarters
Well
Monk's Dormitory
Stables
Cloister
Refectory
Kitchen's For The Poor
Church
Anchorage
Saint Mary's Chapel
Winery
Porter's Houses
Monk's Cemetery
Apiary
Saint Michael's Chapel
Vineyards

PREFACE

At the Porter's Gates of Disibodenberg Monastery

27th of November, Thursday, in the Year of Our Lord 1102

"There are no mysteries here, my son, no secrets, and certainly no romance. The brotherhood will be your new family. Through these gates, you will find only peace and quiet." The words were whispered by the venerable lord Abbot Burchard, whose chilled, wraith-like breath wrapped around the trembling boy like a shroud. [1]

There are truths worth knowing; yet, lies sometimes can feel better than truths. Volmar had seen more in his seven years than most, and knew a lie when he heard one. Nowhere on this earth would he find peace to still the inner torment he felt. Why not welcome this lie from the kindly holy stranger who promised him a new family, peace, and a quiet sanctuary away from the pain of his life?

"Please sir, Anya has a fever and needs medicine." Volmar spoke these words with clarity, having at last found his voice, his diction leaving no doubt of his upper-class pedigree. He reached awkwardly for a coin from his finely-tooled leather pouch, still trying to cradle his younger sister's limp, lifeless head.

The Abbot grimaced, knowing the difficulty any child had in facing the finality of death. "Keep your gold coins, son, only the Lord can save Anya. You must let her go, for she is in His care now."

Beyond exhaustion, beyond hunger, Volmar knew he had no fight left in him to resist. He lowered his deep-set, smoldering blue eyes and surrendered. There were no more tears left in him to be shed. Abbot Burchard gently lifted Anya, the last member of Volmar's family, from his arms forever.

---

[1] Shroud: A burial cloth usually made of linen.

Book I: Young Apprentices

Chapter I: Enticements of the Mind

The Stables of Disibodenberg Monastery

10th of March, Wednesday, in the Year of Our Lord 1104

"Take that, you belching beast!" Volmar swung hard, his long thin stick stinging the air, hitting the imaginary dragon directly between the eyes, cutting it in half.

"Volmar!" Brother Hugo, the Keeper of the Stables, yelled out, his stern voice breaking into the boy's daydream with grim vengeance.

"I'm coming," Volmar said, tossing his weapon into the grove of fruit trees and scooping up the pail of water he'd gone to the well to fetch. He raced back down the path from the well, the bucket cradled steadily in his arms so the water wouldn't slosh over the sides.

Dutifully, Volmar went to the trough in the stable and filled it with the cold water. He nodded to the sheep and pigs, acknowledging their bleating and grunts of thanks. He turned the bucket upside down and sat on it, warmed by the heat of the animals. By tending the livestock at the monastery he had learned the languages of the different animals and how to care for them, appreciating their simple, direct voices. People, though, were different, he mused. There was always tension between their spirits and the world, a tension which caused their voices to be discordant and misunderstood. Not so with animals.

"Come over here, son, I want to show you one of life's miracles." Hugo was a morose, uncommunicative monk and spoke to others only on rare occasions. However, towards Volmar he talked continuously. It was as if he held a never-ending conversation with his young apprentice from sunup to sundown, going from one thought to the next with little pause.

"Let me ask you, Volmar . . . Is reflection a vain pursuit?" he queried his young protégé.

Volmar rose from the upturned bucket he had been sitting on, shaking his head automatically in dissent. He knew what was coming next.

"I think not, my boy, for it allows us frail beings an opportunity to forget death and the endless, relentless march of time. It allows us to reflect on what lives on, beyond our years on God's green earth."

Hugo reached into the compost pile with his bare hands and pulled up a fist full of greyish leathery-looking maggots. "Look here, Volmar. There is such complexity in God's design, that these tiny maggots with their sharp little teeth give us the rich soil that puts food on our table and sustains our lives. Here, son, feel life's mystery." Hugo opened Volmar's hand and dropped the crawling black dirt into it.

Volmar cringed, remembering he had mucked out the stalls of the horses only this morning, while they smelled disgustingly of fresh manure. How could he tell his kindly Stable Master that he could not stand it whenever his hands were dirty?

"Ah, breathe it in, son. Don't you just relish the beauty of God's magnificent plan?"

The rusting iron gate swung open and Brother Paulus, the Infirmarian, [2] walked in carrying a small scroll in his large hand.

"Good day, Brother Hugo," Paulus said, greeting the man whose face had suddenly turned upside down into a frown. Brother Paulus's voice was rich and deep, fitting for a man of his gargantuan[3] size.

Volmar, supremely grateful for the diversion Paulus caused, allowed the fistful of maggots to fall through his fingers and wiped his hands quickly against the front of his loose, white wool shirt. The boy noticed with surprise that Hugo was treating this man's visit warily, as a dog would to another dog who invaded his territory.

"I'm working . . . which I see you are not," Hugo said with little humor, forgoing any polite introductions.

"I shall be blunt, Hugo, for I know you prefer it that way." Paulus unrolled the parchment and handed it over to the stable master. "Abbot Burchard has agreed that Volmar becomes my personal apprentice. His writing, reading and understanding skills far surpass any of

---

[2] Infirmarian: The healer or doctor for the monastery.

[3] Gargantuan: Huge, large in size.

the other young boys, and I am in desperate need of a capable young scribe."

Hugo did not immediately answer. He was listening but with only half of his attention. He stared at the parchment and its cryptic lines, which Volmar knew were beyond his ability to interpret. With a grumbling *humph*, Hugo rolled the parchment up dismissively. "The boy has to have a say in his future, Paulus. It's only fitting that he is given the choice. What say you, Volmar? This man wants to take you away from here . . . "

Paulus quickly interrupted, "Only to the Infirmary, my son, where you can learn the healing arts and use the mind God has given you."

Volmar turned from one man to the other, realizing the enormity of this decision.

"Be off with you, Paulus," Hugo demanded, giving back the Infirmarian the parchment of agreement. "The Good Lord above knows this is where the boy belongs." He made no efforts to restrain the triumph in his voice.

Paulus accepted the parchment graciously, and studied the face of Volmar. "Is it your will that I leave?" he asked courteously, "For one so young and talented as you are there will always be conflicting choices." Paulus himself knew the appeal of many interests. He became a healer at the late age of thirty, having spent most of his youth traversing the world as a traveling scholar. Something too, the Infirmarian failed to consider, was Hugo's obvious affections for the boy. As an orphan himself, Paulus knew the power of such attachments. Wrenching one so young from a secure and predictable environment into one that changed daily, even hourly with the demands of the sick, certainly presented the boy a difficult predicament.

"Thank you, sir, for your offer, I am indeed very grateful, but . . ." Here Volmar's usual eloquence failed him. He searched for the words, turning instinctively to Hugo. Volmar's unspoken feelings communicated his desire to Hugo, his desire to leave the stables for the intoxicating prospect of expanding his knowledge with this learned monk.

Hugo's incomprehension over the boy's changed appearance slowly turned into a burning desire to be rid of his young charge. He finished off the boy's thoughts by saying with a growl, "Be off with you both! But I warn you, child, the enticements of the mind will never replace the euphoria of hard work."

Hugo stood stoically to one side and let them by, silencing their apologetic whispers with a glare and a mouth shut tight.

Chapter 2: The Secret Vision

Country Road Leading to the Village of Sponheim

29th of October, Monday, in the Year of Our Lord 1106

Hildegard of Bermersheim tried not to listen to her parents arguing. The opulent carriage lurched to one side and the young girl slid up against its latched door, suddenly feeling the draft of the cool morning seeping through its cracks. She stretched out her hands and closed her eyes, imagining herself as light as a feather and with no strength of her own, being tossed about by the chilled breath of God.

"From the day she was born, we agreed she would be our tithe[4] to the church," Sir Hildebert said, staring straight ahead. "I told you not to get so attached," he added harshly, his square jaw clenched.

Lady Mechtilde of Merxheim's dark eyes flashed with unspoken hostility. "I am her mother. And I remember telling you I would do no such thing!" She wore a wig made from a peasant's hair and, as was her habit, she touched it nervously to make sure it was still in place.

"You have nine other children, woman! Surely you can part with one. Especially one so frail and . . . " he stumbled as if correcting himself, " . . . mystifying." Cautiously, the old knight eyed his youngest daughter sitting across from him as if he wasn't sure if she deserved his pity or his fear. He loosened his collar and, with unacknowledged discomfort, looked away from her. "Besides, the arrangements have been made. She will be well cared for."

"Are you sure?" Hildegard's mother said, the doubt in her voice audible. "I've heard tales about this fourteen-year-old companion of hers, Jutta of Sponheim."

Sir Hildebert gave an exasperated sigh as he knocked his cane against the ceiling, signaling to the driver that he needed to take the

---

[4] Tithe: A tenth of one's salary given for the support of a church.

curves with less enthusiasm. "Please tell me you're not listening to the servants again."

"Sometimes I think they have more sense than we do," she added sullenly, taking the silver filigreed clasp from her silken scarf and pinning it to the cape draped around Hildegard's shoulders.

"I thought I gave that to you on the eve of our wedding," Sir Hildebert muttered.

"You did. I want our child to have something precious from both of us."

Sir Hildebert rolled his eyes and grunted, "Humph . . . sentimentality, a woman's frailty."

"And cold-heartedness, a man's demise," Lady Mechtilde responded with spite, giving him an incensed glare. She shifted her attentions back to Hildegard. "Poor child, her cape will have to do since we will no longer be responsible for keeping her warm."

Lady Mechtilde dabbed a stray tear with her handkerchief and turned to stare out the window. "Hildegard is such a sensitive child. I'm afraid Jutta will simply overpower her. I've heard that she has behaved scandalously ever since her father's death. Imagine turning down so many eligible suitors! There's even gossip that she wants her own anchor-hold[5], a tomb to live and pray in all the rest of her days."

Sir Hildebert absently twisted his family's signet[6] ring on his finger. "Count Meinhard, Jutta's brother, mentioned all this to me. I told you before, Jutta suffered a near fatal illness when she was twelve and promised God that if she lived, she would serve Him as a virgin the rest of her life."

"Well, she seems quite determined to keep her promise. I've heard they are considering converting the old stables at Disibodenberg monastery into an anchor-hold. I do not approve of my child being

---

[5] Anchor-hold: The name of the living tomb where a spiritual person, in this case, the Anchoress, lives out her days in seclusion and prays for the monks at the monastery.
[6] Signet: A small raised unique crest of aristocratic families usually worn as a ring. It is used as a signature to press on melted wax to seal missals, or letters or indicate ownership on important documents.

someone else's consolation from Heaven. It sounds so . . . " she frowned, "so cold and lonely." She gazed longingly at her daughter, who had her eyes closed and was now humming a lilting tune. "You must admit, Hildebert, more than any of our other children, Hildegard is the most precocious. She has a beautiful voice and a clever mind."

"Yet she possesses a weak constitution, my dear. Hildegard would die trying to give a husband children, unlike our Irmengard or Clementia. We've gone over this several times. I would rather she be someone else's comfort than our grief. Have you not heard what her own brothers say of her?"

"Must you always speak this way in front of the child?" Lady Mechtilde motioned sympathetically to her eight-year-old daughter sitting across from them.

"Why? She didn't mince her words to them! She told them that they walk with the Devil and warned them that their children will one day turn against them. She didn't even stop there! She said she had a 'vision' of them as adults crawling pitifully like spiders into a high stone tower!"

Lady Mechtilde grimaced, "If it was Drutwin and Roricus, I don't doubt it's true," she said, shaking her head with annoyance. "It would do them some good to listen to their baby sister's warning. You must admit, they do act rashly and are entirely disobedient."

"Come now, think, woman! We've all witnessed Hildegard's powers of foretelling the future and have heard her communing with the spirit world. It's unnatural! She's unnatural." He glared across at his own flesh and blood as if she was diseased and now, as a last resort, required amputation. When he looked away, he concluded sharply, "These two young girls will suit one another, whether or not they make their home at Sponheim or Disibodenberg."

Hildegard stopped humming, suddenly fully aware of her parents' painful attentions. She'd heard enough of her father's reasoning and her mother's pleading to know why they thought she was better off as a ward of the church. She opened her eyes, cupped her hands and blew on them, scattering imaginary seeds, remembering the secret vision she had had of her own future; of her own talents spreading and sprouting new growth that would last beyond her lifetime. She knew not what the seeds represented; only that she was destined to plant them. No, she consoled herself, her parents were both wrong. Her future resided not in their hands, as they thought.

BOOK 2: GLIMPSES INTO ONE'S DESTINY

CHAPTER I: A LONE RIDER

Hillside Overlooking Disibodenberg Monastery

18th of October, Wednesday, in the Year of Our Lord 1111

Disibodenberg, the Benedictine[7] monastery, was perched high on a hillside overlooking two rivers, the Nahe and the Glan. There it nestled comfortably in the cold pale sun of the winter morning, between rows and rows of tidy vineyards. Its formidable bell tower stretched upward like a fingernail pointing to God. It could be argued that the monastery was neither fully in this world nor the next, but somewhere in between, keeping a watchful eye on the small bustling village of Staudernheim.

High on an opposing hillside, a lone rider brought his horse to a standstill. Smoke rings escaped from the horse's nostrils as it snorted in protest. Matthias relaxed his grip on the reins. He was in his late thirties, dressed as a gentleman but built like a warrior, tall and deeply tanned with broad, square shoulders.

"There, there, girl, take a rest now," he said, patting his horse's taut neck. He lowered his eyes, keeping to the shadows at the edge of the forest, and surveyed the crowds gathering below on the grounds outside the monastery for the festival.

He envied them. Like sea waves they could come and go with rhythmic ease. Their movements were simple and purposeful; never calculated or deceptive like his.

Once, he had relished the adventure, the thrill and challenge of living a life on the boundary between the law and the lawless. Now, though, he resented the constant peril he had to endure each day. He had become weary, travel-worn, and lonely.

---

[7] Benedictine: A following of monks who promise to live a life of poverty, chastity and obedience. Their customary clothing is a black habit, symbolic of humility.

Matthias stiffened, suddenly hearing a queer noise directly behind him. Between the twisted skeletal arms of a blackthorn's branches, the dark crone of the woods, he caught sight of a bushy whip of a squirrel's tail darting into the safety of a knothole. The nervous squirrel's movements caused more of the blackthorn's dying yellowing leaves to fall helplessly to the ground.

Matthias focused once again on the throngs of moving people below. His extraordinary sixth sense prickled, telling him what his eyes had failed to pick out. His pursuers were near. To him they had a smell, and mysteriously—like a cat known to identify a dying man—he too, had an enhanced sense of death's threatening gaze and could tell when his life was in danger. "Must it always be a game of predators and prey?" he muttered to his horse.

The black horse snorted impatiently.

"I know, girl," he said, patting her black mane absently. "I was hoping that our journey would come to its end as well."

His eyes continued searching, taking in the minute details of each stranger in the long lines awaiting entrance into the monastery and in those erecting tents along the surrounding hillside. He listened as the bells tolled the hour of prayer, Terce,[8] and knew intimately the learned ritual to this melodic signal. He watched as, one by one, the community of cowled black-robed monks dropped their tools in the fields and solemnly made their way to the cloisters. Even those raking leaves under the orchards had to leave their work to join their holy brothers in worship. It was a comforting ritual he had once observed and delighted in.

It was then that Matthias saw his pursuers galloping up the far hillside, heading to the monastery. An older and younger man dressed pretentiously as gentlemen, both on trained warhorses. There was a distinctive, familiar odor to the lust those two possessed for spilling blood. Together the two riders pushed ahead of the crowd of people and passed effortlessly ahead of everyone else through the porter's arched gate.

---

[8] Terce: The office of prayer at 9 a.m. every morning.

Matthias felt exasperated. Now he would have to retreat to the south and return at a later time, after the dismal winter winds and snow had thawed. He knew this was his penitence[9].

He spurred on his horse with the heels of his fine leather boots, thinking bitterly of all the lost years in this chasm of his life. He was a man without a country or a cause, existing alongside the living, but essentially dead. He'd already spied on his younger brother, Amos, who held his estate, his children, and—as he had found out nearly seven years ago—warmed himself at night lying beside the wife of his youth. Matthias had paid handsomely for a deed committed in the terrors of war and now he longed for release, freedom from the burden and obligation he carried tucked inside his belt.

Chapter 2: This Side of Heaven's Ivory Floor

Infirmary at Disibodenberg Monastery

Harvest Festival, Later That Same Morning

It was effortless, really. From years of practice, Volmar slipped his hand under the cloak of the elderly man and lifted his knife. Its blade was thin, unsheathed and as sharp as an angry woman's tongue.

The Infirmary[10] was bustling with activity. Removed from the main buildings of the monastery, it served the people directly. It was the third day of the harvest festival and practically the entire village was present with some sort of gluttonous[11] illness or combative complaint. With patience, Volmar settled the old man beside the open hearth on a small pallet, where the roaring fire lent color and warmth to his ashen dampness.

"Kiss her cheek, will you!" the old man bellowed, taking the shoulders of the young monk in an iron grip and pointing him to the young

[9] Penitence: Punishment for sins committed.
[10] Infirmary: The place in a monastery for the sick.
[11] Gluttony: The act of eating to excess, one of the seven deadly sins.

girl cowering in the shadows. He heaved himself upright and sneered, "She'll purr for you like a kitten."

Volmar ignored the old man's blather and the girl's obvious humiliation. Calmly he removed the old man's worn, muddied boots, appalled at the condition of the man's feet. They were worse than anything the young monk had ever seen in his past seven years at the Infirmary. With care, Volmar continued removing the man's patched cloak and dirty outer garments before tucking him under the blanket with only his stained and frayed tunic on. The old man struggled, jerking and twitching his jaws, which were speckled with stubbly grey hairs and dried food. Pulling free, he yanked a fistful of Volmar's dark black hair and brought the boy's ear close to his swollen lips. "There's a smell to souls," he muttered, his breath a rancid whisper, "and yours is putrid."

"All souls are marred by sin, my good man," Volmar answered, unclenching the man's fist and reaching for a clean rag. "After all, who can say, 'I have kept my heart pure; I am clean and without sin?'"[12] Volmar quoted the Scripture passage automatically. Years of rote memorization occasionally had their value. Gently he wiped the whitish frothy drool from the corners of the old man's mouth as he searched the great hall for Brother Paulus. Their eyes met instinctively, as the older monk clipped the final round of linen bandage he was applying to a drunken man's bloodied cheek. Volmar gestured silently for Paulus to come. Volmar and Brother Paulus shared many hand signals. Volmar gave to Paulus the signal that implied immediacy. The young monk knew gratefully that nothing on this side of Heaven's ivory floor was as fair as Brother Paulus' Infirmary. Rich or poor, it did not matter; one's medical needs took precedence over one's station in life.

The girl, no more than twelve summers old, was still blushing from her grandfather's embarrassing outburst. "I'm so sorry about that," she murmured apologetically, "If it is any consolation, sir, Grandda told me my soul was not only putrid but will burn forever in Hell."

Volmar tried to smile to reassure her but couldn't find a smile inside him. The young girl looked woefully underfed and just as fragile as her grandfather. He could see reason struggling with emotion in her young face. Her eyes were an intelligent, yet turbulent, greenish-blue in

---

[12] Quote from the Holy Bible, Proverbs: Chapter 20, Verse 9.

color, and reminded him of the dark dampness of the earth. And yet her hair, as if to contradict such dankness, was the color of a candle's

glowing ring, cascading around her heart-shaped face. She looked comely except for the crimson scar running like the morning's horizon across her pointed chin. Volmar spoke softly to her. "The old man is talking out of his mind. I'm sure he didn't mean it." He wondered what else the old man had told her and how she had coped, for surely her daily life had been intricately woven into this man's abusive nonsense.

Volmar's kind words broke the girl's composure. Her full lips started to tremble. Then, as if permission had finally been granted, the tears and words came streaming out. "I-I think that there's a fierce and bitter demon in Grandda. He curses in languages I do not know and has been spitting up all this white foam. I didn't know where else to bring him. He didn't want to come here. Maybe he has a fear of holy objects and knows he would not be welcomed."

Volmar struggled with how to respond to her fears and lamely muttered, "You were right to bring him to us, child. Perhaps he is under the spell of demon possession. He is also very sick and needs our help."

"Tell me this, kind sir. There are plenty of evil people in this world, why would demons want to possess my Grandda's soul? He's the gentlest of all men." She curled her hands into small fists.

Volmar knew that feeling well, how little youthful strength could help. "Old age wakens many demons," he added in sympathy, wishing he could command the diabolical legions of Hell to take back its wayward, unwelcome guest. His fingers tightened around his quill, longing to wield it as a sword and defeat all suffering in one fell swoop. Instead, he turned to making notes, first concerning possession of the old man's knife, and then recording his observations of the old man's condition. His effectiveness, he reminded himself, meant he needed to record what had happened, rather than be drawn into that bottomless pit of despair. Paulus insisted that Volmar keep records not only of his successes but his failures as well. It was Volmar's job to record the date, the patient's name, any observable symptoms, the treatment given, and the results that followed. To this purpose he devoted his attentions.

The young girl came over to where Volmar was seated at the end of the pallet and peered over his shoulder, watching as his quill scratched the parchment.

"I need to know. Tell me! Is Grandda's soul no longer his own?" The young girl was unwilling to accept the young monk's abrupt ending to the conversation she'd begun.

Volmar relaxed his grip and put down his quill. Slowly, he ran his fingers through his tangled hair. "You've stumbled on one of life's mysteries. Life is certainly full of contradictions and strange paradoxes. Why does anyone fall ill? Church doctrine tells us it happens when a person permits himself to become alienated from God. He is tempted by greed, pride, fear or any other low moral standards; in such a sinful state, he can easily become possessed. Then again, there are those who purport . . . "

"I thought," the young girl said, interrupting his philosophical discourse and crossing her arms, "I prayed to a merciful and kind Father, not one so disagreeable."

Volmar suppressed a smile. He'd said the same thing when he was her age. "I tell you what, I'm not the Infirmarian. The man in the far corner finishing a wrap on the man's face is. His name is Brother Paulus. He will be here shortly. You can ask him this very question."

"You told me who you are not, kind sir, but have failed to tell me who you are."

"My name is Volmar. I'm a scribe[13] and, for now, Brother Paulus's apprentice." Volmar returned to his writing, conscious for the first time of how his own actions must seem through someone else's eyes. When had he stopped feeling? When had he accepted such dreadfulness as commonplace? The smell was indeed rancid. Bed after bed lined the walls of the Infirmary. Here he came each day, to follow Brother Paulus around recording the pitiful cries of pain, feverish moans, and wild mumblings. The sounds of suffering were his daily chorus. If ever there was an outlying edifice of Hell, it would be here, he thought, where the beckoning shadows of death always seemed to linger.

"May I call you simply Volmar?" the young girl interjected, chasing away the dark thought crossing Volmar's mind.

"Only if you grant me equal privilege in knowing your given name." This time he managed a weak smile. Sometimes he forgot that

---

[13] Scribe: One of a learned class whose job is to record events as a Chronicler, to take dictation for letters, or to copy the writings of others.

he was only sixteen, not much older than this young girl, and yet, he had lived too much to feel as if he was very young.

"It's Sophie. I didn't know where else to bring my Grandda. His name is Silas."

Volmar wrote both of their names down on the sheet of parchment. "And how old is he?"

"He was born in the spring of 1053. That means he's 58 years old," she answered promptly.

"Interesting—you know numbers," Volmar said, impressed. He knew that his Abbot ascribed to the belief that names provide glimpses into one's ultimate destiny. Maybe there was something to his theory. "I shall speak plainly, Sophie, for your name means Wisdom; and as I've suspected all along, you are very wise for one so young." Volmar held her gaze directly. "Your Grandfather is seriously ill; bringing him here was the right thing to do."

"And I, young lady, concur with whatever my able young apprentice has said to you thus far." Brother Paulus approached the two of them, patting dry the beads of perspiration on the back of his neck and forehead with a damp rag. To Volmar, Paulus looked tired and infinitely older than his forty-five years. He stood a head taller than most men and had a brooding expression in his deep-set eyes, the color of blackened pitch. In direct contrast was his long white beard and wild hair; obviously a man of presence and clarity of mind. Volmar longed to acquire the sharp logic and confident manner of his mentor.

Brother Paulus continued, "Shall we find out what's going on with your Grandfather, young lady?"

Volmar was fascinated by Paulus' unique approach to each patient. Paulus had travelled far in his youth and had been eager to study under many teachers before turning his hand to medicine. His self-proclaimed eclectic approach owed much to Hippocrates[14], the Greek healer, and others whose works were harder to come by unless you were a scholar and could read the original Greek, or Latin, languages Paulus had mastered in his youth.

---

[14] Hippocrates: This Greek healer and his theories dominated medicine until the nineteenth century. His philosophy held that all material in the universe, including the human body, was based on four elements: earth, water, fire and air. These humors must be kept in balance; if they are not in harmony, disease results.

Volmar passed over his notes and stood up beside Paulus. "His name is Silas and he is 58 years old. He is suffering from hallucinations and some sort of wasting disease. Take a look at his feet." Volmar lifted the end of the blanket, revealing the deformed feet. "I've never seen anything like it before."

Paulus nodded, his brow furrowed. "It seems his feet are full of scabs and scar tissue from blisters. Hmm, they are still blackened and quite swollen, but, it seems they have mostly healed. We'll need to wrap both of them right away after cleaning them with warm wine."

Paulus had his look of total concentration etched on his face. He knelt beside the pallet and felt for Silas's pulse. He then leaned forward and held his head close to the old man's chest to listen to his lungs and heart. Volmar held the old man's limp hands back just in case he woke and tried to attack Paulus.

"His breathing is erratic, and so are the beats of his heart." Paulus frowned, as he leaned back and began to move Silas's head from side to side, "Interesting, it seems he has a twisted, contorted neck."

Volmar went back to his writing, "The young girl is his granddaughter. Her name is Sophie. She can likely answer any questions."

Silas stirred at the mention of his granddaughter's name, "You-u can't have her. I promised her to that boy first." His stark green eyes fluttered opened briefly before shutting again, his eyes rolling back into his head.

Frightened, Sophie mumbled a prayer of forgiveness.

Paulus turned to her and spoke plainly, "Diseases, Sophie, are not a punishment from God." The elder monk went on. "There's always a natural cause and each disease has its own peculiar nature and external causes. There must be something in your Grandfather's diet, his occupation, or perhaps even the weather, that's affecting him. My task . . . our task," he said, correcting himself with emphasis, "is to find out what's causing this condition. To do so, however, I'll need your cooperation."

"Yes sir . . . Brother Paulus, sir," she stammered.

Volmar whispered to Sophie, "Don't worry. I was terrified of him for years. He's much nicer than he looks."

Brother Paulus grunted obligingly. His thoughts were already racing to make any connections to past cases. The only things that kept coming to his mind were the 'Holy Fire' epidemics of 857 and 1039. Silas had all of the classic symptoms, the gangrenous feet, the twisted neck muscles, the confusion and hallucinations . . . . He'd read of the dreaded disease's devastation at a monastery years ago in Vienne, recalling that no one knew how it started or why and no one knew how to treat it. Nightmare stories abounded on how it spread like a raging fire throughout the Rhine River Valley, mainly affecting peasants in rural areas, killing thousands; leaving aristocrats, monasteries and other more heavily populated villages alone. Disibodenberg was ill-prepared to deal with a plague, especially one so deadly and unpredictable.

Paulus turned to Volmar. He didn't want to raise any alarm unnecessarily so he kept the worst to himself, at least for the moment. "Well, well," he declared, "whatever we're dealing with is not contagious. Otherwise Sophie would be suffering from it also."

"I agree," Volmar replied, making additional notes in his book.

Paulus closed his eyes and prayed silently, hoping his instincts were wrong. He leveled his eyes with Sophie's. "When did your Grandfather fall ill?'

"Outside of Cologne, I think. Three months past."

Paulus gave a sigh of relief. He had it all wrong. No way could a man of Silas's age survive three months with 'Holy Fire.' "Go on, child, tell me what happened," he urged, listening intently.

Sophie nodded, "We've been on the road since spring, looking for work. When the weather was pleasant we would sleep outside. We made camp in a clearing outside of the town when suddenly Grandda was attacked by a demon. He became horribly confused and complained that his feet were burning. The skin on his feet started peeling off. I didn't know what to do. I built a big fire and fed it with branches because he complained he was so cold, but then he started sweating so, saying how hot he was."

"Had he eaten anything out of the ordinary?" Paulus asked, interrupting her story.

"We always ate better when we were in a town. In the woods, we kept to nuts and berries. I got really worried when Grandda couldn't get up and ended up soiling himself. The demon inside him kept cursing. The noise must have alerted a stranger sleeping in a nearby clearing. Grandda would have surely died had it not been for this stranger. He cured him."

"A stranger cured him?" Volmar looked up from his writing.

"The stranger was dressed like a gentleman and never told me his name. I-I'm not sure what he did except he took from his bag a smaller bag made of what appeared to be oiled wool and drew from it a small object wrapped in leather. He told me to pray with him as he held it over Grandda's chest. The next morning, I woke up and the stranger was gone and Grandda was himself again."

Paulus spoke carefully. "Remarkable, truly a miracle. I'd like to meet this stranger."

"Me too," Volmar said, wondering what sort of object would have such amazing healing powers.

Paulus toyed with his beard, thinking through all the old man's symptoms and the miraculous healing. "So for three months your grandfather was well. What ails him now?"

"We found work nearby in Staudernheim repairing the piers on the stone bridge. Late yesterday evening he fell from some scaffolding and injured his head on the rocks below along the river's bank. He doesn't remember how long he was lying there. He was fine at first; but this morning he woke and started talking like when that old devil came to him during that night in the clearing."

Paulus's eyebrows knitted together with worry. "I see." He lifted the hair on the back of Silas's head and only then noticed the raised bump. "A nasty bump, there's likely to be bleeding inside his brain. I've had some success with rosemary, though. It increases the circulation to the brain and might help. I will prepare your Grandda a tonic right away to ease the confusion and the swelling." Paulus turned to Volmar. "Why don't you take our young guest to the kitchens down the hill and find her something to eat while I work? She will need her strength, now more than ever, for what lies ahead."

He placed a hand on his young apprentice's shoulder, and added firmly, "Afterwards, Volmar, take a rest before Vespers[15]. I will too, once I give the old man a tonic and see to his feet. You too, my dear Sophie," he said, turning to her, "may find rest upstairs in the women's quarters. I'm sure your grandfather will want you nearby."

---

[15] Vespers: An evening prayer service around 4:30 p.m. in the late afternoon, held generally at sunset.

Chapter 3: Melancholy in the Air

Outer Court of Disibodenberg Monastery

Harvest Festival, Late Morning

Outside a cool mist rose and hung like melancholy in the air, refusing to leave as Sophie and Volmar walked downhill on the outer court of the monastery. Sophie slipped her small hand into Volmar's. He was unaccustomed to such signs of childish affection and held it limply, unsure of how he should react.

Suddenly, from around the corner and further down the cobblestone road, there were the unmistakable sounds of a whip being snapped and several horses snorting in protest. Moments later, there were hoofs charging towards them, barely visible in the heavy fog. Volmar abruptly lifted Sophie into his arms and held her flat against the stone wall of the Infirmary, protecting her from the elegant carriage that sped by, barely missing them.

As the carriage blew past them, Volmar detected a hint of perfume that, to his knowledge, only women of high birth wore and saw from the family's crest mounted on its door that it was in fact, the Count's[16] carriage. For days, the Count's upcoming visit had been the talk of all the holy brothers. Truly, the most intriguing part of the gossip was not the Count himself, but his beautiful sister who deliberately wanted to forgo all her riches and princely offers of marriage to become a recluse, a humble anchoress at their monastery.

Volmar sat Sophie down, making a mental note to seek out Brother Johannes later. As the head custodian for the monastery, he was privy to the entire goings on of the monastery and would likely know the truth behind this noble family's intrusion.

Unimpressed by the entire ordeal, Sophie dusted off her skirts, which were already crumpled and faded from too many scrubbings, saying nothing as the two continued to make their way down the cobbled road towards the open-air kitchens. As they turned the corner leading there, the distinctive clanking of chisels against rock could be clearly heard, their rhythmic sound reverberating through the court-

---

[16] Count: A European nobleman whose rank corresponds to that of a British earl.

yard as steady as drumbeats. Sophie cocked her head to one side and asked, "Are they adding a wing to the church?"

Volmar gave a light laugh as he paused by the worksite. "They haven't stopped adding on to the sanctuary since I've been here. This time, though, work is underway in transforming one of the old stables into an Anchorage. If you can imagine, it's to be seventy-five feet long, with two rooms, a stone fireplace, and a walled-in garden."

Sophie stood very still, her gaze bright and sharp, clearly entranced by the workmen. "My Grandda was a stonecarver and a mason, too," she said, speaking with pride. "For several years he worked on the capitals[17] of the portal facing the market for Saint Martin's Cathedral in Mainz. He would use the knife you took from him to carve models in wood late at night beside the fire, so he'd have a guide when he'd chisel the stone. When his hands started shaking, I would carve for him. He taught me all that he knew. I completed the face of the angel to the right side of the Holy Throne of Christ on the portico."

"I suppose your Grandfather was asked to leave when they found out the deception," Volmar said, completing her thoughts.

Sophie nodded. And then she added quite wistfully, a secret dream. "One day, I'll show them, I'll carve the most beautiful scenes illustrating the Stations of the Cross."[18]

"That would be a masterpiece," Volmar said, staring with respect at the child's hands, tanned and calloused against the soft supple leather of her purse. He'd heard that there were craftswomen who worked tirelessly on the grand cathedrals, but one so young? "Surely you have other family?"

"No, no, not anymore. That's why Grandda and I left Cologne." Sophie cast her eyes downward. "My mother died having me, and my father went off to war in the Holy Land and never came back. When Grandda started showing signs of his advancing age, he thought it best for me to go and live with my mother's sister and . . . " she added sheepishly, "learn the ways of womenfolk."

Volmar gave Sophie a look of mild surprise. "Did she not take you in?"

---

[17] Capitals: The top part or piece of an architectural column, usually ornate.

[18] Stations of the Cross: Fourteen individual scenes telling of the Passion, or the journey Christ made to Golgotha for His crucifixion.

"Her husband refused, and she couldn't go against his wishes. She had four children of her own to care for and feed anyway so there wasn't any room for me. Grandda and I stayed one night and were told to leave the next morning." Sophie added with an edge of sarcasm, "Can't blame my uncle, really. After all, look at me. I'm a girl. To marry me off, they'll need a dowry[19]."

Sophie's thoughts were cut off abruptly when a cat suddenly jumped down from the roof drains, landing effortlessly in front of the two young people. The creature rubbed up against Volmar's leg, purring. The young monk bent down to pet its soft fur. "Hey, time for another meal, hmm, Samson?"

Sophie moved forward and cautiously stroked the cat's gray back and upright tail. "Samson? What an unusual name."

"Samson showed up at the monastery seven years ago missing an ear and with a dreadful gaping wound on his thigh. I had to shave most of his fur off to apply the sage ointment suggested by Brother Paulus. He looked so pitiful without his hair, so he was named Samson."

"I thought it was forbidden for monks to have pets."

"True. We are prohibited from indulging in such worldly pursuits. However, Samson takes care of the rats that eat our stored grains and the voles that plague the gardens of Brother Albertus. Everyone gives him scraps to show their appreciation, so he's quite well-fed and essentially belongs to all of us."

Thomas, the head mason's red-headed son and apprentice, approached the two from the building site of the Anchorage. He wiped his mouth with his sleeve, unknowingly smearing more mud and mortar across his face. Volmar knew of him, and was always a little wary of his unpredictability. He had the reputation of being both intense and temperamental, the kind of boy who remedied his boredom through arguments. "Couldn't help but overhear the story this girl told you, Volmar," he said, turning his back on Sophie in further insult. "You can't possibly believe that she was allowed to work on a cathedral."

Volmar nodded to Sophie. "I believe her, Thomas. Sophie's grandfather was a stonemason in Mainz." Volmar realized almost immediately that he should have kept out of this, for Sophie was perfectly

---

[19] Dowry: Property that a woman brings to her husband in marriage.

capable of holding her own against this young man's condescending attitude.

Sophie turned to Thomas skeptically. "I don't see how you can use up all that mortar you've mixed. We were never allowed to be so wasteful. You'll still have more than half of it left over after you finish your courses of stone."

"Clever little runt, aren't you?" Thomas said, crossing his arms and leaning up against a pillar. He was actually smiling at her, his teeth surprisingly white despite his worn appearance.

"A runt is a small dog or cat and, in case you haven't noticed, I am neither." Sophie stuck out her tongue at him, lifted her skirts and took off down the hill towards the kitchens.

Volmar inclined his head towards Thomas, who apparently didn't seem to mind being made a fool of. Maybe, the young monk reasoned, the apprentice was grateful to meet a worthy opponent.

Chapter 4: Road-Weary Travelers

Open Dining Hall at Disibodenberg Monastery

Harvest Festival, Late Morning

The smell of warming bread quickened Sophie's steps, and soon she was running ahead of both Samson and Volmar as she hastened to get in line behind several other road-weary travelers.

The dining hall near the open kitchens of the monastery was practically full to capacity. Visitors from all over the region were milling in and out due to the festival and were grateful for the charitable hospitality. Volmar took pleasure in studying those around him and reading their lives in their faces. It did him good to hear laughter and to listen to children crying around him out of greed, not pain. These were mostly peasants from neighboring villages, he judged, mingling with a few merchants smelling of exotic spices and carrying colorful caged birds.

Volmar blessed Sophie's food before sitting silently across from her at the long trestle table. He watched her in amazement as she devoured several bowls of lentil soup and endless slices of thick horse bread, dark and heavily seeded with whole grains.

"This is so much better than rye bread," she said between mouthfuls. "I can't stand the taste of rye, it's too sour." Obviously Sophie had not had any food for days. She ate nearly half of the five-pound loaf before slowing down.

Volmar's thoughts drifted as he watched her eat. With a bit of washing up, Volmar mused to himself, Sophie would probably look something like Anya would have had she lived. It wasn't often he would indulge in such memories, and he let his mind leisurely wander back into the past. Anya and Sophie would be about the same age now and, he reflected, would probably possess the same resilient temperament.

Volmar was jarred from his thoughts as a small commotion started to erupt near the entrance. Two high-born men in navy velvet tunics, black silk tights, and high leather riding boots had stormed into the kitchen's open-air dining area, reeking of ale. They were darker-skinned, tanned, Volmar guessed, by a stronger Middle Eastern sun. The men were dressed as gentlemen, possessing all the signs of returning Crusaders[20].

The young monk watched as the two men glared out across the dining hall, walking purposefully up and down the rows of tables, clearly looking for someone in particular. One by one their stares silenced the room. By the time they reached Volmar's table, the young monk could clearly see their disappointment. One of the men, the older and more muscular one with a short wiry gray beard, reached down and plucked the slice of bread from Sophie's hand and took a bite.

"Not bad, my friend, though I think the village food and its company might be more to our liking." Reaching down with a smirk on his rough features, the man took hold of Sophie's chin and pulled it up, tracing her scar with his finger. "Look here, it seems someone wanted to shut this little girl's mouth, didn't they?"

---

[20] Crusaders: Returning soldiers from the Holy Land. The Crusades were a series of wars undertaken in the 11th, 12th, and 13th centuries, by the European Christians eager to regain the Holy Land from the Muslims.

"How dare you!" Volmar shouted angrily. He rose to his full height and glared at the man across the table. "Get your filthy hands off of her! She was eating that piece of bread!"

The stranger locked eyes with young Volmar. His sneering eyes took in the boy's simple black wool robe, leather pouch, and blackened fingertips. "So she was, Scribe, so she was." He then wiped his hands clean on the hem of Sophie's tattered cape before tracing the slight curve of the girl's neck with his finger, adding hoarsely, "A few years older and rest assured, I would have taken more than just her bread. Think on that, my dear brother, and burn."

The other man coughed loudly, clearly embarrassed by his friend's show of coarse humor.

Volmar planted his hands firmly on the table, icily glaring across at the stranger with righteous indignation. "How dare you speak to a child in such a manner!"

The older man gave out a snort of laughter, taking little notice of Volmar's outrage. In mocked complicity, he reached for Sophie's fist, pried it open and put the half-eaten bread back. "See? There. Forgive my rude behavior, my lady, I've been duly chastened by God's holy scribbler." The stranger then gave a comical bow and straightened up, laughing harshly and bitterly as he did so. As his wild voice rang out over the dining area, the two men made their way back to the entrance and left.

Volmar hung his head. The stranger's laugh had a ring of familiarity, stirring a deep-seated emotion of fear and helplessness that Volmar couldn't put reason to. Outwardly, he fumed over the man's arrogance towards Sophie and murmured a curse under his breath. Volmar hoped God would understand why it wasn't a prayer.

Sophie rose and walked silently over to him. "I don't mind, Volmar. He gave it back and only took a small bite from it. See . . . " Sophie showed him the half-eaten slice of bread. "It still tastes the same, and besides, I'm getting full anyways. Let's head back." She waited until they were outside to take his hand again.

Volmar took a deep breath, still simmering with anger. Were all girls this confusing? With Thomas, Sophie had stood her own ground and did not hesitate to put him in his place, and yet with the older stranger, she had kept her silence, choosing instead to ignore his insult.

Maybe, he thought, she was right in turning the other cheek, realizing the stranger was a lost cause.

He led her back across the courtyard and upstairs to the guest quarters on the east side of the Infirmary, where the women and children slept. Only then did he let go of her slender hand, a small part of him fearing for her future.

Volmar clasped his hands loosely behind his back and forced himself to look into her eyes. Sophie stood before him, rigid and pale. He recognized instantly that she already knew of the enormity of the burden resting on her small shoulders. Her eyes were those of an old woman in a young girl's face.

Chapter 5: Restless Spirit

Clearing Outside of Disibodenberg Monastery

Harvest Festival, Late Afternoon

Exhausted, Volmar felt the branch sigh beneath him as he settled his back firmly against the crook of the old yew's trunk. Over the jovial sounds of the minstrels playing at the harvest festival, he heard the distant rumblings of an approaching storm. It made the air around him taut with expectation. Vespers would be soon, but for the moment he was grateful to be in his own world, away from the reach of the studied rituals, insistent conformity, and peculiar community of the cloistered life.

From his perch, Volmar fixed his gaze on the cobbled road, thinking back to Sophie's story and her journey from Mainz. This road led to a world he only knew from the books he read and the colorful tales of strangers. Was he a mere "scribbler," as the arrogant soldier had indicated, destined to live his life on the outskirts of the real world? How could he effect real change, if he did not know how most people suffered and lived? Although he had completed his probationary period last year, and had made his profession of faith and taken the cowl[21] in spring, for some reason, he still struggled with his faith and his calling to be a scribe. If only God would give him a sign, a message that he was following his true destiny.

Inside his head, the voices of his tutors echoed, rebuking his faithless questioning and his worldly need to intellectualize and seek proof of the spiritual realm. "How can you, a mere child, question the Word of Christ? Such faithless doubting would have me worried over my own salvation; my unclean, broken soul. Faith pleases God. God always responds to faith."

Volmar fumbled for a rag from his leather pouch and started rubbing furiously at his blackened fingertips. These ink stains would always reveal his livelihood as a scribe, as the crude soldier had deduced. Even if he ran away and left the familiar fortress of the monastery of Disibodenberg to explore the unknown world beyond, these stains would always mark him like Cain. Every stranger he would encounter would know he was a faithless, condemned man who had failed the church, and ultimately, God.

"Surely, Lord," Volmar closed his eyes and prayed, a little faintly, "by acknowledging my own weakness, I will find the faith I so ardently seek." For how could he catch a glimpse of the one true God if he was blind to his own misgivings and sins? A boom of distant thunder answered, followed by a stark flash of lightning. The storm was fast approaching, a storm that would surely call off the evening's events at the harvest festival.

The sky darkened. Volmar imagined in its looming, shifting shadows the candle-lit Scriptorium[22]. The clouds transformed into the humps of the backs of his fellow brothers who, like hard black beetles, clicked away in the carrels of the Scriptorium, the tips of their quills scratching against the parchments. At least, he thought with a grateful heart, his apprenticeship with Brother Paulus gave him a wider perspective of the outside world beyond the stuffy, deafening silence of the Scriptorium and the earthy smell of the stables, albeit only through the eyes of the suffering.

---

21 Cowl: A monk's hood and an expression used to refer to becoming a holy brother and following the Benedictine code.

22 Scriptorium: The room in medieval monasteries where Scribes would copy by hand, manuscripts.

The wind quickened, and one of those crusty black humps rose up and changed into an illuminated[23] beast. A jagged gash of lightning became the beast's serpent-like tongue. Slowly, Volmar watched how its body transformed into pure black from nose to tail, and with an unholy grace, the beast unfurled its large, spiny wings like a lady's fan. Of course, Volmar mused, the beast only pretended to pay him no attention, for in a moment's time it suddenly stretched its deadly talons and reared up to peer at his face more closely. Volmar expected the beast's voice to roar, asserting its masculinity, as did all of his imaginary beasts. So, when he heard, instead, a singular, melodic feminine voice carried in the brisk wind, Volmar was jarred out of his own musings. The young monk slowly loosened himself from his reverie as the voice grew louder, and he wondered if it belonged to this world or the world beyond.

Taking a deep breath, Volmar peered down through the branches of the leafless tree, half expecting to be fooled by seeing the familiar, wrathful beast of inhuman stature and demeanor glaring up at him. Instead, in its place, he saw a thin, dark-haired young woman skipping curiously towards his tree, completely oblivious to his presence.

The wind caught her plait and loosened her hair so its dark tendrils fell across her pale cheeks and forehead, softening her delicate, pretty features. She looked a couple of years younger than him, wearing a crown of woven flowers, and she was dressed in richly embroidered velvets, etched in gold thread. Her long, dark blue cape whipped about her freely, pulling against its chain and the silver clasp of filigree at the nape of her neck.

Volmar figured the young woman was play-acting as he observed her coax an invisible companion to the clearing. Curtsying to this apparition[24], she then took its invisible arm and began to dance. Her movements kept time to her plaintive singing, an obscure psalm sung to music. It was beautiful and strange, a melody at once defiant and complementary to the stillness of the forest. Volmar watched, half bemused and half self-consciously, as she twirled about hand in hand

---

[23] Illuminated: Decorated images in a manuscript, painted in gold, silver, or brilliant colors, often elaborate designs or pictures along borders and letters.

[24] Apparition: A supernatural appearance, a ghost.

with this invisible person, all the while laughing and singing, her skirts billowing out from her like a bell.

Volmar sensed an unfamiliar stirring of attraction. Unlike Sophie, whom he saw as a child, this girl was older and shapely like a woman. From where he sat he could see how her bosom rose and fell in time with her movements. Volmar's solemn life knew little of such carefree laughter and even less of the opposite sex. His dealings with women were restricted to only those who were crippled, diseased, injured, or pregnant.

Guiltily, Volmar spied on the laughing young woman with a longing he couldn't put into words as he watched her from a safe distance, mesmerized by her foreign and evocative ways, welcoming for once the protective cover of silence.

When at last the young woman seemed positively exhausted from her dancing and singing, she rested on a rock and urged her invisible companion to sit next to her. "Please, tell me another story," she spoke, glowing from the exertion.

There she sat for what seemed to Volmar like an eternity. He watched her as she nodded, enthralled with what she alone was hearing and seeing. Even when the sky darkened and the wind picked up speed, she continued to sit still, unmoved by the rapidly changing weather.

In the distance, the cloistered bells started ringing. Their insistent clanging announced Vespers. Dinner would soon follow before dark. Volmar knew he would be late and also that he would be reprimanded for his tardiness. However, he feared more revealing himself to this young, evocative woman.

"It is time for me to return to the monastery," she announced to her invisible companion. "Shall we meet again tomorrow afternoon at this same clearing?"

The apparition must have agreed, for she curtsied respectfully, lifted her skirts, and turned towards the monastery's gates.

At that same instant, in an unguarded moment, Volmar's grip carelessly slipped. He lost his balance, and before he knew it, he fell from the old yew tree, landing close to the young woman in a small trench between the largest roots of the tree. He scarcely recovered before she was leaning over him and spoke.

"Who are you, sir?" she said with mild surprise, noting his black robe. "Are you an angel or a demon?"

Volmar looked up, spitting out a mouthful of wet leaves. There she was, staring down at him with interest. "What? Uh, I-I am neither," he stuttered, finding the nearness of her presence and her insightful gaze more disarming than he could ever have anticipated. He couldn't even remember his own name to introduce himself.

The young woman stared over Volmar's shoulder; her grey eyes were unusually dilated and appeared as large black pebbles. "I know of Virgil's warning, 'fear does betray unworthy souls,' but this young man wears a tonsure[25] and shows me no fear, only concern."

Volmar hesitantly turned and peered over his shoulder, confirming that the young woman was in fact talking to no one else.

Overhead, the dark clouds finally opened and a cold, harsh rain began to fall. Fiercer winds blew in from the north, mercilessly tearing at the dying leaves still clinging to the trees. "The storm is upon us. Come with me," the young woman said, seizing his hand and helping him to his feet. She raced forward towards a low hillside running along the outside edge of the forest, dragging Volmar behind. Above the wail of the winds, she cried to him, "Brother Arnoul said there's an entrance here to an underground tunnel. We will be dry there."

"A tunnel? I've never heard of it, you must be mistaken. There are no tunnels around here," Volmar answered as he tried to keep up with her, realizing for the first time he was holding her hand. He let go hastily, and tried to compose himself. The winds had now sharpened the raindrops to the point where they stung through his clothing. He could barely make out her solid form through the curtain of rain even though he knew she was an arm's length away. He slipped both of his hands inside the opposite hand's sleeve and said skeptically, "Since you know this place so well, where is this tunnel? Where does it lead to?"

"Brother Arnoul says it leads to behind an altar, the altar of Saint Peter, inside the church. Come on . . . " The young woman waved for him to follow her before ducking and disappearing into what must have been the cave's entrance, fully concealed by thick relentless vines of ivy that hung down like ringlets of hair.

"Humph," Volmar grunted, resisting the urge to follow her blindly into what appeared to be a hole in the ground. His hair whipped about his face in every direction. The rain came down in torrents, soaking his coarse wool cassock. A branch suddenly wrenched from a nearby tree, followed by another, then another. Volmar shut his eyes, said a prayer, then crawled in.

---

[25] Tonsure: The shaven patch worn by monks on the crown of their heads.

Chapter 6: Invisible Threads

Underground Tunnel Outside of Disibodenberg Monastery

Harvest Festival, Early Evening

"You can stand up," the young woman said with a curious smile. She stood several paces ahead, her face surprisingly illuminated by a burning oil lamp. Somewhat embarrassed, Volmar opened his eyes and rose from his crouching position to his full height. The young monk stared at the flickering flames of the pottery lamp, welcoming its light and warmth but clearly confused. "Where did the lamp come from?"

"I don't know. I found it already lit on the wall in that bracket over there." The young woman pointed to a rough-hewn iron bracket nailed into a finely finished and heavily carved wooden arch. The arch framed an entrance which emptied into a moderately sized cave about ten feet in height, rounded with maybe fifteen to twenty feet in diameter, which then narrowed into a long black tunnel.

"May I?" Volmar asked as he reached for the lamp. He turned it slightly to one side. "Judging by the amount of oil remaining in its flask, whoever left it did so less than an hour ago. There is probably still four hours' worth of oil left."

The girl's lips turned up in a smile. "Earlier, I thought you a simpleton, because you were so slow to speak."

Volmar grimaced; his voice was thick with emotion. "I could say the same of my first impressions of your faculties when I saw you conversing with no one in the clearing." He held the lamp high to hide his embarrassment and pretended to be studying the finer intricacies of the heavily carved wooden arch.

There was no reproach in her voice as she answered. "His name is Brother Arnoul. He's a Benedictine monk . . . or rather was. He died about ten years ago."

Volmar turned to her in disbelief, meeting her eyes. "You mean, my lady, you are exchanging confidences with a dead monk?"

"Yes."

Volmar stood speechless a moment before turning his back to her and muttering under his breath. "Now I am certain you've lost your mind." He circled her, illuminating the darkness all around them, determined to frighten away any unwanted spirit. "Is your dead monk in here with us?"

"No. Brother Arnoul cannot leave the clearing where he died. There are rules in the spiritual world just like there are rules in our world." The young woman twirled her fingers through her long entangled ringlets. "Ever since I can remember, I've had the ability to see and speak with spirits still attached to this world."

"You expect me to believe such nonsense?"

"I expect you will believe only what you see and nothing more." The young woman answered dismissively.

Taken aback by what he interpreted as a slight, Volmar responded. "I see nothing wrong with being dubious. When a storyteller tells me he's met dog-faced humans in a faraway land, I realize that he has merely stumbled onto a leper's colony. Reason and facts are my guides, my lady, not my imagination." Volmar frowned, hearing in his own voice the peculiar authoritarian voices of various monks speaking through him. Why did he turn everything into a theoretical lesson? Why couldn't he simply relax with this young woman and be himself? He let out an exasperated sigh.

The young woman, however, did not seem annoyed by his intellectual postulations[26]. "Our Lord is not one to be limited by human understanding. Think about it, we learn to see and not to see."

Volmar turned to her and raised his eyebrow with suspicion, "What do you mean . . . not to see?"

"Do you have dreams at night?" The young woman asked while tracing her fingers over the raised relief of a winged man carved into the wooden archway.

"Of course. We all dream at night. If we do not, we would go mad."

"That is so. And when you dream at night, your eyes are shut and what you see is not physically present in your bedchamber, right?"

Crossing his arms, Volmar nodded, "Very well, I see your point. Your visions are like dreams."

The young woman tilted her head to one side and thought for a moment before responding. "These visions are more like waking

---

[26] Postulations: Theoretical proposals taken for truths.

dreams. I am not asleep but awake when they come to me sometimes in a fiery light of exceeding brilliance."

"A fiery light? Are you sure you are not witnessing the flames from Hell licking the caverns of Purgatory[27]?"

She blushed more from annoyance than embarrassment. "Humph, I should never have told you."

Volmar put his fingers to his lips and said plaintively, "Please tell me that you don't believe that good and evil come from a creature such as a raven or a cat? Or that you know people who've turned into wolves."

"You are no longer speaking with your mind. Now the conversation has turned from thoughts to fears."

This time Volmar raised both of his thick eyebrows; clearly he had difficulty accepting this bizarre assertion. "If I were you, my lady, I would leave this region at once. The villagers will not welcome a bewitched or demon-possessed young woman, no matter how pretty she may be." He blushed as he realized what he let slip.

"I know. It is why I do not talk of such things with strangers." The young woman turned her back to him and stood gazing thoughtfully into the blank eyes of a stone-carved winged man holding the portico on his shoulders.

Perplexed over her insinuation of their familiarity, Volmar sputtered, "I didn't mean it like that. Surely you must be careful who you share such spiritual revelations with."

She extended her arms out expressively. "There is nothing more than a mere veil that separates the spirit world from our own."

"I see."

"Do you? Do you, really?" She answered, turning to him with enthusiasm. "I knew you were the one when our eyes first met. See," she said, touching Volmar's sleeve, "you wear the humble black robes of a young Benedictine monk and have on your hands the black ink stains of a scribe, my scribe." She turned his free hand over in hers, lightly touching his blackened fingertips and smiled warmly up at him. "We are all connected, the world of the unseen and the seen."

Volmar took a step back, fearful of her sudden intimacy towards him. "Yes," he muttered, slipping his hand from hers and burying it

---

[27] Purgatory: An intermediate state of temporary punishment after death.

inside the sleeve of his habit. "But where do these invisible threads or connections originate? The Devil has many disguises and often invades souls weakened by grief or innocence."

The young woman sighed deeply. "It may be too soon. I assure you, sir, that though I am young, I am as respectful and fearful as I should be of the wiles of the Devil. If you must know, I am in training for the veil of virgins. I was my parent's tenth child and was given to the church as a tithe."

"I didn't mean to be rude but I've never met anyone like you before." Volmar didn't realize that he'd started pacing. "Where are you studying?"

"My name is Hildegard. My spiritual companion, Jutta of Sponheim, is discussing the plans for an Anchorage at Disibodenberg with the Abbot as we speak." At that moment, Hildegard sneezed. Her clothes were soaked through as well, and the coolness of the cave made her shiver uncontrollably.

Volmar stopped pacing, noticing her distress. He removed his own cloak and hung it around her small shoulders, setting the oil lamp on high heat before placing it upright between them. "Forgive me, Hildegard." The young monk bowed low. "My name is Volmar. Please, warm yourself by the fire," he motioned. His mane of shaggy hair fell into his eyes. He pushed it self-consciously over his ear and added, "Like you, I am a charity child, a ward of the church. I was left on its doorsteps over nine years ago."

"You do not remember your parents?"

"Not really."

Her eyes searched for the answer left unsaid.

Volmar shifted his footing uncomfortably and changed the subject. "Surely the storm will be over soon and then we can leave." Volmar motioned again for Hildegard to sit across from him, closer to the warmth of the flame. Outside they could hear the storm continue to rage.

After a long while, Volmar broke the companionable silence. "For the sake of argument, tell me why a monk who has been dead for over ten years insists on having an audience with a young woman during a rainstorm?"

Hildegard warmed her hands over the fire and spoke to the flames that danced in front of her. "Brother Arnoul shared with me a story, which bears witness to your fears and accusations. The Evil One's misdeeds abound even among God's own brethren."

"Go on. I have been duly chastened." Volmar sat down across from her. His eyes, unlike hers, were not fixed on the flame's mesmerizing movements; they were lost in her compelling face.

"Brother Arnoul told me he was a man of courtly manner and noble birth. He was born in a small French village of Amiens and traveled to Disibodenberg to copy a particular book to bring back to his own monastery."

Volmar nodded in agreement, "Many monks do this. It is the only affordable way to improve the collections in monastery libraries throughout the surrounding kingdoms."

"Yes, I have heard of this practice as well. Anyway, in the Scriptorium where Brother Arnoul labored, he became friendly with another young monk who unfortunately was as greedy as he was ambitious."

"Why would he make such an accusation?"

"Brother Arnoul apparently observed this young monk on several occasions, sneaking out of the monastery when the others were asleep. The next day, after he'd questioned his friend on these nighttime adventures, Brother Arnoul was called before the Abbot and was accused of stealing the monastery's rare copy of the *Codex Benedictus*[28]."

"I've heard of this book before. It is legendary. The codex was created at the monastery of Monte Cassino in Italy back in 1070."

"Well, this was the very book Brother Arnoul had been diligently copying for his monastery. He swears by God, he did not steal it."

"But the book went missing."

"Brother Arnoul was incensed. After being accused of theft, he met privately with the Abbot."

"Abbot Burchard?"

Hildegard leaned forward, still captivated by the flames of the fire. "I believe so. The Abbot, uncertain of the circumstances, asked him to return to his own abbey in France. This angered Brother Arnoul. He tried to clear his name by confronting his friend in the very clearing where I met him."

"The clearing by the old yew tree."

[28] *Codex Benedictus*: The codex was a series of stories about Benedict; his twin sister, Scholastica; and Maur, Benedict's first disciple.

"Yes. Their words quickly turned into a vicious quarrel. The two were evenly matched until Brother Arnoul fell from a blow to his stomach and hit his head against a rock, the same rock we sat on earlier together. He was killed instantly."

"More like murdered, than killed," Volmar muttered. The two allowed the horrible word to sit between them, neither one eager to continue. Outside they could still hear the steady fall of rain. The noise echoed and reechoed around them, suggesting that the tunnel went on for a considerable distance.

"I agree," Hildegard said at length. "Brother Arnoul's spirit is restless because this guilty brother buried him unceremoniously and in secret here in the woods outside of the monk's cemetery. His name has been stricken from all monastery records and no one is allowed to speak of it, for many think he committed a theft. It is as if he never existed."

"That doesn't sound like Abbot Burchard," Volmar said defensively.

"I'm sure the Abbot suspects Brother Arnoul returned to his monastery in Amiens and knows nothing of his untimely death."

"And the young novitiate who was guilty of this conspiracy, whatever happened to him?"

"I pressed Brother Arnoul on this very point. All he kept repeating was that 'Judas betrayed me.'"

"Judas betrayed me," Volmar repeated, incredulously. "Was he referring to the Judas from the Bible who betrayed Christ?"

"I am not sure. Judas can be a given name, though one rather unpopular with Christians," Hildegard responded pensively.

"I wonder if the book is still lost." Volmar mused, "I could ask the Librarian, Brother Cormac, if we still possess the book." Volmar noticed in saying this, his conversation with this young woman was nearly as agreeable as it was with other more learned brothers at the monastery.

"Listen," Hildegard suddenly whispered, motioning with her finger for him to be silent. There was a distinct dripping noise on the wall to their left. "Don't you hear it? I believe this wall," she said, rising and motioning to her right, "is not as thick as the one over there."

Volmar got up as well and moved in close to her. There was definitely a small dripping sound of moisture coming from behind the wall.

"Hear that?" she said, her brows knitted together, "that means there's a hidden room behind this wall. It is likely that the chill outside from the storm has caused condensation to gather on its walls."

Volmar nodded. He ran his eyes up and down over the stone wall in question, methodically looking for a potential entrance into what might very well be a hidden chamber. He felt the wall up and down, tapping, feeling and listening, hoping for something that didn't sound solid. His efforts were not in vain. At the far end there was a single stone protruding that did not seem a natural extension of the larger stone it was attached to. He went and felt around it, finding, to his pleasure, a cold iron lever hidden beneath its underbelly. "Stand back," he said to Hildegard, having moved directly behind him, holding the oil lamp. He pulled the lever down.

There was a prolonged groan, like the yawn of a sleeping beast, which echoed throughout the cave. Both Hildegard and Volmar took a step backwards and watched in amazement as the large stone moved forward, dislodging itself and becoming flush with the protruding smaller stone. It was a finely chiseled piece of work, the same particular craftsmanship taken in the carvings on the wooden arch. From inside a chain could be heard moving as if it was turning on a wheel followed by the sound of a weight dropping from inside the hollowed out wall. The large stone started sinking slowly into what now appeared to be a false stone floor, revealing a small doorway clearly opening into a hidden chamber.

The two peered in. Benches lined the side and back walls of this newly revealed chamber with one or two steps leading up to the benches opposite the entrance. More surprising, though, were the skulls. There were at least fifty skulls all yellowed with age lining the benches. Their hollow eyes watched in eerie unison as the two entered and stood in the center of the small room.

"I believe we've stumbled onto an ancient ossarium[29]," Volmar whispered, the thrill of their find evident in his low voice.

---

[29] Ossarium: A chamber or depository where bones of the dead are kept.

Hildegard nodded, clearly moved as well. "Could these be the remains of the founding brothers of the monastery at Disibodenberg?" She blew at the dust which had gathered on the skulls. The tiny particles danced about unnaturally in the sullen quietness.

"It is possible. No one knows where they were buried. It's always been assumed that they would be nearby on our hillside."

Hildegard curiously touched one of the skulls. "Anonymous in death, but not in life. Tell me," she said, her luminous eyes turned to his, "of Saint Disibod and his followers. I know nothing of them."

Volmar reached back into his mind to retrieve what little he'd heard in his early lessons of the monastery's founding fathers. "They were Irish monks, I believe, who came to this region to establish a hermitage nearly five hundred years ago. You know the yew tree that is above our heads?"

"The one you were spying on me from?"

"I wasn't spying," Volmar retorted, blushing shamefully. "Well, anyway, it is said that the old yew tree is Saint Disibod's own gnarled staff which took root after he stuck it in the ground and set up camp. He claimed this foreign soil as his new home and the heathens of this region his new converts."

Only the central part of the chamber was bathed in a warm light filtering through a crystallized rock roof overhead. Its edges, however, were cloaked in shadows.

"Here it is," Hildegard said, excitedly steadying her lamp, "an inscription on the wall." Below a canopied niche that may have held a crucifix or even a small statue of the Virgin and Child, was a plaque.

Volmar went and stood by her side. He read aloud the verse quoted from the Bible: "If I take the wings of the morning: and remain in the uttermost parts of the sea; Even there also shall thy hands lead me: and thy right hand shall hold me. In the Year of our Lord, 8 September 700."

"A comforting passage from Psalm 139, for ones who've traveled so far from home and suffered piously so that strangers' souls may be saved. However, this inscription was only made four hundred and eleven years ago," she added teasingly, "not five hundred years."

Volmar grinned sheepishly. "I was close . . . only off by a hundred years."

Hildegard inclined her head towards the skulls and listened. "The consensus of the group seems to be that they are at peace and do not want to be moved."

"So you can hear them speak as well," Volmar muttered, wrinkling his brow, not sure what to make of Hildegard's professed supernatural abilities.

"Volmar, step to one side. Look at where you are standing." Hildegard knelt at his feet and tentatively touched the outline of what appeared to be an iron floor plate. It measured no more than two square feet.

Suspecting a hollow space underneath, Volmar felt for the iron plate's side handles and slid it open with Hildegard's help. A wickedly cold breath reached up from its earthy darkness, as if it was beckoning them to come down.

"Wait here," Volmar said, taking the oil lamp. The stone steps were narrow and steep, slipping into the darkness leading to another floor below. "I'm not sure what lies down there."

Hildegard nodded, "Watch your head," she said just as he bumped it against the low ceiling.

He rubbed it and muttered, "Thanks," before descending further into the pit below. Cobwebs tickled Volmar's exposed skin as he tore through their flimsy defense. At the base of the steps, Volmar found himself in a rather large room, mirroring the size of the ossarium above. To his left, he saw what appeared to be a passage to a second, much smaller chamber. Clearly the air had been freshened earlier, for there was no musty odor which one would expect when entering an enclosed, unused chamber. He called up to Hildegard, "It's a double cave."

"What else do you see?" Hildegard's voice called tentatively from overhead.

"There's a wooden trunk here in the far corner, with a latch and lock and . . . wait, there's clothing here too." Volmar lifted the cloak, surprised to find that it was a monk's robe. He sniffed the neckline of the cowl. He smelled sweat mingled with a sweet cinnamon scent. The cassock too was folded neatly beside the trunk. It was black and distinctively Benedictine in cut and make. There was no distinguishing tear or frayed hem which gave any specific clue as to who its owner might be. Whoever it belonged to was certainly taller than he was by nearly half a hand's length.

Volmar then turned his attentions to the wooden trunk and jiggled its lock. It held fast, determined to keep its secrets. He tried to lift it but found it too heavy and filled with what sounded to him like coins knocking against one another with a characteristic metallic resonance.

Volmar put the trunk down and froze, sensing that something, or someone, was in the room with him. Whoever or whatever it was must be alive, he thought, as he now heard the sound of its unnatural hum, a noise no human could make. As Volmar listened in silence, he was able to determine that the humming was coming from the adjoining chamber. Slowly, he made his way across to this smaller chamber, carefully placing each step as the flagstone floor was uneven. The stones were pushed on their sides by the roots of the trees overhead which, like living ropes, were intertwined haphazardly across the walls and the floors. His jaw muscles tightened and his heart thundered as he entered the adjoining smaller chamber.

When his eyes did finally adjust, what he saw neither frightened him nor sickened him. It did, however, mystify the young monk. In the corner of the antechamber, a partially decomposed body sat upright on a stone bench, leaning absurdly forward with its arms and legs crossed, ridiculously staged as if it were reading. Curiously, Volmar approached the body, still dressed in the shreds of a robe of a holy order he was unfamiliar with. The body's hands were shriveled like twigs, giving the perception of abnormally long and pointed fingernails. The right hand was positioned so one finger was up its nose and the left hand was turned so it could hold the book it was reading. The facial features preserved by the inner chamber's dry chilly air, however, belied this comical pose. On it was a petrified expression of outright rage. Volmar was grateful Hildegard did not have to witness such disdainful profanity.

Volmar roused himself, feeling a need to speak aloud, to say something to confirm that here in front of him was proof that Hildegard's story of Brother Arnoul was at least in part true. He gave in to the feeling, swallowed hard and said, "Brother Arnoul, we meet at last."

The petrified skin on the back of the body's skull was cracked and showed distinctive bruising suggesting a head injury. But other than a few other skin discolorations, Volmar did not see any visible indications of puncture wounds caused by a knife or sword.

Suddenly, two honey bees flew from the body's left ear, followed by six more buzzing irritably. Volmar backed off quickly, realizing that a beehive must have formed in the folds of the dead monk's habit. He recalled the story of Samson in the book of Judges and the riddle he made up after finding a beehive in the carcass of a dead lion.

"In death there is life, eh brother?" Volmar said, thankful the bees ignored his presence and seemed more attuned to escaping through the ceiling's opening. Whoever visits down here, he surmised, does so on a regular basis, at least enough to allow the survival of this hive. All of this confirmed what Hildegard had said about her apparent conversation with Brother Arnoul's left-behind spirit. He felt ashamed that he had doubted her story.

"May I?" he asked politely, lifting the book from the remains of what he surmised was Brother Arnoul. The book, however, was not the missing codex he half expected to find. Instead, it was a dummy copy with the crudely scrawled title of *Benedictus*, clearly meant to mimic the original missing tome and to further add to this cruel joke. Who would do such a thing? "The very same soul who wants to hoard treasures in this cave rather than in heaven," he said aloud, answering his own question. He slipped the dummy copy of the book into his leather pouch, determined to find out who amongst his holy brethren would have a sense of humor bizarre enough to find such an inhuman shrine amusing to look at for over ten years.

Before turning the lever to seal the entrance to the hidden chamber, Volmar looked around one last time. Hildegard was there beside him. She had said very little after he'd mentioned that he had seen the remains of Brother Arnoul in the chamber below. She had listened to him with her soft eyes shining in the darkness. It was as if he was simply confirming a fact she'd already known. There was a certain analytical logic to her response.

"Do you think you could find out if the codex has been returned to the library at the monastery and report back to us in the clearing tomorrow afternoon?"

He accepted the "us," knowing that this second person was a dead monk trying desperately to right a terrible wrong. "I will try, I promise, even if I will be assigned extra duties to make up for missing Vespers this afternoon. But," he added rather wistfully, "it was worth it."

"Come, Brother Volmar." Hildegard lifted the oil lamp high. "Brother Arnoul assured me the corridor under the wooden arch leads to the Altar of Saint Peter. Perhaps, if we hurry, you'll be able to attend prayers after all." In the warm flickering glow of the flame, Hildegard paused and said frankly, "I've never met one whose curious nature so evenly matches my own."

"I could say the same." Volmar smiled, something he rarely did. He stood gazing into her pale, penetrating eyes, mesmerized by the way the lamp's light suddenly seemed to play with the energy emanating from her soul.

The young scribe reached to carry the oil lamp. "My turn, your arm must be tired." He paused for one brief moment as his fingers lightly touched hers. Together they crossed the cave floor, which was slippery with lichen, and went into the dryer tunnel marked by the stout wooden arch.

Chapter 7: Preposterous Facsimile

Library at Disibodenberg Monastery

Harvest Festival, Evening

After dinner Volmar had plenty of time to think, while serving out his punishment for missing Vespers. He cleared the tables and scrubbed clean the pots and bowls from dinner. The Kitchener, Brother Amos, took to heart his role as the monastery's improvised disciplinarian. He felt, especially towards Brother Volmar, that despite all of his eloquence, this young monk needed to be humbled and reminded that no task was too menial. Volmar obediently carried out Brother Amos's more outrageous orders and served out his sentence in silence, all the while thinking of Hildegard and Brother Arnoul.

Vespers were over and the sanctuary had been serenely quiet as the two slipped out together from behind Saint Peter's Altar. The rain had eased and the clouds parted only to reveal a meager sun setting in the west. Hildegard insisted that he leave her beside the team of carriage horses waiting in the church's forecourt, urging him to join his holy brothers in the refectory for dinner.

It was an awkward moment. Volmar imagined that the horses were stamping nervously to register their displeasure over his and Hildegard's forbidden afternoon spent together.

"I shall come for you in the morning and report on the visit to the library," he had said politely, his hands tucked in the cuffs of his sleeves. Turning back after they had parted, Volmar had caught her eye and in it he knew that she also felt as bewildered as he. Not only had they stumbled on an unsolved murder, it seemed she'd also awakened in him dormant feelings he didn't know he possessed.

An hour later, humbled from kitchen duty, yet determined to find answers, Volmar climbed the winding staircase with its high clerestory leaded-glass windows leading to the Library. Once he mounted the precipice of the last step, he leaned against the wall and knew he had stayed away too long. He missed his leisure study time. It was a high price to pay for being Brother Paulus's apprentice.

The heavy oak doors of the Library stoically served as guardians to the region's most prestigious collection of literary and canonical[30] works. They were propped open to allow the Librarian to participate in the holy offices of prayers without having to leave his post. Reverently, the young monk entered, surveying the vast room hung majestically with iron balconies. Every available wall was lined with leather-bound books and scrolls, top to bottom, stone floor to vaulted ceiling. Volmar breathed in their familiar smell. If only his mind could take in as easily what his eyes marveled at. Among the treasures of Disibodenberg's library was a Latin-German dictionary dating back to A.D. 790, a German translation of the Lord's Prayer, and a copy of the Nicene Creed. The pride of place, however, was reserved for a three–volume giant Bible given to the monastery by visiting brothers from Britain's Tewkesbury Priory. Their library was in a condition of ruin and decay, and many of their valuable books were brought to Disibodenberg for safe-keeping after Brother Cormac became the Librarian and his acquisitive reputation spread.

---

[30] Canon Law: The law governing the Holy Roman Catholic church.

There were many empty carrels[31], but only one heavy table in the center of the large reading room, and it alone had light. Almost everything else was shapeless and lost in the dusty edges of the encroaching twilight shadows. Such austerity suited Brother Cormac, who was seated at the table. He was alone as usual and bent over, dutifully and meticulously writing out his newly revised contents list of the monastery's vast collection. Beside each entry he assigned a mysterious location number and alongside it he inscribed an even more inscrutable symbol of which he alone committed to memory its meaning. Once he completed the last entry he would start all over again, as was customary. In this way, Disibodenberg's incalculable treasures were fully known to only this one man.

"Do not breathe on any of the books," he snapped automatically without looking up. "Hot air curls the pages."

Volmar recalled his first visit to Cormac's library and the dread this man had provoked in all the younger students with his litany of rules. Punishment for disobedience was immediate, severe, and unpardonable: banishment from the collection. To Volmar, such an edict seemed unduly harsh, as if he were being forced to leave Eden. In this way, Volmar realized, Cormac had kept his own contact with the outside bustling world of Disibodenberg on only a need to know basis, nothing more. Cormac went on in his gravelly voice, still not lifting his head up from his work, "Be sure to put on a mask and gloves. They're in the cumdachs.[32]"

Volmar knew all this. Quietly, he lifted the book-chest's lid, finding the mask and gloves in the crimson velvet interior. As he took them out, Volmar wondered to himself how he was going to get this obstinate, surly monk's attention without regretting it.

He cleared his voice and began, "My soul is lost in here. Surely, if God had a dwelling place on Earth, it would be in this Library."

That did it. Even though he had his back to him, Volmar could feel the sting of Cormac's piercing gaze. He had the Librarian's undivided attention. Deliberately, he took his time slipping on the gloves. They were especially soft and supple, made from deerskin. The mask was

---

[31] Carrels: A table with bookshelves often portioned or enclosed for individual study in a library.

[32] Cumdachs: An Irish word for a portable wooden book chest or trunk.

equally soft, with leather straps to hold it over the mouth. No one was allowed to handle the manuscripts without such precautions.

Cormac pushed his paperwork to one side and rose. Who was this young intruder who spoke so well of his own sentiments? He was intrigued. "Speak up son," Cormac said, knowing full well his hearing was impaired simply from disuse.

"Isn't it a shame that most people live and die without ever having the opportunity to set a finger on a book?" Volmar said, scratching behind his ear as he straightened up. He knew Brother Cormac's character flaws, better perhaps than his own. Cormac was a teacher rather than a thinker; a gatherer and distributor rather than one in which new ideas germinated and prospered. His bent of genius, so unlike Brother Paulus's, was in the preservation of knowledge inherited from the past, not the methodical investigation of facts for the sake of new discoveries. Volmar used this insight to his advantage and went on, deciding to come directly to his point. "I understand a book went missing ten years ago."

"Hmm? Oh yes, the *Codex Benedictus.* I haven't had it replaced, still hoping it might show up one day." The skin exposed on the top of Cormac's skull reddened. "It was stolen by a Frenchmen disguised as a visiting brother." Cormac's comments sounded more like a lament. "Do you know," he went on remorsefully, creeping slowly towards the intruder and acknowledging to himself that he missed the thrill of imparting his thoughts, "that over 180 animal skins were sacrificed to produce the parchment for that single book? What a deplorable waste."

"Surely," Volmar continued with fresh determination, hearing the soft approach of the Librarian's leather sandals, "a monk must have spent six hours a day and several years meticulously copying page after page of that book."

Brother Cormac stood behind the young intruder, uncharacteristically engaged. "I cannot help you, sir, if you are after the *Codex Benedictus.*"

"Ah, but I think you can. What if I told you that Brother Arnoul was killed in the clearing outside of our walls?" Volmar turned around to watch Cormac's reaction directly.

The Librarian frowned. "You are mistaken, son. His kind never receive their just rewards until they face the Almighty. His name was stricken from all of the monastery's records, I saw to that myself. Here, now, how do you know of this wretched thief?" he asked, holding the lit candle up to the boy's face.

Volmar pulled back the hood of his cowl and smiled warmly. "It's good to see you again, Brother Cormac."

Volmar had never seen Cormac smile. So unaccustomed was Cormac's face to such a distortion, he was sure if Cormac could manage a smile, it would seem more devious than divine. "Nonsense," he said dismissively. "Go on, Volmar, with your ridiculous tale."

Volmar knew better than to take the older monk's rudeness to heart. Brother Cormac had a powerful intellect but an equally scornful manner. Volmar took the calculated risk by appealing to Cormac's mind. "I have proof of Brother Arnoul's death. His desiccated body sits in an ossarium, buried not far from here." He could tell that this mention of an ossarium was a piece of new information to Cormac.

Cormac hesitated. A response was obviously called for, but he was not quite sure what he should say. "An ossarium, you say . . . There are legends of one nearby holding the bones of our beloved Saint Disibod and his earlier followers."

Cormac studied Volmar, staring at him with wide eyes, and asked with a little more warmth, "Have you come to return the book the Frenchman stole?"

"No, I'm afraid all I found was this." Volmar reached into his leather pouch and produced the hand-written dummy copy of the valuable lost codex. "I came for your advice, in fact, on what I should do about all of it."

The Librarian took from his leather pouch a small magnifying glass he had obtained during the summer months, when he journeyed throughout the region and abroad for the purpose of copying and collecting books. Volmar watched in amazement as he held this round glass piece over the calligraphy title on the cover of the dummy copy, intrigued at how the glass enlarged the lettering below.

A long time ago, Volmar recognized Cormac for who he was. Cormac had made his peace with the passions that were for other men a great hindrance to the monastic life. Socially, he was inept, but mentally, he was on fire. The old monk reserved all of his obsessions for his collection. In here, he was arrested by the words of others safely inscribed on the pages of books, not vigorously spoken or insinuated in face-to-face conversation.

"Ah ha! With this tool, details unseen by our own eyes are suddenly visible," Cormac said, handing to Volmar his remarkable magnifying glass.

Volmar took it and held it over the cover of the dummy codex.

"No, no, no . . . you must close your other eye and hold it close to your stronger eye," Cormac instructed with little patience.

The effect was certainly mesmerizing. Volmar held the marvelous glass steady, seeing for the first time the details his eyes normally missed. Could this be one of the realities that Hildegard had hinted at that were part of the invisible world?

"See here, Volmar," Cormac went on impatiently, "how the letter 'T' is crossed with two strokes, not one, and how the "E" is shorter than all the other letters? One's style of writing is as individual and telling as one's choice of words."

"Can you tell me who wrote this?" Volmar asked in disbelief.

"Humph, never liked the man myself . . . " Cormac mumbled, searching through his vast store of memories, forgetting for a moment that he had an audience. "Thought he was better than everyone else, he did. Come along, I'll show you his work and you can tell me if it resembles this preposterous facsimile[33]."

Cormac led Volmar down a long corridor past rows and rows of bookshelves, explaining as he walked. "You see, Volmar, my objective as a Librarian is to obtain one copy of every important text ever written. I'd like to have here representative works from every civilized culture that has ever existed. When a book is stolen, as with the *Codex Benedictus*, a hole is left behind that injures the entire collection. Ah, here we are," Cormac said, reaching for one of the works under the category of General History of the Roman Empire. "What one enjoys reading tells you also volumes about the nature of one's soul. This particular young scribe had a fascination with powerful emperors, relishing especially their methods of torturing Christians." He handed over the book to Volmar's gloved hands. "You tell me, Volmar, if it is not the same style of writing."

---

[33] Facsimile: A forgery or exact copy of an original work.

Volmar walked the book back over to the table where the light was the strongest, slipped on his mask, and used Cormac's magnifying tool to make the critical comparisons. "*Church History* by Eusebius of Caesarea," he read aloud.

"Eusebius was a prolific writer of that time," Cormac explained. "This is perhaps his most important work covering the history of Christianity from the time of Jesus Christ to the time of Emperor Constantine. I believe this book contains those parts which deal with the ten persecutions."

As Volmar listened, he went back and forth leveling the magnifying glass onto one page after another, carefully comparing each letter with its corresponding match. "This is truly amazing," Volmar said swallowing hard. "There are remarkable similarities between both writings. See how in both the copied book and the phony facsimile, the letter "U" is drawn with a peculiar tail that goes up? One would expect it should go down. It does the same here," he sighed, looking up. "Do you know who was the scribe who copied this book by Eusebius?"

Cormac spoke after a moment, looking over Volmar's shoulder. His manner was as aloof as his reputation. "At the time, he was a novitiate and if my memory serves me well, his name was Judas. Unfortunately, he's no longer here, son, I'm sure of it. He'd always set his sights on Rome."

This was disappointing. Volmar turned in confusion to Cormac, who stared back with a hint of contemptuousness and grimaced. "There's something about human nature. You always seem to remember those who troubled you the most."

Chapter 8: To Let Go

Infirmary at Disibodenberg Monastery

Harvest Festival, Late the Same Evening

Sophie sat beside her grandfather and listened to his breathing keeping time with the distinct rhythmic chant of the masons chiseling stones nearby. During the storm the masons had rested, but now they were back at work on the Anchorage. She then heard the sound of muddy boots being scraped outside the Infirmary's door and the unfastening of the door clasp. Brother Paulus, she thought, must be returning early from Vespers. She watched as Paulus entered, nodded a greeting, then silently took the lantern from the hook, wandering off, muttering to himself. Certain monks like the Infirmarian, she understood, were released from the burden of attending all of the daily Offices of Prayers[34]. They could choose which times were convenient to attend.

Sophie rose and stretched. Slowly, she traced with her long fingers the raised bumps and deep crevices of the carved mantle over the oak hearth, a simple design of leaves and acorns. She felt restless and couldn't sleep, though she was very tired. She thought back to how her days had seemed more complete when she was working alongside her Grandda. Perhaps, she might find at the quarry a discarded stone or even a piece of wood she could take up to carve in order to fill these long, agonizingly empty hours of waiting for her Grandda's health to improve.

For the moment, he was resting peacefully. She guessed the tonic Brother Paulus had prepared for him must have had a sleeping potion in it. It was disconcerting to see how normal Grandda appeared once he lost consciousness; the lines on his face had softened and he seemed much younger, more like she remembered him.

"Drink . . . " weakly mumbled her Grandda. "I need . . . drink."

Sophie took the mug next to his bed and helped him sit up to take a swallow. His lips were cracked and still swollen from the fall. She then took a rag, rinsed it in the nearby basin and rested it back on Silas's forehead. "There, there, that should feel better," she said, fussing with the collar of his tunic.

He smiled gratefully for her kindness, the wrinkles around his eyes moistened, as if he were remembering all the horrible things he had said to her earlier. "Forgive me, my dear," he murmured before closing his eyelids, welcoming, she knew, the blissful oblivion of sleep's comforting embrace.

Sophie leaned forward and kissed his cheek, so cold against her lips. "No matter, Grandda, it's forgotten." Silently she stood and

---

[34] Daily Offices of Prayers: A practice observed at monasteries whereby the monks observe every three hours, or eight times daily, prayer meetings.

stoked the fire, trying to warm the sudden chill in the air. She listened to the familiar strains of music being played outside in the fields surrounding the monastery. The rains must not have dampened everyone's spirits, she thought, throwing open the window and leaning out on its ledge. A cooler breeze caught her hair and tugged at her imagination. She could still hear the excitement of the festival. Surely while her Grandda was resting comfortably, it wouldn't be wrong to go exploring.

Sophie tip-toed past what she knew now to be the laboratory of Brother Paulus, noticing how the scent of the room was both pungent and aromatic due to the bundles of herbs drying neatly in rows on racks. She peered in. Paulus had settled comfortably on a high stool, intent upon what appeared to be a small crucible[35] bubbling over a candle's flame. A scroll was half-unwound beside him on the stone table and a glass of ale rested in his hand. He sat the glass down and picked up some tongs and pushed the crucible he was tending deeper into the flames. What was it exactly that frightened her about Brother Paulus? The answer came to Sophie as she departed from the Infirmary. He had control over her future. That must be it. Her grandfather's future rested in his knowledgeable yet fragile hands. How she hated to let go and allow a stranger to determine her chance for happiness. Is this what it means to become an adult, she wondered, permitting outsiders, not loved ones, to determine your fortune?

Unknown to Sophie, not one, but two souls passed under the threshold of the Infirmary's door. One soul was young and determined; the other, old and protective. One soul was still held prisoner within its frail body; the other soul was free at last from all constraints governing the living, except perhaps love.

---

[35] Crucible: A heat resistant container, like a flask, it can be subjected to extreme temperatures.

Chapter 9: A Fleeting Smile

The Festival Grounds at Disibodenberg Monastery

Harvest Festival, Late Evening of the Same Day

The rainstorm had left in its wake a chilly wind, so Sophie wrapped the warmest part of her torn cape around her head and neck and set off down the slimy cobbled road. She was determined to satisfy her curiosity and see if the stone quarry had any promising stones or wood to work with before it got to be too dark.

The monastery's bell chimed loudly, announcing Compline[36]. Sophie stood motionless for a moment, watching, by the light of a rising full moon, the monks moving in unison to the cloister with their black cowls covering their heads. To her, they were like mystical travelers moving effortlessly between two distinctively different worlds, one of chaos and one of order. In less than an hour, she knew, the monks would retire for rest and would sleep until the bells of Matins[37]. There was comfort in such disciplined rituals, she thought straightening up, comfort and timeliness.

There were fewer festival-goers. Many had abandoned the evening's activities due to the unexpected storm and were now forming a lengthy supper line outside the open kitchen's dining hall. Sophie quietly moved between their noisy chatter, admiring the women's colorful dresses accented with scarves, beads, and tassels. So intent was she on such spectacles, she almost bumped into a scowling old man with a basket of flopping fresh fish.

"Out of my way, child," he said, kicking at her shins.

Sophie, however, was quick and sidestepped the blow, disappearing into the throng of families. She weaved behind fathers carrying children on their shoulders and in baskets affixed to their backs. She could hear the conversations of those children old enough to walk, tugging on their mother's skirts, begging for more attention. Sophie stepped out of the crowd and hung back against the wall, watching and listen-

---

[36] Compline: One of the daily offices of prayer around 6 p.m.

[37] Matins: The darkest hour office of prayer given between 2:30 and 3 a.m.

ing with an avid curiosity. Women especially, were a novelty to her, she found them sadly puzzling. Those she observed did not seem content with their lives. They were hurried, tired, or annoyed most of the time, treating their husbands more like children than companions. She winced in pain as she saw one young mother discipline her child with a reddening slap on his cheek.

In the world she and her Grandda had shared, there were only stonemasons with their familiar and predictable ways. She knew little of such family closeness and its apparent discord. Grandda was the only real stability she had ever had in her short life. They had travelled far, visiting many towns and staying as long as there were great carvings to create. Now, with her Grandda's failing health, her world was crumbling like thin layers of slate. Sophie suddenly felt alone in the crowd, different from everyone else. What would she do if the unthinkable happened and Grandda passed on?

"You would survive," she heard her Grandda whisper in her heart. Sophie turned around, half-expecting to see his dancing eyes. Instead she saw in the distance a trainer guiding his chained bear up a wooden ramp and back into its iron cage.

A minstrel[38], with fiery red hair and a bushy beard, winked at her as he passed by. He must have sensed her pensive mood, she thought, for suddenly he switched to singing an old love ballad. She lingered longer, listening attentively and watching in awe as his fingers moved over the strings of the lute[39]. It was effortless for him, like it was for her when she sculpted. It was as if the fingers had a mind of their own. The people all around her also grew quiet to listen to the song's familiar, evocative story. The melody was so sad and full of longing that Sophie wanted to cry. In the song, the poor wench[40] discovers that she has fallen in love with a young man who loves another. The pitiful wench, like all young children, has no memory, and lives entirely in the present. She feels pleasure and pain, and bears great hopes and wishes. However, when she witnesses her love in another's embrace, her world shatters as easily as glass. She is unable to recover, for she has no

---

[38] Minstrel: Or Troubadour, were singers who would sing simple ballads or songs, while playing an instrument for entertainment.
[39] Lute: A medieval guitar; a stringed musical instrument with a large pear-shaped body and a fretted fingerboard.
[40] Wench: A young woman or female servant.

depth of experience to draw upon. In the end, she suffers with such intensity she ends up taking her own life.

"If such a tragic fate should overtake you," the minstrel concluded as he serenaded Sophie, "then know that you, like she, will live on for a time in a song."

The dismal fate of the young wench tugged at the cobweb of common sense Sophie possessed. There were times in life, her Grandda used to tell her, when there were only poor choices; but nevertheless, the world was a place of beauty and mystery, and always there was hope.

The minstrel gave Sophie a fleeting smile, then moved on unhurried through the crowd to sing to another troubled soul.

Only then did Sophie sense that someone was watching her. She searched the crowd, clearly feeling the uncomfortable gaze of a stranger. Her eyes met up with a young woman, a few years older than herself, who was taller than her and was dressed richly in a velvet cape of navy blue with a silver filigreed clasp at her neck. She had long, luxuriant auburn hair that fell about her shoulders loosely as if it had just been combed through. Sophie stiffened, feeling suddenly exposed in this woman's intense gaze. She felt at once shabby and as poorly dressed as a leper. She also felt an overwhelming need to flee.

"Wait," the young woman called out to her, as Sophie took off down the hill. She stumbled in front of a performing juggler, causing—to the utter delight of his young audience—his red, blue, and yellow leather balls to tumble from their arcs and roll up to their feet. The young woman called out again, this time with more urgency, "Sophie!"

Sophie froze. How did this strange woman know her by name? She held her breath and turned around to face the young woman's flushed but relieved face.

"I have a message I'd like you to give to Brother Volmar," the woman said, handing her a rolled parchment tied with a golden string. Then she did a most astonishing thing. She took Sophie's hands in hers, squeezed them and prophesized, "One day, you will achieve recognition for your gifts; hold fast to that as the darkness rises and the storm clouds gather." She turned from Sophie and spoke to the space next to the young girl. "She is stronger than you realize. You've given her a great start in life. Go in peace, knowing this."

Before Sophie could question this woman's insights into her future, a carriage, the same elegant one that nearly trampled her and Volmar earlier that day, stopped directly in front of the young woman.

A footman dismounted and said with a sigh of relief, "My lady, we've been looking all over for you."

"Forgive me," the young woman apologized meekly before turning to Sophie. "Your grandfather wants you to know he loves you very much."

"What do you mean?" Sophie sputtered. "How do you know of Grandda?"

"I know, because he is there standing beside you." The young woman hesitated, "and will always be there, he says, to look after you." She smiled sadly and accepted the footman's arm as he assisted her into the coach.

The horses snorted, their warm breath coming out as small trails of smoke in the cool night air. Moments later, Sophie watched as the carriage clambered away down the darkened road leading to the porter's gate and out from the protected walls of Disibodenberg.

Chapter 10: The Darkest Corner

The Infirmary at Disibodenberg Monastery

Harvest Festival, After Compline the Same Day

Paulus's very black eyes started watering and his cheeks grew red. He smashed his fist down on the table and muttered, "Send for Sophie. She'll need to know right away." Brother Paulus was unaccustomed to losing a patient and it took him more than a moment to find his composure.

Volmar had only just returned from Compline to prepare the patients for bed when he found to his horror that Silas, Sophie's grandfather, had died in his absence.

Volmar gently shut the lids of eyes no longer dulled by the confusion of delirium and pulled the sheet up over the old man's face. He said a prayer for his soul and remarked as if the value of the life suddenly lost needed to be reaffirmed, "Silas was a stone carver in Mainz. He and Sophie worked on a portico at Saint Martin's Cathedral."

Paulus slumped forward, muttering absently, "The bump on Silas's head merely hastened Death's arrival. It was just a matter of time, really. When trees grow old they begin to lose their inner greenness. Likewise, when a man ages, his brain shrivels and dies chamber by chamber, eventually leaving the skull a hollow shell."

Paulus reached for the poker and used it to stoke the fire. There was such a cold finality to death, he thought, watching as the embers glowed with renewed warmth and life. He put on another log and stood back, watching as the flames devoured it slowly. The intense heat reddened his face even more and finally he drew back, unable to repress an unworthy flash of malice towards God for permitting such suffering. He lowered his head until he was able to conceal his private sentiment, the losing war he waged against God. Still trying to rein in his temper, he asked quietly, "Did you say that Sophie also knows how to carve in stone?"

"Or wood," Volmar said, genuflecting[41] and making the Sign of the Cross. "She apparently finished the portico when her Grandfather's hands started shaking."

"It takes skill, patience, and a great deal of artistic talent to sculpt in stone. I wonder . . . does Sophie have any other family?" Paulus queried, straightening his shoulders, gathering his resolve to help the living, rather than grieve over the dead.

"I am alone," a small voice answered him from the darkest corner.

Brother Paulus blinked in momentary confusion, and saw in the shadows how very pale Sophie had become. "I am so sorry, my dear child. Your grandfather passed on a short while ago." Paulus motioned with his head for Volmar to go to her. "She's still afraid of me," he said.

Paulus stood back as Volmar approached Sophie. Both were surprised by her reaction. At first, Sophie gave Volmar her hand and a scowl that trembled very slightly. She then wrapped her arms around the young monk and held him snug to her small frame as if such an action made possible her desire to squeeze the life from one to nourish the other.

---

[41] Genuflecting: To bend the knee in worship.

Volmar whispered to her, blinking back his tears. "Sophie, do not let this grief steal your dream."

Chapter II: A Remembrance Candle

Saint Peter's Altar at Disibodenberg Monastery

Before Matins the Next Morning

Uppermost in Sophie's mind was the need to burn a remembrance candle and to say a prayer for Grandda's soul. It troubled her how his illness and injury made him curse and say such wicked things, and she wanted to remind God that he was not himself the past year. Could God remember a man's soul before it was spit upon by a demon's sickness?

Sophie couldn't sleep, though she pretended to do so. Patiently she waited until everyone else went off to bed before quietly reaching for her tattered cape. So that no one could hear her footfalls, she slipped on her wooden clogs once she was safely outside. She then turned her back to the Infirmary and followed the moonlight as it directed her path to the church. She shivered uncontrollably as she entered the cooler sanctuary. Women were strictly forbidden to enter the church after Compline. Tonight, she didn't care.

It was much smaller than the Mainz Cathedral but imposing nevertheless with its looming ceilings, frescoed walls, and high, leaded-glass windows. Even on such a bitterly forbidding night, God's house at that moment felt more welcoming and familiar to Sophie than the harsh world she'd left outside. Its serene stillness embraced her trembling soul and stilled her wayward thoughts. The stones beneath her feet smelled comforting, of lingering incense. After spending a year traveling, dare she allow herself to feel she had returned home at last? She knelt on the small knee bench and folded her hands. She had witnessed many ceremonies and knew she needed to make a vow[42],

[42] Vow: A solemn promise or assertion, one by which in this case, Sophie binds herself to an act, service, or condition in respect to the church.

promising to the Almighty her commitment to furthering His Kingdom on Earth for saving the soul of her Grandda.

The alcove[43] was dedicated to the memory of Saint Peter, the founding Saint of the Holy Roman Catholic Church. Surely Saint Peter would understand her suffering and intercede[44] on her behalf.

"Unworthy as I am." She prayed in earnest, knowing very well that her presence before the altar might be interpreted by some as blasphemy. "I beseech thee, Saint Peter, to call to mind that sickness my Grandfather suffered. Pity me for my spirit is anxious. Thou, who art standing on the eternal shore, behold my dearest Grandda. When all others abandoned me, he stayed. Place him where light abides and life reigns eternally, and I swear to serve the Lord God Almighty with my gift cheerfully all the rest of my days." Sophie breathed a sigh and knew the enormity of what she had just promised. Not many servants of the Lord, no matter how enlightened, would accept a stone-carver so young and especially one that is a female.

She opened her eyes when she sensed a movement in front of her. There, in front of her, stood Saint Peter, glaring down at her as if she were a boil on the end of his nose. In the half-light she saw that he was alive and fully dressed as he once was, as a poor fisherman and not the revered saint. He watched her silently a moment longer. "Did you take my lamp?" he demanded. "I couldn't see a thing down there." A cold force emanated from his body.

Sophie stood bravely despite the tears brimming over in her eyes. "Please," she pleaded, "keep searching for my Grandda. Turn away thine anger, and have pity on thy servant's frailty. Deliver him, O Saint Peter, from the malice of the Devil down there, and from all sin and evil, and grant him a happy end for thy loving mercy's sake."

In a flash of insight, the man who Sophie addressed as Saint Peter muttered, "Go, child, and speak nothing of this to anyone." He waved her off with his hand.

Sophie hurriedly left the Saint behind her in the sanctuary, feeling only a sense of secrecy and discordance emanating from him. There was doubt, too, as a disturbing awareness washed over her. Maybe

---

[43] Alcove: A small chapel off to one side of the church.

[44] Intercede: To act in behalf of another with a view to reconciling all differences.

what she had encountered was not supernatural at all. She would have to ask Brother Volmar; he would know if it was, she thought.

Chapter 12: The Devil is Still Afoot

Clearing Outside of Disibodenberg Monastery

Before Compline

Volmar sunk his hands into the sleeves of his robe and stood alone in the clearing under the old yew tree. His mind wandered back to Hildegard's words and now agreed that people's minds do create their own realities. The world is so much more than what he could experience.

After Terce, he'd looked in on Sophie and found her clearly agitated by an apparent encounter with Saint Peter. He had listened and concluded with her that she had seen a man, not the revered Saint, who had used the secret tunnel behind the altar. Her description could describe any one of the seventy monks at the monastery and that didn't include the fifty-odd male attendants that worked at the monastery and lived in Staudernheim. The conversation fascinated Sophie and lifted her spirits. She had spoken animatedly of other secret passages she'd seen in various churches she and her Grandfather had visited. She'd also given him the message from Hildegard.

In it, Volmar had read what he already had heard from gossip amongst the brothers. Jutta's mother had fallen ill, and their party had to return to Sponheim immediately. However, it was gratifying to read that Hildegard regretted having to leave him without saying goodbye. She had also enclosed a secret code, a message only he could read. It ended up being an alphabet. Hildegard wrote that they could use it to communicate about Brother Arnoul, in a way no one else would be able to decipher. Volmar had folded it away and kept this secret even from Sophie.

In the clearing, Volmar held his oil lamp high into the air. Its light danced back and forth in the restless chilly wind. It was an unusual gray twilight, caused by the reflection of the moon on the barks of the trees surrounding him. "Brother Arnoul, I didn't find the book in our library," Volmar said aloud, listening for a moment to any reply from the spiritual world. "Our Librarian," he went on, "Brother Cormac, remembers you and Judas, and is convinced that your murderer left the monastery for Rome. I am not so sure. I sense that the Devil is still afoot within the monastery's walls." He paused, kicking at the rocks at his feet, trying to piece together all the known facts. "We're making progress, though. Sophie met a man returning to the monastery late, using your secret tunnel. Hildegard and I had taken his lantern from the tunnel and he could not change back into his robes."

Volmar touched the back of his neck. Was it the cold presence of a dead monk or merely a chilled wind? He went on. It was indeed difficult to address someone he could not see. "There is no monk in the Benedictine order here at Disibodenberg who goes by the name of Judas. Perhaps, Cormac has it right and he has left for another monastery. However, I do not think so. I am suspicious that someone still uses the secret tunnel to come and go as they please." He paused and concluded, "Brother Arnoul, I will not give up until justice is served and your good name is restored."

Chapter 13: Blackbirds

Cemetery Near St. Michael's Chapel

21st of October, Saturday morning, shortly after day-break, the

Year of Our Lord 1111

There were blackbirds everywhere. Their strong beaks pecked hungrily in the fallow fields surrounding the cemetery. One blackbird, set apart from the others, stood guard as it watched over the burial proceedings from the stone steeple of Saint Michael's Chapel.

A watery sun shone fitfully through the gathering rain clouds. A cold, weak light streamed down on a small group as they stood around the grave. Hot tears streamed down Sophie's cheeks. Behind her stood Thomas, who had surprisingly put down his tools and crossed the pasture to attend the ceremony, without saying a word. Volmar and Brother Paulus stood on either side of her like great stone pillars. There was no money to afford a coffin. Her grandfather's body was wrapped in a simple shroud. Several monks stood across from her and sang a tuneless psalm as the body was lowered into the grave.

Sophie straightened her back and lifted her head as the scoops of dirt toppled onto her grandfather's dead stiff body. She was so stricken by her grief, she could not even bring herself to respond to Brother Volmar's or Brother Paulus's caring gazes. She knew now that she was completely alone.

Abbott Burchard concluded the simple funeral service and sprinkled holy water from a silver aspersorium[45]. As the other monks and Thomas left to continue their work for the day, the Abbot knelt beside Sophie, admiring her handiwork. She'd spent the last several days chiseling a plaque for her Grandda's headstone. On it he read aloud the perfectly inscribed words: "*Vale in Christo semper memor nostri amen,*[46] Silas of Cologne, 1053–1111. Do you know Latin, my child?"

Sophie collected herself with an effort, hesitated and asked plainly, "Would it make a difference if I said yes or no?"

"I suppose not, though it is highly unusual for a girl to know how to write and understand Latin."

"I've lived all my days in the hallowed grounds of cathedrals and have listened daily to the monks reciting their prayers. Grandda taught me all that he knew, so I could make my own way in this world when he was gone."

"He was a wise man, your grandfather." The Abbot cleared his voice, clearly uncomfortable with what needed to be said. He searched and found the eyes of Volmar and Paulus lingering at the gate of the cemetery, watching respectfully from the distance. Both of the monks nodded to him, and he continued. "Err, I and another wise man, our Brother Paulus, have had a lengthy consultation on what to do with you here, Sophie. What he asks is contrary to our usual practices, but I do see the logic in the arrangement. Sophie, Brother Paulus requires many precise instruments to use in his healing practice and would like your help in creating these tools. In exchange, of course, you would receive room and boarding in the Women's Guest House. I told him I would ask you if this arrangement suits your plans for the near future."

Sophie dropped her head into her hands and murmured a prayer.

---

[45] Aspersorium: A holy water bucket, a liturgical implement, often used with a small ornate ball that holds within it a sponge. It is shaken over a gravesite as a way to offer blessings for the recently deceased.

[46] *Vale in Christo semper memor nostri amen*: A Latin inscription that reads when translated into English: *Farewell in Christ, always mindful of us, Amen.*

The Abbot inclined his head, and spoke hurriedly. "Evidently, I've offended you. I beg your pardon. It is an unusual request, my dear child, and made to you at such a delicate time. If you need time to consider our proposition . . . "

"Oh no, Father," Sophie blurted out, barely able to contain her excitement.

"No?" the Abbot repeated, shaking his head dismally towards Brother Paulus and Volmar.

"Wait, I mean, yes. The arrangement to work for Brother Paulus suits my plans and my promise to God, perfectly. Thank you so much!" She hugged the Abbot, flagrantly disregarding his esteemed status and his blushing discomfort towards such an outward display of gratitude.

Book 3: Before God's Throne

Chapter 1: A Time of Outright Corruption

Abbot Burchard's Private Quarters

One year on, Feast of All Saints, 1st of November, Friday, the Year of Our Lord 1112

"All ages are troubled," Volmar said, crossing his arms and warming his hands between the folds of his cassock's sleeves. " . . . and ours is certainly no exception." He nodded in disgust at his last entry in the monastery's register.

The last year had brought many changes. Sophie now assisted Brother Paulus in the Infirmary, and Volmar had been given the honor of assisting Abbot Burchard in his correspondence and recording of Disibodenberg's activities. Volmar was grateful for this position, because it gave him a perspective on the outside world that few of the other brothers at the monastery shared. For one who had just turned seventeen years of age, it was an impressive yet daunting duty.

"We cannot change the world overnight, my son," the Abbot answered as he busied himself with his cincture[47] in front of his full-length mirror and frowned. "I just don't understand. No matter how I tie it, it still makes me look fat. How can I be gaining weight in the winter when we're only allowed one meal?"

Volmar persisted, unwilling to change the subject. "Father, we live in a time of outright corruption. King Henry the Fifth treats our Pope as a mere commoner, throwing him into prison when the Pope refuses to give in to the King's requests to appoint the bishops he wants instead of the ones the church selects. Not only that, but just last month the Pope went back on his word and now the King has been excommunicated from the church!"

---

[47] Cincture: The velvet-waist scarf worn by Abbots.

"I wish I could say that all of this was unexpected, my son. Such bickering is in part how equally powerful institutions come to terms with each other. Eventually you'll see that the church will settle a truce with the King. If you want my advice, son, hold your tongue around the Bishop when he gets here. From what I've gathered, he's a shrewd politician and has been a staunch supporter of the Emperor, not the papacy."

"All of this is as foolish as trying to build a tower to reach heaven. How did we stray so far from the church's original mandate to spread love and forgiveness, the very tenets of Christianity?"

"Brother Volmar, you listen too much with your heart. We are only temporary travelers in this world. History is tension; in it we find the roots of our problems, our anguish, and yes, perhaps if we are fortunate, we even find the sleeping seeds of our salvation."

"And then there's Jutta of Sponheim," Volmar said, waving the parchment the Abbot had asked him to prepare for the evening's ceremony. "Why must we allow an anchoress to live at Disibodenberg, and one who is a professed ascetic[48]? Does the church now condone self-inflicted mutilation? It is an archaic ritual. We're living in the 12th century, not the 3rd!"

"You read yourself the edict from the Bishop. Jutta of Sponheim is well-connected. She comes to us from a wealthy family of upper nobility. Furthermore, she served her three years as a novitiate under the tutelage of her mother Sophia and another widow woman, Uda, both by all accounts devout." The Abbot went to his wine cupboard and pulled out a bottle, checking the date on its label. "Last December when her mother died," he continued, putting the bottle back and selecting another. "Jutta wanted to make a dangerous pilgrimage to the Holy Land. Her brother, Count Meinhard, understandably intervened and arranged instead with the Bishop that she come to reside here with us at Disibodenberg as our Anchoress. Just between you and me, her brother is hoping this will be a passing fancy of hers and that after a short while she will be more willing to accept one of the many marriage proposals she has been given." The Abbot, satisfied with the third bottle he selected, placed it on the table and went for the goblets. "You may remember," he added, "Jutta and her young ward, Hilde-

---

[48] Ascetic: Practicing self-denial for religious reasons.

gard, were here last year. Apparently, they both left with a favorable impression of our modest monastery."

Volmar of course remembered. It was a rare moment of warmth in his life. How could he forget? It was a stormy day when he'd met Hildegard in the clearing, and now the dark clouds were gathering for this storm. Hildegard was the very reason why he protested this ceremony. He did not want her to be locked away with the Anchoress.

"Do you think the Bishop will be traveling with more than two companions?" the Abbot asked, breaking Volmar's ruminations, as he surveyed his modest collection of tarnished silver goblets. He selected one and began polishing it with his stole[49].

"I think in his letter he mentioned two young men would be accompanying him."

The Abbot placed four silver goblets on the table next to the wine bottle and returned the fifth one, making a mental note that he'd have the Cellarer[50] use the mixture of ashes and soap to polish them for next time. "Volmar, you may stop frowning at me, I had nothing to do with this. The decision for this enclosure ceremony is out of my hands."

"Father, I was just thinking about something else . . . " Volmar hesitated, remembering his promise to Hildegard and Brother Arnoul. Deciding against caution, he blurted outright, "Do you recall a novitiate who lived at the monastery nearly eleven years ago named Judas?"

The Abbot was used to Volmar's peculiar conversational habits and thought nothing of the abrupt changes in their topic. He took a horse hair brush and used it to dust off the chairs. "Judas, you say? Hmm, the only Judas I remember was a young novitiate who left for Rome. I did not find in him a 'worthy vessel of God.'"

"You declined his desire to become a monk?" Volmar was both impressed and curious.

"I did. Not everyone who begins the novitiate should become a fully professed monk. His attitudes provoked criticism and hostility from within our community. Come, come, Volmar, why would you be interested in such a person?"

"No reason in particular, just something I heard."

---

[49] Stole: Is a long narrow rectangular garment, Abbots drape stoles around their necks.
[50] Cellarer: The monk responsible for all the food supplies in a monastery.

"Well then," the Abbot sighed, settling into his chair and appreciating the warmth from the roaring fire, "as for Jutta and her decision, I too think it is radical of her to go from an ordinary pilgrimage to a life as an 'exile.' Though, I must say, I admire her willingness to live the austere life as an Anchoress. Christianity warns us often that when one has all one cares to have, there is little need to think of an afterlife. Don't get me wrong, wealth is a great blessing and a means of doing good. However, it can be a serious distraction in faith."

"Father, don't you think it is a shame when the church is guilty of such a distraction?"

The Abbot sighed. "Volmar, this arrangement isn't all about these young women's dowries. Besides, you know as well as I do, the additional land will allow us to plant more vineyards, and the extra monies will go a long way towards adding more wings to our library. These are all blessings. We can't always come to expect funds from our anonymous giver."

"I know," Volmar said, "and yet . . . " he stubbornly asserted, "I can't help but feel the church is being mercenary."

"Brother Volmar, that is enough said. This is not like one of our lessons where there is a clear right and wrong answer. As you know, monasteries are homes for imperfect people to come and learn how to serve our most perfect Savior. I will take your objections into consideration. Nevertheless, the solemn induction[51] ceremony you speak ill of will take place this evening after Vespers." Abbot Burchard slumped forward in his chair. The skin on his bald skull left by his tonsure was so clear and thin you could see the pulsating blue veins below. Volmar had forgotten how old he really was.

"I am sorry, Father. I understand that your hands are tied in all of this." Volmar went and kneeled before his Abbot. "Forgive me."

The Abbot patted his shoulder good-naturedly, "Until I pass on, Brother Volmar, I am the chosen shepherd of the community of Saint Disibod." He gazed over at the flames licking the grate. "It is my responsibility to feed the fire on the altar of the Lord. Remember this, my son, the three young women you speak so passionately for are of

---

[51] Induction: The formality by which Jutta will be enclosed as an Anchoress at Disibodenberg. It will also involve Hildegard and Hiltrud, who will be enclosed as her spiritual companion and servant.

the age of consent and have asked for this life of prayer, celibacy, and praise." He straightened his back as the distant bells announced the arrival of the first of their guests. "It is time."

Volmar rose and checked the water clock. Its steady, relentless drip reinforced the sense of inevitability. He went to the window and peered down into the Abbot's garden. "I believe it is the Bishop and his entourage."

The Abbot straightened his cincture, thankful that the Bishop was of his generation and perhaps more forgiving of how one's proportions are altered by time. "Many persons of high and low degree will be in attendance," he said with some trepidation. "The entire village of Staudernheim will find these proceedings very curious, indeed. Come now, my son, we must put on a brave face."

Chapter 2: Air of Mistrust and Secrecy

Abbot Burchard's Private Quarters

Feast of All Saints, 1st of November, Friday, the Year of Our Lord 1112

Moments later, there was a knock at the Abbot's door. Brother Rudegerus, the Guest Master[52], ushered in Bishop Otto and his two distinguished-looking traveling companions. All three had cloaks with ermine collars and hems edged in gold tracery. They had journeyed nearly two hundred miles from Bamberg to preside over this ancient rite.

Bishop Otto breezed by Volmar, dropping his heavy cloak into the boy's arms. His heavy-lidded eyes focused only on the Abbot. "Good evening, Abbot Burchard."

---

[52] Guest Master: The one who welcomes and sees to the needs of visitors to the monastery. His duty was to receive any strangers and conduct them to the hospice or guest-chambers. The Benedictine principle of hospitality, expressed in chapter 53 of the Rule of St. Benedict reads: "All guests who present themselves are to be welcomed as Christ, for he himself will say: I was a stranger and you welcomed me (Matt 25:35). Proper honor must be shown to all, especially to those who share our faith (Gal 6:10) and to pilgrims."

Volmar noticed how the Bishop's thin, hawk-like features smiled continuously. To him it seemed artificial and tasteless. The Bishop extended his left hand.

"Your Grace," the Abbot responded, rising from his chair and bowing, kissing the ring on the Bishop's middle finger in deference. For the first time, Volmar examined the face of his Abbot anew. Here was a determined man lacking the meekness, patience, and humility that he normally portrayed. It was as if the occasion had suddenly energized him, rekindling the Abbot's spirit with a breath of fresh air. Maybe these visits were necessary, Volmar reasoned, if only to give the Abbot stimulating contact with the world beyond his monastery and with superiors he could confide in.

"Abbot Burchard, may I present my traveling companions, Adalbert of Mainz's son, Reginald, and his friend Atif." Reginald was a short, stocky man, looking barely out of his teens, and Atif was taller, leaner, and at least a decade older.

"Ah, it is an honor to meet you Reginald . . . Atif." The Abbot extended his hand to both men in a hospitable gesture. "I hope you will find your stay at Disibodenberg a comfortable one."

"I'm sure we will," Reginald answered for both of them, sourly noting the humble furnishings of the Abbot's private chamber.

"Atif . . . that's an unusual name," the Abbot mused aloud. "Tell me, do you know what it means?"

Volmar rolled his eyes in amusement, finding his Abbot's obsession with names and their meanings rather eccentric. By far, he put too much emphasis on a person's name being a window into their soul.

"I am not sure, Father," Atif said, bowing low, his dark eyes focusing above the Abbot's head. "Does it matter? Is not a man supposed to be judged by his character instead of his name?"

"Perhaps," the Abbot answered with a feigned smile.

Atif appeared genuinely ill at ease with everyone's attention suddenly focused on him. Quietly he helped Reginald with his heavy cloak and approached Volmar with it. He smiled stiffly before draping his own cloak over the young monk's arm.

Volmar quietly slipped into the nearby dressing room to hang up the overcoats. As he was hanging Atif's cloak on the hook, he heard the faint sound of something dropping to the floor. Kneeling discreetly, Volmar picked up a small rosary[53] and studied it, surprised to find it had the distinctive markings of a crucifix from the Knights of Hospitaller[54]. He slipped it back into the hidden pocket he guessed it had been in, hung the cloak up on the hooks behind the door with the others, and returned promptly to the Abbot's study.

"You may recall," the Bishop continued, "nearly two years ago, Adalbert went to Rome to arrange Henry the Fifth's coronation as Emperor. The Emperor, in turn, has gratefully appointed him the Archbishop of Mainz."

The Abbot turned to Reginald and clasped both his shoulders. "I hadn't heard. Give your father my heartiest congratulations. Tell him that he deserved such recognition a long time ago."

When Volmar returned, he noticed that Brother Rudegerus had moved quietly from his corner over to the Abbot's desk. With pursed, thin red lips he began rearranging the correspondence Volmar had been working on. Volmar felt annoyed by this obvious intrusion and watched with disdain as Rudegerus furtively read excerpts from the Abbot's personal papers.

Rudegerus had that quality of not caring what other people think, or at least acting like it didn't matter to him. In his late twenties, he had made it perfectly clear to anyone who would listen to him that he was infinitely more qualified than Volmar for the role of the Abbot's personal assistant, and would have made a better choice than the precocious younger monk. Such back-stabbing remarks troubled Volmar, and now, silently, he made his way behind Rudegerus, snatching up the pages he'd been working on earlier. Rudegerus turned and glared at Volmar. Protectively and silently, the young scribe gathered up all of the scattered pieces of correspondence and locked them away in the Abbot's desk drawer.

---

[53] Rosary: Prayer beads used in saying a Roman Catholic devotion consisting of meditation on sacred mysteries during recitation of Hail Marys.

[54] Knights of Hospitaller: Brotherhood of St. John of Jerusalem. This military religious order of monks founded by Blessed Gérard thought of the hospital as a community of saints: the brothers extended God's loving care to the needy.

Kneeling discreetly, Volmar picked up a small rosary and studied it, surprised to find it had the distinctive markings of a crucifix from the Knights of Hospitaller.

Out of all the holy brothers, Rudegerus was Volmar's least favorite and perhaps the most infuriating. Everyone knew that whenever Rudegerus was late for Mass, he was simply hiding behind his position, using it as an excuse to absent himself from holy affairs.

Bishop Otto continued. "Well, it should come as no surprise that Reginald has expressed interest in the church and wanted to accompany me on this journey so he might observe one of our more arcane rituals."

The Abbot looked ruefully at Reginald and said, "Weren't you one of the more persistent of Lady Jutta of Sponheim's suitors?"

Reginald replied stiffly, "Our families had discussed the possibilities of marriage. But Lady Jutta chose to keep her promise to God."

The Bishop took his cue and continued his introductions. "Atif is an Aramaic[55] scholar from Rome. He is Reginald's good friend and confidant. He is also interested in our practices and is considering the cloth."

Volmar checked his impulse to verbally disagree with the Bishop's false pronouncement of Atif's background. If he was who the Bishop said he was, then why would he carry a rosary of a very obscure and secretive society of monks from Jerusalem?

"Please, join me in a drink," the Abbot said congenially, scooting up two more chairs and placing them beside his and the Bishop's. He uncorked the bottle and poured wine into four goblets. Handing Reginald his drink, the Abbot asked, "What were your father's impressions of our new Roman Emperor, King Henry the Fifth?"

"Truthfully," Reginald said, sitting upright, his eyes luminous under his thick eyebrows, "my father regrets supporting the Emperor in his quest to regain the rights to investiture[56]." He emptied the glass in a single gulp and set it down with an impatience that belied his outward appearance of calm. "Roman Emperors are all alike. They are dull-witted, egotistical, and completely ungrateful! It is shameful how this Emperor has systematically gained control of our imperial castles by enlisting the help of our own countrymen, bribing them with ridicu-

---

[55] Aramaic: The Arameans, ancient people of Near East who inhabited Palestine and Syria, speak the Aramaic language, a Semitic language closely related to Hebrew dating as far back as 900 B.C.

[56] Investiture: The act of ratifying or establishing in office, a confirmation of the King's right to be King.

lous privileges. If this continues, my father is seriously considering rallying all the bishops and leading them in an anti-Imperialist movement."

"I couldn't help but notice the renovations you've made to the sanctuary, Burchard," Bishop Otto interjected, visibly ill at ease with the sudden turn in the conversation. "I myself am deeply invested in the improvements for the Bamberg Cathedral. You may have heard that a fire left it in a smoldering ruin thirty-one years ago."

"I did," the Abbot said, interested in the sudden air of fear that enveloped the room. "If Your Grace is willing, I would be overjoyed to show you and your companions around tomorrow shortly after Prime[57]. The Anchorage is but one of our more recent projects we've completed here at Disibodenberg."

The Abbot refreshed Reginald's drink, and then sat back, perplexed over how to continue diplomatically. The cloud of animosity that had formed still lingered in the room. When distant bells announced the arrival of more guests, the Bishop gave a strained laugh and genuflected, motioning the sign of the Father, Son, and Holy Ghost. "In homage of the divine Trinity, I am ready to conduct this ancient rite."

Abbot Burchard's gaze momentarily met Volmar's eyes. His young assistant had moved to the wall opposite the Abbot and the seated guests and was propped up against the heavily carved wooden mantel, fully engaged in all that was happening. The Abbot then turned his attentions to his goblet. He twirled it around and around in his hand, staring down into it . . . wine was a rare indulgence. In a low voice he broke the tense atmosphere and addressed Bishop Otto. "Your Grace, enclosure is a frugal life for young women accustomed to being the daughters of a count and a knight. I must admit, I do not know how long their vows would sustain them under such hardships they are not used to. The Anchorage has but three small windows to the outside world, a pitiful substitution for life."

Bishop Otto shifted uneasily in his chair. "Are you saying, Burchard, that you are not ready for tonight's ceremony?"

---

[57] Prime: The Office of Prayer around 7:30 a.m., shortly after daybreak.

"No, no. It isn't that at all. We will be ready. I am simply questioning whether the three young women are ready."

"They are of the age of consent, and all of their dowries have been registered, approved, and taken care of. So, that is that . . . the ceremony is all that is left to do."

Abbot Burchard turned to Volmar and, with a resigned expression, signaled to him that there would be no more debate. "Brother Volmar, be sure all is in proper order and is prepared for tonight's ceremony."

Volmar bowed formally as a sign of respect, though no one was paying particular attention to him. He turned and saw that Rudegerus had no intentions of leaving with him. Such political intrigue, he could tell, had the Guest Master mesmerized. Volmar then left his elders so they might converse further about the details of the ceremony.

Chapter 3: Odd Sort of Insolence

Preparation Room in the Chapter House

Feast of All Saints, 1st of November, Friday, the Year of Our Lord 1112

Hildegard shivered as she stood next to the window. A steady rain blurred the cloisters below into a grey labyrinth of competing shadows and pools of water. A familiar cowled figure with the determination of youth cut across the knotted garden. Stopping, as if sensing her gaze, he lifted his head up towards her window. With only a light towel wrapped around her to cover her nakedness, Hildegard stepped back, more though from confusion than shyness. She could not meet his eyes. They were at the crossroads where their two paths were to converge. However, it was not in the direction the young monk's heart was willing it to go. Hildegard saw how Volmar stood motionless in the rain and knew instinctively, the young monk was grateful for the downpour, for it masked the tears welling up in his eyes. Nothing, though, could hide her own tears that streamed slowly down her cheeks. Quietly she reminded herself that her God was a sovereign God, and that if she bore direct witness of the Spirit, all strands of her tangled, muddled life would eventually come together.

Hildegard's turn was next after Jutta's, who was sitting motionless on a stool, having her hair shorn. Jutta's reddish gold locks fell to the floor like a heap of autumn leaves. They were preparing themselves to step from the lush green fields of Eden, the rich world Hildegard adored and knew she would sorely miss, into what would surely be like a parched landscape of the Egyptian desert: the stark, stony confines of an Anchorage. The enclosure ceremony would take no more time than it would take for a small mound of sand to accumulate in the base of an hourglass, and yet, for Hildegard, the vows she was about to make were to last a lifetime.

Jutta had tried to explain it all to the servant girl, Hiltrud. "I am sorry to have to put you under such a strain," she had said gently to the fourteen-year-old girl, "but there are causes greater than our own needs. By bidding farewell to an ordinary life, you will be given the opportunity to live at the gates of heaven."

Hildegard knew the truth. Jutta was headstrong and wanted to be the one devoted to God in a highly conspicuous way, to wield power as a spiritual intermediary for the faithful. As Disibodenberg's Anchoress, Jutta would be sought after for her advice and her wisdom, becoming the focus for the communal religious life of the village. For an ambitious woman of twenty, who spurned the love of men, this was the answer to her dream, not Hiltrud's. Hildegard thought of it as an odd sort of insolence that could hardly be reprimanded.

Hildegard did not share in Hiltrud's misgivings. Like Jutta, she felt this was where she should be, especially on such a fortuitous occasion[58] as All Saints Day. But her reasons were altogether different. At last she could devote herself completely to the love of God. She craved the separateness and mental independence given to an incluse[59]. Ironically, in a world where silence and passivity were the highest ideals for women to aspire to, sharing a stone cell with Jutta

---

58 All Saints Day: In the Catholic traditions, this was the night when all the spirits who dutifully served their time in Purgatory could finally seek passage into heaven.

59 Incluse: An arcane term used to distinguish between recluses in a more social setting such as a city church and incluses, Anchoresses tied to a monastery and under the rule of an Abbot.

and Hiltrud would give Hildegard the freedom and a life of contemplation she had been looking for.

Jutta walked back to a large tub filled with scented hot water. Hiltrud rose from the tub, red-faced and dripping, her eyes still puffy from having seen her own ghastly, hairless appearance in a mirror. Jutta passed Hiltrud the towel as she leaned forward to touch the water. It was still warm. In a small gesture of one used to getting her way, she ordered the room's servants, "Take all of our clothes and give them to the poor," before immersing herself into the pool of purification, heavily scented with rosemary[60], sage[61] and lavender[62].

"Wait," Hildegard said, rushing over to her long blue cape. She was in the habit of keeping her drawing utensils and books inside its many hidden pockets. "Please, if you will, take these to the Anchorage." She handed the elder servant a stack of small codices,[63] bound parchments, and various writing instruments. A pressed clover and a single leaf of wormwood fell to the floor. She picked them up and carefully placed them back in her journal on herbal remedies that she was compiling. She smiled apologetically as she kept digging further into the myriad of deep pockets in her cloak, finding more and more oddities, such as a string of pearls, some jasper, chalcedony, and an old feather from a cuckoo bird.

"Please take my wardrobe to the Infirmary. I'd like my clothes to be a gift to a certain young lady named Sophie." She unfastened the silver filigree brooch and unobtrusively tucked it between the leaves of parchment to be taken to the Anchorage. "Thank you," she replied before turning away to take her turn on the small stool.

---

[60] Rosemary: Represents faithfulness, love and remembrance. Rosemary is usually symbolic of feminine love because the herb is very tough and strong, and grows very slowly. It is also the symbol for prudence and sensibility.

[61] Sage: Symbolic of strength.

[62] Lavender: Possesses a strong aroma and is thought to curb many evil things and because of it, malign spirits are terrified.

[63] Codices: A bound booklet, or small journal.

Chapter 4: Time's Rude Hand

Nave of the Disibodenberg Church

Feast of All Saints, 1st of November, Friday, the Year of Our Lord 1112

As Brother Hans rehearsed the psalm to be sung in accordance with church traditions in celebration of All Saints Day, Volmar went about his duties in silence, thinking of Hildegard.

Volmar had taken many precautions to prepare for this night. He knew it was to be a continual struggle for a monk to exert mastery over his carnal desires and to remain dead to the delights of the world, but he didn't think it would be so difficult. He'd taken cold baths, refrained from eating meat, which was known to inflame desire, and had even contemplated harming himself, hoping that the wounds of the flesh might heal the wounds of his wayward obsession with Hildegard. And yet no matter what he tried, she kept dancing her way into his mind, caressing his lonely thoughts, and setting aflame his passions. Would he never find peace from these fiery, fitful temptations?

One by one he replaced the usual yellowing candles with long white ones. He then smoothed out a wrinkle in the altar cloth, before turning to survey the nearly empty sanctuary. The words Brother Hans so plaintively sung *a cappella* in Latin, shattered the stillness and all hope.

Who are these like stars appearing?
These, before God's throne who stand?
These, whose robes of purest whiteness . . .
Still untouched by time's rude hand . . .
Following not the sinful throng . . .

Chapter 5: A Life of Angels

Nave of the Disibodenberg Church

Feast of All Saints, Dusk, 1st of November, Friday, the Year of Our Lord 1112

An hour later at dusk, the three young women entered the sanctuary. They followed the Bishop, his entourage of lesser priests and monks, and the Abbot from the Sacristy[64] into the Chancel[65]. Volmar stood alongside his fellow brothers in the individual stalls of the choir, witnesses to this most ancient of rituals.

The young women stood barefoot before the stone altar and the cross, humbly attired in white linen shifts. Their heads were bowed, reciting prayers as they prepared to become brides of Christ. The words of the Psalm hung in the chilly night air: *untouched by time's rude hand.* Volmar was close enough to see that the young women were shivering. He was shocked at Hildegard's transformation. He knew that all three of them had to have their heads shaved as part of the ritual preparations for the ceremony, but nothing really prepared him for how other-worldly this made Hildegard appear to him.

Volmar stirred himself, realizing suddenly that he was not the only one suffering because of this spectacle. He searched the people standing in the nave watching the ceremony and was arrested by the pained expression etched on Reginald's face. He wondered how deep Reginald's affections had been for Jutta. Rumor had it that the Archbishop's son had courted Jutta for over five years, since she was fifteen.

Taking turns, Jutta, Hildegard, and Hiltrud knelt and made their professions of faith, followed by the Bishop repeating, "*Confirma hoc Deus.*[66]" After each affirmation, five collects[67] were said. Three times,

---

[64] Sacristy: A room in a church where sacred vessels and vestments are kept or meetings are held sometimes referred to as the Vestry.

[65] Chancel: The part of the church including the altar and choir.

[66] *Confirma hoc Deus*: In English, it requests like a refrain, "Confirm in us, O God." in part taken from Psalms 68.

[67] Collects: Short prayers comprising an invocation, petition, and conclusion.

Bishop Otto invited them "to come," and three times they replied, "and now we follow with all our heart."

Volmar recognized excerpts from the Book of Job and bore witness to the solemn kiss of peace given to each on their foreheads during the Mass[68]. The Bishop then administered communion. There was a hush over the gathering crowd. It was the most sacred and mystical part of the ceremony where the three women entered into a supernatural union with God through the Eucharist[69]. By eating His body and drinking His blood, they became one with the heavenly Father.

Following the communion were more prayers and blessings; these, though, were associated with the last rites and the Office of the Dead. The Bishop gave to each woman a cross, placing it in their arms as he spoke. "Receive this image of the crucified one, taking care to always keep His passion and death in your heart." The Abbot followed behind the Bishop and pressed the candle of death into their hands. All of these rituals symbolized their vow to live out the rest of their lives on the threshold that stretches between life and death.

Three funeral biers[70] were then lowered. One by one, the young women stretched out on the biers. Over each of their bodies, the bishop genuflected, motioning the cross and intoning more Latin prayers. His censer[71] swayed forward on its long golden chain as the smoke from the sweet-smelling incense rose in unity with his prayers up to God.

Over Jutta, the Bishop spoke aloud into the hazy, thickening silence. "Grant, O Heavenly Father, that the Devil, our adversary, may never find Disibodenberg's Anchoress, Jutta of Sponheim, off her guard, or out from under Thy protection. Make her mindful of her weakness and fortify her soul against all temptations of the world, the flesh, and the Devil."

---

68 Mass: A sequence of prayers and ceremonies forming the Eucharistic office of the Roman Catholic Church.

69 Eucharist: Communion, a Christian sacrament in which bread and wine are partaken of as the body and blood of the crucified Christ, in remembrance of His supreme sacrifice.

70 Biers: A stand or pallet bearing a coffin or corpse.

71 Censer: A vessel for burning incense in a religious ritual.

Bishop Otto paused, clearly in command of the people's attentions, before posing his question. "Jutta of Sponheim, do you wish to live in seclusion as Disibodenberg's Anchoress until you die?"

Jutta of Sponheim responded in a confident voice. "I do indeed."

Volmar watched as Reginald hung his head, acknowledging what the young monk suspected was final defeat.

The Bishop passed the censer to the Abbot and clasped his hands in prayer. His loud yet tremulous voice echoed through the stone cavern and rose up as if it were knocking triumphantly on heaven's golden doors. "Our Father, we deliver unto Thee Jutta of Sponheim, Hildegard of Bermersheim, and Hiltrud of Rupertsberg."

Volmar felt the hot tears welling behind his eyes and held back a cry of anguish. He had also prepared for this moment. He reached into his pocket for a small peppercorn and popped it in his mouth, while pretending to cough. His teeth went to work, grinding down the beastly hot and bitter seed, hoping to deceive his own spirit from what he knew it could not swallow.

"In their hearts," the Bishop continued, his voice sealing Volmar's heart forever, "they have promised to live apart, separated from the errors and vices of the age we live in, choosing to dwell in Your house and for Your glory apart from worldly infidelities, wicked principles, profanities, heresies, and the faithlessness of this Godless age." The Bishop's voice grew more passionate as he continued. "O Christ, our Refuge and Strength, in this hour of their deaths, grant the beginning of eternity, of true faith, sure hope, ardent love, unshaken fortitude, deep humility, unconquered patience, and whatsoever other virtues they will need to reside at heaven's doorstep."

The Bishop dramatically raised his hands towards the heavens. "And into Thy Hands, O Lord, I commend their spirits; and whatsoever sins they may have committed through the frailty of their mortal natures, in Thy merciful loving kindness blot out forever; through Christ our Lord. Amen."

Volmar watched as the biers were carried aloft in a solemn processional by twelve hooded brothers all dressed in black robes. From the church it was only twenty-odd paces to the Anchorage, the young women's earthly tomb. As each of the three young women made their way down the aisle through the fog of incense and extinguishing candles, they began chanting in turn: "This is my resting place forever, here shall I dwell for I have chosen it." The psalm was shortly followed by another. "I shall go up into the place of the wonderful tabernacle." And another: "Let us enter the house of the Lord with rejoicing."

Volmar winced as he heard Hildegard's voice rise above the others, its lyrical tone resounding strong and true as she recited the mantras of denial and death. So final, he thought, bearing in silence the guilt of his sinful affection for her. From now on Hildegard and the other women would live isolated from the outside world, the door of their cell bolted tight, and the windows covered with black leather curtains and shutters. Tradition dictated that they live as if at the gates of heaven, praying day and night while in the seclusion of their cell. A *Vita Angelica*, a Life of Angels. The Bishop sprinkled dust on them as they passed under the entrance of the church.

Chapter 6: A River of Many Waters

Forecourt of Disibodenberg Church

Feast of All Saints, 1st of November, Friday, the Year of Our Lord 1112, Evening

Volmar had observed many religious rituals, but this was his first enclosure ceremony. As the villagers filed out in an orderly fashion following the processional, Volmar lingered, observing the rest of the guests. Reginald had backed himself into a corner and was staring ahead with a frown, seemingly waiting at the empty altar. It would be his right, Volmar thought, for Reginald to walk away from this ceremony, which should have been his wedding, condemning love and feeling justified in his own self-pity. It was impossible to tell from this distance which direction Reginald's mind would take.

Why would God create male and female? Was it simply to complicate our lives, plague us with consuming passions, or distract us from contemplating paradise? This mystery troubled Volmar as he also wondered why Reginald's friend Atif was not standing there beside him. Instead, he noticed, the Aramaic scholar was across the room meeting with a messenger of some sort, who looked as if he had just slipped in from the outside road, judging by the red clay still clinging to his muddied boots. Volmar watched as the messenger reached under his cloak and gave Atif a bound set of small papers. Atif took the booklet quickly from the man and flipped to the first page. He read through it, his expression suggesting nothing less than elation. After he had finished, Volmar watched as Atif held the small book up to his lips and kissed it softly before tucking it safely under his heavy cloak. As the messenger quietly took leave, Atif slipped back silently into the throng of people and disappeared. Volmar held back, wondering what would motivate a man to kiss a book, unless it represented something more to him than simple words. Such misplaced passion reminded him of his own guilty passions towards Hildegard.

Volmar exited into the forecourt, relieved to find that the rain had eased and a quarter moon was valiantly trying to peek through the ominous gathering of clouds. A slight rustle from behind was the only warning Volmar had. He turned with a start the very moment an old woman grabbed his arm and pulled him into the shadows.

"Hear me out," the old woman spoke in earnest, placing a papery thin finger to the young monk's mouth before Volmar could complain. "I have a message from God, meant only for your ears and yours alone. Her life, I've been told, is intricately woven into your own."

The old woman's strange words at first did not sink in. "Whose life, dear lady . . . the Anchoress?"

"No, brother; not the pretty one named Jutta nor the servant girl Hiltrud." The old woman's breath smelled of rotten plants and decay. "I saw it all in a vision. The frail child with the gray eyes, the one they call Hildegard."

Volmar blanched. How could this woman know of his sinful obsession?

"God has poured out His grace into this child like a river of many waters. Someday, she will compose and sing chants to the praise of God and his saints. Through the favor of God, those wise eyes will see through the diabolical fog that oppresses the church and will serve all, both rich and poor, well."

Volmar swallowed hard. Often when he was on duty in the Infirmary he would hear the idle ramblings of the elderly and suspected that this old woman was sleepwalking and confused, having awoken and wandered into the middle of the enclosure processional. And yet, she knew of Hildegard and his affection for her. The old woman's uncanny insights had him stumbling for words. "Please, kind woman, may I help you back to your pallet?"

She refused his proffered arm. "I'm not dreaming," she chided, making a disapproving sound with her tongue against her few remaining teeth. "Hear me out, Volmar. Do not trivialize this meeting, for these are the words God spoke to me."

"Who told you my name?" he said, facing the old woman directly. Only then did Volmar become aware of the milky clouds floating in her unfocused eyes. He passed his hand over her eyes several times, but she did not blink. The old woman was blind.

"It is not your name, but Hildegard's name that will be remembered in centuries to come."

Volmar pictured Hildegard, the unconventional, peculiar girl of last year, dancing and singing in the clearing. She'd become his fantasy; a coveted, secret image so intoxicating that he had to say many prayers to beg forgiveness for his errant thoughts. "Our lives have intersected before," Volmar admitted, finding the woman's blindness even more distressing. "She was here, a year ago, when they laid the cornerstone for the Anchorage."

"Hildegard will become a cornerstone for the faithful, young Scribe. Kings will seek out her wisdom and Popes will ask her advice. She will not give in to the oppression of this corrupt religious order. She will live separately and be a voice for God through her music, her healings, her writings and drawings, and her visions; but first she must learn from your teachings and compassion. You will always love her deeply."

"Love her deeply?" Volmar repeated. These were foreign words for one who had promised to forsake the love of a woman for the church.

Suddenly there was a hush, as if everyone were holding their breath. The Bishop arose from the Anchorage's entrance, returning after walking through all three rooms with the Abbot, blessing the place with holy water and burning incense, a practice echoing once again the final ritual practice of blessing the corpse before its burial.

One by one, the biers were carried under the door's archway, the Bishop confirming each of the young women as they entered with five prayers of blessings and signs of the cross.

Volmar turned to challenge the old woman directly, but saw to his surprise that she was gone. One moment she was by his side, the next moment she had mysteriously disappeared.

Sophie approached and gave Volmar's wavy black hair a small affectionate tug instead of taking his hand as she once did. "Hmm, what's troubling you?" she asked. She could always read his mood.

Volmar turned to Sophie and gasped. She had on the same dark blue cloak and exquisitely embroidered dress worn by Hildegard over a year ago!

Sophie blushed deeply and smiled back. "It was a gift from Sister Hildegard. You do like it, don't you? She had all her clothes sent over earlier to the Infirmary especially for me." She twirled around, allowing the heavy brocade skirts to billow out. "Come now, Brother Volmar, don't you love it! Brother Paulus thought I was one of the esteemed visitors, at first. I feel so spoiled!"

Volmar was speechless. Although the monastic life demanded austerity and self-denial, he was pleased that Sophie didn't have to comply. Her nature responded to beautiful things—he knew it to be the artist inside her. Over the past year, he had marveled at how Sophie had given up many of her childish ways. While occasionally he missed the comfort of her small cold hand in his, he admired now how she would use her hands. They were like magnificent drawing instruments, moving through the air to draw for him pictures or busily carving a delicate hollow tube for Brother Paulus, so he could hear with more clarity the sounds a stomach or heart were making. Sophie's face, though, had matured the most; with a sense of purpose, it had a charm all of its own, at once lively and animated, or solemn and thoughtful, like it was now.

"I've never had anything so warm or soft. And look at all these pockets, Volmar. Wait, there's something in this one." She reached in and removed a roll of parchment. It was sealed and addressed to Volmar. "For you," she said, handing it over to the young monk's trembling hands and added teasingly. "Is there something you're not telling me, Brother Volmar?"

Volmar responded with a pained, guilty expression, which she took to be merely disappointment over her bold accusation.

"Sorry," Sophie added hurriedly, "I'm just curious, that's all. Please let Hildegard know how eternally grateful I am for her beautiful wardrobe. Let her know the clothes fit perfectly. Brother Paulus has kindly offered a cupboard to be moved to my cell, so I can store and care for them properly."

Volmar tucked the missive inside his leather pouch. "Thank you," he said, closing the clasp on his leather pouch. "You do look lovely, Sophie. I'll let Hildegard, err, Sister Hildegard know how grateful you are for her gift."

"I've never witnessed the rituals of an internment," Sophie went on, her eyes shining from his rare compliment. She gazed over towards the Anchorage.

Volmar nodded. "It is hard for us mere men to know God's intentions," he mumbled, the token answer she expected from monks whenever they faced something they felt was wrong.

Sophie wisely left it at that, seeing how Volmar wore his look of total concentration that she knew so well and had learned to respect.

At length, Volmar turned to her and asked as calmly as he could, "Sophie, is there a blind elderly woman in the Infirmary's care?"

"No," she said, putting a finger to his lips, "shush!" She turned to the Anchorage and became very still as the final moments of the ceremony took place.

The last robed pallbearer exited the Anchorage. Abbot Burchard heaved the massive oak door reinforced with iron plates hard enough to close it. The Bishop took the key from his ring of keys and turned it securely, locking the clasp, saying, "May God protect your entrance and prevent you from coming out."

Book 4: Vows

Chapter I: Removed from the World

Common Room of the Anchorage

Feast of All Saints, 1st of November, Friday, the Year of Our Lord 1112, after Enclosure Ceremony

Hildegard jutted out her lower lip and blew gently, trying to remove the dust Bishop Otto had sprinkled on her and which clung stubbornly to her eyelashes. As she heard the key turn in the lock on the door, Hildegard felt her racing heart slow to a steadier, relaxed pace. She attributed the aching sensation in her stomach to hunger and the unaccustomed chill to the stout stone walls which now enveloped her. In preparation for the ceremony, Jutta had insisted that they fast for three days.

Hildegard lifted her hand, stiff from the lack of movement over the past few hours. Tentatively, she ran her fingers over her bare head where her hair had once been and thought fleetingly of the superstition of combing one's hair to comfort one's brain. Living in the Anchorage would hold few if any of the familiar comforts. In here, the three women were completely removed from the world. Then again, Hildegard thought, as she set aside the stub of the candle which she earlier had to blow out and the cross which was to be hung over the head of her bed, she had always felt set apart from others.

The waxing moon broke through the clouds and streamed in through the small window, bathing the room with its soft and lingering light. For the first time, Hildegard could survey her surroundings. They were sparse, as she anticipated, but adequate. She was grateful to see in the far corner the massive silhouette of what she recognized to be her glass-fronted bookcase. She was pleased to see the shadowy stack of her writings and drawings, finding comfort in their presence. Here was the room in which she would spend all her waking hours. In the gloom she could just make out a couple of dark objects on a table nearby.

Hildegard stood and felt her way over to the heavy wood trestle table. On it she found one of the objects to be an oil lamp, its wick trimmed and filled with oil. The second item was a large basket filled with items of food and a small flask of wine. The moon slipped behind the clouds, plunging the room into darkness. Thankfully, though, from where she stood, she could see on the other side of the table a smoldering rustic glow in what appeared to be the remains of a fire in a wide stone fireplace. She went and took a piece of ember, blowing on it coaxingly until a flame darted from it. Using this to light the lantern, she then threw a few more logs onto the fire to warm the room and welcomed its warm glow.

It was ever so slight but unmistakable; a moan had come from Jutta, whose bier was placed on the stone floor between Hildegard and Hiltrud. Hildegard took the oil lamp and knelt down beside her Anchoress' side. Carefully, she lifted the now blood-encrusted shift up to Jutta's thigh so she could survey the extent of the leg iron's damage. Jutta had insisted on wearing it regardless of the ceremony, much to Hildegard's chagrin. Suppressing a sigh, Hildegard examined the wound. It was an old familiar wound, deep and jagged like the teeth marks left behind by a raging bear. It had never been given the chance to heal properly. Thankfully, Jutta would not be protesting her ministrations this time. The new Anchoress appeared to be in a self-induced meditative state in which physical pain could not be felt. Softly, Hildegard took the key from around Jutta's neck and loosened the leg iron, gently releasing the last lock and drawing it away from the woman's thigh. Hildegard knew she had to work quickly. Otherwise, the wound would get worse if she left it unattended.

As a child Hildegard remembered Uda commenting once on how the Disibodenberg monks were excellent beekeepers. She said a small prayer, went back to the table, and lifted the food items one by one from the basket. There was bread, cheese, nuts, lentil beans, and . . . "Yes," she said out loud, "honey. Thank you, Lord." Placing the honey on the table top, she uncorked the pottery jar and took one of the wooden spoons from a hook to stir it.

By this time Hiltrud had moved and was now curled up on her bier, her knees to her chin, softly crying. Hildegard had questioned the wisdom of forcing a servant girl to comply with a life of enclosure. No one had listened to her. The consensus was that two young noblewomen could not go without a handmaiden, no matter where they lived. Hildegard crossed the room to her and gave her a wooden spoon dripping with honey.

"It's so sweet," Hiltrud said, putting it to her lips. She handed the spoon back, grateful for the unexpected kindness.

Hildegard dipped the spoon in the jar once again and gave it back. "Our heavenly Father has given us nature and in it, healing. There's bread and cheese on the table. Help yourself."

Hildegard left Hiltrud licking the spoon and knelt once again beside Jutta with the honey jar. Carefully Hildegard ripped off the edging on her own white shift. Using it as a cloth she dipped it into the jar of honey. Gently she smoothed the honey over the area of the wound, wrapping it within a crystallized protective shield. When she had completed this task, she corked the honey and left the rag nearby to apply another layer in a few hours. She then reached for the oil lamp and motioned for Hiltrud to follow her into the next room. They both nodded with satisfaction when they saw the small adjoining privy with three wash basins. However, the rest of the furnishings were bleak compared to what they were both accustomed to. Three straw pallets sat on sturdy wooden platforms. There was a small bedside table and, on it, another oil lamp which Hildegard lit. The extra glow from the light made the high ceiling and the plastered walls feel less cavernous. On each of the beds were folded thick woolen blankets. The two of them dressed the beds, shaking the mattresses to check for bugs before folding and tucking in the blankets.

"Much better," Hildegard remarked after the last bed was made. "Hiltrud, I don't know about you, but I'm exhausted. Why don't we take time to rest?"

"What about Sister Jutta?"

"Let her sleep. When the bells of Matins sound, we'll see if she's strong enough to join us for our devotions and prayers." Hildegard squeezed Hiltrud's hand, worried over how cold and clammy it felt. "Don't worry. We will make a comfortable home for ourselves here, Hiltrud. Rest now; there will be plenty to do in the coming months."

Hildegard pulled the coarse wool blanket up under her chin, letting her mind wander back through the day's momentous events. Beside her, in the next pallet, Hiltrud was soon snoring steadily, having finally given in to sleep's tyranny.

Hildegard turned to her side, tucking her arm up under her neck, trying to get comfortable. Often in quiet moments like this, her thoughts strayed to Volmar. She'd sensed his pain during the ceremony and knew a door had closed between them. "Anything worthwhile, child, takes time and sacrifice," Uda had gently reminded her, as she often did when the doubts overwhelmed her. Surely, this was her destiny; not the one young Volmar's heart yearned for. She needed confirmation, reassurance. In the darkness, Hildegard stretched out and with her mind she tentatively reached across the chasm between this world and the next, searching for the familiar warmth of the Living Light, a comforting presence she'd known since she was three.

Chapter 2: Rule of St. Benedict

Volmar's Cell

2nd of November, Saturday, the Year of Our Lord 1112, Before Matins

Volmar tossed and turned on the narrow mattress, finding it impossible to surrender to sleep. Giving up, the young monk sat up and fixed his eyes on the crucifix at the foot of his bed without really seeing it. Volmar wondered whether he was now regretting taking his vows. Had he sworn to follow the Rule of Saint Benedict[72] prematurely? The severity of monastic life had never troubled him before: The frugal diet, the lack of sleep, the life of service and contemplation. All of these restrictions had seemed perfectly normal. After all, he'd been blindly abiding by the rule most of his life. Yet now, his vows demanded that he control his thoughts as well as his deeds, and this he knew was impossible. Even the act of saying penance against the desire he felt for Hildegard seemed only to make his

[72] Rule of St. Benedict: A set of rules which governed medieval monastic life, the main ones include: chastity, poverty and obedience.

suffering stronger and more insistent. Cantilevered between Heaven and Hell, a monastic existence demanded all worldly desires be rebuked, as he was only to lust for spiritual communion with God the Almighty. Illicit feelings and intentions were considered as worthy of censure as misdeeds; a glance, a gesture, or mere touch were strictly forbidden. Deep down, he knew, simple prayers and holy meditations were not going to be enough for him to exert control over his inflamed passions towards Hildegard. Volmar struggled to keep his thoughts pure, and yet the images kept tumbling out from the remotest places in his mind: The turn of Hildegard's neck, her full, parting lips, her deep sighs . . . so powerful was her hold on him that it could elude his reasoning and his resolve like a dream.

Silently he reached for the few worldly possessions he kept hidden under his bed in a simple wood box with an iron clasp. Usually, on a sleepless night, it gave him comfort to touch objects that revived memories of long ago. He opened the clasp. Inside was the leather pouch he had with him the night he arrived at the monastery with Anya. He emptied its contents out on his bed. In it were several gold coins, a locket of his dead sister's hair, a rosary, and the parchment disclosing Hildegard's secret alphabet. He laid it out carefully and, using it, translated the note she had written to him and left in the pocket of Sophie's cloak:

Try as I may, I cannot get Brother Arnoul's predicament out of my mind. Please come to me, Volmar, when you have a chance, so we can work together to free his tortured spirit. Your sister in Christ, Hildegard.

Volmar turned it over in his hands and smelled its lingering, heavenly perfume, thinking back over what the old woman had told him earlier about Hildegard's future. She was right about one thing, he thought, ruefully; he loved Hildegard deeply.

Attempting to redirect his sinful thoughts, the young monk turned to the rosary. He stared at the eight-pointed star below the head of Christ, the emblem of the Order of the Knights Hospitaller of Saint John. It was the same eight-pointed star on the rosary he'd seen earlier that fell out of Atif's traveling cloak. He ran his finger over the scrawled name of his father, Symon, etched in the ebony. A messenger had given this rosary to his mother a year after his father had left for the Holy Land. All he knew of his father was that he had given his allegiance to the Order of Knights Hospitaller of Saint John in Jerusalem.

Volmar had been barely three when his father left. Try as he may, he could not remember the man's face. Even his own mother's beloved face was blurred from time's inevitable passage. The thin straw pallet and single burlap blanket provided little comfort or warmth. Volmar reached for the overweight tabby sleeping at his feet and stroked Samson's soft gray fur. He thought back to the blind woman's revelations and remembered how Hildegard had happily declared him her scribe during the storm in the cave. It was like an eerie conspiracy. Everyone seemed to know of his future but him.

Samson stretched and yawned, knowing full well it was too early to awaken for prayers. He turned over while purring contentedly, his grey belly exposed and his paws extended straight up in the air. "I know, Samson, I know, but I can't seem to fall asleep," Volmar explained. He leaned forward and aimlessly scratched under Samson's chin. "In a way," Volmar mused, yawning, "those moles you love to hunt travel through a realm of silence and darkness, trusting their paths only to what they hear. Should we not act likewise? Should we not simply let go, listen, and trust God to direct our paths?" Volmar yawned again and curled up next to Samson, the rest of his words dying in his throat as a restless sleep finally overtook the troubled monk.

Chapter 3: Numbing Touch of Cold

Courtyard and Common Room of Anchorage

2nd of November, Saturday, the Year of Our Lord 1112, Before Matins

Jutta collapsed; her naked body had finally given in to the numbing touch of the cold air. The courtyard of the Anchorage had but one tree, and there she lay, crumpled like a leaf in a stupor of painless sleep. The moon still hung overhead, lending its ghostly light to the small courtyard, a time closer to midnight than morning.

Hildegard heard the noise and awoke in their sleeping chamber. Instinctively she rolled over and saw to her dismay that Jutta was no longer in her bed. This was worrisome, for Hildegard knew quite well what had likely happened. Rising quickly, Hildegard wrapped several blankets around her and went to investigate.

When she finally found Jutta at the base of the tree, the Anchoress was lying face down on the stone pavement, unable to be awoken. Hildegard sighed and wasted no time in wrapping the unconscious woman in several layers of blankets before going back in to enlist Hiltrud's help in moving her in from the cold.

Hildegard leaned over Hiltrud, whose eyes were still puffy and swollen even in sleep. She hated having to stir the young girl from her peaceful slumber.

"Hiltrud, wake up. I need your help."

'What's wrong?" Hiltrud sputtered, moistening her dry lips.

"Could you please start the fire and boil some water? It will be a long night, I'm afraid. Sister Jutta has wandered into the cold of the courtyard and has stayed out all night meditating in this dreadful weather."

Once the fire was burning brightly, the two young women carefully carried Jutta in and laid her in front of its warmth, her body cocooned in multiple blankets.

"It's below freezing out there. Why would she do such a foolish thing?" Hiltrud asked, fumbling for the nearest jug in the fire's light, still bleary-eyed and half asleep.

Hildegard shrugged. "It is her way of coming humbly before our Lord and Savior." She unlocked the leg iron and began to slowly clean the widening lesion with a soft pad of linen before adding more honey and applying a new dressing.

"If she keeps this up, she'll be standing in front of the Holy Throne before her time," Hiltrud said resentfully as she set a jug of water on the grate above the flames.

Hildegard inclined her head, cognizant of the folk wisdom of Hiltrud's simple ways. Rolling the bandage over the wound and finishing it off neatly, Hildegard then felt Jutta's forehead and the back of her neck. Her temperature was dangerously high even in the cold. Her condition was becoming worse. Hildegard knew if she didn't get some proper herbs to bring down her temperature soon, Jutta would not make it through the night.

Book 5: On the Defensive

Chapter 1: A Formidable Dance

Clearing Behind Guest Quarters, Disibodenberg Monastery

2nd of November, Saturday, the Year of Our Lord 1112, Mid-Morning

Sunlight caught the blades as they twirled and sang in the air. Two men sparred without the protection of heavy armor in a small clearing behind the Hospice. Effortlessly they moved from one dangerous moment to another without fear or concern, their sparring looking so ingrained and natural that it seemed almost reflexive in nature. The sharp stinging noise they made was so regular and timed in such a way that it was obvious the two knew of each other's strengths and weaknesses. Back and forth they parried and returned strikes, acting like young wolves at play. It was a formidable dance that Volmar had witnessed only a few times at the monastery, and each opportunity fed in him a desire to learn to move with such grace, purpose, and agility.

To establish such a bond would have taken years to master, Volmar reasoned, as he sat down on the stone wall to watch. He studied the strangers' fighting movements, delighted by this unexpected diversion. He deserved a rest, having been back and forth three times since Terce delivering messages from the Abbot to Brother Andres concerning the winter's food supply for the poor. The younger of the two men suddenly took a scrape on his sleeve. Blood darkened the ripped shirt. Raising his free arm in a signal to stop the fight, he peered closely at the wound. The older of the two men started shuffling his feet, his sword down to the left side of his body. He moved from side to side, circling his opponent as if he were his prey.

"Tired, my friend?" the older man asked. His breathing was barely apparent as he kept his feet and wits agile in case it was a ruse. He had broad square shoulders and a slightly dappled gray beard. He would have been considered a handsome man had his expression not seemed so sinister and somehow familiar. Volmar couldn't place him in his memory.

"No, it is but a scratch," the younger man said with a grin, a thick Italian accent coating his words. Without any further delay, the Italian brought his sword well above the level of his head and swung down at the older man with considerable force, and the two were at it again. They each continued to parry every strike comfortably away from their bodies, allowing for the easy movements of their blades. Finally, the older man rotated his arm at the elbow to the left and brought his entire arm, sword in hand, pointed straight out onto his opponent's shoulder, making abrupt contact with the other's sword. At the other's quick block the older man's sword was knocked out of its line of attack and away from his opponent's torso.

"Ah ha, old man, thought you had me there," the Italian gleamed.

Both men, clearly spent, collapsed to the ground. "You're getting stronger, my friend," the older man admitted, breathing hard. "It won't be long before such play will become dangerous for me."

The older man turned to Volmar, who had quietly witnessed this unusual admission. "Be careful who you choose as your friend, brother, for there are those who cannot draw a line between an adversary and a friend in competition." He stood and extended his hand to his opponent and helped him to his feet.

"So tell me, my young brother, have you ever even held a sword? Or has a stylus been your only weapon?" the older of the two men said with a chuckle as he approached Volmar, handing to him the sword of his younger opponent. He appeared eager to amuse himself further.

"Words can be as powerful as a sword, if not more so, in my opinion," Volmar said evenly, taking the younger man's sword in his hand. The young monk swung it in the air a few times, finding its heft, balance, and its maneuverability more satisfying than the wooden ones he'd been accustomed to when play fighting as a boy with visiting squires and knights. He took a stance that indicated he had more than simple book knowledge of how to spar and readied himself.

"Be careful, my young brother, you do not want to parry with this man," the Italian man warned. He had a young face that had seen too much sun, with a light crinkling of skin around his dark, intense eyes.

"He is the one who knows no friend in competition. See?" the Italian slipped off his leather glove, revealing that he was missing both his forefinger and half of his middle finger on his right hand. The Italian man bowed graciously to his opponent and left the clearing, whispering as he passed Volmar. "So be it, it is your funeral."

"Ha, you answer me with arrogance and nerve! Formidable qualities for a spineless holy brother," the older man said, his eyes twinkling with mischief. "Tell me, what is your name, boy?"

"It is Volmar, Volmar of Bermersheim."

At this the older man faltered, briefly betraying a look of agonizing insecurity. However, he recovered briskly. His cajoling demeanor returned, though it had a distinctive, more lethal edge to it. "Son of Katherina of Bermersheim?"

"Yes. Did you know her?"

The old man raised an eyebrow. "No one in this region, save those without eyes in their head, would claim not to have known her. She was a beauty and a viper."

"How dare you speak of my mother in such a manner!" With that, Volmar sprang forward, catching his opponent by surprise and leveling a loud crack that could be heard from the Infirmary as the older man's sword met his. The commotion caused a few guests to step outside and congregate around the stone wall to view the sword play firsthand. The swords clanged even louder as the two matched each other's swings, Volmar clearly on the defensive. The old man laughed as he playfully deflected Volmar's best efforts. The crowd that had started to gather began to cheer for the obvious winner, encouraging him to put the inexperienced boy in his place.

"There is more to sword fighting than mere desire to win, my boy," the old man said, his smirk still in place as he acknowledged the youth's enthusiastic, yet feeble attempts. "Keep moving. Do not stand still or you will become an easy prey." He dipped forward, the tip of his sword barely missing Volmar's neck, as if to emphasize this very point.

Some who had gathered in the crowd started chanting for blood.

"So, you are Katherina's son, eh? Well, well . . . " the older man said over the uproar. His eyes clouded over and, in their gaze, Volmar saw something he'd never seen before: a desire to kill, and to kill without mercy.

"Volmar!" Brother Paulus shouted. His voice was thick with anger as he hurried into the clearing, "Both of you; stop this nonsense at once!" Paulus crossed his arms in the sleeves of his habit, clearly incensed by this brutal play, and stood immovable between the two. "I'd rather not have to stitch up another injury; one is quite enough!"

Volmar let his sword drop forward and fall awkwardly to the ground. He was truly spent. He bent over, hands on his knees and heaved a deep sigh of relief, grateful to be able to breathe after realizing he'd been holding his breath through most of the battle. He stared at the ground, imagining himself lying prostrate in the clearing, impaled by this stranger's sword. His impetuous nature had almost ended his life.

Sophie had followed Brother Paulus from the infirmary and now stood beside Volmar, glaring up at the older man with an expression of deep hatred and disgust. "He's the man who stole my bread last year," she whispered to Volmar between clenched teeth. "You should never have acted so foolishly as to parry with such a beast."

The older man chuckled as he left the clearing. "The little wench is right, son. Keep to your words; for you will surely die by the sword." He paused suddenly, locking eyes with Atif, who, in the midst of the gathering crowd, stood silent in front of him.

"Well, well," the older man chuckled, "it is barely noon and the day is already full of many surprises. Tell me, Atif, are you still the water boy for kings?"

"No. But I can see you still haven't lost your delightful sense of humor."

"How can I," he queried in jest, "when life can be so deliciously ironic?" The older man laughed heartily as he pushed Atif aside and made his way towards the Infirmary.

Brother Paulus stooped over Volmar. He took the boy's shoulder and asked more gently, "Are you all right, son?"

Volmar hung his head in shame. "Nothing a good dose of common sense couldn't amend . . . I am sorry, Brother Paulus. Sophie's right, I feel so foolish."

"Good," Paulus said, his gruff attitude returning, "and very well you should. You were way out of your league. Those two men are professional warriors; they have seen and caused more death and destruction than you could possibly imagine. Now be off with you before you get another mite-brain idea."

Paulus glared at the few onlookers remaining. His white mane of long hair and his flowing beard made him appear in the sunlight like a fierce territorial lion protecting his pride. His voiced roared. "And all of you should be ashamed of yourselves as well, cheering on such preposterous fighting! Surely such savagery will put an end to us all." As the crowd meekly dissipated, Paulus marched past Atif back to his Infirmary. Sophie followed, scowling first at Volmar and then at every face daring to meet her gaze.

Chapter 2: Smoldering Pride

Clearing Behind Guest Quarters, Disibodenberg Monastery

2nd of November, Saturday, Mid-Morning

Volmar closed his eyes and prayed in earnest as the crowd dispersed. Soon, everyone had left, with the exception of Atif. "You forgot the most important thing, my young friend," Atif said as he picked up the sword, his voice heavy with an Arabic accent. "Rhythm. All things in nature move in harmony. By working with the rhythm of a situation you can turn it to your advantage with little effort."

"Rhythm?" Volmar said, searching Atif's dark, impenetrable eyes.

"That, and you must learn to parry."

"I thought that's what I *was* doing," Volmar said, letting out a deep sigh as he sat down gingerly on the wall.

"Yes, but with little consistency. You must practice a rhythmic attack like step-parry-thrust-parry. Furthermore, it is a good idea to parry after lunging, since your enemy is likely to counter your attack with one of his own."

"Are you, sir, willing to show me what you mean by this?" Volmar decided what discomfort he felt was less important than salvaging his smoldering pride.

"Only if we use wooden sticks," Atif grinned, offering Volmar a hand.

Rummaging through the wood pile behind the kitchens, the two found a couple of sturdy sticks and sought privacy in a small clearing behind the bread ovens.

"Were you once a water boy for a king?" Volmar asked, taking his position on the other side of the rocky clearing. "I couldn't help but overhear the gentleman's pronouncement."

"First of all, that man is no gentleman." Atif spat onto the ground with disdain. "I had the misfortune of knowing him in Jerusalem a long time ago, after the invasion." He ran his fingers through his dark hair, trying to untangle the past with more clarity.

As the sun went behind several gathering clouds, the air suddenly became chilly. "You perceive the war with the infidels as an invasion?" Volmar asked, surprise in his voice.

Atif sighed deeply. "History will not be kind to such brutal occupiers. It did not matter that my family was Christian or a part of the Arab aristocracy, our lives and properties in Samaria were seized nevertheless. I became a slave, the property of the court and of the European kings Godfrey of Bouillon and his merciless brother Baldwin."

"I did not know. What needless tragedy." Volmar was bothered by how insincere and shallow his own words sounded. "War never leads to peace, only more wars."

"I was fortunate though. An old monk took pity on me and brought me to Rome." Atif patted the small bulk of what Volmar knew to be the codex given to him the night before by a messenger. "Now I will be able to return to the ruins of my homeland and start over."

Volmar recalled Atif's rosary. "What do you know of the Knights Hospitaller?"

"You are a curious lad," Atif said, eyeing the boy suspiciously. "What makes you ask me such a question? I am a mere Aramaic scholar."

Volmar said quietly, "Sir, I do not believe you are who you say you are."

Atif paused, balancing his answer and his voice carefully to a neutral tone before answering. "And what, pray tell, do you base this on?"

"Few scholars ever touch a sword, and when they do, they are like me, pitiful warriors."

"Is that all?" Amusement danced in Atif's eyes as he paced back and forth in front of Volmar.

"All right then," Volmar said, "a test. Was Paul's letter to Rome, what we know as the Book of Romans, written in Aramaic before it was translated into Greek?"

Atif shook his head. "I do not know," he answered, seemingly unperturbed at having been caught posing as someone he was not. "My turn. Tell me, my young interrogator—such accusations do not explain why you think I am of the Knights Hospitaller?"

"A rosary fell from your pocket last night when I was hanging up your cloak. I couldn't help but notice the distinctive eight-pointed star of the secret brotherhood."

"Ah, of course. The rosary was a gift from the monk who brought me to Rome. I owe him a great debt. He was kind to me when no one else cared." He paused and changed the subject abruptly. "Now, my friend, you must learn to parry with your sword just as well as you wield your words. Your back is not straight." He went and physically straightened Volmar's posture. "When you lean forward, you are compressing your backbone. Here and here," he said, patting the space below Volmar's neck and the small of his back. "It weakens each swing you make."

Volmar lowered his stick and laughed bitterly. "Maybe the old man was right. I should keep to my letters."

"Trust me. That old man speaks only in half-truths and lies," Atif said curtly before swinging his stick and knocking it against Volmar's. "Come now, don't give up. Sword fighting takes practice and patience. Do not take this the wrong way, Volmar, but," Atif smiled, his teeth remarkably white, "you seem to have little of both."

Chapter 3: Poor Souls

Behind the Bread Ovens of the Kitchen Gardens, Disibodenberg Monastery

Sunday, 3rd of November, the Next Morning

Bloodied rags were thrown onto the refuse heap. Volmar watched mesmerized as the flames eagerly consumed the bandages, helplessly spitting and sputtering in protest.

"Those all came from the Anchorage?" he asked in disbelief, as Brother Johannes, a heavy-set man with a disfiguring harelip, hastened the rags' demise with his poker.

"Yep, it seems our new Anchoress wears one of those nasty leg irons that bite into yore flesh and causes yore wound to always fester and burn. Not exactly what I'd do ta get closer ta our Lord, if I do say so myself."

"I'm of the same mind . . . and what about the other two young women? Do they have ascetic habits, too?"

"Not that I can tell, little brother. They don't seem to be starving themselves . . . at least not that servant girl, Hiltrud. She has a figure, that one, if you know what I mean." He grinned rather sheepishly. Volmar wasn't sure if he was blushing or if the warmth from the fire was turning his face red.

"What about the other one?" Volmar pressed on, more concerned over what Brother Johannes thought of Hildegard than Hiltrud's curves.

"That Hildegard girl seems to be the most sensible of the three. Yesterday mornin' right away, she requested some seeds to grow a few herbs and vegetables in their own garden. She told me 'erself that she's developing some sort of a calendar ta let 'er know when ta harvest certain herbs. In all, I've spoken with her twice and on both occasions she'd request practical items like blankets and linen strips and candles, and, strangely enough, a psaltery,[73] so she can sing Mass with us, she said."

---

73 Psaltery: A stringed-musical instrument, an ancient harp that may be plucked or played with a plectrum or pick.

"A psaltery . . . " Volmar repeated, bemused, remembering her lilting voice in the clearing a year ago.

"A second-hand one would do nicely, she said. She made it clear that she appreciated old things and could fix the psaltery if it was broken. She also was a wondering if she could have a wax writing tablet and stylus to write down the words of the Holy Scripture." Johannes grinned. "Imagine that, little brother, a girl knows more letters than I!"

"Sounds to me like you have found a new friend," Volmar said.

"Maybe she's attracted to old deformed men, who knows?" Brother Johannes chuckled. He wiped his sweaty brow, and threw the last shovelful of garbage onto the fire before remarking more seriously. "No woman ever looked at me with longing, I can tell you that, little brother. But, no matter, she's a smart one."

"And with good taste," Volmar added, holding the handles of the wheelbarrow as Brother Johannes scraped clean the insides with a rag before tossing it into the fire. "I suppose, if I had to live in an enclosure, I would want to use the time to learn all I could, too. Only an active mind can avoid the trap of boredom."

"That and active hands, Brother Volmar. They'll need to find suitable work for those three. Otherwise, they'll all slip into madness, and Lucifer will find three open doors, mark my words. I myself need a reason to rise up each day; otherwise, I'll fall victim to the hordes of airy spirits looking for weaknesses such as pride and arrogance. If you ask me, we were put on this earth to do good works however humble and however mundane in His name, not our own."

Johannes took the poker back in his hand and started turning over the rubbish, letting the air whip up the flames, sending sparks of light into the foggy grey morning air. "You would be surprised by the number of our own who are not abiding by the Rule, trying to seek their personal fortunes here on earth."

"How could there be such greed among us?" Volmar said gravely, shielding his face as the pile of burning garbage threw off more heat.

"Well, it's not my place to spread rumor, but let's just say that I've witnessed a certain brother who takes to disguising himself and spending an unholy amount of time down in the village. Never gotten a good look at his face, mind ye, but I know it was one of us anyways."

"Do you know what he does in the village?"

Johannes paused and scratched his chin. "All I know is that he comes back in the dead of night."

Volmar thought of the clearing and Brother Arnoul's unfortunate death after accusing a fellow brother of sneaking out at night. "Brother Johannes, you grew up in the monastery, right?"

"I certainly did, for nigh over half a century! I was a foundling, and was dropped off in a basket at the Porter's[74] hut. Poor soul, this face of mine must've scared me own mother."

"Perhaps you remember a holy brother by the name of Judas who lived here at the monastery over eleven years ago."

"Judas," Johannes repeated with a frown. "I don't recall someone by that name. Me distant memory has never been clear. There were many novices who came and went, finding our strict observances of the Offices difficult to bear. They also didn't want to work none, spoiled they were since most of them were the second sons of aristocratic families or such like that . . . used to servants doing everything for them, even dressing them."

From the far end of the burning garbage heap a small voice called out, "Brother Johannes . . . "

Johannes listened for the familiar rustle in the bushes nearby. "I hear ye. Hold on, boys, I've a few scraps saved for yore family." Johannes motioned for Volmar to keep quiet. Reaching around, he retrieved a heavy burlap bag, lifted it to his strong shoulders with ease, and flung it into the woods.

"God bless thee," the same small mysterious voice answered.

"God bless ye both," Johannes added, wiping his coarse hands together. The brothers watched in silence as two young boys, dressed in what appeared to be oversized cassocks, scurried off like field mice through a small gap in the wall, disappearing with the bag of food scraps.

"Those two were as thin as broomsticks last spring. Poor little 'uns, caught them drinking from the streams. Didn't know better, it could kill you I says to them, so I sneak a few bottles of ale into a sack, with blankets and anything else that's thrown away around here."

"To them, our garbage is a feast of plenty," Volmar muttered, moved by what he'd witnessed.

---

[74] Porter: The gatekeeper at the monastery.

"Well, they haven't any money, and as far as I can tell, there're about five or six of them. Their mum and dad both died of the fever last winter. Those two are the eldest and are good scavengers, they are." Brother Johannes wiped his forehead, the sweat soaking his hair and the neckline of his habit. "Wish I could do more to help them," he said, returning to his work.

"You're keeping them warm and well-nourished."

"They're proud, those two." Brother Johannes gave a wide grin. "That's why they never want to show their faces . . . that, or they're scared of me. Don't know which as of yet."

Volmar acknowledged that with a grim twist of his mouth. Given the stories told in the villages, someone like Brother Johannes could be perceived as something of a frightening ogre.

"The eldest boy calls himself Michael, and his younger brother's name is Gabriel . . . two feisty little archangels, eh?"

"God have mercy on their poor souls."

The last of the morning mist was rising. The clamor of the bells in the tower announced Terce; their relentless clanging calling everyone to prayers. Brother Johannes suddenly stood, staring at the flames in front of him. He grabbed Volmar's sleeve and spoke eerily. "Don't you smell it, little brother?"

"Smell what, Brother Johannes?" Volmar queried, noticing how the old monk's voice quivered uncharacteristically.

"It's in the air, little brother. Been there for several days now, I warn ye, that ol' woily devil is up to no good. Be careful, Brother Volmar, watch your back." Then he whispered. "As a favorite of the Abbot, you have many enemies."

Chapter 4: Rude Statues

Cloisters and Sanctuary of Disibodenberg Monastery

Sunday, 3rd of November, Terce, Around 9 a.m.

Reluctant to leave the warmth of the fire behind, the two made their way to the rusting Iron Gate. There they were joined by their other brothers, also interrupted from their morning chores, filing in from various parts of the monastery. Light streamed in through the high and dramatic arches of the cloister, turning the black hoods of the monks a shimmering grey as they lifted them over their heads, obscuring their faces. It was an orderly, quiet processional. Even the center stones of the pavement reflected this ritual with their well-worn patina.

Volmar had time now to think through Johannes's warnings. Was he, in fact, a favorite of the Abbot? Could jealousy exist even amongst the holy brethren? The monastic life wasn't meant to be overly severe; yet, its imperatives certainly were. It was an unnatural way of life, solely devoted to meditation and contemplation. No wonder those who turned to the cowl thinking it was a haven of tranquility were disillusioned. Everything inside Volmar rebelled against such artificial restrictions; and yet, here he stood with his hands clasped, following the usual rituals. Why?

Impulsively, Volmar whispered to Johannes, "Dear brother, you have given me an idea."

From under his hood, Johannes shook his head, a black hole where his face should have been. He began in a low voice, "Now, now, little brother . . . " then he saw a mischievous glint in Volmar's eyes and trailed off uncertainly. "Huh, what sort of scheming have I seeded, eh?"

Volmar lifted his hood over his head, joining the end of the line with Johannes. "Don't worry. I will be careful." At that moment, he made a personal pledge to find a suitable psaltery and wax tablet to give the sensible young lady who desired only to stimulate her mind with God's words and teachings. His sense of what is just and right felt relieved.

The sanctuary seemed darker and cooler than Volmar expected, especially after the warmth of the bonfire. He followed after his holy brothers in silence. In the house of God they came together as a unified community. No longer were they individuals. Here they moved together and sang together; dark, shapeless, identical shadows with disembodied voices that rose in complete harmony, in unison and in prayer to one God. Reverently, the monks passed the marble font where, each in turn, dipped their fingers into the cool pool of holy water and muttered a prayer, giving the sign of the cross. Such comforting rituals, Volmar knew, kept the mind and the spirit submissive to God. The brothers took their assigned places in the choir loft. Few villagers at this time were in the nave,[75] where the congregation stood. Volmar recognized Reginald, the Bishop's entourage and their servants, but also noted Atif's absence. He must have already left, Volmar reasoned, and as a free man. The bound codex was the legal confirmation of having satisfied the last of his indentured requirements; though under what circumstances, Volmar wasn't sure. The Bishop stood beside the Abbot in the chancel at the altar. It was to be the last Mass they would share together before the Bishop left the next morning to return home. They nodded to one another before taking turns reading the scriptures associated with the Crucifixion. Terce commemorated different moments in Christ's Passion.

Volmar knew most of the Mass by heart, so he was looking up from his service-book when two soldiers under the command of a knight dressed in the Emperor's colors entered the sanctuary from the forecourt.[76] The massive wooden doors had creaked open and light now flooded into the dark entry. But it was the unaccustomed sound of metal rubbing against their scabbards that brought everyone's eyes to the back of the sanctuary where these soldiers stood immovable, like rude statues, their swords drawn to block the exit.

Volmar turned and watched as the Abbot and the Bishop leaned forward, ready to rise from their stalls, as they exchanged questioning looks in the dimness. Seeing that the soldiers respectfully stood their ground in silence, the Abbot nodded for the Mass to continue. No one would argue the reality that the Mass was said in a more hurried fashion than usual, or contradict the fact that few if any of the brothers were able to ponder what was being said, knowing full well that they were all under the oppressive scrutiny of the Emperor's soldiers.

At the end of the Mass, the holy brothers rose and exited the choir stalls, chanting in unison about the promise of the Resurrection. Reluctantly, they filed by the soldiers, exiting into the Cloister to return to their work, wondering what would bring the Emperor's men to their humble monastery. Volmar broke line and, keeping a reasonable distance, went and stood in the shadows to be within earshot of the exchange as the Abbot and the Bishop approached the soldiers.

---

[75] Nave: The central part of the church running lengthwise.
[76] Forecourt: The front entrance to the church.

The knight bowed formally to both holy men before handing to the Bishop a parchment. "By order of Henry the Fifth, I present ye with this message."

The Bishop broke the wax seal of the letter, imprinted with the Emperor's own insignia. For a few embarrassing moments, he held the letter first close, then far away, trying to bring its tiny script into focus. The Abbot understood the failure of old eyes and quickly motioned for Volmar to come out of the shadows and over to read aloud the letter's contents:

This is to inform you that Adalbert, Archbishop of Mainz, has been arrested by imperial troops and is being held on charges of treachery and intrigues. He is imprisoned in the castle of Trifel and has formally requested the presence of his son, Reginald of Mainz. The Emperor, Henry the Fifth, has graciously conceded to this arrangement and is providing safe escort for his son to the castle.

Volmar returned the letter to the Bishop, searching the empty nave for Reginald. During the reading of the message, Reginald had approached the altar, knelt before it and prayed. Stoically he rose, crossed himself and then turned to face the others, with no visible signs of distress. It was, the young monk thought, as if he'd anticipated such an arrest and was somehow relieved that the endless waiting was over.

"Is that all?" said the Bishop, as he sternly addressed the knight.

The Abbot piped up, equally incensed. "Has there been a trial? Has the church been notified?"

For the first time, Volmar saw how quickly the Bishop's smile could turn ugly, into a malicious sneer. "Burchard, this sounds to me like a trap! I insist that Reginald stay put." He turned to the knight and declared so all could hear, "Tell your King that Reginald of Mainz chooses his right of sanctuary and will not move from Disibodenberg."

Reginald came forward and put his hand on the Bishop's shoulder. "It is I who will make such accusations, and will do so in person." He turned to the knight, who already seemed somewhat flustered by his lack of knowledge. "Do not torment the messenger, my friend. I am ready to face my enemies, those who see my father as a traitor to the crown. In the kingdom of God, motive matters. I will go with these men willingly, and inform the Emperor myself of his foolishness."

"Reginald," the Bishop said, clearly worried. "Are you sure you want to take your orders from this King? I'm sure Abbot Burchard would not mind you seeking sanctuary until we have the support of the church. I will take this to my superiors right away, and we will all plead your father's case together."

"Thank you, Bishop Otto and Father Burchard." Reginald nodded to the Abbot, "But no. I will not rest on my hands in here while my father rots in a dungeon." Reginald kissed the Bishop's ring and embraced the Abbot before being led outside into the bitterly cold morning air, cut off from the safe confines of sanctuary.

Volmar stepped aside and watched with a growing sense of admiration as Reginald and his servants were escorted out and led into a waiting carriage marked with the imperial crest of King Henry the Fifth.

Abbot Burchard muttered so only the Bishop and Volmar could hear. "This is proof of the King's determination to drive one more nail in the coffin of the church."

The driver whipped the horses, the carriage rocking from side to side on the uneven cobblestones as it made its way past the Anchorage and further down the hill to the Porter's house. Volmar thought back to the freedom papers of Atif. Were they a gift from the crown for one more dutiful mission? He couldn't help but feel that Atif was the Emperor's pawn used to seal the fate of this troublesome family. Volmar doubted that this would ever be achieved. Both father and son had a cause and a stubborn determination that prison would only strengthen.

As they watched the carriage amble away, the Bishop turned to the Abbot. "Burchard, my friend, I will need to leave within the hour." He turned to his entourage, and with a swift and decisive wave of his hand he said, "Go on. Prepare for our departure."

The Abbot hesitated for a moment longer, then gestured for the Bishop to follow him. "There's an abbey close to Trifel Castle, isn't there?" The two walked side by side back into the church and down the aisle of the sanctuary to the Abbot's private chambers. Their steps seemed more measured, less confident about what the future might hold.

Volmar had a terrible premonition of what would come next. The Emperor was not known for compromising and neither was the church for that matter. "God preserve us," he prayed.

Chapter 5: Shadow of the Devil

Infirmary, Disibodenberg Monastery

Sunday, 3rd of November, Terce, Mid-Morning

The lengthening shadows of the cloistered walkway chilled Volmar to the bone. He felt torn, wondering if he should wait to visit Brother Hans to request a psaltery for Sister Hildegard until this disastrous development faded from everyone's memory. As he turned the corner, he ran into Paulus coming from the Abbot's garden, carrying an armload of various bottles. Volmar felt he owed the man an apology after the sword fighting incident. "Can I help you with those?" Volmar offered, taking several of the cruets, flasks, jugs, and pots from him. "By the way, I am truly sorry for the sword fighting spectacle yesterday morning."

"Don't worry, it is all forgotten." Paulus sighed. "Thank you for helping. I know I should not be carrying so many at one time. I suppose my thoughts are elsewhere."

"Is it one of your patients?"

"No, thankfully everyone is recovering as expected. It's probably nothing . . . nothing at all."

"Nothing?" Volmar said with disbelief, knowing full well that whatever was troubling Brother Paulus was not trivial. "If it distresses you, there is a reason."

Brother Paulus paced along the cloister walk, head bowed, watching the paving stones pass under his habit as he went on. "For the past two mornings I've discovered that someone has entered my laboratory between the offices of Compline and Matins and has helped themselves to some of my herbs and potions."

"Who would do such a thing? I will be sure to mention this to the Abbot."

"I have just come from discussing this very thing with him. In the past fifteen years, I never felt like I needed to lock any of the cabinets in that room." Paulus sighed deeply. "Perhaps it is time to reconsider. It will take several days to change out the doors and place locks instead of latches on them. As you know, in the wrong hands, these concoctions can be quite dangerous. The distinction between poison and medicine is very narrow. More often than not, it is simply a matter of dosage."

They took the shorter route around the kitchens and together crossed the road before entering the other world, the Infirmary.

Volmar couldn't help but notice a woman with disheveled red hair sitting on a stool by the hearth of the fireplace, rocking back and forth humming. Her face was painted bizarrely with black charcoal, a sign of mourning. Sophie sat close to her, trying unsuccessfully to feed her.

Brother Paulus motioned for Volmar to follow him into his laboratory with the bottles he was carrying. The acrid smells, the gurgling sounds of liquids boiling over small flames, and the amazing array of labeled pots and urns furthered Volmar's sense of suddenly being transported into another world. It was a room like no other. During the winter months, Paulus spent most of his time in this room investigating new combinations of various herbs and potions and reading through his large leather-bound tomes, the exhaustive observations of healers who came before him. There was even whispered speculation that Paulus was working on a remedy for sleep, so he would never have to waste any of his time.

With a western exposure, sunlight was still streaming in through the cracks around a narrow rear door, which led to Paulus's summer work, the Infirmary garden. Mostly dormant this time of year, it was a living testimony to his tireless dedication. The garden covered nearly an acre of land as it cascaded down the hillside, offering every conceivable species of known medicinal plants, all neatly organized in structured beds, one for each species. Paulus had managed to purchase all that he needed in hospital supplies from selling such things as the seeds of leeks, mustard, hemp, colewort, onions, and grafted fruit trees to the villagers. By keeping such an organized nursery trade, Paulus was also able to purchase new species of plant life that captured his fancy. Often this trade would take place in the guest house, where travelers who knew of Brother Paulus's reputation would pay for their lodgings with interesting plants and herbs from exotic places such as the Far East and Africa.

"What miraculous potions are you working on now?" Volmar asked, curiously lifting the lids of a few of the jars and wrinkling his nose in disgust at some of their horrid stenches, placing them quickly back on the shelf. He missed the days when he was Paulus's apprentice, assisting him in his experiments and helping him record the details of various medicines, salves, and tonics that he had concocted.

Paulus scanned the top shelf of his laboratory and said ruefully, "That shelf, as you know, represents my failures—potions I'd rather forget. But that doesn't quite answer your question. I've had a couple of recent travelers from the Holy Land who, in exchange for lodging, have given me some interesting seed specimens."

"Are they the sword fighters from yesterday?" Volmar asked sheepishly. He hated bringing up the memory but was curious about the new travelers from the east.

"Yes, I believe they're the men who nearly put you out cold in my mortuary, Ulrich and his younger companion Donato."

Volmar hung his head in mock humility. "I'll stay out of their way, I promise."

"Good. Thankfully they keep to themselves and are gone most of the day. Both of them, however, impressed me with their knowledge of the healing arts."

"Really?" Volmar replied, intrigued by this juxtaposition of opposites. "Warriors and healers, an odd combination, wouldn't you say?"

"An implausible, dangerous combination if you ask me." Paulus walked out into the Infirmary's courtyard and over to his hot house, a lean-to set against the Infirmary's chimney. Its constant warmth helped germinate the more sensitive seedlings through the cold winter. He changed the topic abruptly by proudly pointing out the bounty of his recent trade, a seedling tray where he had planted the traveler's seeds. "They're much too fragile to set in the ground. I'll have to wait until spring. Supposedly, the salve from their seed spores can cure blindness. I'm not sure about that, but it is worth trying, eh, my friend?"

They returned to the laboratory and Volmar couldn't keep his eyes from studying the shelf that always held his interest more than any other. It was the shelf of dried specimens. There were exotic reptiles, birds, and other small mammals, including a dried bat. Their shriveled skins, nails, hair, and even tissues provided Brother Paulus with ingredients to prepare his healing remedies.

Suddenly there was a cry from the women's infirmary followed by a crash of what sounded like shards of pottery shattering on a stone floor. Volmar and Paulus rushed to the room, aghast at what they saw. The bowl Sophie was holding had been flung to the floor by the red-headed woman she was trying to feed. The woman now stood inches from Sophie's face, screaming over and over, insisting that the girl "feed my babies."

"Providence, I feel, has brought us together," Paulus said, as he placed his hand on Volmar's sleeve. "Come, I need your help."

The two approached the frantic woman from either side. Paulus quietly and firmly whispered in the woman's ear. "I'm here to care for your children also."

The whispered words of comfort were surprisingly louder than her rage. With the woman's face purple from grief and anger, Volmar gasped at how hideously the ashen lines accentuated her inner torment. With remarkable ease, Paulus led the woman back to her cot.

Sophie, clearly shaken by the ordeal, reached for several rags and started wiping up the mess the woman had made with the porridge all over the floor. Volmar bent down to help her retrieve all the broken shards and listened sympathetically as she filled him in on the strange woman's condition. "She came to us last night. Her neighbors brought her in, saying that she'd lost her entire family to a fever, four of her babies and her husband. She herself, though, seemed healthy enough, except when Brother Paulus examined her. On the side of her right arm, there's an unusual growth that ended up being a home of sorts for worms."

"Worms?" Volmar repeated, wrinkling his nose in disgust.

Sophie continued, "Yes. However, she is quite fond of these worms. She treats them as her children and she refuses to let Brother Paulus clean out the wound. She has given the worms names and she talks to them as if they were her own brood."

"She lives in the shadow of the Devil."

"I'm afraid so," Sophie added, mopping up the last of the sticky porridge.

Paulus approached Sophie and Volmar, shaking his head. "It is a perilous condition. If her madness is not arrested soon, she will surely become divorced from our reality for the rest of her life . . . poor soul."

"How did this happen, Brother Paulus? I mean, worms to my knowledge only feast on dead flesh."

"The wound is self-inflicted, my boy. I've seen this sort of transference before, but never to this degree." Brother Paulus selected one of his bound reference books and handed it over to Volmar. "I'd like you to record this case for me and accompany me to her side."

"Maybe, Brother Paulus, we can convince her that the worms need a new home, in this empty flask." Volmar picked up one of the few empty flasks from the shelf.

"Yes, it is worth a try. Go along with me when we approach her. Perhaps, this will save her arm. Otherwise, I will have to amputate her arm in order to save her life from the infection which is spreading."

Brother Paulus approached the young woman, bowing slightly. "Milady, I have one of the greatest scribes in this region with me. His writing is flawless and authoritative for he is the Abbot's own personal assistant. Would you allow me to extract your family from your arm, if he recorded each of their names? We will give your children this fine new home, where they will have more room to mature." Brother Paulus gave her the jar to assess.

"Oh no, they are not ready to be weaned. It is too soon," she protested, giving the glass flask back to him.

Sophie went to the other side of her cot and spoke gently. "You really should listen to these two men. They are very learned, Isabella, and want to help."

Volmar met both Paulus and Sophie's questioning eyes and decided it was his turn to try. "Greetings, milady, my name's Brother Volmar. I have vowed to be a faithful chronicler. I am taking a census of all who are in our Infirmary this day. What is your name and date of birth?"

The young woman stopped humming and smiled up at him. "My name is Isabella of Staudernheim. I was born the 13th of April in the year of our Lord 1088."

Quietly, Volmar wrote her name and the date of her birth into his book and then went on, "Isabella of Staudernheim, I understand that you have a large family. Help me with their names, please?"

"...She has given the worms names and she talks to
them as if they were her own brood."

"Is that the church registry?" she asked, suspiciously eyeing the big book he held open and expectantly in his hands.

"It is where we write what needs to be remembered," Volmar replied.

"The names of my children, if written down in that book, could still be read even when their little bodies have turned to dust?"

"Yes. Written records such as this outlive all of us. They are more truthful than memories."

"Can angels read?"

Her question was spoken so softly that Volmar had to drop to his knees beside her to hear. "Yes, Isabella, angels have powers that far surpass our own. I'm sure they already know that you've cared deeply for your children and will not be careless with their young souls."

"Very well. Write their names down as I say them."

One by one Isabella lifted out a worm from the wound in her arm and announced its name and date of birth. Dutifully Brother Paulus took the worm from her and put it in the glass flask Sophie held, while Volmar recorded the information.

"Their precious souls are not lost, are they?" Isabella asked suddenly.

"God is a loving Father. He doesn't condemn those too young to know him."

Isabella then abruptly untied the red ribbon from her own hair, ran her fingers through Sophie's long straight blond hair as if she were combing it, then tied it into a lovely small bow at the nape of the young girl's neck. Sophie touched the bow lightly, unsure how to react. She had never had any feminine adornments in her hair before, and clearly felt touched by this mad woman's gesture.

"There," Isabella said with an air of satisfaction, "You look beautiful, child." Her face suddenly softened and the need for sleep overwhelmed her. "Take good care of them, will you?" she murmured, curling up awkwardly at the head of the cot. "I will rest now."

Paulus quietly proceeded to clean and bandage her arm. Volmar left with Sophie and the jar. They returned as Paulus was draping a blanket over her. Inside the flask, Volmar and Sophie had added food for the worms, sprigs of moss and dead leaves. He placed the flask on the small table beside the sleeping woman.

"Thank you, son, and you as well, Sophie," Brother Paulus said, nodding towards the girl. "Your simple reassurances gave her the ability to let go. Memory is a gift from God; however, sometimes the ability to forget is also a blessing."

Chapter 6: Unsuspecting Traveler

Countryside Beyond Disibodenberg Monastery

Sunday, 3rd of November, Late Afternoon

Sometime during that first day of riding, Atif broke his silence and began confessing his sins to his horse. "Reginald, and for that matter, his father Adalbert, had trusted me and yet I rewarded their trust by coldly betraying them to the Emperor. Tell me this, friend: Is my freedom worth more to me than the freedom of others?" The horse listened with the patience of a true friend and wisely kept its own counsel.

Atif drew in a deep satisfying breath. The air smelled like snow. He pulled on the reins, as they came to the edge of the cliff. He patted the side of his horse's face as he pulled out a map and turned to face south, trying to get his bearings. "I know you are tired, boy. It will be slow going down this hill. In nigh under an hour, it'll be as black as the inside of an iron pot. We won't make it to Altenbamberg. We may as well make camp at the base of this hill beside the river."

Slowly Atif guided his horse down the rocky hillside. When he came to a rise, he suddenly met up with a riderless horse. The horse was oversized, clearly a warhorse. It was fully saddled; its reins hung limp about his neck. As Atif approached cautiously, the jet black horse reared its head and neighed, clawing the air with its hoofs. Atif couldn't help but wonder if this was a trap. The hairs on the back of his neck stood on end in anticipation. He'd heard of elaborate snares gypsies would use to rob an unsuspecting traveler. Instinctively, he felt for his scimitar[77] tied securely to his belt. In battle he could take a

[77] Scimitar: A curved sword used by Arabs.

man's arm off with one swing of its blade; however, out here, all alone and at dusk, it seemed little protection against an ugly ambush. Atif proceeded with caution, peering both upwards into the trees and downwards into the quiet underbrush, looking for signs of someone hiding. In the distance he could hear the wailing of wild dogs, vicious creatures that when driven by hunger could attack and kill a man with their razor-sharp teeth.

Not more than ten paces ahead, he saw a man lying face down next to a stream. The stranger was dressed in gentlemen's clothing and was not moving.

Atif steered his horse alongside the man and withdrew his scimitar. He waved it into the air and bellowed, "Come out, you scurrilous thieves! Fight as men!" With cold regard he listened, surprised to see no movement in the deepening shadows of the surrounding woods. The fallen man rose up on his elbows and flipped himself over. He gulped for air along with hope as he looked up into Atif's face. "Atif, is that you?"

"Matthias," Atif said in disbelief. Returning his scimitar to its sheath, he dismounted and knelt beside the old man. "After all these years we meet again, my friend."

Chapter 7: Dark Recesses of his Mind

Library at Disibodenberg Monastery

Sunday, 3rd of November, After Compline

Cormac held onto the iron banister as he climbed the steps slowly up to his library. With his other hand he tightened his grip on the rag he held up to his nose. It was drenched in blood. He pinched it with growing impatience, breathing heavily through his mouth. "Growing old has so many indignities," he muttered, remembering the humiliation he now felt, being relegated to the retrochoir[78] loft for the sick and infirmed. However, he reminded him-

[78] Retrochoir: Situated behind the monks' choir, this was the area for the elder brothers who weren't expected to follow the rigid routines of the community.

self, this arrangement did allow him the privilege of leaving the prayer service earlier than usual to retire for the night. So, as with many things in life, it was a mixed blessing.

At the top of the landing the elder monk was astonished to find a suspicious glow coming from around the door into his library. Few rules at the monastery were as strict as the ones he observed in his library. He, alone, decided who saw what, when, and where. Access was strictly regulated and controlled. He entered and instinctively armed himself for battle by reaching for his infamous cane formed from a contorted filbert tree branch. For more than a decade, his cane had served him well, striking painfully the careless knuckles of those who dared to touch a manuscript without wearing the proper gloves or face mask. Worldly concerns of theft and vandalism were certainly a real threat. There were travelers who would take advantage if they could of monastic hospitality. For this very reason Cormac was grateful that all of his manuscripts were chained to their small cubicles. Whoever this foolish intruder might be, Cormac assured himself, it would take the strength of a leviathan to unclasp the rod and locks which held the library's treasured books firmly clasped to their shelves. To his chagrin, Cormac realized the light was not coming from the common reading or circulation section. The glow was coming from the restricted reference collection in the rear of his library. These works were more fragile and considerably more valuable; they were devoted entirely to first-century church history.

Cormac moved soundlessly with practiced stealth, no longer worried about his bleeding nose. He passed the arched closets cut into the stone walls that stored small statues and miscellaneous treasures, and crisscrossed around the labyrinth of reading desks. When at last he turned the corner to face the intruder, he breathed a long drawn-out sigh. The culprit had disappeared!

Cormac studied the scene with annoyance. The invasion was certainly not imagined, for the wooden seat he felt was still warm, and beeswax from a burning candle had left its telltale droppings. He noted with alarm that these wax drippings ran across the stone floor leading indisputably to a secret passageway formed within the thickness of the walls, hidden behind the bookcase. It was an obscure escape route, one that a stranger to the monastery would not know. Few brothers even knew of its existence. It was a throwback to earlier times when the monastery was newly built, when there was a necessity to flee in times of war, disease, or rebellion. Cormac bent over the open book. Its title in Latin disclosed its obscure subject: *Ancient Holy Relics.* Blood dripped from his nose onto a small torn parchment lying beside the book. On it, words were scrawled out, in a hurried but recognizable hand—the same distinctive writing style he'd recognized over a year ago with young Volmar. He read and re-read their meaning: *Those in possession of this ancient blood relic, the Spear of Longinus, are invincible against all human frailties . . . the 'Spear of Christ' or 'Spear of Destiny' is believed to have acquired tremendous mystical power.* He read the notes further and shuddered. *Whoever claims the Spear 'holds the destiny of the world in his hands for good or evil.'* It took but a moment before the full implication of these written words illuminated the dark recesses of his mind: Judas had returned!

Chapter 8: Promise of a Remarkable Mind

Common Room and Sleeping Quarters of the Anchorage at

Disibodenberg Monastery

Sunday, 3rd of November, Late Afternoon

Hildegard slowly reread the letter she had found folded and sealed on the food tray with their supper. The words were beautifully scripted and written in High German, not Latin; probably, she reasoned, because the person may have doubted her ability to read Latin.

Sister Hildegard, It has been over a year since our last face-to-face encounter in the woods. I beseech you to pardon my boldness and not to disdain but to accept this message: another friend in Christ recommended me to you, saying that I may be of service as your humble teacher; for you have an able mind and would benefit from a higher level of education. I am willing to do what pleases you and, if by God's Grace, to help serve Him better in doing so.

Respectfully yours, Brother Volmar

And then in Hildegard's own secretive language Volmar had written an addendum, on a small folded piece of parchment:

We have much to discuss concerning our mutual friend Brother Arnoul. The book in question is still missing after all these years and I am no closer to unraveling the true identity of our deceptive Judas. Last year I questioned Brother Cormac the Librarian and Abbot Burchard. Both suspected that Judas left Disibodenberg for Rome. However, circumstances may have changed. After all, ten years is a long time. Brother Cormac came to me just tonight to confirm my growing suspicion that Judas has returned. Sophie, the girl you met at the festival last year, saw a disagreeable man leave Saint Peter's Altar, the very same night we found the tunnel. He asked who had used up his lamp's oil . . . so, as you can see, there is much to discuss on this matter. By the way, Sophie in her own words is 'eternally grateful' for the wardrobe you gave her.

Hildegard held this smaller note to her breast and sighed. It was a rare moment that quietly illuminated everything. It surprised her how gratifying it was that she and this young monk shared a way to communicate with one another outside of the church's rigid conventions of decorum. In this way she would stay connected to the world outside. Quietly she took the small parchment and, while the other two women were occupied over a dropped stitch, she burned it in the open flames of their hearth. "This is only the beginning of the answer," she whispered, watching the parchment curl, before burning to ashes.

In her hand remained permission to continue her studies. She could feel the excitement well up within her. From childhood on she had studied grammar and the other liberal arts, and hoped by perseverance to attain a perfect knowledge of religion, for she was well aware that the gifts of nature are doubled by study. She'd read eagerly the books of the Old and New Testaments, and committed their divine precepts to memory; but she wanted to further add to the rich store of her knowledge by reading the writings of the holy Fathers, the canonical decrees, and the laws of the church. There was so much more she could learn, and she knew enough to understand how little she really knew.

Hildegard took Volmar's letter and approached Jutta, who was patiently showing Hiltrud how to mend an unsightly tear in one of the monks' undergarments. Hiltrud had a willing spirit but not much delicacy of touch; so mending was all she could manage. Embroidery tasks were set aside for Jutta to do, for she was far more accomplished with the needle. Hildegard regarded several large baskets full of mending neglected for years. Clearly, Hiltrud's days were laid out before her, spent in the honorable tradition of the Benedictine rule of work and prayer . . . but what of her own days? Hildegard knew that she needed purposeful work as well. She considered idleness a poison to the soul. She waited until Jutta returned the needle back to Hiltrud. "Jutta, may I speak with you in private?"

"Of course." The two women left Hiltrud bent over and in complete concentration on her next stitch, and entered the sleeping quarters. Jutta's request for a kneeling bench and altar table had been promptly answered, and they knelt together and faced the standing crucifix placed on an altar cloth woven in gold thread by Jutta many years ago. Though it was their third day of enclosure, it was Jutta's first day of being entirely conscious and moving around. Hildegard noticed how she winced in pain as she knelt, but did not complain or cry out.

Jutta spoke first after they both said silent prayers. "You've received a message. Are you prepared to tell me of it?"

"I am. As I told you, I did not know how it was to happen, I only foresaw his gentle face and knew him to be my teacher."

"Ah, Hildegard's scribe, the young monk haunting your visions?"

"Yes."

"Remember, your visions do not exist to tell you what to do, they are only there to guide. It is up to you to listen, and it is your actions that can take advantage of their wisdom. I have taught you all that I know and so did Uda, God rest her soul. She admonished me many times and made me promise to ensure that you continue your studies; for in you alone she saw the promise of a remarkable mind and feared the prospect that it would be wasted."

"And in you, Jutta, she often remarked to me how your sacrificial nature would attract many followers."

Both of them fell silent, lost in their memories. The sudden death of Jutta's mother, Sophia, was tragic; but mentioning Uda's death brought with it a flood of recollections not easy to look back on, for Uda had suffered greatly under the wasting disease of old age. Health was so fragile and so important. Hildegard wished that Jutta would not take hers so lightly, but she knew forcing her will onto Jutta would be a waste. Suddenly, Jutta went pale. Her eyes fell out of focus. Hildegard rose and supported her arm. "Do you need to lie down?"

Jutta waved off her concern. "I'm fine."

Hildegard knew Jutta held with disgust anything having to do with "the flesh." To Jutta, suffering from malnutrition, dehydration, and a collection of maladies brought on by the neglect and abuse of her own body only brought her closer to the Almighty. On the other hand, Hildegard saw her own body as a "temple of the Holy Spirit"; to Hildegard it should always be cared for out of respect. It was nearly impossible to explain or understand the mystery of these contradictions. Quietly, Hildegard handed Volmar's message over to Jutta and regarded her as she read it through. Joy was never an emotion Jutta expressed openly. She'd even gone so far as to forbid laughter in her presence. To Jutta, life was to be lived soberly, and suffering was its only reward.

At length Jutta responded. "Very well, I will write to Abbot Burchard on your behalf. We should come to some arrangement for your continued education here at the Anchorage."

Hildegard's hands wrapped around the letter Jutta handed back to her, feeling assured that so long as her life was in God's hands all would be well.

Chapter 9: A Violent Manifesto

Abbot Burchard's Private Quarters at Disibodenberg Monastery

Sunday, 3rd of November, Evening, Before Compline

Volmar scraped clean from the ivory-colored parchment yet another portion of what he had written. He was already regretting the size he'd cut the parchment into. The dictation was more involved than he anticipated, so every word needed to be carefully chosen.

"Brother Volmar, is something troubling you?" The Abbot sat across from his young protégé and held his hand to his brow. He rubbed his temples, a habit, Volmar noted, the Abbot exhibited whenever he was perplexed. "It's so unlike you to make so many mistakes."

"Father, I am troubled. If someone you knew had a remarkable mind and musical talent, should that person not be taught to use their talents: to learn to read and write better in Latin and to study musical notation?"

"By all means, my son, Christ taught us to use, not squander, our spiritual gifts. It would be a sin to knowingly repress such abilities."

"I thought so," Volmar mused.

"How so?" Abbot Burchard adjusted his weight, finding the wooden seat less tolerable than usual.

"I am not ready to disclose all as of yet, Father. I wrote a letter to this person and am waiting anxiously for a reply."

"Patience is not one of your virtues, Brother Volmar. That much I do know." The Abbot chuckled and the two men resumed the chronicle, or recording, of the week's events. "What day did we leave off?"

"I believe, Saturday the 2nd of November."

"Good. Be sure to add that I've discussed with Brother Andres the need to increase our provisions, since the farmers predict a long and bitterly cold winter ahead. All signs point to freezing temperatures well into the Lenten season."

There was a knock at the door. "Enter," the Abbot said, recognizing immediately the young man who came in as being from the Bishop's own personal entourage. "We have word already of Adalbert's release?" He rose and offered the young man a chair next to his.

"No, Father," he said, with a wave of his hand. "I cannot stay long. I'm afraid the circumstances are quite grim for the Archbishop."

"And Reginald, how is he holding up?"

"As well as can be expected, Father, under the circumstances. The Bishop wants you to keep him in your prayers. The Emperor has issued a violent manifesto against the Archbishop and all his treasonous followers."

The Abbot hung his chin in his hands. "His followers are many: the Pope, the church, and the nobles, particularly in Saxony. Any word from Rome, as of yet?"

"It is too soon, Father. There's snow just south of here. Word has it that the only pass through the Alps that isn't blocked from the recent landslides is treacherous due to ice."

"Has the Emperor made clear where he will celebrate the Nativity of the Lord this year? Last year, it was held in Mainz."

"This year he is planning to celebrate the Nativity of the Lord in Goslar, Father."

"In the Duchy of Saxony? Oh my, he is asking for trouble. God be with you, my friend. Tell the Bishop that we will pray for Reginald and the Archbishop's timely release. Go in peace." The young man knelt before the Abbot. "May you travel with His hedge of protection around thee. In the name of the Father, the Son, and the Holy Spirit, Amen." He motioned the sign of the cross before touching the man's forehead.

Still thinking, Volmar said, "More than ice needs to melt. None of it sounds hopeful."

After the young man had disappeared down the stairs, the Abbot laid a hand on Volmar's arm and said, "It is getting more difficult each year to keep our own little corner of the world free from the battleaxes chipping away at its very mortar."

"Come now, Father," Volmar said, absentmindedly twirling his quill. "If I remember correctly, Reginald spoke all too freely of his hatred towards the Emperor. I'm sure his father too had difficulty holding his tongue."

"I know. Both men thought little of their own safety. Do you suppose that other man, the Aramaic scholar, had something to do with all of this?"

"He was not an Aramaic scholar, Father. This I can assure you of. I questioned him the next day and found his scholarly knowledge lacking. His weaponry expertise, though, was exceptional. He even gave me a few sword-fighting lessons."

"I suspected as much. He did not know what his name Atif meant in Persian. A man gifted in languages should know such trivia."

"I'm sure you've already been to the library to look up Atif's name. What does it mean, Father?"

The Abbot grimaced. "What the man is obviously not: compassionate and sympathetic."

Chapter 10: Visitors of Importance

Stables at Disibodenberg Monastery

Monday, 4th of November, Early Morning, After Prime

Everyone knew that the Keeper of the Stables, Brother Hugo, still held a long-standing grudge against Volmar. Hugo felt betrayed ever since Paulus requested the boy's assistance in the Infirmary.

Still, Volmar knew he couldn't afford the time to wait for Hugo to come back from the village market to ask permission to borrow the small stool. Hildegard was waiting for him, and this was to be their first introductory lesson together.

Feeling the pressure of time, he walked quickly to the stables. The distinctive livestock smell hit him as he swung open one of the large wooden doors. He lifted the iron latch and locked it firmly behind him so the wind wouldn't disturb the resting beasts. He couldn't help but notice two fine black steeds, handsome animals for mere villagers from Disibodenberg. He studied the insignia on the saddles, an eight pointed white star on a red shield, the same symbol he remembered from Atif's and his father Symon's rosary. They must be travelers from the Knight's Hospitaller visiting the monastery. There were two other horses without any insignia. Judging by the horses' care and breeding, there were two more visitors of importance. By the Benedictine Rule, the monastery was required to give food and shelter to any traveler who asked for them. Hopefully these strangers might leave a few coins as a gift to compensate for their brief stay. Generosity, though, could not always be expected, especially from those of power and position.

"Good day, Brother Volmar." Brother Albertus' eyes fell upon the stool.

"God's Grace to you, Brother Albertus. Please inform Brother Hugo that his stool will be returned promptly before prayers will be said during Nones[79] at three."

"You're taking quite a risk there, are you not?" Albertus added with interest. "You of all people should know that Brother Hugo has a

[79] Nones: Office of Prayers said between 2 to 3 p.m.

good arm with a whipping stick." Albertus sighed, then started massaging his lower back.

Volmar waited, anticipating a comment about the weather. No one could forecast the weather with such accuracy as Albertus. His body was a remarkable gauge. An ache here or a pain there gave his predictions the exactness of a sage.

Sure enough, Albertus turned towards the leaden sky. "Ah, we should have snow tomorrow night. I should water," he said, and added dismissively, "I'll mention the stool to Brother Hugo if I see him in the fields." He took off down the hillside. Albertus looked after the kitchen gardens and the paradise garden outside of the monk's cemetery. It was his duty to keep the traditional altar flowers and the lilies required for burials. To Volmar it didn't make sense how Albertus always watered his tender plants before a freeze. Miraculously, though, it worked. The next morning they would lie well protected in a thin layer of ice.

Chapter 11: A Sweeter Mission

Anchorage Window at Disibodenberg Monastery

Monday, 4th of November, Mid-Morning, After Terce

Volmar approached the Anchorage. Samson showed up and curled lazily next to him as he sat on the milking stool in front of the small arched window. A panel at each end was hinged and was now swung open. The leather flap used to block the chill of the winter winds was rolled up and tied. Hildegard's face was obscure in the dark shadows of the window's opening. Hiltrud was sitting with her mending in her lap, illuminated by a beam of late morning light. Her presence was necessary in observance of the unspoken rule that a nun should never be alone with a man. There was a long and awkward silence between them.

Volmar took a moment to consider where they should begin. "Very well, Sister Hildegard, let's start with conjugations in Latin. Repeat after me: *amo, amas, amat, amamos, amatis, amant.*[80]" Volmar listened to Hildegard's flawless recitations. As they continued the lesson, Volmar realized that he had greatly underestimated Hildegard's knowledge of Latin.

He concluded their lesson with the ninth stanza of an old hymn, *Vexilla Regis Prodeunt*[81]. "*O Crux ave, spes unica, hoc Passionis tempore! Piis adauge gratiam, reisque dele crimina.*[82]" She had understanding far exceeding what he had expected of a young girl trained by widow women. It was incredible how she repeated the words, they were not entirely spoken. The recitations were being sung. Her voice sounded clear, tuneful and strong, the same haunting voice he'd heard in the tree, only richer and with more emotion. The music moved through her entire body and somehow reached out to his soul, calming his restlessness.

When the lesson came to its conclusion, Volmar furrowed his brow, noting his young student's distraction. "Did you receive my message about Judas?"

"Yes, a tragic tale of greed, power and betrayal. Do you feel, dear brother, he is in our midst?" she inquired, almost playfully.

Volmar paused, intrigued once again by the thought that his new student possessed the ability to somehow see future events and to "hear" the thoughts of others. This, coupled with her obvious love of being taught new things and absorbing whatever he said with great enthusiasm, was truly remarkable. For a moment he had to catch his breath. It was something he had never attempted before. He was to be her mentor, her adviser, her faithful scribe. The thought brought him considerable trepidation. Of all people, he was most unworthy. How could one so contrary to acceptable wisdom and teachings be entrusted with such a great responsibility?

"Silence can speak volumes, you know," Hildegard said with a smile.

---

[80] *Amo, amas, amat, amamos, amatis, amant*: Latin conjugations for "I love, you love, he loves, we love, you love, they love."

[81] *Vexilla Regis Prodeunt*: Ancient Roman hymn to the True Cross of Christ dating back to the 6th Century.

[82] "O hail the cross, our only hope, in this Passiontide! Grant increase of grace to believers, and remove the sins of the guilty."

Volmar grinned sheepishly, his heart beating rapidly. He was scarcely able to speak, so ensnared by her charms. Then he added slowly, searching for the right words, "I have something for you, for your studies." Through the window's opening he passed a ten-stringed psaltery. "Brother Hans, the choral director, made me promise to give it only to one gifted in music. It is yours."

"Oh, it is beautiful." Hildegard had difficulty suppressing her joy. She leaned forward into the beam of light. Volmar could see how she cradled the instrument like a child. "Look, Hiltrud," she said, lightly running her fingers over the strings, "there are ten of them, each with a different sound and when you hold the handle like this, the strings have even a richer, deeper sound." She turned to Volmar. The look on her face far exceeded any repayment for the personal effort he'd gone to. "I will learn to play it right away. Thank you so much, Brother Volmar."

"Music," Volmar answered, recalling the old woman's prophecy. "I cannot fathom a sweeter mission to have, in a world lost to decay and disharmony."

Book 6: Deception

Chapter 1: Humble Ministrations

Infirmary at Disibodenberg Monastery

4th of November, Late Evening, After Compline

Paulus drew back the blanket as Atif laid his old friend, Matthias, down onto the cot. The Infirmarian watched as the Persian leaned forward and whispered something in the older man's ear, which caused Matthias to smile. Atif moved away, frustrated that he could do no more for his friend. "Do all you can for him, Brother, I owe him my life."

Sophie, in her nightdress and embroidered coat, brought Paulus clean towels and stared down at their new patient. "The miraculous healer," she uttered in surprise. Sophie turned to Paulus. "He's the one I told you about, the stranger in the clearing, who healed my Grandfather two summers ago."

Matthias met the young girl's eyes with recognition and a steady gaze, remembering too that night long ago in the woods. "I remember well the incident in the clearing . . . the last stages of holy fire. How fares your grandfather now?"

Sophie swallowed hard. "He died from a fall last year—he hit his head." She hadn't mentioned her grandfather to anyone since the funeral.

"I'm so sorry." Matthias leaned forward, attempting to straighten his hurt leg, and winced from the pain.

Sophie noticed that on both hands he wore thumb rings of gold. Quietly she resumed her duties, turning to the barrel and drawing out a mug of ale for the Arab foreigner. Paulus studied Sophie with consternation; rarely did he think of her as she once had been, a fragile little girl who showed up at the Infirmary clinging to her dying grandfather. Now she was like his right hand, sitting up late into the night feeding the elderly and wiping their feverish foreheads with tireless patience. Her sensitive nature made her a natural comforter for suffering women and children especially, who came to the Infirmary seeking

Paulus's help. As he predicted, her skillful hands could turn a mere wooden stick into a delicate instrument he could maneuver and use to hold back the healthy flesh while he cut off the dead or diseased parts.

Where he was lacking, she was not. When did she become this capable young woman? Was it the way she filled out her new clothes that accented her maturity, or had her rich wardrobe only brought it glaringly to his attention? This must be like the feeling fathers have for their grown children, Paulus thought, with fond admiration.

Paulus gazed down at his patient with renewed respect. "When you are stronger, I'd like to hear more of your remedies, especially in dealing with holy fire. For now, you must accept our humble ministrations; even healers need help now and then." Paulus turned to Matthias's injured leg. "You seem to have suffered a bite of some sort, more than likely from a wild dog. Is that right, sir?"

Matthias grimaced and said between his clenched teeth. "A pack of them caught me by surprise two nights ago."

"That must have been some fight. Some of those males can stand a full three feet high at the shoulder. It is a testimony to your courage that you survived."

"I'm well protected," Matthias said, mysteriously patting the pouch under his shirt. "I will not die so long as it's with me."

Atif was in such a dark mood and so engrossed in watching Paulus's ministrations that he didn't bother to question Matthias's strange assertion. He accepted Sophie's mug of ale with nothing more than a brief nod of gratitude.

Gently, Paulus removed Matthias's worn boot. Then, with a small knife, he cut through the cloth Atif had wrapped around the wound and, with a sponge, he slowly began bathing the wound in warm wine he had boiled and allowed to cool.

Matthias's eyes pinched closed in pain, but he said nothing.

"Atif," Paulus said, "why don't you take that sweet substance there on the nightstand and simply rub it on Matthias's teeth while I dress his wound. It will help with the pain, and soon he'll be able to sleep."

Atif lifted the small dish. "What's in it?" he said, sniffing it with interest.

"Believe it or not, the original recipe had at least 70 different ingredients. I've been playing around with the necessity of each of them for years."

"Let me guess. There's honey, castor oil, opium, myrrh, frankincense, the dried flesh of a viper, and spikenard, the very ointment Mary applied to the feet of Jesus."

"I'm impressed. Where did you learn of the healing arts?"

"I had a remarkable teacher. I was Matthias's young assistant, many years ago in a hospital in Jerusalem. Back then we called this mixture Theriac."

"That it is. Galen's own recipe," Paulus said with pride.

Atif carefully smeared it over Matthias's gums.

"The longer he stays off of that foot, the quicker it will heal." Paulus rose and stood over Atif, watching as he administered the last of the salve.

Atif looked up. "Is that enough?"

Paulus nodded.

Atif put a hand to Matthias's forehead. "You'll feel light-headed in a moment, my friend; don't fight it. Give in to the sensation. It will help you sleep." He extended his hand and gripped Matthias' frightfully cold palm in his. "Life is long. We will meet again another day, in a better place than this."

Matthias nodded with understanding and struggled to reply. "You've been away too long from your own people. God be with you."

Atif rose hesitantly. Paulus showed him a basin where he could wash his hands, and gave him a towel to dry off. "Come, we will know by morning if our efforts have helped. You need a good night's rest as well, my friend. The cot beside your friend is free for the night."

"Thank you, Brother Paulus, you have been most kind. If my friend is better by morning, I'll take my leave."

As was customary after Compline[83], Paulus left his new arrivals and began sprinkling each bed with holy water and saying a prayer. Sophie returned to bed, her sensitive nature deeply conflicted. She couldn't shake the feeling that something terrible was about to happen.

---

[83] Compline: The Office of Prayers said around 6 p.m.

Chapter 2: Death's Insistent Murmur

Infirmary at Disibodenberg Monastery

During the Night of the 5th of November, Before Matins

Atif stretched out on the cot, appreciative of not having to sleep another night on the cold ground. With no need to seem strong for anyone to see, he lay down on the bed with a groan and curled onto his side. The fire in the hearth gave off a steady glow. For a while he listened attentively to the uneven breathing of Matthias. One good deed could not erase the damage he'd caused for so many, he thought grimly. This was certainly the last place he should have returned to. He thought again about his terrible treachery and how he had betrayed his friend Reginald's resistance to the Emperor's cause. Now they were wasting away imprisoned because of his own desire to return home to Jerusalem. Surely, the Abbot, a friend and ally of the Archbishop, would not take long to point fingers at him. The chasm of hatred he'd created could never be undone.

At long last, Matthias's breathing settled into a steady, predictable pattern. Atif sighed. His friend must be mercifully asleep. Shadowy movements of strangers settling down on their cots for the night suggested a world he was eager to leave behind as he too drifted off to sleep.

Atif awoke sometime during the night. He opened his eyes and saw two men staring down at Matthias. He watched in horror as they searched through his old friend's travel bag at the foot of his bed. Atif gingerly reached for his scimitar in the satchel by his knees. He drew in a hissing breath of anger and flung himself on the man closest to him. "Don't move," he whispered into the ear of the thief, "or you will feel how sharp this blade is. You?" he muttered in disbelief. He turned the head of the man in his grasp. "What are you two still doing here, and why are you searching my friend's belongings?"

The older man went on smiling. "So, we meet again, water boy." With a look to his partner to be sure of his agreement, he stared down at Matthias, still asleep, and said in a cheery voice, "I was just checking to see if this is who I thought he might be."

"And who do you think he is?" Atif asked, still holding his knife to the throat of the younger man.

The older man shifted his narrow look to him and said with no particular interest, "He's simply a tired old soldier. We will leave him alone. He's not the man we've been waiting for."

Atif studied the older man, feeling there was something he wasn't letting on—or was he reading more into the situation than was necessary? As a spy, he ended up suspecting that everyone was as deceptive and cunning as he was.

The older man saw the glint of uncertainty and changed the subject. "I've heard about the Archbishop's arrest. You spent a great deal of time with that family in Rome and then in Mainz, did you not?"

Atif released the younger man with a shove and put his knife back into its sheath. "Where I choose to live and who I choose to know is none of your business. Leave me and my friend alone, understand?"

"Of course. Let us put this unfortunate incident behind us, shall we?" The older man bowed courteously and approached Atif as if to shake his hand in agreement. "It was an easy mistake to make." He reached over, but instead of a friendly handshake, the old man shoved a knife through Atif's ribs and directly into his heart. "Good night, my friend. Sleep well."

Atif crumpled to the ground. Images of his ill-spent youth darted through his dying brain as his own warm blood seeped through his fingers and began to soak through his shirt. At this solemn moment, he could feel his soul loosening itself from the shell of his body to return to God. There were voices, though, whispering voices of his assailants arguing with one another.

"Now why did you go and kill him?" The younger man whispered, clearly distraught.

"He knows too much. After all these years we've finally caught up to Matthias. I am not going to walk away now."

"All right then, what are we going to do with his body?"

"You ask too many questions, just like him." The old man kicked Atif's body so that he fell forward, his face nearly under Matthias's bed. "Don't worry, no one misses a spy. He'll have no mourners: He has no past and now no future."

There was a stifled gasp. The two men turned from their victim and saw clearly in the shadows the anguished look of two very young,

yet perceptive green eyes. The younger man went immediately to the girl and seized her arm, bringing her into the light of the moon streaming in from the window. "She knows too much," he countered, tightening his grip as she squirmed to get away.

"Who do you have here, Donato?" spoke the older man, lifting the girl's chin to gaze into her upturned face. "I recognize you," he crowed. "We meet again." He snatched the blanket from around the girl's shoulders and flung it to the floor. "I see you've matured into a pretty young thing," he said, clearly admiring the curves of her young body, suggested in the flimsy folds of her long delicately embroidered undergarment.

The younger man hastily interrupted his companion. "Ulrich, this isn't the time to think of such pleasures; we've just killed a man!"

"You are right as usual, my friend. We will take her with us." He grinned down at Sophie, who was shivering uncontrollably. He reached for her blanket and held it mockingly from her. "Give me a kiss right here and you may have it," he said, pointing to his cheek.

Obediently, Sophie leaned forward and gave him a quick peck. He smelled of strong ale. The white hairs on his cheek felt scratchy.

"See, that didn't hurt," he said, before whispering menacingly, "and don't even think of screaming or you will suffer the same fate as our friend here." Once more he kicked at Atif's crumpled legs.

Atif felt for the rosary in his inside pocket. Soaked in his own blood, he used it to scrawl an "S" just under the bed before closing his eyes and giving in to death's insistent murmur.

Chapter 3: A Caged Animal

Village of Staudernheim

5th of November, Early Morning

From the back of Ulrich's horse, Sophie watched the townspeople ducking out of their low doorways. They were dressed in their heavy cloaks of coarse wool, shuddering in the chill of the morning air as they gathered their pails and headed down to the river to draw water. She tried in vain to make eye contact with one of them, hoping to communicate somehow that she had been kidnapped by these two finely dressed gentlemen. In the past she'd depended on the blindness of strangers, concealing from them for as long as she could the fact that she was her grandfather's apprentice. Now, she wished they would notice her. Unfortunately, her captors were both knights and noblemen. Such status, she knew, meant they could do as they please. Few if any of the peasants raised their heads as they laced up their boots, and no one stole even a glance up to the height where she sat high on a chestnut warhorse. One man, however, did come right up to the flank of her horse and spat on the ground before turning to a nearby shrubbery to relieve himself. She interpreted this as an act of defiance. Ulrich and Donato chose to ignore the incident, she assumed, because they had more pressing business on their minds.

Sophie reasoned that these were simple hardworking people, keeping to themselves out of a sense of hopelessness. They were like her aunt's husband, leading lives controlled by poverty and fear inflicted on them by the wealthier classes. She forcibly turned her thoughts back to her captors. Ulrich and Donato had said little else to one another since leaving the Infirmary. Donato had saddled up the two horses and had tied her into Ulrich's saddle while Ulrich apparently had disposed of Atif's body. There was an unspoken urgency between the two men, though neither one of them seemed too terribly upset by killing the foreigner in the Infirmary. Their impatience had a greater purpose. They had left the monastery by riding upstream through a gap in the fortress wall surrounding the fields of Paulus's herbal garden and had turned towards the village just as the sun rose behind the distant hills.

At least whatever they were up to had taken priority over her. She blushed shamefully, remembering the look in Ulrich's eyes. How she longed to hold her pale hands out over the fire in the comfort of Brother Paulus's Infirmary. Even his giant aloof presence was preferable to this refined man's lewd comments. Now, however, she remembered her Grandda's words. "What you do, what you say, even what you think, girl, has a direct influence on what those around you may do."

Ulrich disappeared into the merchant's hovel. Donato stayed mounted next to her, holding onto the reins of her horse. She decided that she ought to now take advantage of the opportunity. It would be easier to win over this man than his fiendish friend.

Donato reached into his saddlebags and retrieved a simple oil cloth. "Eat up," he said, handing her a hunk of wheat bread and a small onion. Sophie pulled her blanket closer around her and ate, grateful for the nourishment. She tucked up her sleeve a chunk of the bread for later, not knowing when she might be offered her next meal.

After a short while, Donato appeared clearly uncomfortable with his new role as warden. "What is your name, child?"

"It's Sophie, sir," she answered. Could there be some truth to her Grandda's teachings? Could she somehow change her circumstances by influencing Donato? Maybe, if she shared something of herself, he would see her as a real person. It was worth a try. "You have a foreign accent, where are you from?"

"Florence, Italy," he said, proudly.

"I've heard they have beautiful cathedrals there. What is it really like?" she asked.

"Warmer than here," he added quickly, pulling up his collar and reaching for his own slice of bread. "There is a color, Sophie, to the sky that suits me. It is always tinged with blue, not so heavy with clouds and so grey."

"You miss your home very much. Do you have any family?" she went on encouragingly.

"I do," he said wistfully. "I have a big family, with many brothers and sisters, and a wife. I left her to go fight in the Holy Land. She was pregnant. I do not know if I have a son or daughter, for I haven't returned in nigh eleven years." There was regret in his voice.

"Your son or daughter would be but two years younger than me," Sophie said with sadness. "I wish I knew my own father."

Ulrich re-emerged, this time carrying what appeared to be a large wicker basket with iron hinges. It was covered in burlap, so it was difficult to tell what species of creature was making all the weird squawking noises. Without saying a word, the older man strapped the basket behind her. Likewise, she too was strapped down and had essentially no choice. Maybe, she thought, to Donato she was more than just a caged animal for someone's amusement.

Chapter 4: Shattered the Peace

Refectory at Disibodenberg Monastery

5th of November, Sext, Mid-Day Meal

Volmar quickened his step to fall in line with Abbot Burchard. Both were on their way to dine in the Refectory. The bells were chiming the noon hour of Sext.

"And how, Brother Volmar, do you find your young student?" Abbot Burchard said with mock annoyance.

"More clever than I was at her age, Father."

"Clever, you say? Humph! Funny you should use such a word. I see it all so clearly now . . . you came to me with a plaintive case of unused talents and even had me quoting Scripture supporting the sin of wasting God's gifts. The entire time, however, you omitted one important and relevant detail. Namely, this was not a man, but a girl you wanted to teach; and one imprisoned for life in an Anchorage!"

"I apologize for the deception, Father."

"Yes, yes, but nevertheless, I see now, that it is *you* I need to be wary of." Abbot Burchard wagged an accusative finger under the young monk's chin.

Volmar looked sheepishly at the Abbot, aware of all the other holy brothers who were now silent, listening in on the conversation. "Father, you and I both know it was a wise decision on many levels."

The Abbot let his voice drop and motioned for the young monk to walk beside him. "It will be perceived by the Bishop as an outrage. Not even one week has passed since their enclosure, and we're already talking about turning the Anchorage into a school! The Bishop is not as young and idealistic as you are, Brother Volmar."

"Father, Jutta is still an Anchoress; she will not leave the Anchorage. Hildegard is the only one I will be instructing in Latin. There is a window through which we can conduct our lessons. All proprieties will be insured because her servant girl never leaves her side. And, in turn, Hildegard will teach the other young women the *Opus Dei*[84] in

[84] *Opus Dei:* A musical composition in Latin sung in praise of our Holy Father.

Latin as it should be sung; that way they can join in with us from their Anchorage."

"I suppose, I could appeal to the monetary benefits. If we could attract more young noblewomen to the Anchorage we could acquire more land, and in turn, more vineyards. The dowries these young women would bring with them will likely help the Bishop see the benefits of this new arrangement."

"Precisely," Volmar continued enthusiastically. "The Anchorage would no longer be a remnant of times past but a beacon for the future, a school for young women to learn of the ways of God. Certainly this change will be more aligned with our sentiments, Father, and should breathe new life into this old monastery."

The Refectory glowed in the torchlight, and the heady smells of food and fresh rushes on the floor wafted through the corridor, reminding Volmar that he hadn't eaten since yesterday and was now very hungry. One by one, the monks took turns washing their hands in a small fountain by the entrance and wiping them dry on a white linen cloth. They filed into the room with its high ceiling and stood behind their places on the simple wooden bench. Quietly they lowered their cowls over their faces and buried their crossed hands under their sleeves. The Abbot went to stand at the head of the long table. Not everyone was present, but once the Abbot arrived, it was time for him to give the *Benedicite.* He called on all creation, from the angels in the height of Heaven down to the fish in the depths of the sea, to give glory to God.

Behind him on a raised platform, Brother Albertus took his turn and read as the Precentor.[85] He'd chosen a passage in the Book of Daniel to read aloud, the one where Daniel interprets the handwriting on the wall, predicting the death of the Chaldean King Belshazzar. At the reading's conclusion, the Abbot raised his hands and said the final benediction. Everyone sat down to a meal that was to be enjoyed in silence. Many of the brothers used hand signals to greet one another, but tradition urged everyone to hold their tongues and to take time to reflect on their souls as they nourished their bodies.

"Father Abbot!" Brother Rudegerus's voice shattered the peace as he rushed into the dining hall. All the monks suddenly stopped chew-

---

85 Precentor: A leader in the reading of the scripture.

ing their bread and held their wooden utensils suspended in midair so as not to miss one word of this brazen interruption. Rudegerus the Guest Master continued, "Father, there's a stranger in the Infirmary who's speaking out of his mind! I fear he might be possessed by an evil demon."

The Abbot bent his head slightly and said, "Now, now, let's not make more of the situation than necessary, Brother Rudegerus." The Abbot gave a hand signal for everyone to continue their meals and rose from the table. "Is this man able to speak?"

"When he was not raving, he apparently asked to speak with you, Abbot Burchard."

"I see. Show me this beleaguered man and I will give him counsel. Brother Volmar, you may want to accompany us in case this stranger has a request that needs to be recorded."

Volmar reached for the bread and tore off a few chunks to slip into his pockets for later. "Thank you, Father. I assume I'm in your good graces again?"

"I never said that," the Abbot remarked lightly as he led the way to the Infirmary.

Chapter 5: Mystified

Infirmary at Disibodenberg Monastery

5th of November, Mid-Day

Brother Rudegerus walked with them to the cavernous room of the male Infirmary. He motioned to the man lying on the cot in the far corner. "If it were up to me," he grumbled, "I would've bound him with chains. Brother Paulus felt it was unnecessary and refused to listen to my warnings."

The Abbot simply grunted in dissent and left Brother Rudegerus's side, walking directly towards the sick man. Lining the walls on both sides were humble pallets raised on wood platforms and tied together with knots of rope. A fire burned brightly in the open hearth. It lent a warm glow to the noisy, bustling hall. The Infirmary was crowded with homeless men and boys, their skin lined and toughened prematurely like old leather. Respectfully, they were silent as the Abbot and the two monks walked past, then they continued what they were doing.

Brother Paulus waved his hand from the far corner of the room. He put down the spoon he was using to feed one of the elderly residents and went to wash his hands in a basin. Volmar admired how his movements never seemed hurried, but instead were methodical and careful. It was as if he walked in another plane of existence, where scientific discipline ruled and challenged the noisy confusion of pain and poverty that surrounded him daily. He was disappointed, though, that he couldn't see Sophie anywhere.

"I wish his friend was still here, he could tell you more of the man," Brother Paulus said, joining the Abbot and Volmar.

"His friend?" Volmar asked.

"The stranger who brought him in, a personable younger man of Persian descent, said he owed his life to this man. I gathered he was Matthias's assistant in a hospital in Jerusalem during the war. By the way, Sophie recognized Matthias as the man in the forest who saved her grandfather's life two summers ago."

Volmar registered both facts with wonderment. He turned to the Abbot. "Atif?"

The Abbot shrugged. "Quite possibly. There are few men around here who would fit such a description." The Abbot turned to Paulus. "Did the stranger tell you his name? You see, we think he might have had something to do with the Archbishop's arrest. There's hearsay that he may have been a spy for the Emperor."

Paulus wrinkled his brow. "No, I don't believe we exchanged names. That's a serious accusation . . . a spy for the Emperor. Could be why he left so abruptly. My knowledge of his language is limited, let me see . . . " Paulus continued. "Matthias claims that he is a soldier returned from the Holy Land. He was attacked three nights ago by a pack of wild dogs. The Theriac I gave him last night seems to have arrested his fever but it's the injury to his ankle that has me puzzled."

"Has it become infected?" the Abbot asked, knowing the likelihood of surviving a wild dog attack to be minimal.

"No, his wound has healed remarkably. Quite frankly, Father, I am mystified. I've never seen anything like it before. It is as if it hadn't happened. Which brings to mind Sophie's insistence about this man's remarkable healing of her grandfather, which quite frankly, I cannot fathom, since he possessed all the deadly symptoms of 'holy fire.'"

The Abbot smiled. "Come now, Brother Paulus, you are being modest. Give yourself some credit."

"That's just it. It is not my doing whatsoever. In all my years as an Infirmarian, I've never seen a wound that jagged and deep heal completely on its own within a few short days."

The Abbot put his hand on Paulus's shoulder. "We cannot presume to understand all the mysteries of God, my friend."

Paulus held out his hand to guide the two over to Matthias's bed. "About four hours ago, I gave him an infusion of linden flowers in a tea. He was going on about being followed, and it has been only in the last hour that he has started to finally talk more sense."

Matthias opened his eyes. Volmar saw that they were small for the size of his face but intensely blue. His face had the complexion of one who had been in the sun many years and the graying of his beard indicated that he was a grown man, his youth already spent.

"Father, is that you?" Matthias's voice was deep and arresting, not easy to ignore.

"I understand that you are feeling better, my son." The Abbot sat at the edge of the bed. "My name is Abbot Burchard, and I am willing to hear what it is you would like to tell me. Brother Volmar, my scribe, will record our conversation if you will permit it."

Matthias nodded weakly in agreement.

"Very well, then," the Abbot said. "Brother Paulus and Brother Rudegerus, you may leave us and return to your work. Brother Volmar and I will be fine."

Rudegerus bit his lip in disgust, but slowly turned to walk away. What is Rudegerus hiding? Volmar mused, intrigued. There was more to this situation than simply a man desiring a confessional.

Chapter 6: This Cursed Relic

Infirmary at Disibodenberg Monastery

5th of November, Mid-Day

Matthias sat up in bed, propped up against the stone wall. To Volmar, he seemed a man who at one time could have inspired terror in his enemies and commanded respect from his men. Yet, Volmar sensed, he was clearly uncomfortable with the story he was about to tell.

"Father, I've recently returned from the Holy Land and have in my possession a relic. I'm sure it would be of interest to you and your monastery here at Disibodenberg."

"Go on," Abbot Burchard said impassively. There was a plethora of religious relics returning with soldiers coming back from the Holy Land. "Is it a nail from the Blessed Cross or a napkin from the Last Supper?"

With a distinct edge to his voice, Matthias responded. "Do not make light with me, Father. What I possess is the real thing. It carries with it great powers." The man wiped his brow with his sleeve.

"Powers," Volmar repeated, looking up from his parchment.

"Yes, whoever possesses it and calls upon its power for their own selfish use as I have, will rise to a position of great authority and prestige. However, it possesses a darker side, a curse really, for it can turn a normal man into a heartless, ruthless monster."

"My son, I have no doubt that you feel you have a sacred relic in your possession; however, you must forgive me for my resistance to believe what you say is the truth. Each month we have young men returning from the war in the Holy Land trying to sell us the bones of animals, not the holy apostles."

"Heed my words Father. You may feel differently after you hear my story." Matthias took a deep breath and began, "On the 10th day of June in 1098, I was a mere foot soldier in the ancient city of Antioch. We were besieged by the Muslims, trapped in a city we had just conquered, and completely out of supplies. Our horses and donkeys were dying of thirst. We all knew the hopelessness of the situation and knew our days were numbered. Then a poor monk, a servant of Count

Raymond's army by the name of Peter Bartholomew, came to me. He described a series of visions he had in which Saint Andrew told him where to find the legendary Spear of Longinus, the lance said to have pierced the sinless and holy body of Jesus Christ after He died on the Cross."

"Saint John records this testimony in his Gospel," the Abbot said, obviously finding Matthias's story more captivating than he first thought.

"Well, we told our leader of these visions, and I was ordered to follow Peter Bartholomew to the cathedral of Saint Peter, where he said that the Holy Spear was buried under the floor. There was great opposition to this; gossip amongst the other soldiers had it that Peter Bartholomew had buried a simple spearhead himself, just so he could find it. Nevertheless, I had my orders, so we lifted up the flagstone flooring and dug. I remember both of us were more than waist deep in a hole in the place Saint Andrew had indicated in the vision. Suddenly Peter Bartholomew cried out. In tears he pointed to an object still half-buried. We were both on our hands and knees furiously using our fingers to unearth this object. If I knew what was in store for us, I would have left it in the ground." Matthias looked away momentarily. Volmar saw on his face either grief or fear, he wasn't sure. The man was actually reliving the moment. Perhaps, it was a blending of these two terrible feelings.

"Our return to the camp was preceded by a miraculous meteor shower in the shape of a long spear," Matthias continued. "We took this at the time as a providential sign from God."

"There are many legends surrounding the Spear of Longinus," Abbot Burchard said, rubbing his chin. "The Old Testament scriptures prophesized that the Messiah would be pierced, but his bones would not be broken. When the Roman centurion, Gaius Cassius Longinus, saw that Jesus was already dead at the time of his crucifixion, he unwittingly fulfilled this scriptural prophecy."

Volmar added, "He wanted to show the soldiers that Christ was already dead and that there was no need to break his bones as was customary to do to hasten death."

"Yes," the Abbot continued, "and when Longinus's lance pierced our Savior's side, it is written that blood and water poured out and into Longinus's face. This unbeliever's eyes were opened and healed of partial blindness. At that moment he was converted by our Lord's precious blood." Abbot Burchard glanced at Volmar, relieved to see that he was dutifully making notes of this strange conversation. "I have not heard, however, of any lance from Antioch. Go on, my son, I'm listening."

Matthias resumed. "What happened next is unbelievable, Father. I swear an oath to God every last word is true. Back at camp, we rallied behind this Spear of Christ with such enthusiasm. I remember how the lance itself was affixed to a pole and carried into battle as our Christian banner. It inspired our march against the deadly Turkish horsemen." He wiped his forehead, and backtracked for a moment. "I told you that we were greatly outnumbered and surrounded, and yet, during the battle, I swear our dead rose up on the battlefield and fought with the living! God was on our side. We defeated this powerful enemy and felt as powerful and as invincible as the ancient Israelites were against the hordes of Philistines."

"Legends do say that whosoever possesses the Lance of Longinus will never be defeated," Abbot Burchard mused, and then he lowered his voice. "A Holy Relic of unspeakable power and potential destruction."

Matthias's eyes were glazed over. He was living in the past, hearing alone its incessant march through events unfolding in the same horrible way. "Of course with this taste of victory we felt we were unstoppable. With the Sacred Lance we could drive on to Jerusalem and take the city entirely. Outside of the great city's gates, however, and human nature being what it is, Peter Bartholomew announced that he alone was the only one holy enough to enter Jerusalem carrying the Lance of Christ. Suddenly, our soldiers began to question the Holy Spear's true origins. Peter Bartholomew insisted on the Holy Relic's authenticity and to prove it, he agreed to take a trial by fire."

"A trial by fire?" Volmar reiterated, glancing up from his writing, fearing the worst.

"Yes," Matthias replied grimly. "That night, in the cold of the desert evening, we all surrounded a path we had set on fire. I watched in terror as Peter Bartholomew took his eyes off of heaven and looked at the flames. I could see that he was being led by his humanity, not his godliness. Needless to say, he did not survive. Peter Bartholomew lacked faith. The flames destroyed his life and with it went the devotion of our men. Each one of them dispersed after that. No one felt any ambition to take on even a small regiment of Turks, let alone the vast city of Jerusalem."

"And the Holy Spear?" Abbot Burchard asked, staring down at the floor. "What of it?"

"I alone buried Peter Bartholomew. However, I did not bury the Holy Spear with him as the others suspected."

"No one witnessed this?" the Abbot asked.

"I was alone, Father, the others had fled into the night. I took the Holy Relic from my dead friend's fleshless, blackened hands, and my life was changed. I am truly haunted by the images of the years that followed. Battle cries such as 'It is God's will' and 'It is no sin to kill an infidel' left my lips as they did others before me; such wretched sentiments burn in my conscience, night after night disrupting any calm of sleep. It was a dark and wicked time." He bowed his head. "I am ashamed, Father, that I had a part in it."

"I cannot absolve your guilt, my son." The Abbot inclined his head, thoughtfully. "For any religion to offer a theological justification for war is irresponsible. Wars should cause shame no matter what the rationalization."

"Father, there is more. I was a member of the Order of the Knights Hospitaller of Saint John in Jerusalem for a while until Brother Gerard and I quarreled. As you probably know, the Knights of St. John have a philosophy of healing, and are trained in medicine. Caring for God's people is seen by the knights as their primary purpose for existence – yet they too have failed this higher calling and over time have become more militant and unscrupulous. As caretaker of the Holy Relic, I rose in rank from an unimposing, simple foot soldier, to a trusted advisor in the Court of Godfrey of Bouillon, the first King of the Kingdom of Jerusalem, in a very short time."

Volmar interrupted. "I heard from a pilgrim that Godfrey of Bouillon refused the presumptuous title of King, saying that no man should wear a crown where Christ had worn his crown of thorns; instead, he took the title Defender of the Holy Sepulcher."

Matthias eyed the younger monk with a newfound respect. "Yes, and God-fearing Godfrey of Bouillon died the next year. His brother and successor, Baldwin I, was not so honorable. He had himself immediately crowned King of Jerusalem. I lived in opulent luxury in a seized palace, my slaves were Arab aristocrats. We weren't going about God's business and spreading His Holy Word. Instead we became what all conquerors become, greedy occupiers and careless philanderers. We took whatever we wanted without opposition and hurt anyone who stood in our way. I've since learned that a rule of terror is no rule at all."

"War is a human sickness, we must learn to rise above such human failings and stop assuming we know the mind of God," Abbot Burchard murmured, clearly moved by this account.

"Father, I credit my survival to this Holy Relic. It has made me invincible. I do believe in its power and am fearful of the consequences should it fall into the wrong hands. That is why I am here and not in Rome, handing it over to the Pope. These are dubious times for the Papacy. I have been followed since leaving the Holy Land; believe me, I've left hastily in the dead of night many times." Matthias paused, before adding, "All I ask for now is peace. I want to be free of this cursed relic and live a life untainted by its blood. I have grown tired. I want to return home to farm my own land and embrace my own wife and children, if they'll still have me."

Volmar caught Abbot Burchard's eyes and did the calculation. "You've been living abroad for nearly fourteen years?"

"Too long by anyone's measure," Matthias responded, with a catch in his throat.

"In all that time, did you ever meet a knight named Symon of Bermersheim?" Volmar ventured, having asked every returning knight from the Holy Land that he met this same question.

Coldly, the words came, before Matthias thought much about them. "I've heard the name—the devil incarnate, by all accounts. He climbed high in the ranks, a shrewd, heartless man. Apparently, he is Brother Gerard's most trusted confidant, eager, they say, to do all of his deceitful work. Why do you ask? Is he a relation of yours?"

"Yes, but that was a long time ago," Volmar said, visibly distressed. "Please continue your story."

"Well, I've heard many good things about your monastery. The villagers think highly of you, Father. They say you are a fair and wise man. It is said that the Holy Relic loses its power unless it is freely given. I am willing to turn over the Holy Spear into your care without any payment. Consider it my alms to the church. To outsiders, no one knows what happened to the Lance at Antioch; it will be lost to history. Whether or not its legend is resurrected will be entirely left up to you and your conscience."

"Your faith in my goodness is flattering," Abbot Burchard said, watching as Matthias reached under the band of his wide belt and retrieved what appeared to be a soft black leather pouch from a hidden pocket. It measured slightly less than a man's foot and was about as thick.

"Father, may I have a word with you in private?" Brother Volmar said abruptly, interrupting the formal exchange from proceeding.

The Abbot studied the inscrutable face of his young scribe, curious as to why for once he showed so little emotion. He rose apologetically. "Of course. We will return momentarily, Matthias."

Volmar led the Abbot to one side of the room, away from listening ears and in a low voice said, "Father, I suspect we're being watched." He told him about his suspicions of Brother Rudegerus, insisting that they devise a simple plan before returning to Matthias.

"Well, Matthias." Abbot Burchard spoke in a loud, firm voice as he moved to temporarily block Brother Rudegerus' view of the old soldier. "I do not make any important decisions on an empty stomach. I will have to discuss your terms with my superiors."

Leaning down, Volmar whispered hastily to Matthias. "We fear we're being watched. When I drop my quill and bend down to pick it up, slip the Holy Spear into my hood." Volmar dropped his quill and bent down in front of Matthias. He arose only after he felt the slight heaviness of the leather pouch drop into his hood, its folds concealing the relic according to plan. What Volmar hadn't expected was the sudden rush of excitement, something his more studious nature knew little of. Could these newfound feelings of exhilaration have something to do with the fact that he now possessed the Spear of Destiny and was its new caretaker? Even his surroundings had sharpened and became more distinct, as if he possessed a third eye. All of his senses seemed alert, more intense, his sense of smell, sight, even intellect. As he looked around the Infirmary, he could hear all of the conversations going on, even ones drowned out by the roaring fire at the end of the far wall. He found all the prattling intrusions equally undiminished and awe-inspiring!

Abbot Burchard continued. "Give me until tomorrow before I let you know what I have decided. Until then, sleep well, my friend."

"Father," Brother Paulus called out from across the room, "could I have a word with you before you leave?"

The Abbot waited patiently for Brother Paulus to approach. Volmar bowed to take his leave, eager to test his enhanced sensitivities. While his head was down, though, the reflection of a small metallic object caught his eyes. It lay just under the foot of Matthias' bed. Volmar bent over, pretending to adjust the straps of his boot and reached under the bed for what he realized was a small rosary, lying in a pool of red. A single letter was written beside it, the letter "S". Volmar slipped the rosary into his pocket, rose and tuned in to the conversation the Infirmarian and the Abbot were having.

Brother Paulus had come closer. "It happened again last night, Father . . . you may stay, Brother Volmar. It is something you and I have already discussed at some length. This time, however, some peach pits were stolen; whereas, on the other nights burdock seeds, parsley, and the essential oils from sage, rosemary, and thyme went missing. I'm not sure what to make of our elusive nighttime Infirmary thief."

Volmar, although attentive, was troubled more by his sudden act of secrecy. Here he had found an obvious clue and, for some reason, felt indifferent about sharing it with his two most trusted brothers. He stared back down at the floor. There were more red stains on the stone; not many, but enough to be seen by someone who was looking for them. He shifted it all around in his mind and kept his silence. The confusion was overpowering in and of itself. Let no one into your confidence, it kept insisting.

"Yes, and deeply troubling," the Abbot added.

"Peach pits? What would anyone want with peach pits? It is far too late in the season to plant fruit trees," Volmar muttered, forcing himself to return to their conversation.

"Precisely. The others I can understand." Brother Paulus looked puzzled. "They are traditional remedies for a great many illnesses, including infections. However, peach pits can be highly poisonous. Fruit pits in particular hold the distinction of having such an ominous duality. The seeds of apples, cherries, plums, and peaches all hold within their pits the poison cyanide."

Volmar suddenly remembered a passage he'd read while copying and translating Brother Paulus's codices, several years ago. It seemed as if it were only yesterday. "Didn't the ancient Egyptians soak peach pits in water to create a poison to give their enemies?"

"Poisons . . . break-ins . . . Oh dear, please stay alert and keep me informed, Paulus. Come along, Brother Volmar," Abbot Burchard said, "we have much to discuss."

"Please tell Sophie I'm sorry I missed her," Volmar added, remembering how striking she had looked in Hildegard's clothes the night of the enclosure ceremony. He blushed. What was happening to him? Thankfully, neither man noticed his discomfort.

Paulus gave Volmar, then the Abbot, a worried look. "I haven't seen Sophie since before Compline last night. I meant to ask you, Volmar, where she might be today. It is so unlike her to leave without letting me know."

"This is worrisome," the Abbot concluded. "Please let us know if Sophie doesn't show up by this evening. For now, let us all keep our suspicions to ourselves."

Chapter 7: His Evil Seed

Window of the Anchorage at Disibodenberg Monastery

5th of November, Before Nones

Outside the Refectory, Abbot Burchard turned from Rudegerus to Volmar and asked his young monk, with an imperceptible wink, "Is it not time for your lesson at the Anchorage, Brother Volmar?"

"My lesson at the Anchorage . . . ?" Volmar repeated, taking a moment longer before catching on to the Abbot's plan. "Oh yes, in all the confusion of the past half hour, I forgot the time. I am truly late for our afternoon recitations. Please excuse me." He bowed politely and turned from the Refectory's entrance.

Volmar hurried away, impressed by Abbot's Burchard's insightful thinking. Rudegerus wouldn't suspect a thing. No one would. An Anchorage would be the last place one would think to look for a disputed, long sought-after Holy Relic. Matthias's hounds would likely sniff out the Abbot's belongings and his own meager dwelling in hopes of finding it, once they realized Matthias no longer had it. But who in their right mind would think of coming across it in an Anchorage, in the care of three young women?

Volmar could see his own breath. The temperature, he knew, was dropping and yet as he walked briskly through the cloisters, the cold did not seem to bother him. He'd never felt better. Samson bounded after him as he passed by the entrance to the store room at the Kitchens for the Poor and rubbed affectionately against his leg. "Found any rats?" the young monk chuckled, scooping up the cat with ease. Samson squirmed and wiggled free, jumping uncharacteristically from his arms and disappearing into the shade. How strange, Volmar thought, Samson had never turned down a petting before. It had been a day full of oddities: First Matthias's story, then Sophie's strange disappearance, and now this, Samson's unfriendliness.

Why wasn't he more worried about Sophie, or more eager to go off and find her? It was so unlike him to be careless about a friend's welfare. Was he suffering under the illusion of the Holy Spear's legacy, or was he actually being changed by it? Was this part of its entrapment, making him squirm and wiggle free from the bonds of attachments around him? Claiming his soul for its own, parsing it off from everyone else. Was the Holy Relic offering him freedom from the messy securities of relationships and responsibilities towards others? Its guiltless allure certainly was strong.

Volmar quickened his pace as he headed down the hill towards the Anchorage. Could he really have hidden in his hood the very spear that pierced his Lord's side? He tried to rein in his galloping thoughts. Hildegard was not expecting his return. In their parting words, they had settled on one morning lesson per day during the short winter hours of daylight. He felt assured that she would be able to care for this precious relic, at least until he and the Abbot decided its fate. But, was it wise to give such a powerful relic to a mere woman, and . . . what of its future? Such a renowned relic would bring travelers from the far reaches of the world to Disibodenberg. Surely these pilgrimages would bring the faithful closer to the Lord's teachings. Or would it? His thoughts were suddenly arrested by a gentle haunting melody, a barely audible song, coming from the Anchorage. Volmar paused, allowing the music to surround and still his conflicted soul. He dreaded having to interrupt it.

"Sister Hildegard," he called through the window. "It is I, Volmar. I am truly sorry to bother you at this hour; however, I have a request to make."

The music from within stopped and a shadowy face, pensive and pale, looked out to where the young monk was standing. Volmar checked to make sure no one else was around before he slipped his hand into his hood and held the wrapped Holy Relic for the first time. He remembered how Matthias had said he felt invincible with the relic in his possession. He stared down at the unassuming pouch, thinking how its humble leather exterior belied its true significance. He knew legendary treasures were always protected by tests of worthiness. Was he a worthy caretaker? His mind was racing wildly with plans of stealing off into the night with this holiest of relics. He could leave Disibodenberg and become a great leader under the Holy Spear's influence. Who hadn't heard the legends of how Constantine and Charlemagne conquered their ancient worlds while in possession of this very Holy Spear? After all, it had been willingly given to his care. He was the rightful heir to its powers, was he not?

Then, just as unexpected, his mind's eye diverted his attentions to his past. For a brief and terrifying moment he relived that fateful night long ago, the sobbing of Anya, as the two clutched their lifeless mother, trying to find warmth in her cold arms. Anya's face was contorted in anguish. What was happening to him? It had been years since he had allowed that ghastly memory to intrude and surface. Could this mystical object also be stirring up all his dormant emotions?

Brazenly, Volmar looked down and gazed at Hildegard's upturned face, lit only by the single candle she held. He admired the soft curve of her chin and the delicate balance of beauty and wisdom etched in her features. His eyes wandered further to her neck and thoughts of how delicious it would be to trace its gentle curve with his lips intruded, and then . . . he smiled without shame.

Hildegard's graceful features hardened under Volmar's lusty look. The candle's flame flickered as if caught by the draft of her cold, knowing stare. When she spoke, her voice clamored for control over his wayward attentions and his thoughts of ambition, lust, and power.

"I will keep safe the Holy Relic, Brother Volmar. It has had a long and bloody history."

"How do you know that's why I'm here?" Volmar was caught off guard by her foresight.

"Don't you remember? We see in our dreams, even though our eyes are closed, do we not? Don't worry, Hiltrud and Jutta are sleeping. For their own safety, they will know nothing of our encounter or the Holy Relic's presence."

"Yes, of course. I will come for the Holy Relic when the danger has passed." Volmar was still feeling overwhelmed by his heightened senses. He lifted the leather wrapping from the Spear of Destiny, and gazed longingly at its most precious blade, unimaginably old and believed to have been lost to the world for centuries. This blade of iron had drawn blood—and not just anyone's blood. This blade had borne testimony to the greatest crime ever committed by man.

Solemnly, he draped it again with its humble wrapping, his hands trembling, as he passed the Holy Spear through the small window and into Hildegard's outreached hands. "Sister Hildegard, you are now its caretaker. I give it over freely to you. I should warn you, the Holy Relic has a curse on it."

"I know," she answered softly, cradling the Relic gently in her hands. "But it is cursed only when the power it radiates is used for selfish reasons."

For a wordless moment, Volmar stood very still, feeling the sudden loss of the Relic's power. He felt awkward, vulnerable, and very weak. Volmar drew himself up to his full height and reached into his leather pouch. "Sister Hildegard, you may read this parchment. It is the conversation the Abbot and I had with a soldier named Matthias in the Infirmary. In his own words, he explains how this Relic came into his possession. Please guard it as well."

"Brother Volmar, this man, Matthias, I fear his life is in grave danger. He must leave Disibodenberg at once."

"Matthias is planning on leaving as soon as he is well enough. He is tired and wants to return home to his family."

Hildegard's piercing pale grey eyes searched the young monk's weary features. "Something else is troubling you."

Volmar sunk his hands into his sleeves. "I am not used to having someone read my thoughts so easily. I did a foolish thing. I asked Matthias if he knew my father, Symon of Bermersheim."

"And did he?"

"What he knew of him was not flattering. Apparently, my father is one of Brother Gerard's closest companions. He belongs to the Order of the Knights Hospitaller of Saint John in Jerusalem. Rumor has it that they have become more militant over the past few years. They are no longer the noble healers they once were."

Hildegard spoke reassuringly. "I would question, Brother Volmar, a son's responsibility for his father's failings."

"Perhaps so; but a son possesses the same tendencies as his father." Volmar spat on the ground, as if trying to get rid of a bad taste in his mouth. "I carry his evil seed. My earliest memories are of him slapping my mother and making her cry. I remember him with hatred, not kindness. The feeling must have been mutual, for my mother often protected me from his explosive temper. I am the reason he deserted us for the battlefields of the Holy Land."

"This is in the past, and told from a very young child's eyes. Dear Volmar, I sense in your temperament a strong desire for the truth. Evil cannot consume a life bent on serving justice. Remember that."

"I am forever indebted to you, Sister Hildegard." Volmar bowed formally, nearly tripping over the stool. He smiled at it and then at Hildegard's smirk. "Until our next lesson . . . .sleep well." He picked up the stool and rounded the corner before taking off up the hill. The chill in the air was invigorating, as well as Sister Hildegard's expressed warmth towards him.

Once inside the common room of the Anchorage, Hildegard listened to the rasping, irregular breathing of Jutta and the even less harmonious snoring of Hiltrud, reassured that what she was about to do would go unseen. She walked over to her exquisitely carved glass-fronted bookcase. From underneath her plain linen undergarment, she took a key hanging from a gold chain around her neck. Quietly, she turned it in the lock, opening the secret drawer where she kept her writings, drawings, and paintings, as well as the silver-filigreed clasp given to her by her parents. In reverence, she bent and kissed the Holy Relic, before draping it in its leather cloth and concealing it among her few worldly treasures.

Chapter 8: This Unholy Fiend

Village of Staudernheim

5th of November, Afternoon

Donato recognized the look in Ulrich's eye. After years of traveling together, he knew the signs. Never though had the old man chosen one so young and so inexperienced before. The thought of Sophie in this man's embrace troubled his conscience, what little he had left of one. Ahead he saw the village tavern's lamp. The wind knocked it against the sign cut out to resemble a frothing wooden mug. There were rooms for rent in the attached inn, and he knew that was where they were headed.

"Buy you a drink," Donato proposed, as they slowed the horses into an easy saunter.

"What about the girl?" Ulrich said, inclining his head towards Sophie, who had already loosened her grip around his waist, fearfully anticipating the worst of what lay ahead.

"She'll keep with the horses in the stable. If you like, I can tie her to the basket. That way they'll both be fine while we eat and drink in preparation for tonight."

The stable reeked of stale ale and human feces. It was cold and damp, and as black as the night. Sophie huddled under the blanket Ulrich had wrapped around her after he had tied her snugly to the basket. He leaned over and kissed her mouth, briefly but hard. "I'll be back," he said hoarsely.

Sophie turned away, tears streaming down her reddened cheeks. Never had she felt such pain; it was as if he had slapped her.

Donato squatted down beside her, making the final twist of rope around her ankles. He couldn't bear to make contact with her terrified eyes, but he whispered instead in confidence. "I'll see to it that he'll drink too much. Nothing will happen this evening, I promise."

Ulrich traipsed off, his arm around Donato's shoulder. Outside, Ulrich blurted out a verse to some vulgar ballad Sophie wished she could not understand.

It was a long while before her entire body stopped trembling. By then, her eyes had adjusted to the darkness. The basket was next to her, like a mooring anchor in the straw. It was a half-sphere in shape and at least four hand-lengths across. The top side was made of very open wickerwork woven around flat strips of iron.

She spoke softly, more in an effort to calm her own nerves than the beast she heard scratching incessantly from inside the basket next to her. "Hello there, my little friend," she said as gently as she could.

The basket pitched violently from side to side. Whatever was inside must have sensed her fear and was responding aggressively.

Hesitantly, she peered inside through a gap that appeared from the burlap being thrown off to one side. All at once, a beak the size of a grown fist shot out and snapped at her. She jumped back, unfortunately moving the basket closer to her rather than gaining any distance from it. Whether she liked it or not, she had to somehow rid herself of this unholy fiend.

Regaining her nerve, Sophie leaned forward, noting the creature's reddish comb and wattle. "This is no ordinary rooster," she muttered. The rooster lunged forward again, making an unearthly guttural cry of war. Sophie then saw a large metal spur the length of a man's finger attached to a talon on one of its feet. This claw scraped frantically at the rope fastening the lid on the basket, savagely trying to claw its way to freedom. The sharp spur had already left huge gouges, splitting the willow branches. Sophie backed away slowly, thinking of how that talon was certainly sharp enough to free her ropes. If she could only maneuver her wrists so the rooster could claw through the rope's knots and not her skin, she would be free!

In the distance, she heard the coarse noise of men's voices, rising and falling in bawdy unison, carrying on under the influence of heavy drink. She knew there was little time to make her plan work. She remembered listening to her Grandda's stories about fighting cocks. "Fighting cocks are bred to be mean and are trained to be dangerous, attacking anyone who invades their territory."

She remembered questioning such cruelty and having Grandda laugh at her for feeling sorry for the rooster. "I do not understand the reasoning behind such savagery," she had said.

"There, there, my little friend," she cooed softly. 'You're hungry, aren't you? Here, I have some bread crumbs for you." With great discomfort, she managed to reach up her sleeve with two of her fingers and pinch off enough bread to get the rooster's undivided attention.

She then tossed the crumbs into the rooster's basket and watched as he feverishly clawed away, shredding the straw even after he'd eaten all she had given him.

"That's it," she said, taking more crumbs and this time sprinkling them over the rope that held the two of them together. "I have plenty, don't worry." She added more crumbs as the rooster pecked and clawed furiously.

The rope became the plate upon which she poured more and more bread crumbs. This went on for several long minutes. With each feeding, the strands on the rope became frayed and then, finally, the silver claw cut through the very last strand and the tautness of the rope around her wrists relaxed.

"Well done, my little friend," she said, pulling her small hands through the last of the knots. Deftly she untied the rope around her ankles. At last she was free!

Sophie stood, having trouble regaining her balance in her wooden clogs. The burns from the rope around her wrists weren't all that bad, she reckoned, feeling a rush of optimism. In silent exultation, she wrapped her blanket snuggly around her shoulders and took off into the night. Her only thought at that moment was to put as much distance as she could between her and the tavern.

Chapter 9: The Red Ribbon

Disibodenberg Monastery

5th of November, Dusk

Samson caught up once again with Volmar and trailed behind him, following him to the stables. This time the cat warmed to his touch and allowed Volmar to pet him. "Let me know when you come across Sophie, will you?" Samson purred in response.

The stables appeared deserted. During the winter months, the animals were kept closer to the kitchen, where Brother Johannes's rubbish fires could warm them and the kitchen scraps could feed them. The young monk peered in and saw now only two fine horses tethered in the stall; curiously, the two oversized warhorses were gone. Also, there was no sign of Brother Hugo. Relieved, Volmar quietly circled around back, being careful to avoid stepping into the steaming compost heap beside the wall. It was as if it were breathing.

The flood of memories faded as he approached the water trough. It was covered with a thin, cloudy sheet of ice. Volmar went back inside the stables from the rear entrance, wondering where best to leave the milking stool. Only then did he notice something red in the straw. He went over to investigate and found, to his dismay, a red ribbon. He recognized it immediately as the ribbon Isabella had given to Sophie in the Infirmary. He tucked it into his leather pouch and suspiciously looked around for other clues to suggest what may have happened.

In the distance he heard the sound of bells struck by a monk's wooden mallet announcing Vespers. Volmar trudged off obediently, promising himself that after prayers he would go to all the familiar places where he might expect to find Sophie.

As soon as the last "Amen" concluded the ceremony, Volmar turned and questioned all his holy brothers temporarily assembled in one place. Slowly, he pieced together the fact that no one had seen Sophie since the day before. Her sudden disappearance did not make sense. He left the sanctuary, noticing that already the sky was leaden, a sure sign that Brother Albertus's aching back was correct. The sky was heavy with snow.

Why would Sophie leave the monastery so abruptly, telling no one of her whereabouts or her plans? Volmar was deeply troubled now more than ever. He left the rubble of the stone pile where often he would find Sophie watching the builder's son, Thomas, mixing mortar and annoyingly counting aloud the number of scoops of sand he'd put on the board. When the weather was warmer, Volmar would often see them talking amicably, taking turns simply drawing in the sand with a pointed stick. He kicked at the board, dried and hard from an earlier than expected winter. Could someone have said something hurtful to Sophie that angered her enough to make her want to leave? Outside the Apiary[86] were stairs leading to the forest, a vast expanse of scrub and rough woodland, cascading sharply down to the road. Volmar

---

[86] Apiary: A location where the Apiarist, the beekeeper, works to collect honey and beeswax for making candles.

stood at the ledge and gazed into the woods below, knowing the birds, weasels, foxes, rats, and other creatures were warily watching his movements. He held Sophie's red hair ribbon to his cheek, wondering if she had left unwillingly. He recalled the two missing warhorses, appalled by the turn his thoughts had abruptly taken. Could Sophie have been kidnapped?

With his hands on his hips, he stared across the Monks' Cemetery. In the distance he could see the twin towers of the Porter's gatehouse. Perhaps, he thought with some hope, Brother Cornelius would know if Sophie had left of her own accord.

Never had the high stone walls surrounding Disibodenberg seemed more in opposition to him than now as he scrambled downhill. Like a fortress they kept the monastery separate from the outside world, yet in doing so, they also provided sanctuary for all God's people. The monastery was a haven for outcasts of one kind or another, especially the widows and orphans, of which one very special orphan was now missing.

Volmar made his way past the iron gates and into the Lay Chapel. It had a vaulted ceiling and a stained-glass window at the far end over a more modest wooden altar. He knelt before the image of the Holy Mother and lingered on the all-knowing eyes of the Christ child. The thought came to him, as he prayed for Sophie's safety, that if everything were easy, men would no longer need God's guidance.

He rang the bell to announce his need to speak with the Porter. The bell's deep baritone voice reverberated down the empty, drafty corridor. Volmar blew on his hands, trying to warm them while he waited for the Porter's arrival. The temperature was dropping fast.

Brother Cornelius was a thin man with a wispy white beard and dark, belligerent eyes. His position suited his personality, Volmar thought, pacing back and forth, dreading the encounter. Brother Cornelius preferred his own company apart from the other brothers. He did not like people and treated rich and poor alike . . . with utter, unapologetic disgust. Volmar would have preferred not to have awakened him, but felt he had no choice.

Cornelius arrived, carrying a lamp. His hair sprouted in every direction like weeds. "What do you want, brother?"

"I was hoping you could tell me if a young girl with long blond hair, about thirteen summers old, left the monastery at any time since yesterday afternoon?"

"No one of that description came or went, alone," he muttered, turning to leave.

"Wait!" Volmar rushed forward to stand in front of him, blocking his passage back to the comfort of his hearth and cot. "How about with someone—did you see a young girl answering to that description leave in the company of others?"

Brother Cornelius thought a moment and responded. "I did." He rudely turned to push the young monk out of his way.

"Please, Brother Cornelius, I need to know more. Who was the young girl with?"

For one so old, his recall was undeniably clear. "There were two well-dressed gentlemen. One wore leather boots with a cruel spur on the buckle. Both were on fine warhorses. May I?" he grunted.

Volmar stepped aside, and watched in dismay as the disagreeable old monk took his leave. He was observant but otherwise not much help. Only then did Volmar discover the impossibility of shedding just one tear. "There will always be a companion," he muttered, brushing the dampness from his cheeks. Even after recovering the red ribbon and finding the strangers' two horses missing, Volmar had refused to let his mind process the evidence. Now he had no choice—here was irrefutable testimony that Sophie had been abducted. Volmar knew of the hearts of men like those two; if given the chance, they were capable of much evil.

The bell to the Iron Gate suddenly started clanging wildly. This time it went on and on with such vehemence that Volmar wondered if it might be announcing the end of time. He heard the thick door to the Porter's room slam shut down the long corridor followed by the scraping sound of the Porter's sandals on stone. The young monk hurried to see who could possibly be arriving at such a late hour and on such a dismal night.

There, dressed only in her nightdress and blanket, stood the most incredible sight. Volmar ran to Sophie and lifted her high into the air.

"You're alive," he said, pushing the tangled hair from her face and cradling her chin in his palms as he placed her gently back on the ground. "Did he in any way defile your innocence?" As he asked this, he recalled that man's lecherous intentions towards her the first time she had encountered him.

"No, but he wanted to," Sophie answered, allowing—only now that she was safe—the tears to stream down her pale cheeks. "Oh Volmar, I do not know how to be good enough so that this will not happen to me again."

Volmar held her back at arm's length and searched her face with tenderness. "Don't feel that way, Sophie." Words failed him. Although he was not her big brother, he wanted so badly to protect her from life's injustices.

"I know," she said with no real conviction. It was a familiar yet maddening refrain. "We are not meant to understand in this life the mind or ways of God."

"Humph!" the old Porter grunted, turning around. "Two wretched fools," he muttered as he disappeared down the long corridor, his lamp showing the way, clearly the only warmth in his solitary life.

Book 7: Stark Winter Landscape

Chapter 1: Blood on a Rosary

St. Mary's Chapel at Disibodenberg Monastery

5th of November, Before Compline

Volmar found Abbot Burchard in Saint Mary's Chapel kneeling in front of the altar on a prie-dieu[87]. The Abbot was alone in the dark, brooding, slumped forward, his chin resting in his hand.

Silently the young monk went and stared out the arched window, missing entirely the magnificence of the quiet winter landscape. Even the distant mountains, normally visible in the expansive grey sky, had all but disappeared in the whirling mass of snow now falling. "Thank you, Lord," he murmured, acknowledging God's hand even in the timing of nature's fury, "for guiding Sophie home before the storm."

After what seemed like an eternity, the Abbot responded to Volmar's presence. "The Holy Relic is safe?"

"As safe as it can be in these turbulent times."

Brother Volmar turned and passed under the arch separating the small chapel from the Abbot's private study. He returned his leather pouch to the desk drawer before locking it. He re-entered the chapel and gave the keys to the Abbot, who slipped them under his wide belt. Volmar took a matchstick from the nearby silver brocade holder and lit the wick of the hanging oil lamp. The golden light transformed the heavy gloom. "Father," he went on, staring mesmerized at the flame, "are you familiar with the Order of the Knights Hospitaller of Saint John in Jerusalem?"

"I have only heard of their service in the hospitals, helping our injured soldiers and pilgrims. I did not know a relation of yours was a part of the secret Brotherhood."

---

[87] Prie-dieu: A small prayer desk he used for his own private devotionals.

"My father, the devil incarnate," Volmar muttered, visibly distressed.

The Abbot lowered his voice. "What people may hear isn't necessarily the truth, my son."

"I know," Volmar said, kneeling next to the Abbot. "My father left for the war in 1098. I was three." Although he looked up at the crucifix, his eyes were focused on distant events in the past. "I spilled wine on the floor. My father lifted me up high in the air and was shaking me. My mother rescued me, screaming for him to leave us."

The Abbot nodded with understanding. "Frightening memories for a boy of three. Surely son, you do not feel responsible for your father going off to war?"

Volmar continued, ignoring the wisdom of the Abbot's words. "Over the years, I've questioned many travelers returning from the Holy Land and have learned a little of this organization through these conversations. The Knights Hospitaller chose the shape of the cross as their emblem, to represent the spiritual qualities blessed by Christ in the Sermon on the Mount. And so the four arms of the cross stand for the four Virtues: Prudence, Justice, Temperance, and Fortitude. The eight pointed star represents the eight Beatitudes, and the color white is for the purity of the soul. I've been wondering, though, about Matthias's suspicions towards Brother Gerard. Other travelers, too, have mentioned how militant he's turned over the past couple of years."

"Forgoing their Christian heritage is a serious accusation, my son."

Volmar rose from his knees and began pacing the room. The Abbot remained kneeling, closed his eyes and listened intently. "Father, earlier this morning I noticed four horses in our stables. Two of the horses were warhorses and each had the Order of the Knights of the Hospitaller insignia; two did not. I checked before Vespers and now only two horses remain tethered in our stables, the two unmarked horses."

"Go on."

"Don't you see? The two horses with the emblem of the Knights Hospitaller belong to Ulrich and Donato. Paulus told me their names, after I had the misfortune of sword-fighting with the older knight, Ulrich. Also, we know from our conversation, Matthias wants to have nothing more to do with the Brotherhood. So, I reckon, one of the unmarked horses must be his. That leaves us with an unclaimed, unmarked horse. And according to Brother Paulus, Atif left yesterday morning. And yet, how could he, if his horse remains?"

"You do make a point, my son. Rarely do we get travelers this time of year, and who would leave on such a dreadful day, especially with a winter storm brewing?"

"There's more, Father. Forgive me, I hesitated to show this to you in the Infirmary, but I found this at the base of Matthias's bed." Volmar handed the rosary over to the Abbot.

The Abbot turned it over in his hands, knowing his old eyes were hopeless in making out its tiny inscriptions. "Knights Hospitaller?"

"Yes." Volmar nodded. "Father, you can see the cross and the eight-pointed star. Atif had such a rosary in his possession, or one just like it, the night of the enclosure ceremony."

"Go on," the Abbot said, peering at it more closely. "How did it get these red stains?"

"It was like that when I found it. Father, also, a letter 'S' was scrawled on the floor, next to it in red. I suspect it is dried blood."

"Hard to tell, could be wine," the Abbot said, sniffing it.

"The facts do not make sense. We know Atif rescued Matthias the night before last. Matthias had a nasty bite wound on his ankle. But why would there be blood on a rosary Atif kept close to his heart in an inside pocket? And why would there be other bloodstains on the floor next to it?"

"Other bloodstains, my son? Now, now—we mustn't let our imaginations take over. Somehow we must find a way to reconcile our observations with the dictates of reason." The Abbot handed the rosary back to Volmar dismissively. "Besides, you would expect to see blood stains on the floor of an Infirmary."

Volmar gave a helpless shrug as he slipped the rosary back into his pocket. "If the rosary belongs to Atif, and I believe it does, then, why would he scribble an 'S' on the floor, in blood, next to where he left it? All Atif said to me was that the rosary was a gift from a monk who brought him to Rome. He said that he owed him a great debt and that he was kind to him when no one else cared."

The Abbot laced his slender fingers together. "And you think this kind monk is none other than our Matthias?"

"Well, it does seem likely. Why else would Atif risk returning to Disibodenberg? He must know there's danger here because his part in the arrest of the Archbishop has now become known. And you heard yourself, Matthias admitted to belonging to the Order of the Knights Hospitaller of Saint John in Jerusalem. But, Father, why an 'S,' of all letters?"

"Sin, Savior, Salvation, comforting words of redemption for one torn in his allegiance and affections for an old friend. Maybe it is some sort of ritual, a Persian religious belief, perhaps?"

"I wish I could be as certain, Father." Volmar paused before announcing, "There's more. Sophie has returned."

"Well, that is a relief, son." The Abbot made the sign of the cross. "How is she? Tell me, where did she go, and why did she not tell Paulus of her absence?"

"Brother Paulus has given her a sedative, and she is resting now. Father, Sophie woke last night and observed two men, Ulrich and Donato, searching through Matthias's travel bags. It was dark, but, from where she was, it looked to her like Ulrich killed a man with a knife. I think the man killed was Atif."

"Ulrich killed Atif in the Infirmary?" The Abbot rose and stepped into the light, taking Volmar's shoulders into his hands. "Are you certain, Volmar? Sophie saw one of the traveling Knights of the Hospitaller kill the Persian spy?"

"All I can honestly say is that Sophie saw the glint of a blade, and the man slumped forward. Then the man, Ulrich, with his traveling companion Donato, took her as a captive to Staudernheim, fearing she was a witness to the crime. Fortunately, Sophie escaped while the two men were getting drunk in the tavern."

"Why, pray tell, is there no body?" Then the Abbot turned to Volmar with a flash of anger. "Volmar, why did you wait so long to tell me of Sophie's ordeal in all of this?" The Abbot's face paled even in the warm glow of the oil lamp.

"Forgive me, Father. It was unintentional. I'm only now just making sense of what Sophie blurted out to me. She'd been through a great deal and was in shock when she showed up here a short while ago at the Porter's gates. The tonic Paulus gave her to calm her nerves had her speaking even more bizarre things before she drifted off to sleep."

"How so?" the Abbot asked, his eyes matching Volmar's quizzical look.

"Something about a rooster."

"A rooster?"

"When she wakes, I'm sure she'll make more sense and we can question her further."

"This is very strange. We have a witness to a murder that took place in our Infirmary early this morning, but no body. The two suspects are none other than Knights Hospitaller desiring the Holy Relic and are obviously willing to kill for it. And, Brother Cormac has informed me that one of our own brethren had secretively gained entry into the library. Cormac discovered open on the table ancient writings about the Spear of Longinus. Who among us would be privy to such wickedness and knowingly allow fellow brothers to kidnap and terrorize a young girl?"

"Have you a plan, Father?"

"I have only one. That is to pray to the Almighty for guidance." The Abbot stared back up at the crucifix. He waved his hand to dismiss Volmar.

Volmar bowed respectfully and approached the exit. Before turning the iron handle of the door to leave, he stopped for one more question. "Father, do you really think we have in our possession the true Spear of Destiny?"

"I do not know, my son. I do fear, though, that there are those who think we do and will stop at nothing to take it from us."

Chapter 2: An Accursed Brood

A Monk's Cell at Disibodenberg Monastery

5th of November, During Compline

Not far from the Abbott's study, a single oil lamp burned in a cell in the monks' dormitory. The troubled holy brother found that he could not attend Compline at 6 p.m., certainly not in the state he was in. He went to his basin, filled it from a pitcher of water, then lifted a small flask and perfumed the water before splashing it on his face and neck. No matter how hard he tried, he couldn't rid himself of the stench.

He started pacing from one end of his small room to the other. The flagstone floor was beginning to show a wearing away from this, his frequent habit of worrying. The monk turned every now and then to his narrow bed where the distinctive shape of a man lay under his own blanket, apparently asleep. The sleeping figure's hand suddenly fell, dangling from under its meager covering. The monk yelped, slapping his own hand to his mouth in horror of being overheard. He listened to the apparent silence around him. With shaking hands he kissed his rosary and attempted once again to concentrate on saying more "Hail Mary" prayers.

"Stop laughing at me, Lucifer," he replied firmly, throwing his rosary to the floor. The delicate string snapped and the tiny carved beads scattered everywhere. He sunk his head into his hands murmuring, "I know I'm of an accursed brood . . . "

Chapter 3: Tortured Soul

Sanctuary of Disibodenberg Monastery

6th of November, Matins

The morning was bitterly cold. Snow already lay heavy on the ground and was still falling as the bells rang out announcing Matins.[88] Volmar stood in his place in line beside the other holy brothers in the Sanctuary. Bleary-eyed, he was finding it difficult to stay awake with the heady scent of incense and the rhythmic chanting enveloping him. His thoughts drifted, wrestling with chaos. He deliberately tried to organize their randomness. There was Sophie, of course, and her shocking kidnapping, not to mention the distinct possibility of Atif's cruel death . . . And what of Samson? Although he did not place his relationship with his cat on the same level as that of his two friends, Samson had disappeared, unusual for such a frightfully frigid night. It was his cat's first night away in seven years.

---

[88] Matins: The Office of prayers said at 3 a.m.

Brother Albertus, standing sleepily behind him, chanted on, completely flat. The notes hung menacingly in the air, triggering for Volmar the vivid memory of a horrific dream, a nightmare he had had earlier just before waking. He remembered trying to cry out, but no sound would come. In the dream, he was in Jerusalem and the city was engulfed in flames. Innocent men, women, and children were there, walking the streets beside him, droning on and on, eyeless skeletons, shuffling about in rags. Blood fell from the heavens instead of raindrops and seeped into the street's flooding gutters. It was a shocking apocalyptic scene. Volmar shifted his weight to his other leg and thought to himself how Matthias's account of the taking of Jerusalem from the Infidels had made him ashamed of his own countrymen . . . and he had to admit, of his own father, for surely his father was there, participating in the ghastly slaughter.

So many lives stained by so many horrific crimes. How could such actions not jeopardize the order of a civilized world? Could this be the Hell on earth the scriptures foretold of as the end times? Was Matthias's possession of the Spear of Destiny a power too tempting for mere mortals to possess? Volmar joined in with the others as they bowed their heads in prayer. Instead of mumbling the Mass of Matins, Volmar formulated a question and put it to God. "My Father in Heaven," he murmured. "Is the relic's power inspired by the Devil? If so, surely it will only hasten man's downfall. Or is it a gift from You, Father? Is it an artifact of divine knowledge which will, in the end, enhance the lives of all men? Please, Father, I need to know Your purpose for the Holy Relic here on Earth."

No sooner were the words spoken than a peculiar throaty cry was heard. Brother Hugo rushed into the Sanctuary. Silhouetted in the shadows, his hair was wild and his belt was missing from his cassock. He bent his knee towards the altar and made a quick sign of the cross before blurting out to the others, "There's been a hanging!"

Time stood still in the high-vaulted sanctuary. The chanting came to an abrupt discordant end. Brother Johannes gripped Volmar's arm. "A hanging?" he repeated in disbelief.

"Where?" someone said more loudly.

"In the stables." Brother Hugo's knees finally gave out, and he collapsed at the Abbot's feet.

"Be respectful of our brother's age and the weariness of his mind," the Abbot said, his voice both solemn and ominous, motioning the others to keep quiet.

At length, Hugo looked up, his eyes narrowed with revulsion. "It's the traveler, Father, the one you counseled in the Infirmary." Hugo's face was flushed and his breathing came quickly. "The man's gone and hung himself from the rafters in my stables!"

Hushed voices repeated the dreaded word which in turn eerily echoed throughout the great vaulted roof of the austere sanctuary and back again to their intimate circle.

"Matthias hung himself?" Brother Paulus uttered in disbelief. "Why would he go and do a fool thing like that?" He cupped his hands together thoughtfully, suppressing an inner tension that the others around him found impossible to contain.

Brother Albertus blessed himself with an expression of disgust on his face and said aloud what the others were thinking. "This man's tortured soul is eternally damned. We all know how the church views taking one's own life. It's considered a cowardly act of avoidance and not one of martyrdom."

Volmar remained silent. Even a highly decorated Knight of the Brotherhood such as Matthias would be forbidden to be buried in consecrated ground if he committed suicide. "S" for suicide; could this, in some bizarre ritual, be the meaning of the blood message left at the base of Matthias's bed? Had he been preparing himself for an act scorned even by his better self?

"God protect us," cried one of the brothers, and a few others joined in, repeating the same prayer in a despairing lament.

The Abbot pulled a linen handkerchief from his sleeve and patted the beads of perspiration on his forehead. Even in the shadowy glow of candlelight, Burchard had a pale cast to his features, clearly distressed by the news.

Brother Paulus approached Volmar and put his hand on the young monk's shoulder. Under his breath, he said, "We have lived in splendid isolation in Disibodenberg, but not any more. I fear we've been caught up in a game of strange and wicked alliances."

Volmar couldn't help but feel that here, playing before him in all its evilness, was the burden of God's answer to his question. The Holy Relic and its sordid history now seemed a poor excuse, an inflated lie, to justify man's selfish greed and self-destructive tendencies. "The story is certainly becoming more complicated," Volmar answered, allowing no expression to be read on his young face.

Chapter 4: Hedge of Protection

Sanctuary of Disibodenberg Monastery

6th of November, Matins

The room was alive with whispered speculations. Abbot Burchard went and stood before the richly adorned high altar and raised his hands, awaiting silence. It took a few moments before an unnatural hush came over the gathering.

In the moment of silence, Volmar prayed to himself. "God give me a discerning spirit." He then searched the other brothers' faces, specifically looking for that of Brother Rudegerus. His absence was duly noted. He turned to the Abbot, who met his eyes with the same understanding.

"Please, dear brothers," the Abbot said, taking charge, "I think we've given enough time for idle conjectures, none of which, I'm afraid, will bring us any closer to the facts. We will need to involve the district Magistrate in this. I do not want to risk any confrontations between civil and ecclesiastical justice. Brother Julius, let the Porter know what has happened and ride with Brother Andres to Bermersheim to alert the Magistrate[89] of our predicament. We need his help."

Brother Albertus shook his head. "Father, can't we simply take care of our own and not involve the outside world?"

"That would be all well and good, my son, but leaving the district Magistrate out of this would further the perception of those who are convinced that our message is only about the next world, and has little bearing on how we live our lives in this world."

Like the dogs they kept for hunting, Brother Julius and Brother Andres knew the countryside well even though it was blanketed with

[89] Magistrate: An official entrusted with administration of the laws.

snow and the river was indistinguishable from the fields. These were sensible men who quietly nodded to one another and took their leave.

"I'd like only three brothers to accompany me to the stables. The rest of you may want to continue your prayers in your cells. We will all meet back here in a short while to further discuss what has happened."

"Father, it would be blasphemous to lay such a body here in the Sanctuary." A few of the other brothers nodded in agreement.

"Please, dear brothers, it is premature to discuss burial arrangements when we haven't even seen the body. For the sake of my sanity and the law of this land we need to proceed cautiously, observing all manners of propriety and care. I do not look forward to opening our gates to the people of Staudernheim and the district Magistrate for an investigation, but it now seems that we have no choice."

"What do we tell those in the Guesthouse and Infirmary when they wake up, Father?" Brother Albertus asked.

"For now, hold your tongues and let them sleep. It is best if we all refrain from speaking untruths to one another until we know more of this frightful situation." The Abbot sighed with resignation. "No one, I repeat, no one, will touch the body until a clear verdict has been ascertained by Brother Paulus. God has led us all into this mystery; and we must believe that He will protect us while we try to unravel it. And, regardless of the ruling, I will not allow this man's body to be desecrated in any way."

The Abbot searched the faces of the brothers, sensing in them a wide range of volatile emotions. He paused for a moment, trying to decide what else he should say. "I'd like to have someone who is skilled in medicinal arts and someone who is familiar with the goings and comings of all our guests, so I'd like Brother Paulus and Brother Rudegerus to accompany me. Brother Volmar, we will also need a chronicler to record what has happened, so please retrieve your writing instruments and meet us at the entrance to the stables."

There was silence, followed by quiet murmurs as the other brothers now noticed that Rudegerus was not among their numbers. Someone in the back mumbled. "I think the Abbot needs to find out where that one was last night."

"Very well, then," Abbot Burchard said, ignoring the scandalous accusation. "Brother Paulus and Brother Volmar will accompany me.

The rest of you will need to gather your wits and pray for the Lord's guidance."

Keeping a stranglehold on his growing sense of dread, Volmar grabbed a torch and, for the first time, walked quickly through the hushed nave of the Sanctuary in the direction of the Abbot's private chamber. The young scribe's thoughts were racing as fast as his booted feet once he exited God's Sanctuary. Why would a man returning home after fifteen years hang himself? Surely Matthias knew that the church condemns suicide. None of it made any sense. Paulus was right, it was a foolish man's recourse. Why would a man leave a heroic battlefield promising an honorable death only to commit suicide in an obscure monastery's stables? Other questions darted in and out of his thoughts like moths around a light: What of Matthias's suspicions that he was being followed, and the strange disappearance of Atif's body? And what, pray tell, was Rudegerus's involvement in all this? More than likely, Volmar concluded, Matthias's death had more to do with the Holy Relic's curse than a wild moment of cowardice. Once Matthias had parted with the Holy Relic and the hedge of protection around him was lifted, he died in mysterious circumstances!

Chapter 5: Weary Pilgrim's Heart

Abbot's Quarters of Disibodenberg Monastery

6th of November, After Matins

As Volmar turned the corner and approached the Abbot's quarters, he could see that the heavy oak door was left ajar. He stood at the entrance and noticed right away a drop of wax on the floor from a taper someone must have been carrying. He bent down and touched the wax. It still felt warm.

Volmar stood in disbelief on the threshold of the Abbot's private chamber. His keen eyes picked out each and every detail. The room had been searched, turned inside out. Papers from the desk were scattered about and drawers were dumped onto the floor, their contents strewn everywhere. Even the straw mattress where the Abbot slept had been dragged off of its wooden platform and stood leaning upright against the far stone wall. Toiletry items, too, were spilled and lay in waste beneath the bedside table.

Someone desperately had been hunting for something. Volmar studied the scene in silence. He grasped that whoever had done such a thing knew of the Holy Relic and was hoping to find it in the Abbot's possession. He was grateful that it was safe in Sister Hildegard's care. Volmar approached the desk and saw that the drawer he had locked the night before lay wide open. His leather pouch was still there, although there was a tear in its leather stitching. At least he had safeguarded as well all of the notes he had taken of the details concerning Peter Bartholomew and the Holy Spear; for otherwise, the history of the Holy Relic would now be in this thieving scoundrel's hands.

Volmar then remembered why he'd come. Hastily he gathered a quill and ink and a small clay jar to hold the ink, and rolled up a blank sheet of parchment before tucking it into his leather pouch. As he headed for the door to leave, he stopped suddenly.

Only then did he notice that someone was sitting in the Abbot's chair. The person was seated with his back to him facing the fireplace. It was difficult to determine the man's features silhouetted by the glowing embers of last night's fire. The stranger sitting in absolute stillness sent a chill up Volmar's spine. Even from this distance he could tell that the man was obviously dressed as a gentleman in fine velvets and brocades.

Volmar spoke with authority. "Sir, the Abbot has been detained. I am his Scribe. My name is Brother Volmar; may I be of service?" There was no answer, not even a simple nod in acknowledgment. Volmar had a sinking feeling. He spoke even louder, in case the stranger was hard of hearing. "Sir, how may I help you?"

The realization did not come in an instant. Somehow Volmar's mind knew he had to experience the horror in small increments. He went to the firebox, reached for another log, and threw it onto the grate before taking the poker and positioning it onto the center of some ash-covered embers which seemed to have retained a spark of life. Quietly, he blew on them. Cinders flew here and there, spitting and crackling with new life, illuminating the dark corner.

"It's amazing how a simple fire can warm a soul," he said, the dread now almost unbearable. Still there was a deafening silence.

Slowly he turned and gazed up at the face of the dead man, ashen grey even in the warm glow of the fire. A wave of sadness came over him, deeper than any he had anticipated.

Atif's hands were folded across his chest, so life-like, and yet Volmar could tell there was no blood coursing through his once nimble fingers. He had to remind himself that this was but a body, a soul-less husk of the man who had taken an afternoon to instruct a mere beginner in the art of swordsmanship and, more importantly, giving him a lesson in how not to give up.

Stoically Volmar approached his friend, went to his knees, and held Atif's cold, gray-green lifeless hand in his. He prayed, "O God, be merciful. Bring comfort to this weary pilgrim's heart." Volmar forced himself to peer up at Atif's discolored features, then at his chest. Out of respect, he closed Atif's eyelids. He did not need any medical knowledge to see that his friend had died from a knife wound to the chest as Sophie had described and that his death was at least a day old. The wound appeared sharp, not jagged, indicating that it had been the result of one single thrust. The murderer knew exactly how to kill.

Atif's mouth hung partially open as if he had one more secret to impart. Volmar reached inside the Arab's hidden pocket and retrieved the small codex. One look confirmed his and the Abbot's suspicions. The Emperor had in fact granted Atif his freedom, but at what cost? He slipped the codex into his leather pouch. He felt around in the pocket for Atif's rosary and confirmed its absence. In his own blood he must have wanted to communicate one more word.

"Your death, my friend," Volmar said soberly, "will be as a thorn in my side. I will personally hunt down the man who did this to you and will bring him to justice. The forces of darkness have misjudged my determination."

The Abbot's window suddenly blew open, its leaded-diamond pane knocked against the wooden frame by a harsh cold wind. It threatened to put out the fire. Volmar shivered, rose and went to close it. In the courtyard below he noticed at least a dozen or more yellow lights illuminating the misty white flurries of snow sweeping through the Abbot's withered garden. He squinted through the slanting snow below, a view all the way to the Porter's gates. He could tell that villagers dressed in heavy dark cloaks were making their way up the hillside to the stables. Several more seemed to be coming up the hill, their lanterns swinging, like many rips in a black cloth. Volmar knew their intentions: To shed light on this sickening gloom which seemed to be spreading. Could outsiders be the only ones capable of unraveling the evil lurking in the recesses of this once holy stone fortress?

Volmar stared back down into Atif's face and for the first time felt as if Disibodenberg had somehow abandoned its calling as a center of civilized life. The sight was so unnerving, he couldn't move. How could God's people fumble something so central to their mission? They alone in this dark, dismal world were obligated to ensure that the Devil could not establish his kingdom in places consecrated to God. And now instead of peace, there was discord; instead of godliness, there was strife; and instead of charity there was senseless slaughter.

Chapter 6: Deep-Seated Fear

Cloister of Disibodenberg Monastery

6th of November, After Matins

Volmar closed the gate to the Abbot's garden and headed off towards the stables. Now more than ever he was determined to make sense of what was happening. The shock was absolute: A possible suicide and now a cold-blooded murder. The Devil walked amongst them. The wind gathered strength as it blew great white clouds of snow onto the cobbled path that led to the Cloister. Volmar screwed up his eyes against the blinding ice pellets and walked on, nearly bumping directly into Rudegerus.

"Why aren't you at Matins, Brother Volmar?" Rudegerus's words were carefully enunciated and held a certain disdain.

Volmar noticed the color rise in Rudegerus's face. An odd smell emanated from him, covering up what seemed to be a much more disagreeable smell. With a puzzled grimace, Volmar answered, "I was, and where were you, Brother Rudegerus?"

There was no answer for a moment, then Rudegerus mumbled barely above the whistling of the wind in the white air. "I was detained by business."

Volmar looked hard at Rudegerus. His face was marred by heavy shadows which ringed his eyes and gave his crooked nose a more pinched, sickly look. "The Abbot has requested our presence at the stables. I'm not sure if you heard the news, but the traveler the Abbot and I spoke with yesterday evening, Matthias, has been found dead there." Volmar said this taking in finally what his eyes and nose were sensing. Rudegerus had recently washed. There was that faint smell of a freshening herb and his hair was slicked back, wet from having been recently cleaned. Three in the morning was an odd time to be bathing, he thought.

"I have not heard," said Brother Rudegerus, a trace of worry slowing replacing his calculated look. "The church is very clear about suicide. Why would anyone choose to hang himself?"

"There is much still unknown about this man's motives," Volmar asserted, wondering if Brother Rudegerus realized he'd stumbled. Something has unsettled him, he thought. He's acting too careless, for how could he deny hearing of this man's death and yet know that the stranger had hung himself? Swirling pellets of ice continued to fall.

Brother Rudegerus rattled on, oblivious to his apparent contradictions. "Surely Matthias was fleeing his responsibilities. His motivation was despair, a fatal vice inspired in him by the Devil."

Behind Rudegerus's smug attitude, Volmar heard the fear. Not blind ambition but plain, deep-seated fear lurking behind every absurd accusation his fellow brother was making. He knew the monk was a man of narrow mind and total self-absorption, but an accomplice to murder? What was Rudegerus so fearful of? Rudegerus must be hiding some kind of lie. Volmar didn't know what exactly, only that it left an acrid taste in his mouth. Suddenly uncertain what to say, Volmar added softly, "Suicide, like murder, is an act counter to nature, and an affront to God. He alone gave us life and He alone should determine our moment to face death."

Chapter 7: Demons Present

Stables of Disibodenberg Monastery

6th of November, After Matins

"Come in, brothers," Abbot Burchard said, approaching the two of them. "I was hoping, Brother Rudegerus," he continued, handing Rudegerus a lit torch, "you might be able to shed some light on this gruesome situation. I need to know the names of all those visiting our monastery." The Abbot rested his hand on Rudegerus's shoulder and also noted, Volmar could tell, the fact that he had recently bathed.

"Father, may I have a word with you?" Volmar said, stomping the snow from his heavy leather boots. He was well aware of the under-currents of emotion in the room and was certain now that Rudegerus was involved somehow, some way with Atif's untimely death.

"Now?" The Abbot asked, clearly stunned.

"Yes, it will take but a moment."

Outside, the violence of the wind softened to a moaning whisper. Brother Rudegerus stood to one side, his dark restless eyes downcast. If Volmar had to make a judgment, the man seemed genuinely terrified by his current circumstances.

Brother Paulus stood in silence beside his fellow brother, clearly aware and concerned over Rudegerus's demeanor. He studied his brother's features, noting that he had not once looked up into the face of the victim. Instead, his eyes were fervently scanning the area in which they stood, as if he half-expected a demon to come charging out of its darkened crevices and corners.

Abbot Burchard's lips twitched as if he wanted to say something more, thought better of it, and said nothing as he stepped aside to talk to Volmar in private.

Volmar wasted no time whispering to the Abbot how he'd come across Atif's dead body seated in Burchard's own chair. He reached into his leather pouch and pulled out Atif's codex, the papers acknowledging his freedom and his deceit. The Abbot took this news with considerable self-control, though, Volmar noted, he switched hands, for the torch he held in his right hand suddenly started shaking.

"So, our young Sophie was not dreaming. She observed a murder. And we've finally found the body." He sighed deeply. "I've gone ahead and brought Brother Paulus into our confidence about the events we discussed last evening. For now, son, please tell no one else of this unfortunate death." The Abbot returned the codex to Volmar for safe-keeping. "There is much we do not know as of yet."

Volmar nodded, adding with equal seriousness, "We're witnessing the Holy Relic's curse." The two turned back to the others, clearly upset by the turn of events, yet determined to sort it all out and bring justice to the architects of this terrible violence.

Volmar had come face to face with death only a few moments ago, and still it didn't make walking up to Matthias's body any less disturbing. He looked up and met the old soldier's narrow blue eyes, staring down at him sightlessly.

Brother Rudegerus mumbled. "Most unfortunate situation, Father. As I said yesterday, the man was demon-possessed."

The Abbot responded thoughtfully to his theory. "There are certainly demons present, but whether they were controlling Matthias, I seriously doubt it. When we spoke, he was in full control of his faculties. Volmar," he said, looking over to his Scribe, "be sure to record our conversation. These observations may prove helpful to the Magistrate and his advisors when they arrive."

"Interesting," Brother Paulus interrupted, holding his torch higher and staring up at the body. "There are none of the usual physical signs of hanging present."

Volmar glanced up from his writing. "Has anyone else been in here?"

"I think other than Brother Hugo, we are the only ones," the Abbot said. "Why?"

"Well," Volmar paused as he formed his thoughts, "when someone hangs himself, wouldn't he require a stool to stand on so he could hoist himself up higher before kicking it to the side? In this case, there is no stool or chair present." Volmar went to the back door, opened it and peered out, confirming his suspicion. "The milking stool is unmoved. It is where I left it the evening before. It could have been suitable for such a ghastly deed."

"Are there any indications of the victim's effort to resist an attack, such as bruises or torn clothing?" Abbot Burchard asked, turning to Brother Paulus.

Brother Paulus nodded. "The neck is obviously broken; yet, as I commented a moment ago, the man's eyes are not bulging, nor his tongue blackened or protruding. The man appears to have been dead before the hanging, Father. My guess would be that someone wanted to make this killing appear as a suicide."

Abbot Burchard grimaced. "If Matthias was trying to leave, as his traveling clothes suggest, where are all the rest of his belongings?"

"Father," Volmar said, interrupting, "all four horses appear to be missing."

"So it seems," Abbot Burchard said in measured tones. "Rudegerus, as the monastery's Guest Master, you're aware of the goings and comings of our civilian population. Who has visited the monastery in the past couple of days?"

"Father," Rudegerus said, apparently worried, "without referring to my sign-in book, I cannot confirm or deny any of our recent visitors."

"Please make that a priority," the Abbot said sternly, "especially before the Magistrate arrives. I'm sure Wolfe will need the names of all those who are recent boarders in our guest house."

"So," Volmar said, thinking out loud, "if there were two murderers, not one, then they left the monastery on horseback with two horses in tow. It will certainly slow them down."

The Abbot exchanged a knowing look with Volmar . . . Atif owned the third horse.

Brother Paulus added, twirling a strand of his long flowing beard, "I know of at least two breaks in the outer walls. Each would provide a way for men on horseback to leave without having to go by the Porter at the gate."

"Surely once our two messengers get word to the Magistrate, he can have his search party track down these two or possibly three men, and see if they have Matthias's horse and belongings with them." Abbot Burchard sounded more hopeful than he felt.

"It has been snowing all night," Volmar mentioned. "It may prove nearly impossible for a search party to follow our suspects' tracks."

Brother Paulus returned to the body. "You would think an old soldier like Matthias would not be easy to overcome, even if two men surprised him. There are no facial contusions, strangulation finger marks, or bruises on his neck or fists." Brother Paulus stood close, eye level with the only noticeable injury. "Father, take a look at his right leg. The trousers are shredded and heavily caked with blood. There appears to be a single gash up the calf of his leg that runs about the size of a man's hand."

"Is this the injury you treated several days ago?"

"No, those were bite marks on his other ankle. This cut seems fresh, so it must have occurred within the last fortnight."

"Could that have caused his death?" Abbot Burchard asked.

Paulus shook his head. "Highly unlikely. Such an injury, while painful, is seldom life-threatening. Remember, this is the man who already survived an attack by wild dogs. Though I must say, this injury is puzzling. If in fact Matthias died before he was strung up, then the broken neck did not kill him—something else did. Without thoroughly examining the body, Father, it is difficult to say how this man died."

"A cut that deep must have bled heavily," Volmar said, examining the bloodstained cobblestone floor below the body of Matthias. He followed the path of the bloodstains across the stable floor and saw how they came from the stall where the horses had been earlier yesterday afternoon. "Judging by this trail of bloodstains, it appears that Matthias had the cut before he was lifted and hung from the rope." Volmar stood inside the stalls where four horses had been tied up. "This is where Matthias must have encountered the two men, perhaps while he was saddling his horse. The struggle, and perhaps the stabbing, took place in here."

"This is ridiculous!" Rudegerus loudly countered, his face a deeper shade of red than usual. "There's no possible way you can determine that!"

Abbot Burchard was already on his hands and knees with Brother Paulus and Volmar, examining the irrefutable blood droplets. "Then how else would you explain these bloodstains, Brother Rudegerus?" the Abbot said, looking up at him. "I am open to all possibilities."

Volmar stood up and drew a simple diagram of the stables on his parchment, indicating where the bloodstains were in reference to where the body was hanging. "Don't you think it is odd how the bloodstains vary in size? Underneath the body there are large stains. Then medium bloodstains all the way up to here," he said pointing to the stall, "and then, inside here we see that the bloodstains look like small kernels of corn."

Brother Paulus rose to his feet with some effort given his advancing age. He stood next to Brother Volmar and studied the younger monk's diagram. "Bloodstains vary in size, depending on how far they have to fall. If a person is standing, and blood is dripping from his calf, there is only a small distance from the floor, such as these small bloodstains here," he said, pointing to the area inside the horse's stall. Slowly and together the two monks walked the distance from the stall back to the body. "However," Brother Paulus continued, "if our victim is carried, the distance to the floor is greater, so the bloodstains will be larger in size, like we see all along this portion of the trail." He pointed to the medium-sized bloodstains.

"And," Volmar continued, "The bloodstains should be larger as we see here under the victim's body since it is hanging much higher. So, taking the size of the bloodstains into consideration, it would confirm our suspicions that someone must have carried Matthias's body from the point of death inside the stalls to hang him out here from a rafter after he had already died, to make it appear as a suicide."

"Well done," Abbot Burchard said with clear admiration. "Brother Rudegerus, do you have anything to add?"

"All of this is mere conjecture, Father! How can you possibly believe that this tragedy is any more than a mad man hanging himself out of despair?" Rudegerus crossed his arms defiantly, though his voice betrayed apprehension.

"What is even more curious and deeply troubling, Brother Rudegerus, is how you are determined to hold onto such falsehoods even in light of these facts." Abbot Burchard studied Rudegerus as he continued. "The poor man I spoke with yesterday evening wanted to return to his family. He expressed no intentions of killing himself. I am grateful that the evidence suggests that his soul is not condemned to burn in Hell. There are no longer questions in my mind. Matthias's body is to be buried in consecrated ground. We are investigating a murder, not a suicide."

Chapter 8: Merciless

Lodge Outside of Staudernheim

6th of November, Before Dawn

Yanking on the reins of his horse, Ulrich came to a full stop in a clearing outside the village of Bermersheim, due west of the monastery at Disibodenberg. They had reached the crest of the hill and the force of the wind was almost unbearable. The village lay below, blanketed in a snowy peaceful slumber. Ulrich turned to Donato and spoke authoritatively, over the whine of the wind. "If I remember, there's a hunter's lodge about a mile up the way in that direction. There we can search Atif's and Matthias's belongings for the relic."

The younger man nodded in agreement, his nose red and numb from the cold. The trek up the hillside was slow going, as both men were dragging the leads of reluctant and tired horses. Ice beneath the snow made it even more dangerous. Ulrich was the first to dismount. He hitched the reins of his two horses to a post before heading to the door. The wind had blown the snow into high mounds nearly waist deep against the lodge's sturdy log walls. If he hadn't known where to look, the lodge would have been lost in the storm. The door swung open after a swift kick.

"These blizzards are worse than I remember," Ulrich said, waiting a moment so his eyes could adjust to the dim light. He gazed up the stairs to the loft above, half expecting to see someone from his past come down the steps to greet him.

The room provided a reasonable amount of comfort. There were two heavily carved but faded tapestry chairs in front of a stone hearth, a modest table, a cupboard and a large wardrobe. Cobwebs hung from the beeswax candles swinging overhead on a chandelier fashioned from antlers.

Donato stomped his boots on the floor, trying to warm his feet. "This old lodge may have once afforded its owners a modest sense of luxury, but given its present state, I dare say the only satisfied inhabitants are the rodents."

"It is gloomy. But at least we are out of the wind," Ulrich said, sweeping the table clean with his arm. Shards of crockery crashed to the floor. He tore open Atif's traveling bag that had been strapped to his horse, pulling out everything that was in it.

Donato went to satisfy a more pressing need. He found some flint in a tinder box beside the hearth and took several logs from the nearby woodbin and placed them on the iron grate. "I thought Brother Gerard warned us, saying the Holy Relic loses its powers unless it is given willingly to its new owner. Matthias's dead fingers didn't exactly bestow the Spear of Destiny into our blood-stained hands."

Ulrich ignored the comments and frantically turned to Matthias's traveling satchel. He ripped it apart, exposing multiple inside pockets. With more care, he took his knife and unraveled the stitched hems. "Ah, my friend, you're forgetting about accidental death. Legend says that if the original owner dies by accident such as being torn apart by a wild beast, then the Holy Relic's powers are passed on to the next man who finds the spearhead." Ulrich was growing more fanatical in his search. He flung dried fruits and salted meats from the satchel across the room.

"Hey, what are you doing? I'm hungry! Let's salvage some of this. We have a long night ahead." Donato squatted down and picked up some of the remains off the dirty floor. He found an oil lamp, grateful that it was partially full, and lit its wick with a twig from the raging fire. He adjusted its flame and took it with him to the wooden cupboards hoping to find some sort of earthenware plate or jar and watched in dismay as several mice went scurrying when he opened it. What he would have given for a cup of warm cider and a slice of fresh bread! "Of all nights to be snowed under—we should be distancing ourselves from this region, not spending the night here, right under their noses."

"Nothing!" Ulrich bellowed, sinking his knife into the table. Skins lay strewn about as if from a wild animal's feeding frenzy. The older man raised his fist into the air and cursed Heaven. "I will not surrender to such trickery," he cried out with a fierce anger. "Do you hear me? I will not give up!" He crossed the room and sank into one of the two chairs.

Donato went to the table and searched through the scattered mess, all that was left of Matthias's earthly belongings. He thought about the edicts he swore to uphold. His soul was far from pure. "All my life," he ventured, "I trained to heal those in pain. When did I start wishing for their deaths?"

Ulrich stared into the golden flames, now breathing hot and licking the grate, swallowing the chill in the air. The glow had brought not only life but memories as well into the room. For a moment, the older man saw a specter of a woman watching him from the opposite chair. He had felt her presence ever since he'd entered the lodge. Her face was drawn and much older than he remembered. She was cradling their daughter who was asleep in her arms. Suddenly she drew back the blanket and revealed to him the corpse of their lovely child, Anya. The little girl's yellow hair hung like catkins from a bleached skull.

Donato dislodged this ghastly mirage when he sat down in the chair opposite the older man. "There's a line that you can cross between God's mercy and God's wrath," he said ruefully. "I'm not sure about you, but I fear the eternity of torment in Hell for the evil we set about and accomplished these past two days."

Ulrich brought his fingertips together, trying hard to stay focused on the present moment and to keep the younger man from seeing how shaky they'd become. In fact he was trembling all over as if he himself, like a snake, was shedding one skin to reveal another. "We've committed unforgivable sins before," he murmured.

"But that, my friend, was in the name of war. This is something else. I know, in the name of Brother Gerard we were sent to hunt Matthias down and seize the Holy Relic for our just cause. Yet, now that the deed is finally done and we still do not have the relic, I can't help but feel our actions will not go unpunished."

"It is far more foolish, I think, not to have known our enemy better. Matthias must have grown tired of the hunt." Ulrich chuckled, a bitter, mirthless sound. "Now, I'll have to return to the monastery."

"Are you mad? I'm sure by now the district Magistrate and his lynch mob are searching the countryside looking for us, even on such a night as this. Thank goodness it's still snowing. Our tracks will soon disappear." Donato shook his head in despair. "Ulrich, you must have a death wish, going anywhere close to that monastery tonight. You'll be arrested, tried, and hung before noon tomorrow if you so much as take another step inside Disibodenberg."

"You may be right. But, not if I decide to wear a disguise." He staggered over to the massive wardrobe and flung it wide open. Clothes musty and moth eaten were neatly folded on its shelves.

"You know this place," the younger man asserted, watching his partner change his clothes.

"I was wondering when you would catch on," he smiled. "Long ago I knew this place well. I went on hunts here in the surrounding forests with my father and later brought my own family here for a breath of fresh air."

"Fresh air . . . "

"It could be rather stuffy living under the auspices of a vain and rich family. Speaking of vanity, how do I look?" Ulrich hunched his back and traipsed about the room with an obvious limp, his clothes hanging from his frame like foul rags.

"Frankly, you look like a very disagreeable hunchback." Donato crossed his arms, clearly disturbed by the direction their plans were taking.

"Do you remember that monk we recognized?"

Donato answered warily. "Yes, the nervous one with the crooked nose . . . by now he's found the body we left him tucked neatly under a blanket in his bed."

"I'm beginning to suspect he must have not only overheard our conversation but decided to seize the Holy Relic himself." Ulrich added with a sneer, "He should be more willing to talk now."

He was so close to Donato, the younger man could smell the stench of his old clothes and the turn in his thoughts. "I wish we didn't have to kill Atif."

"Couldn't be helped, an accident really." Ulrich spoke from underneath his eerie hood. "We couldn't have him tell Matthias we were so close." All that was visible were his remarkable deep brown eyes flecked throughout with gold.

Donato studied his hands, turning them over in disgust, answering Ulrich crossly and with genuine regret. "More innocent blood."

Ulrich tore off his hood, ignoring his companion's pitiful display of remorse. He went and stood thoughtfully staring at something propped up in the back corner of the wardrobe. "I remember this cane," he said, reaching for it, knowing full well that doing so put him on another path, a much more dangerous one. Ulrich rubbed the cane against his cheek, a boyish ritual of affection. Quietly he turned its handle, removing a long thin sword hidden inside its clever scabbard. He touched the edge of the sword with his finger, testing its sharpness and was pleased. "Speaking of innocent blood, I got my first taste of it with this sword when I was five. I never knew rabbits could scream." He swung the sword about, severing the air with satisfaction.

"So young and merciless," the younger man said, aghast. "And you came from a long line of gentlemen?"

"As old and revered as time." Ulrich laughed, long and loud. "The difference between me and you, my good friend, is quite simple. I do not have a conscience. It neither squirms nor is repelled by the shedding of innocent blood. It is your strength and your weakness." And with a single thrust, the older man sunk the long needle-like sword through Donato's heart with the same precision and skill he had taken Atif's life two nights before.

The younger man's mouth formed the word as he gasped in revulsion at his friend's unexpected deed. "Why?" he asked, falling to his knees, the pain only now being felt as if a hard boot was stomping on his entrails.

"Plainly stated," Ulrich hissed, "I want to make history, not be its squirming victim. Whosoever possesses the Spear of Destiny has the power to shape the destiny of this world. Do you think I would want to share such incredible power with another man?"

"What about Brother Gerard?" Donato said, now coughing up bright red blood.

"This search was never for him. I possess loyalties towards no man. It is better this way, my friend, for you will never have to face the humiliation of being caught off guard again."

Donato crouched over, the pain like lightning shooting through every blood vessel in his body. All the lights had been put out except one, and here he fixed his attention. His vision blurred before the darkness fully consumed him. In the meager light coming from the hearth, he saw Ulrich returning to his chair, his fingers laced together, watching him die. The young man stiffened slightly. Someone else was in the room and she too had the same look of horror on her face as Ulrich burst out laughing.

Chapter 9: Night-Time Vigil

Anchorage of Disibodenberg Monastery

6th of November, Before Dawn

Quiet was what Volmar wanted and needed to collect his thoughts. He waved to the others as they all parted company. Rudegerus took off in one direction towards the Guest House, apparently to find his log book of the monastery's recent visitors, so he could report back when the Magistrate arrived. The Abbot had discreetly informed the Infirmarian that there was another body to investigate. While they each kept their own counsel, so as not to arouse any panic or fear amongst the other brothers, Volmar knew as he watched the two trudge up the hill towards the cloister, each of them was considering the solemn ramifications of another murder at the monastery.

Volmar assured the Abbot that he would catch up later. He held his torch to the ground and stepped from the path he and Rudegerus had tromped through earlier. The snow was deeper now. "If ever there was a night when the Devil walked about this monastery, this is such a night," he muttered, thankful on the one hand for the quiet of the falling snow, yet aware that if it continued, it would hide any evidence of footsteps, barely visible, but nevertheless telling in the newly fallen snow. Now, with a little time, he wanted to see if somehow they too would offer any answers to the questions he had swirling around in his mind about these two wretched murders.

"Snow is like a parchment," he said out loud to himself, coming across a pair of footprints. They were small and delicate, not at all the expected length of a man's foot, but more the size of a woman or a child. He thought of Brother Johannes's "archangels" and prayed that the boys would have had enough sense not to be wandering about on such a frigid night. He followed the footsteps closely as they led down the hillside from the stables and concluded to his horror that they had come directly up the hill from the Anchorage. He walked the ascent once more, this time more slowly, retracing the footsteps to reach the same conclusion. The footsteps originated from the Anchorage's window!

Disturbed, he called through the leather flap hanging from the Anchorage's window. "Sister Hildegard, it is I, Brother Volmar, may I have a word with you and you alone?"

There was a movement in the shadowy darkness and soon a voice emerged, singular but not musical. "Brother Volmar, I'm so glad it's you. I've been so distraught, not knowing what to do."

"Sister Hiltrud, where is Sister Hildegard?" Volmar asked, holding up the leather flap.

Hiltrud stared down at her hands resting in her lap. She dared not look into Volmar's face. "I don't know where to begin," she said through tears rolling down her reddened, puffy cheeks.

"And what is this?" Volmar held up a wreath of garlic, hung just inside the window's opening.

"Garlic, brother. It is to draw away disease. It is what my mum taught me," Hiltrud said defensively.

Volmar wondered if Hildegard also believed in such a silly superstition. He tried to keep his voice as calm as possible given his agitated state. "Hiltrud, you will soon hear word of a death, a horrible death here at Disibodenberg. Actually, there have been two deaths. I must speak with Sister Hildegard right away."

"Sister Jutta is ill, very ill." Hiltrud spoke quickly between shaky breaths, her words running over themselves in an attempt to be heard. "On the first night of our confinement, Sister Jutta removed all of her clothes and stood out in our small courtyard in the freezing temperatures for hours. When she finally collapsed and slipped into unconsciousness, we warmed her body, yet saw that she would not survive without certain medicines."

"Go on."

"Sister Hildegard and I could not bear to see her suffer. While the monastery and the monks all slept, Hildegard decided to put on a monk's cassock, one left here for us to mend, and visit the Infirmary's laboratory for herbs."

"It hasn't even been a week and she has already broken her vows of enclosure?" Volmar said with a wry grimace.

"Judge her not, brother," Hiltrud sputtered, between her tears. "There was no other choice, if Jutta was to live."

Volmar sighed and stared upwards towards the stable. Beyond it was the Infirmary. "Tell me, Hiltrud. Was tonight her fourth visit to the Infirmary?"

"Oh no, this was only her third visit. Jutta felt better on one of those nights," she told him, plainly using her fingers to double check her memory. "Sister Hildegard promises to replace what she has taken in the spring, once we plant our own garden here at the Anchorage." The conversation Volmar had had with Brother Paulus inserted itself into the young scribe's mind.

"Did she take any peach pits?"

"No. She only took herbs that she knew would bring down Sister Jutta's fever and infection."

Volmar knelt close to the window. "Hiltrud, I'd like to speak with Sister Hildegard myself. Tell her I will not condemn her act of charity. Please wake her; it is important."

"I cannot." Hiltrud wept bitterly. "I cannot for she is not here."

Volmar stood upright. Fear suddenly threatened to paralyze him. "At what hour did she leave?"

"It was sometime between Compline and Matins."

"The darkest hours of the night, and the very hours we think one of the two murders was committed," Volmar added, clearly distressed.

Hiltrud whimpered, finding little hope in this realization.

"Hiltrud, I intend to find her." Volmar turned from the window, picturing in his mind the inevitable turn of events. Hildegard had left the Anchorage for medicine and on her return trip from the Infirmary she encountered Matthias's murderers. She must have—why else hadn't she returned to the Anchorage?

Snowflakes clung stubbornly to Volmar's eyelashes. He realized that in a short while the footsteps would vanish and all evidence of Hildegard's night-time vigil would disappear. With an urgency he'd never felt before, Volmar rushed back up the hill, retracing Hildegard's steps all the way to the entrance of the Infirmary. Ulrich, he knew, would not hesitate to take another young woman as his prisoner. This time he might have his way with her.

Chapter 10: Wraithlike Figures

Kitchens and Cloister of Disibodenberg Monastery

6th of November, Before Dawn

Over and over Volmar retraced Hildegard's path, determined to make sense of her every movement before her footsteps were erased forever by the continuing snowfall. Volmar frowned and headed once again from the Infirmary entrance down the hill towards the stables, bits of snow clinging to his brow. There he saw that Hildegard's footsteps ended abruptly. He held his torch high, deeply troubled by her disappearance. If the murderers had taken Hildegard as a hostage—or worse, injured her—surely there would be some physical evidence of a struggle, some sort of confrontation. She wouldn't have simply vanished!

Volmar sighed with relief; the snow told no such story. It was a dry snow and had been driven by the wind, banking high up against the walls, hedges, and troughs, filling in all the hollows, except, and there he hesitated, except for the inside of a cart. A two-wheeled delivery cart sat outside the old kitchens with only a mere dusting inside it. There were deep crevices near its wheels suggesting that it had been used within the last hour. He followed its tracks and discovered that it had taken a circuitous route towards the cloister. Why would someone be anxious to make a delivery in the middle of the night? Upon closer investigation, Volmar noticed a small trace of a red velvety fabric clinging to a loose nail on the cart's wooden rim. Volmar reached for the fabric and carefully turned it over in his hand. He wrapped it in some linen and placed it within his leather pouch, realizing that Atif had worn a red velvet cape. Could this be how Atif's body had been transported to the Abbot's chamber? He'd have to mention this to the Abbot and Brother Paulus so they could see if there was a tear in Atif's outer garment.

With a growing sense of confidence, Volmar started piecing together the other discrepancies in the snow. He stood just inside the entrance to the stables, reliving Matthias's fateful last minutes on earth. There were the footsteps of two men who seemed to be walking side by side coming from the Infirmary to the stable doors. Hildegard's footsteps followed the same path down the hill from the Infirmary. Here the two men must have stood, he reflected, and here they parted company. One of them, presumably Matthias, entered the stable, while the other left. His footsteps wound around the back of the stables.

So, Volmar mulled over the known facts, drawing upon his observations and his knowledge of human nature. Where had Hildegard gone? Certainly she would have wanted to hide from anyone awake at such an hour. Across the slippery cobblestones was the entrance to the old kitchens attached to the larger open air kitchens and dining hall. Against that building's wall was the delivery cart and next to it a water barrel. Then he saw something of a slight indent in the snow bank behind the water barrel, suggesting that maybe someone had been there, preventing the newly fallen snow from piling up higher against the wall. Maybe, he reasoned, this was the very place Hildegard had wisely taken cover, so as not to be seen by Matthias and his assailant.

He crossed over and bent down in the snow, intent on seeing if he could find Hildegard's distinctive footprints. Not only was he thrilled upon seeing her two small footprints there, he also found a few bits and pieces of green leaves sprinkled about. Carefully he picked up several of the small leaves and smelled them, sighing with relief. "Thank you, God." The leaves smelled of rosemary and thyme. Volmar stood and swung open the kitchen door. As he hoped, it had been opened earlier, for there were puddles of water inside, where the snow had apparently blown in and melted.

Volmar brought his racing thoughts under control. He walked slowly forward, half-expecting to find Hildegard shivering in one of the corners. But she was not there. He had a look around, eyeing the oversized vats of salted food, jars of oil, stone crockery of flour and oatmeal, and other dry goods. Volmar reflected for a moment then exited from the other side which opened onto the cloisters. The entrance to the church would probably be the most direct path back to the Anchorage. He considered: Hildegard would desperately want to return to the Anchorage before the bells of Matins.

Volmar entered the church from the cloisters. In the dim chapel, flickering flames from the candles revealed other wraithlike figures scurrying from the shadows and grouping themselves with the holy brothers encircling the Abbot. Methodically, one by one, Volmar searched the faces of the strangers and his fellow brothers as they filed in, hoping, by chance, one of them would be a bewildered young woman masquerading as a monk.

Chapter II: Of Two Minds

Sanctuary of Disibodenberg Monastery

6th of November, Dawn

With outstretched hands the Abbot addressed the assembly, first asking for calm and then begging for patience. "In good time we will have more answers to this puzzling death, which for the moment does not appear to be a suicide."

One of the Guest House visitors in back, an elderly man in a ragged cloak, his face obscured under a tattered snow hood, spoke up. "Is it murder, Father?"

The question had been swift and caused the Abbot's eyes to widen. He peered into the dark shadows which seemed to envelop him, as did the atmosphere thickening with fear. "I cannot mislead you or anyone else present this morning. I'm afraid there has been a murder in our stables."

There was silence. It took the crowd a moment to digest this information. Suddenly the unease grew and a few women gasped, causing many to murmur prayers for forgiveness. Brother Paulus recognized the potential for panic and stepped forward, standing close to the Abbot and giving him his unspoken support. Paulus opened his mouth to speak, but the Abbot motioned for him to stay silent.

The Abbot's jaw tightened before he continued. "The Magistrate from the village has been notified and should be joining us shortly. There will be an investigation. I ask that everyone be as cooperative as possible. Understand, these proceedings are likely to cause disruptions to our daily offices and routines. I hope," he warned softly, "each of you will pray unceasingly not only for the soul of the one lost to us sometime during the night, but also for the condemned souls of the man's murderers."

"There was more than one murderer, Father?" the same old hooded man asked, his voice unwavering in the cold.

The Abbot paused, concentrating his gaze into the gloom ahead. "It would seem so. Our resolve will be tested until this unlawful death is punished."

Volmar crossed the room to stand directly behind the hooded old hunchback. Something about him seemed familiar yet so out of place. He noted the old man was wearing a signet ring. If only the lighting were not so poor. Volmar couldn't make out any of the ring's distinctive details, although it was odd that a poor guest traveler would possess this sure sign of a noble birth.

The crowd seemed to have suddenly turned into frightened children. A few stated out loud that they were packing up and leaving the monastery to find shelter somewhere safer in the village.

The Abbot responded reassuringly, "Please, stay calm. No one needs to go anywhere, especially on a night such as this. The Magistrate and his soldiers will secure our monastery. God willing, it will be the safest place for us all."

The hooded hunchback stepped forward, supported by his cane. Volmar regarded his boots thoughtfully. They were well-polished and of high quality leather. Volmar couldn't help but wonder about these inconsistencies. His cloak looked shabby, even frayed and moth-eaten in spots, yet his shoes were well cared for. Interestingly too, his shoes were laced all the way up the calf. In Volmar's experience, seldom do old men take that kind of care in the wee hours of the morning, and frankly who would take such time when they are roused from sleep to attend an unexpected meeting in the dead of night? He took in the other guests—all clearly out of sorts, much as expected. Some were even hiding the fact that they were still in their bedclothes with oversized blankets wrapped around them, braving the cold. Thankfully, Sophie wasn't among them. She would still be blissfully sleeping off her ordeal in the Infirmary. Volmar was grateful that for once, she was missing this dangerous turn of events.

The Magistrate suddenly swept into the Chapter House with an entourage of burghers[90]. Obviously he had also dressed in a hurry for his long silk cloak was flung about his shoulders inside out. Regardless, his disheveled presence did not distract from his air of confidence and his intelligent blue eyes. All mumbling ceased. The hall fell into a disquiet-

[90] Burghers: Prominent townspeople, like the wealthy merchants and landowners.

ing hush as the holy brothers and the guests moved aside, clearing a path for the Magistrate and his attendants to approach the Abbot. The whole power of the state was embodied in this one person.

"I came as soon as I got word, Father," the Magistrate said, brushing back a thick clump of charcoal gray hair that fell across his face. The Magistrate was not a tall man but his heft carried with it a sense of an inner weight that proved he was not easily swayed one way or the other. In Volmar's opinion he was the classic enigma.

"I wish our meeting could have been under better circumstances, Wolfe." The Abbot nodded with appreciation and clasped the man's hand in a friendly way.

"Seldom are circumstances in our control, eh, Father?" the Magistrate answered. "As you instructed, I've sent an armed scouting team with torches down the hillside to see if they could return with the suspects before they leave our valley."

Brother Rudegerus rudely pushed his way forward to the Magistrate. "My Lord," he said, kissing his outstretched hand, "you must not let them convince you of this man's murder. He was an unstable, demon-possessed man. What we have here is surely a regrettable but undeniable suicide."

The crowd repeated the dreaded word "suicide" with a rush of renewed apprehension.

The Magistrate raised an eyebrow and removed Rudegerus's hand from his forearm, which the monk had clutched in his impassioned spectacle. "I prefer to make up my own mind," he answered Rudegerus, dismissing any further speculation. "Which way are the stables, Father?"

"This way, My Lord," the Abbot said, leading him by the arm through the parting crowd of monks and disheveled guests.

For a brief moment, Volmar and the Magistrate's eyes met. The young scribe bowed his head in respect. He thought curiously that there was something else in that short look they shared, something more tragic than even the present circumstances. He watched as a servant adjusted the Magistrate's cloak. Perhaps, this curious expression had to do with the fact that the Magistrate must be mentally checking his emotions, for in a few short moments he had to stare directly into the face of death and not flinch.

Volmar stepped back into the shadows behind one of the stone columns and watched as the other brothers and guests began to disperse. He was of two minds. If Hildegard wasn't among this crowd, then where was she? Should he approach the Abbot and also burden him with the fact that not only had there been two deaths, but one of the sisters in the Anchorage was missing? Maybe, he reasoned, he should wait until he knew more. Who knows—perhaps by now Hildegard could have made it back to the Anchorage and was safe within its comforting walls, nursing the Anchoress back to health.

Chapter 12: A Feeding Frenzy

Sanctuary of Disibodenberg Monastery

6th of November, Dawn

Volmar paced back and forth slowly, keeping to the shadows, keeping an eye on the Abbot and the Magistrate as they assigned their assistants various duties. He read the Magistrate's lips easily. Many years ago Volmar had mastered the art of reading lips. It was a skill developed out of necessity, for in his training in the Scriptorium, Brother Thaddeus had insisted on silence. And now what was once only an amusing game became a godsend.

"No one is to leave the grounds of this monastery, understand?" the Magistrate said, turning to his men. "Report back to me if anyone should try to leave."

Volmar knew that over the years the Abbot had nurtured a relationship with the Magistrate. They were really quite close. Few knew how often they would disappear for hours and come back with a string of fish. Those lazy afternoons were well-spent, Abbot Burchard would confide to Volmar. For, he would say, when a man is relaxed, he is also open to new ideas, such as how everyone will eventually appear before God as an equal and people should be the same in the eyes of the law.

If the two suspects who apparently took off with Matthias's and Atif's horses and possessions after murdering them were in fact

Knights of the Hospitaller of Saint John, then these murders would certainly test the Magistrate's resolve for justice. And if, as Matthias had implied, these two knights were on a secret mission ordered by the Blessed Gerard of Jerusalem to retrieve the Holy Relic and the church was somehow implicated, it would be highly unlikely that the Magistrate would publicly try them for murder. The Magistrate's hands would likely be forced to heed the church's authority and would simply fine these knights before sending them on their way. These men would never come before an inquisitor. Such injustice, Volmar knew, was commonplace in an era enamored with status, power, and personal fortune.

Volmar watched as many onlookers trailed after the Magistrate, his entourage, and the Abbot to the stables. It was as if they were hungry for each detail of this grizzly murder or suicide. Certainly, this incident would incite the village gossips and would likely feed that most contemptible quality of human nature, a morbid fascination with others' misfortunes.

"Like hungry bloodhounds," he mumbled. "Wait until they find out there have been two murders," he said under his breath, with growing contempt. "It will turn into a feeding frenzy."

Paulus approached Volmar, having overheard the young monk's harsh appraisal. He put a hand on the young scribe's shoulder and patted it. "Human history," he said thoughtfully, "is full of such evil deeds. I agree. It would be better if people would look upon such wickedness with deep sadness rather than an obsessive fascination."

Volmar was perplexed by the unreality of the entire situation. Wasn't he, too, caught up in the thrill of unraveling this vile transgression? Then he remembered the cloth that he'd found on the thick wood rim of the delivery cart. "Brother Paulus, I found this outside the stable on a delivery cart. It looks like a torn piece of velvet from Atif's cape. The murderer may have used the cart to deliver his body to the Abbot's personal chambers."

"A quirky sense of humor, wouldn't you say? Who in their right mind would position a dead body in a relaxed pose in front of the Abbot's hearth?"

"Interesting, isn't it?" Volmar answered, thinking back over a year ago, when he found the mummified body of Brother Arnoul in the chamber under the clearing. Could this be a pattern suggesting that the murderer of Atif and Brother Arnoul was one and the same person?

Paulus turned the scrap of material over. He licked it; then sniffed it before he rubbed it against his hand. "There's a faint but distinctive sweet smell to it. I dare say it smells like Theriac, the ointment I had Atif apply to Matthias's gums the night he brought him into the Infirmary." Volmar watched, bemused. There was much he could learn from this scientific approach to everything. Paulus was an avid follower of Aristotle and the Arab physicist Alhazen, and had spoken often with Volmar about the powers of simple observation, the need to formulate a hypothesis, and the value of experimentation.

"Well done, Volmar. I see our talks have found fertile ground. I will check for rips in Atif's cloak." Paulus took the wrapping with the scrap of cloth and carefully placed it in his pocket before lifting his hood, readying himself once again to brave the cold wind. "Rest assured, my young brother, justice will be served, if not in this life, then in the next."

A few guests lingered. Those at the altar took a few more moments to pray for mercy, while the others decided that there was nothing more they could do but return to bed, comforted that they were now not only protected by the church but, perhaps more importantly, by this august, fierce representative of the law.

Volmar's troubled eyes came to rest on the benevolent gaze of Saint Disibod, the frescoed features of their founding saint above him reading in a cell with a rosary. Reaching out over four centuries, the young scribe felt the saint wanted to help. "Where is she?" he asked Saint Disibod, knowing the rush of people around him were not paying him any attention. "Is she tied up on Matthias's horse, being dragged through the snowstorm by two murderers?" The depth of his feelings for Hildegard surprised him. Sophie, he knew, had certainly found a space in his empty heart; for he loved her as he had loved his sister Anya. But, his feelings for Hildegard were deeper and less easy to put into words. Volmar wondered if Saint Disibod could read these forbidden thoughts as well. Surely, Saint Disibod had struggled with his own human failings. He knew of life's bitter hardships and broken dreams. "More will follow," the saintly reformer seemed to say, with wry cynicism. "For that is the way of human discourse."

"There's a faint but distinctive sweet smell to it. I dare
say it smells like Theriac, the ointment I had Atif apply to
Matthias' gums the night he brought him into the Infirmary."
GMD

Chapter 13: The Lion and the Lamb

Sanctuary of Disibodenberg Monastery

6th of November, Dawn

The chanting finally died down and there were no more echoes of conflicted voices. It was as if the Sanctuary were holding its breath in awkward anticipation. Volmar lingered, watching the old man with the polished and laced shoes move out of the shadows to approach the lone hooded figure of Brother Rudegerus. Unobtrusively, the young scribe fell into line behind the last group leaving. Moments later he ducked behind the last stone column and stood in the curve of St. Peter's alcove, beside the stone altar. Here he had a better view of what was happening between these two suspicious men.

"I know you," the old man said abruptly, his voice loud in the quiet of the now deserted Sanctuary. He approached the hooded monk.

Rudegerus backed off, petrified. As he did so, his hood fell away. The monk's appearance shocked Volmar. Rudegerus' eyes appeared hollow and his face seemed drawn as if he was dying of thirst. Rudegerus replied in an astonished rasping whisper. "Are you a messenger of Satan, sent here to torment me further?"

"What if I am?" The old man laughed; a long, heartless laugh. Volmar recognized the laugh, he too had fallen victim to its apathetic sneer. Could this old man be Ulrich, the one he'd dueled with behind the Infirmary? If so, here was their murderer, hiding in plain sight. The hooded hunchback abruptly snorted and said, "I will haunt you to your death until you return what is rightfully mine, the Holy Relic. Give it to me."

Again Brother Rudegerus murmured fearfully. "What Holy Relic? I possess no relic! Leave me, demented demon!" The monk collapsed at the feet of the stranger, his knees surely bruised by the hard fieldstone floor. He began weeping uncontrollably. His sobs echoed throughout the empty hall, sadly unanswered.

The old man's voice was cold, divorced from feelings, from sympathies. "I am neither angel nor demon." His hunched back straightened and with a practiced hand he held his cane menacingly under the monk's chin. "You have until the bells toll for Prime to place the Holy

Relic in the bucket at the old well behind the stables. Otherwise, another grave will need to be dug in the Monks' Cemetery."

Rudegerus nodded in agreement, gasping from the pressure of the cane against his throat.

Volmar sensed that whatever evil stood before Rudegerus had the power to crush more than a human spirit. The old man tapped his cane against the stone in rhythmic time, while humming a macabre funeral march as he exited the sanctuary.

Volmar panicked, realizing that he needed to hide; otherwise his eavesdropping would surely be discovered by Ulrich as he passed by. Hastily he tripped the lever behind the Altar of St. Peter. In turn, a stone slid to one side, revealing a small polished brass door handle in the shape of a lion. Volmar lifted the handle, relieved by how silently it revealed an entrance through a hidden door. "The Lion and the Lamb," the Abbot had said in one obscure lesson, "symbols of our Lord and evidence of the duality of our own natures as well."

Chapter 14: Prayer Closet

Sanctuary of Disibodenberg Monastery

6th of November, Dawn

Volmar slipped inside a tiny room built specifically for monks who were to say penance for misdeeds and were to suffer in isolation sometimes for years—a practice, thankfully, Abbot Burchard disagreed with. This was the same small room that connected to the underground tunnel he and Hildegard had stumbled upon a year ago. Volmar hadn't visited it since that fateful day.

After a moment, he pulled back the velvet curtain, to watch as Rudegerus lay prostrate on the floor, his arms splayed in the sign of the cross. Seeing him suffer so made Volmar's entire body ache in sympathy. Fear was a powerful weapon, he observed, for it could paralyze a grown man. Volmar sat very still, thinking through the scene, when suddenly he was surprised by a movement in the far corner of the prayer closet.

"Volmar." He recognized this voice instantly. Hildegard reached out in the darkness for his hand.

Volmar stooped to kiss the hand he held so warmly and brought it to his cheek. Then he cupped her small chin in his hands and lifted her face towards his. "I thought I would never see you again," he said, his voice hoarse with emotion.

"No, Volmar, we mustn't," Hildegard whispered, her eyes clearly wanting what her voice forbade. She put her finger to his lips. "Please."

Volmar sat back on his heels and was silent, waiting for his heart to stop racing. At last, he spoke. "I've been searching all over for you. Hiltrud told me of your nightly visits to the Infirmary. Hildegard," he said earnestly, "if ever you need anything, if Jutta falls ill again, please send for me first."

"I will tell you next time," Hildegard said plaintively. She paused and reflected. She was grateful that she had someone she could confess her sins to. Holding her silence was one of the hardest things she had ever done.

"Abbot Burchard is correct. Matthias was murdered, but the murderer, I'm certain, is not human."

"Not human? How can that be? Sister Hildegard, please trust me as I have trusted you. Last night you saw something on your way back from the Infirmary. Please tell me what happened."

"When I left the Infirmary and had just turned the corner passing outside the entrance to the stables, I overheard two men in a heated disagreement. It was dark. I could not see the men's faces, but I could hear them speak. One man was telling the other man details concerning Blessed Gerard's master plan. Apparently Brother Gerard is ambitious and wants to leave Palestine to create a new order of the Knights Hospitaller on the island of Malta."

"Did you hear any names?"

"No, but the man who spat on the ground and whom I took to be Matthias wanted to leave. From what I could understand, Blessed Gerard wants very much to acquire all that he can both in land and Holy Relics of great spiritual value. Acquiring the Spear of Longinus would be the highlight of his career."

Volmar's voice shook. "So the church is involved, as I feared."

"It is more than that, Brother Volmar. I do not understand such struggles within the church. Why has neither man obeyed the Rule of Saint Benedict, to disavow oneself from the petty allure of power and greed."

"None of this surprises me. Political posturing in the church has weakened our spiritual message in the eyes of man and surely in the eyes of God. This is the very thing Matthias tried to warn us about. What happened next?"

"It is of considerable significance that the island of Malta is shaped like a spearhead, for the man who supported Brother Gerard said that the Spear of Longinus is destined to reside there permanently in the care of a few select Holy Brothers of the Knights Hospitaller of Saint John. It is there where this secret brotherhood plans to train young knights to rule the world. And both of them have been counted among the chosen ones. Malta, he said, is destined to become the ladder to Heaven, the new center of the world, the gateway to the ethereal realm of the immortals under the Pope's blessing. He went on to assure Matthias that work on an underground city has already begun as planned."

"An underground city?"

"Yes. Those were the words he used, and its entrance is to be across from the Grandmaster's Palace. He also reminded Matthias that St. Paul himself was shipwrecked on this island, so it is only fitting that the spearhead should be venerated on an island which saved the great saint's life."

"How could the Pope condone such corruption and greed?"

"My sentiments exactly. I believe Matthias at this point scoffed, saying how he never regretted leaving Brother Gerard's inner circle and renouncing all ties with the order and its insidious plans to rule the world. He had given all the years he cared to give to their heretical cause, insisting that he was going home and asking the other man to step aside and let him pass. The other one laughed out loud, a cruel, heartless laugh. He said he would gladly let him pass if Matthias gave him the Holy Relic. Only then could he live to see his family again. Matthias told him he was a fool, for he no longer possessed the relic."

"So, Matthias tried to leave last night and ran into one of the two Knights Hospitaller. Well, we know Matthias told this man the truth, he no longer had the Relic in his possession."

"There's more. The next part of the conversation was very strange indeed. The other man said a prayer for Matthias. He then gave him a kiss on both cheeks and simply stepped aside, allowing Matthias to enter the stable. Matthias entered alone. The other man waited outside for only a moment, then left, disappearing into the woods behind the stable. I heard horses then and feared I would be seen if I tried to cross the path towards the Anchorage. So I came here instead. It is a safe place to hide, to observe, and not to be seen."

"So you were here when Brother Hugo announced the death of Matthias?"

"Yes. But what I do not understand is Rudegerus's part in all of this. I fear all of this is only the beginning of the answer to this mystery."

Volmar's brow furrowed. "And now, the hooded hunchback wrongly accused Rudegerus of possessing the relic. We know differently. However, Rudegerus is not an innocent bystander. He has had some association with this man and is frightened of this man's malice."

"Brother Rudegerus's fear is more than the grave. It is as if his life is a lie that is unraveling. I think, Volmar, Rudegerus fears more the humiliation of the retelling of his past deceptions."

"Could Rudegerus have murdered Matthias for this old man? Could he have been the one to commit such a crime in cold blood, at such an hour?"

"I think not. Granted, nothing gives a fearful man more courage than the fear of another. No, whoever is committing this crime lives in a world of his own making, where there are no absolute truths. When you think about it, the mind is such a paradox. You can think your way into a corner and never figure out how you got there. The heart, however, isn't so indecisive. Either you love someone or you do not; you don't entertain a half-baked, partial, sometimes, maybe attitude about love, respect, appreciation, gratitude, warmth, forgiveness, or any other qualities this person has chosen to ignore and belittle as well. The person we are searching for trivializes the most important things in life, Brother Volmar, while maximizing the least. This is his nature and his personality, formed long before he arrived here to Disibodenberg."

"Sister Hildegard, you mentioned earlier that what killed Matthias was not human. Why would you say such a thing?"

"I do not know. At the time, I heard a noise, a sound I could not place. It is also a feeling I have, which I cannot fully explain. Only after I heard of Matthias's hanging did it make more sense."

"You are musical, so your ears are more sensitive to sounds than perhaps my own. Think: Are you certain it was not voices inside the stable you heard?"

"I am sure. I heard something inhuman. I am sorry. I didn't think at the time that the man was letting Matthias leave, knowing he was walking into a trap. And the hooded hunchback we just witnessed, the one who wants the Holy Relic by Prime, he has the same laugh as the man confronting Matthias outside the stables."

"I've heard it before as well. The man's name is Ulrich."

"Oh, Brother Volmar, what are we going to do?" Hildegard reached out again for Volmar's hand and squeezed it. "I remember watching how snowflakes seemed to fall away from him, almost as if they knew of the evil that emanated from him."

Volmar took her hand and stared down at it, so small in his. "Are you cold?"

"No—why do you ask?" She looked across at Volmar.

"Your hand is trembling." Gently he kissed each fingertip. How could he repress such strong feelings, they stirred in him a desire beyond words, beyond vows, beyond the physical confines of his soul. He had lived in books so long that having his spirit leap beyond its boundaries moved him deeply. He drew Sister Hildegard towards him as he was willing this moment to stand still in time.

Hildegard regarded him with a faint smile but held back, her face full of a pale and gentle transcendence.

"I feel like a man compelled by an addiction. I cannot get you out of my mind." Volmar knew she was looking directly at him and through him with that uncanny ability of hers to read his thoughts.

"We've taken vows, Volmar," Hildegard whispered, studying him, unable to find the words to express all that she was feeling. For the first time in her life, she questioned her decision to deny herself the affections of a flesh and blood man. She was shivering and longed for his warm embrace. Could she set aside her promised vows and the strict dictates of the church for one man's love?

At long last, Volmar began, slowly at first, and then, fighting hard to keep his voice from cracking, he said, "Pray for me, for I am shaken by my shortcomings."

"You are like a dark cloud next to the sun. There's a ring around the iris of your blue eyes. They are fiery eyes, clever, hot-tempered, energetic, and keen-minded."

"I am but a man with a man's desire," he countered, clearly flustered. "I may be mad, for given the way that I feel I'm not entirely confident of my hold on reality. Would we truly be causing a violation in the order of things to give in to these feelings? Is what I'm feeling towards you so unnatural that it should be considered a sin? Why must our faith deny our life? Feelings are never as black and white as the constructs of our religious order dictate."

"With God's help," Hildegard said, pressing her forefinger to his lips to quiet him. "I will pray for both of us that this love we share be always expressed as charity and true kindness to one another." She tenderly touched his cheek. "My beloved brother in Christ, you and I are two halves of one whole, called upon to dwell together in a sanctified unity of mind, not body. Spiritual love will help us aspire toward our Creator. Through our ascent, we will glimpse a higher, more perfect love which is free from the bonds of fleshly passions and more perfect in His eyes. You will see . . . I will make you see . . . "

Volmar both envied and despised Hildegard's certainty at the same time. How could she be led by a perfect clarity and he be so consumed by ambiguousness? He coughed nervously, regaining his composure. "I will need to escort you safely back to the Anchorage, Sister. In a short while this place will be taken over by the village Magistrate, his men, and the concerned citizens of Staudernheim. Word of murder travels quickly; pray that justice will be equally as swift."

Hildegard nodded in agreement and lowered her hood close down over her face. Soundlessly she followed Volmar's lead as the two left the alcove of Saint Peter's altar. Rudegerus, if he heard or felt their presence, did not respond. He did not open his eyes or speak. He lay motionless, sprawled out face down on the cold stone floor, his hood over his face.

They parted at the window of the Anchorage. "Brother Volmar, please be careful. I have a feeling your life will also be threatened by this inhuman murderer. There's been so much death, for truly the

"...Would we truly be causing a violation in the order of things to give in to these feelings?"

Holy Relic's curse lives on." Deep down, she knew her warnings could not hold him and keep him from harm.

Snow floated down, belying the depth of horror now surrounding them. Volmar felt numb, but he forced himself to smile back at Hildegard, trying to humor her and shed his own embarrassment over his confession of attraction towards her. Maybe it was the protective womb of living within a prophecy, or the supernatural power of possessing the Spear of Destiny, or perhaps it was more the careless feeling of the invincibility of youth. Whatever, Volmar did not feel a need to proceed with caution.

Book 8: Beyond Redemption

Chapter I: An Empty Vessel

Outside the Anchorage at Disibodenberg Monastery

Dawn

Uda's words echoed from the past in Hildegard's mind as she watched Volmar slowly trudge up the hill, ascending the snowy bank leading back to the stables. "Listen, child, to the stories people tell you. There will be stories of horror, of courage, and yes, even of joy. It is in the retelling of these stories, these most enduring life stories, that you'll come to appreciate who these people are, what troubles them, as well as what inspires them. Once you hear their life stories, you are no longer in the company of strangers. It is this connection which binds us all to the Almighty."

Uda was a big part of Hildegard's most enduring life stories. She was the parent who refused to reject her strange child, a teacher who saw in her a mind of great potential and promise, and a master herbalist who instructed her on the value and respect for all of God's miraculous creations. Uda knew the right potions to mix to cure any ailment, even those hidden from others and only apparent in one's mind. As a child, Hildegard never left her side, assisting her as she ministered to the poor, dressing the wounds of the villagers, as Jutta now ministered to the eternity of their souls. Uda's teachings, to young Hildegard, expressed the practical side of faith, the side where one's handiwork held precedence over one's private prayer life. Hildegard knew that she owed much of her own yearnings to Uda's down-to-earth folk wisdom and now more than ever, she longed for the old woman's sage advice.

Volmar was now a smudge in the blurry drifts of snow that relentlessly fell about her. She did not have the heart to tell him of her own visions, those that foresaw the return of the lost father of his youth. This she knew to be Volmar's most persistent life story, and one she knew would surely end in tragedy. And yet, there was more to Volmar's story, another man she could not identify, his role still shrouded in mystery.

Hildegard shivered uncontrollably, longing for the warmth and certainty of the heavenly light. She could not call upon a vision, it had to seek her out, and for the moment she felt like an empty vessel, wanting and abandoned. Deliberately, she brought the fingers Volmar had kissed to her lips. Was she deceiving herself? Could Disibodenberg be her safe spiritual harbor, or was she merely accepting a future as a caged bird? In time would her song fade perhaps to a whimper?

It was so tempting to run away with Volmar. Wouldn't their life together be so much more than the prospect of being locked away in a damp and cold Anchorage attending to the self-inflicted wounds of her Anchoress? Could she survive such a dismal future?

Hildegard felt for the herbal remedies in the pouch under her habit. In all the turmoil, she'd forgotten the reason for her mission. Their crushed leaves and seeds had the power to heal, and yet Jutta resented her efforts and made each of her attempts to restore her to health a lost cause. She contemplated her breath as it escaped in great wisps of smoke. Are not all the arts serving human desires and needs derived from the breath that God sent into the human body? God gave her, a female, a peculiar charge to use her mind, her hands, and her music to reach Him, and by example inspire others to do so. And yet, He also gave her a singular vision that alienated others and set her at odds even with her own Anchoress. If she hadn't been given to the church, surely she would have been locked away as mad, or worse, burned as a witch. The enclosure ceremony formally confirmed what her unique gifts had always dictated: She could only survive here, at an Anchorage, locked away and on the thin, fragile border between this life and the life hereafter.

Hildegard lingered outside the ice-coated wood-framed window. Behind the leather flap, she heard the deep, steady sleeping sounds of Jutta and Hiltrud's less elegant snoring. Both were blissfully oblivious to the chaos going on around them. They knew nothing of Matthias's murder or the Holy Relic and nothing of the love deepening between her and Volmar. Was this how her life would be? A life lived in the midst of others, yet always separate and lonely?

Volmar in his anguish had rebuked her high-minded, reclusive life. As he put it, "Is what I'm feeling towards you so unnatural that it should be considered a sin?" Had she been too hasty in making the decision to stay the course and not give in to love and stray from her vows? And yet, there was also something to be said for love from afar; love without hope of consummation. Could this be love in its purest sense?

There was an unexpected noise behind her, footsteps of one trying not to be detected. She turned around a moment too late. In an instant, a large cold hand seized her wrists and knotted her arms behind her back; a sharp knife pressed at her throat. A deep voice whispered fanatically into her right ear. "Boy, where is the Holy Relic? I saw you conspiring with Volmar. I must have it now!"

Hildegard knew who her assailant was even though she could not see him. She detected a strong smell of distrust emanating from him towards all human beings. Rudegerus must have witnessed Volmar and her leaving the altar of Saint Peter and stalked them, hoping they had the Holy Relic, which could save his life. She sensed that Rudegerus's soul was in a stupefied sleep and did not know what his flesh was doing. A demon was warping him into insanity and was moving his limbs outwardly with its clever ways. God had allowed this to happen because of the man's own arrogance. Somehow she must confound this malevolent spirit.

Indignantly, Hildegard lowered her voice, attempting to sound like a boy, and answered him deliberately. "Sir, if you let go of my hands, I shall give you what you deserve."

Rudegerus had plunged so far into madness he'd lost all sense of reason. He relented, dropping his knife to his side and waited as Hildegard reached inside her habit. She fingered the leather pouch of herbs she'd stolen earlier from the Infirmary for Jutta. "Lord, help me," she whispered before flinging a fistful of herbs into the shocked face of Rudegerus.

The terrified monk let out a yelp and cried, "My eyes! What have you done to my eyes, you fiend!"

Hildegard wasted no time. She lifted the leather flap of the Anchorage's window and within seconds slipped through into safety.

By the time Rudegerus opened his stinging eyes, his victim had disappeared without a trace. He held his face upward, welcoming the cold flakes of falling snow as they soothed the burning sensation in his eyes and growled bitterly at God.

Chapter 2: Ruse

Stable at Disibodenberg Monastery

6th of November, Lauds

Bells of Prime would ring in less than two hours. Rudegerus's existence, Volmar reasoned, however miserable, was not beyond redemption. Inaction was not the answer to this frightful predicament. Volmar quickened his steps, determined to uncover this nest of serpents. The heavy snowfall made his hike back up the hill more arduous. Halfway up, he paused and spread his arms wide. He twirled about several times, lifting his head to the heavens, tasting the cold flakes of snow and thanked the Holy Spirit for Sister Hildegard's safe return to the Anchorage and for her professed love towards him, even if it was of a spiritual nature only. And he also prayed for guidance.

Volmar stomped the snow from his boots as he entered the stable. Several men were standing on the edge of a cart, under Matthias's corpse. As one held a burning torch aloft to shed light, another one supported the body, and the other one cut the rope. Matthias's body collapsed with a heavy thud onto a cloth. Conversation in the stable fell silent out of respect for the fallen knight, as one of the men wrapped his body in a clean cloth.

The Magistrate raised his hand to keep the silence and announced in a voice well accustomed to diplomacy and leadership, "Matthias's body will not be desecrated in any way. In my educated opinion, I believe we have been called at this early hour to investigate a heinous crime of murder, not suicide. Matthias's body will be carefully laid out in the Infirmary where it will be further examined by Brother Paulus and our own learned village physician. Perhaps this examination will throw further light on this dreadful mystery."

Abbot Burchard looked visibly relieved to hear the Magistrate declare this verdict, the same as his own. The heavy wheels of the wagon jerked forward as the sturdy mules strained and tugged, pulling the wagon through a snowdrift, its wooden wheels crunching on the crisp surface.

Several horses suddenly entered the courtyard beside the stable's entrance. The steam rising from their nostrils and panting mouths made it difficult to make out their exact number. The soldier who seemed to be the leader of this search party dismounted and went directly to report their progress to the Magistrate.

"Quite a storm . . . I'm surprised to see you back so soon. Any luck?" the Magistrate said, his voice almost silenced by the howling wind.

"We've been tracking two horses all night. Come to find we've fallen for a simple ruse." [91]

"Explain yourself," Wolfe said, trying to keep his disappointment at bay.

"Men, you may all take a break." The leader dismissed the others with a wave. Turning to his superior, he said with little emotion, "I will do better than explain myself, I will show you. Come." Volmar approached with the others, noting all but one of the search team had dismounted. The leader walked up to the powerful warhorse and took its reins from his sergeant. The man left in its saddle was slumped forward, his face indistinguishable under the wrappings of woolens.

The chatter slowed down, then all the voices around died. There was a brief moment of bewilderment. The Magistrate put his arm on the Abbot and the two watched as the sergeant hoisted himself up into the saddle and pulled off the mysterious rider's woolens. In the light of the torches Volmar saw the poor man's face. It was the very image of death—rigid, taut, and dry, the color of his cheeks yellowing into shades of brown, like a bruise. The eyes were fixed, staring sightlessly at the audience who beheld him with shock. The Abbot and Volmar crossed themselves.

Volmar approached the body and slipped the leather glove off the dead man's right hand. He could see the man was missing both his forefinger and half of his middle finger. He turned to the Magistrate.

---

[91] Ruse: A wily trick.

"Justice has been only partly secured. This is the body of the murderer's accomplice. I believe his name was Donato."

Chapter 3: A Devil's Triangle

Infirmary at Disibodenberg Monastery

6th of November, Lauds

"His companion did in fact call him Donato. He, like Mathias, was a brother of the Knights Hospitaller. He spoke with an Italian accent and fondly recalled his family in Florence." Paulus drew up the sleeve on the dead man's arm and showed the severe cut he'd bandaged. "I dressed this wound on Saturday. This man's so-called friend had cut him while sparring outside my Infirmary."

"Do you know the name of his dueling companion?" the Magistrate asked. His brows were knitted intently after instructing his men to lay the two soldiers out on the stone slabs in Paulus's laboratory.

"His name is Ulrich, and he too belonged to the secret order of the Knight's Hospitaller of Saint John. Both were paying guests here at Disibodenberg." Paulus decided to leave Sophie's ordeal out of the discussion for the time being. She had been through enough torment for a while, and even if she could be awakened, he knew she would be in no condition to answer questions. "Ulrich has, in my opinion, the temperament of a python, docile and placid until he feels in danger. Then he will strike with a vengeance. As you know, despite an owner's affection, snakes will not build a relationship with people. These two had been on the road for years, and you see what Ulrich has done to his friend."

Volmar bent over Donato's corpse for another moment, seeing the same clean, expert wound as Atif's in this man's heart. "He tried to warn me, but I didn't really listen." He backed off. It was hard to believe that all this had happened within the past two days. "Three deaths," he whispered in disbelief, "a devil's triangle. Father," Volmar said, lightly touching the Abbot's shoulder. Abbot Burchard jerked from the touch but instantly relaxed upon seeing Brother Volmar. "Father, could I have a moment with you? I must speak with you—it is urgent."

Volmar took the Abbot's arm and led him to the common room by the roaring fire, well out of hearing range. He gave the details of what he observed and overheard while hiding in the secret chamber, and then he paused. "Father, there is more, but I must beg your forgiveness first before I reveal how I found out."

"Brother Volmar, please tell me that you have not engaged in wrongful acts trying to unravel this murder." His voice was both sharp and protective.

"I have not; but you see, Sister Hildegard . . . " Volmar began.

"Oh dear, what is it with you two and having to abide by the dictates of the church's rules? Is the Holy Relic safe?"

"It is, Father. But Sister Hildegard is the one who has been visiting the Infirmary late at night."

"Go on, I am listening," the Abbot said sternly, focusing on the crown of thorns carved on his Savior's head on the crucifix which hung around his neck.

"Sister Jutta endangered her health so much that she required immediate medical attention. Sister Hildegard disguised herself as a monk and went between Compline and Matins to find the herbs she needed to concoct the healing remedies which have strengthened and returned a modicum of health to our Anchoress."

"I see. To her credit, she is a young woman of action. So, last night on one of her Infirmary pilgrimages, she must have seen something, for it is between those hours when the Magistrate feels the hanging took place."

"She actually saw very little, but she overheard a great deal. She was hiding in very close proximity to the stable doors, so she was able to eavesdrop on the conversation between Matthias and the man whom we suspect to be Ulrich." Volmar went on and explained the link between Brother Gerard's desire to retrieve the Spear of Longinus and his plan to move the Knights Hospitaller of Saint John from Palestine to the island of Malta. Abbot Burchard listened intently. Volmar also told of the chance meeting he'd overheard in the sanctuary between Ulrich and Brother Rudegerus, and the fact that Rudegerus's life was in considerable danger because he did not possess the Holy Relic.

"You are right, it doesn't bode well for our own misguided brother." The Abbot rubbed his brow. "He is acting stranger than usual out of guilt, I am sure of it; but guilt over what exactly?"

"I do not know. Ulrich must have been sorely upset when he did not find the Holy Relic on Matthias's person and now feels that Rudegerus knows something of its whereabouts, which we know is not true."

"Nevertheless, Volmar, Rudegerus's life has been threatened, and we must do everything in our power to protect him."

"I know. That's why I've come up with a plan," Volmar continued, explaining how he was going to entrap the murderer.

The Abbot nodded a firm assent. "I'll explain it all to the Magistrate, and we will be there at the well at Prime. Go with my blessing, my son. But be careful, we are dealing with a man who would think nothing of taking a human life to satisfy his own personal greed."

The Magistrate eyed the two suspiciously as he approached and cleared his voice loudly. "More revelations?" he asked, studying Volmar's features, as if looking for answers to a much deeper, more inscrutable question.

This was the first time Volmar had been so close to the Magistrate. Before, his encounters were always perfunctory. He would simply bow politely and leave the Abbot to discuss important matters without listening ears or recorded words. Yet for some reason, right now, Volmar felt exposed in this man's gaze. It was a feeling he'd never experienced before. What did the Magistrate know that he did not? It was as if a part of his soul were under this man's thumb. "He knows of my past," Volmar thought suddenly. "He already knows of my father's connections with the Knights Hospitaller and his evil deeds in Jerusalem. Could I have such wicked yearnings in my own soul that he is cautioning me with his gaze to keep them under control?"

Instinctively, Volmar stepped back into the shadows and gave the Magistrate a wider berth. He was thankful for the Abbot's protective wing and wondered how long he could hide beneath it.

"Come, Wolfe, my friend." Abbot Burchard turned to the Magistrate. "There have been further developments. We must discuss them in private over a light meal." The Abbot squeezed Volmar's shoulder, before taking the arm of the Magistrate and leading him and his entourage back towards his private chambers. Many already were murmuring to themselves, speculating as to what the new developments could possibly be.

Chapter 4: Resurgence of Grief

Infirmary at Disibodenberg Monastery

6th of November, After Lauds

Isabella heard nothing of the conversations of murder swarming around her. Nor had she truly acknowledged the two dead bodies that had moments earlier been carried through the common room to Paulus's laboratory. Her consciousness still slept deep within her wakened self, and yet it had a desire, a restless yearning, for change. She rose quietly and slipped her skirt on over her tunic.

In the pallet next to hers, an elderly woman murmured darkly to her in a heavy Celtic accent. "In my country on a night like this, banshees[92] will come howling up our mountain at the smell of a dead soul. Listen," she paused, "do you hear them singing?" She inclined her head to the window. "If you want my advice, I'd stay close and not wander off. Those banshees will surely try to use their feminine wiles to trick those poor men's Heaven-bound spirits into taking the Devil's own road to Hell!"

"Shush, mother," the elder woman's daughter said, yawning and stretching. We're guests in this monastery; such pagan beliefs are not permitted." The daughter gave Isabella a weak smile. "Surely, the worst of the storm has passed."

The old woman snorted at her daughter's discomfort. She lay back, folding her arms to make a pillow for her head. Slowly a smug look of satisfaction spread across her face. "I told you I saw that man's death in the fire last night and said there would be more murders. Mark my words. Death is not finished here."

---

[92] Banshees: Female spirits in Gaelic folklore whose wailing warns a family of an approaching death.

"Please forgive her," the daughter said regretfully. "She's always had these strange nightmare sights; frightening visions whenever she stares too long at any fire."

Isabella nodded as if she understood and went over to wash her hands and face in the rose water kept in a wooden trencher on the stool beneath the clothes pegs. Curiously, she studied the dressing Brother Paulus had wound around her forearm earlier yesterday afternoon, completely oblivious as to how it got there or why. She knotted her long red hair and slipped on her shoes. "No matter," she reasoned stolidly, "it is time to go." Time, she knew, was like a river and no one can stand still against its current. She reached for the jar of worms, knowing she could brave any winter storm to find a home for her children.

Isabella turned her thoughts away from the throbbing pain in her arm. In her mind, all else had been silenced in order to listen for the cries of her children. No one interrupted her movements or even saw as she passed by, their huddled voices low behind the screens in anxious whispers or prayers. Isabella slid a latch on a plank door leading to the common corridor between the two halls of the Infirmary and shouldered it open. It swung heavily and not smoothly. She searched the corridor and saw the door to Brother Paulus's laboratory had been left ajar.

Isabella entered the Infirmarian's laboratory with a single thought once she had taken in the two dead bodies stretched out on the slab: Here was a place where the division between God and man was less distinct, and only here would her children be happy.

"There, there, my dears," she said, puckering her lips and cooing softly at the jar of worms. "You'll rest soon."

She went to the body of the man with a deep gash on his calf. In a flash of insight she knew she'd found a better home for her children.

She turned over the jar above the gaping wound. The worms squirmed around for only a moment and then went deathly pale and stiff. Isabella reacted to this in slow motion, finding for a second it was almost as if she couldn't feel she was there. It was as if the cumulative effects of so much pain had shocked her into an emotional numbness. When she could feel again, it gave her such a resurgence of grief, she collapsed to the floor. The lantern she held tipped to one side, sending the candle inside tumbling with her to the floor. Its darting flames singed and started to burn the folds of the linen cloth draped at the dead man's feet. When she started screaming, she stretched her arms out above her head, trying to claw down God in all His power from the heavens themselves.

This was how the men found her, screeching piteously, surrounded by a ring of fire. The men crowded through the entrance, falling over each other as they rushed to put out the flames. Thankfully, parts of the linen cloth were still damp from the falling snow, and the heavy wet cloth suffocated its own flames.

Sophie breathed smoke in the cold air as she leaned in closer over Isabella, cradling the grown woman in her arms like a baby. Sophie's own eyes had grits of sand in them and her mouth was sour from her heavy sleep. She did not understand Isabella's words but felt their meaning nevertheless.

Brother Paulus's massive stature commanded order even before any words were spoken. He covered his mouth and nose with the sleeve of his cassock and went to open the window—a blast of cold air filled the room and began to lift the choking smoke. Paulus thanked the men for putting out the flames and advised them to step outside a while to breathe in fresh air and clear their lungs. Fortunately, the flames had been put out before they had caused much damage to his beloved laboratory.

When the last of the men left, Paulus bent over and saw Isabella's jar lying empty and overturned on the floor below Matthias's untouched body. Only then did he fully understand what had transpired: Her worm children lay white and rigid in the open cut on Matthias's calf. Here was all the proof he needed to verify what had killed the knight and what could have just as easily killed him.

Chapter 5: Addressing Death

Stables at Disibodenberg Monastery

6th of November, After Lauds

Volmar waited until the last of the onlookers left the stables. He then slipped unnoticed into the tack room just off of the stall where the horses had been the day before. His idea was simple. If he could find a suitable spearhead to substitute for the real Holy Relic, he could slip it into the well's bucket. Then when the bells chimed for prayers at Prime and Ulrich came to pick it up, the Lord Magistrate and his men would be there waiting in the woods to arrest him.

Volmar held his torch high, scanning the open shelves, knowing there would be no chance of finding any weapons amongst Brother Hugo's tools and harnesses. However, there was one tool in particular, he remembered, one he had used many times to turn over the compost as a stable boy years ago. When altered, he figured it could pass convincingly for a thousand-year-old spearhead.

There were the usual tack supplies such as saddles, bridles, reins, and halters. "Now where's that spade?" he muttered, opening and peering into cupboards and drawers. The hook where it usually hung was empty. It was in no way sharp enough to be a spearhead, but a thousand years would take the edge off of most weapons, he imagined. Finally when Volmar looked under the work bench behind the table, he found the gardening spade sitting upright in a bucket with the rake. He turned it over in his hand. It was so unlike Brother Hugo to leave his tools unwashed and not put away properly. He wondered who had been there using it and for what reason. And why hadn't it been put back where it belonged?

Volmar prayed under his breath, "Forgive me, Brother Hugo," before twisting loose the spade's small wooden handle. With a few more turns the handle fell away from the iron-forged blade. He reached for a clean leather polishing cloth and thought after carefully wrapping it that he had a convincing-enough relic to carry through with his plan.

The well was situated less than thirty paces beyond the compost pile out back. It was comfortably centered between the kitchen gardens and the stables. With his torch in hand and his hoax under wraps, he quietly exited the stables. The cobbled path had several inches of newly fallen snow. As Brother Hugo's stable assistant, Volmar remembered taking many trips down this very path, carrying heavy buckets full of well water for the trough or picking up rotten apples that fell from the trees of the orchard to feed the pigs. The clearing provided a serene setting for the stone well. He entered it, envisioning how the arrest would take place. In less than two hours, he reckoned, dropping the fake relic into the old bucket, the well would not be granting this murderer's secret wish.

Volmar stood back and stared at the well, his mind drifting back to the scene in the sanctuary. In his opinion, Rudegerus had behaved in a cowardly way towards Ulrich's threat. Surely he could have reasoned with the hooded hunchback and told him that he had no idea where the real Holy Relic was. Volmar couldn't understand why Rudegerus had given up so easily and lay sniveling like a bewildered child on the stone floor before the altar.

Snowdrifts surrounded him. Returning to the stables the way he had come, Volmar trudged back past the compost pile. His torch's light bounced off of something silvery partially buried in the compost heap. He broke off a twig from a nearby tree and used it to unearth the shiny silver object. Curiously, a handful of peach pits rolled away from it. Volmar caught a strong whiff of almonds. As soon as he cleared the dirt from the silvery object, he knew at once what it was. A silver claw-spur from a fighting cock! He remembered Sophie's warning about a rooster. He turned it over with his stick. Again a musty smell of bitter almonds seemed to be coming directly from it. Volmar thought back to what Brother Paulus had said and backed away, thankful he had used a stick to unearth the silver spur. So, he reasoned, Matthias's murderer was indeed not human. Hildegard had been right! Matthias had been fatally wounded by a cyanide-dipped claw on a fighting cock! What mind could conceive of such horror?

He tripped over what appeared to be a gray stone and fell backwards. He froze. There, lying off to the side of the compost heap was Samson. A dusting of snow lightly covered his furry body. Volmar sank the torch upright into the compost heap before lifting his cat. Instead of Samson's welcoming warmth, he felt a cold stiffness; a stiffness that told him the cat was already dead and had been for a while. "Samson," he murmured, burying his face into his cat's strange smelling fur. "My little friend." His face quivered and melted suddenly. Tears fell, dampening his cheeks.

His breathing increased almost to the point of panting. Just as swiftly, an overwhelming dizziness came over him. Volmar touched his head. His eyes started to itch and burn. He felt weak, intensely weak, as if his insides were rebelling against all their usual actions and had decided to retreat from duty. He coughed. Fear suddenly enveloped him. In his grief he had failed to register that Samson smelled of bitter almonds. His cat had been poisoned, and now so was he! He rose, stumbling away from Samson's tainted body and the compost pile.

There was a rustle, followed by the sound twigs make when they're snapped. Out from the cover of a large tree, Michael and his younger brother Gabriel emerged. "So sorry to disturb you brother, but are you all right, sir?"

Volmar raised his horror-stricken face and tried to say something. His throat ached. He shook his head instead before collapsing into the snow bank.

"Go find Brother Johannes, and hurry!" Michael instructed his brother with authority. The older boy bent down and turned Volmar over, cradling the young monk's head in his lap. He loosened Volmar's collar and cleared the hair from his eyes. Volmar's eyelids fluttered. Instinctively, the boy started talking to Volmar, somehow knowing that he shouldn't fall asleep. "Help is on its way. Gabe's quick. He even runs in his sleep, he does. At night I hear him panting and sweating. In the morning he remembers nothing, which is probably a good thing."

The boy heard the Iron Gate creak open in the distance. "Brother Johannes will know what to do. Come on, wake up, brother," he said, gently nudging Volmar.

Volmar inclined his head, but kept his eyes shut. He heard the boy but, only as if he was speaking to him through water.

"Wake up!" Michael said, fierce with determination, this time slapping Volmar's cheek. He rocked back and forth erratically with no rhythm. "Do you hear me?" he said, loudly addressing Death in the eerie silence of the orchard surrounding him and added with a roar, "Stay away!"

With tears welling up in his eyes, Gabe swung the Iron Gate wide open and took off towards the kitchens. The boys knew Brother Johannes's schedule by heart. Often they would follow him on his rounds, observing his gentle manner from a safe distance, somehow taking comfort in their deformed caretaker's routines. Sure enough, Brother Johannes came around the corner of the stables pushing a wheelbarrow, carrying food scraps to discard from the kitchen, just as Gabe anticipated. Johannes was whistling, enjoying the prospect of having a meal of roast fowl. The cook, in honor of the Magistrate's unexpected visit, was preparing a rooster that was left mysteriously on his doorstep overnight. The cook had promised to save Johannes a wing after serving the Abbot and the Magistrate their special meal.

"Come quick!" Gabe said, running up to the old monk and tugging fervently at his sleeve.

Johannes was flattered to see the boy trust him enough to approach him. He'd been secretly praying for months for the boys to get over their fear of him. "What is it, little Gabriel?"

Gabe blurted out, "Your friend is hurt!"

Propelled by fear, Brother Johannes had little difficulty keeping up with Gabriel. Soon, the two arrived behind the stables. Brother Johannes knelt beside Michael and met the boy's eyes with an understanding that the situation was serious. Volmar retched suddenly and barely had time to twist to his side, before vomiting violently. Thankfully, his stomach was nearly empty and all that surfaced was colorless bile with the same peculiar stench of bitter almonds.

"Brother Volmar!" Johannes cried, lifting him up with his rough hands. Volmar's legs buckled. Brother Johannes knelt with Volmar's limp body over the water trough. He broke the thin layer of ice with his fist and splashed the water all over the young monk's face. "Your heartbeat sounds as if you've swallowed a hundred crickets. What happened?"

Brother Volmar formulated the words in his head. "I must find the Magistrate and the Abbot." A thick fog swirled about, causing mischief with his thoughts. "I must tell them of the fighting cock, the poisoned silver claw, and the bloody gash in Matthias's leg." Yet his words came out all garbled.

"Don't you worry, little brother, I'll carry you myself to see Brother Paulus, he'll know what to do. Come along boys, I need your help."

Chapter 6: Old Wounds

Abbot's Personal Quarters at Disibodenberg Monastery

6th of November, Before Prime

Wolfe sat across the table from the Abbot. There had been much to discuss after Atif's body was removed and taken to the Infirmary. Wolfe was prepared to make an arrest when the murderer returned for the fake relic at the well. He sat closest to the fire smoldering in the grate. There was a fine dew of sweat breaking on his high forehead. "Did you say that Matthias knew Symon of Bermersheim?"

"He knew of him—there is a difference," the Abbot answered, nodding to Brother Andres, the cellarer, who placed on the table in front of the two a platter of a roasted capon[93] and refilled their wine goblets. The Abbot lightly touched Brother Andres's arm and requested, "Before returning to the kitchen, would you please find Rudegerus and ask him to come here right away? We need to talk to him."

The Magistrate stared down at the glowing ashes, taking in the pungent smell of the fresh fowl and wondering if it would be rude to say he had suddenly lost his appetite.

The Abbot lifted the carving knife and slowly started apportioning the breast meat of the bird, neatly cutting thin regular slices. He addressed the Magistrate, finishing his thoughts. "Brother Volmar fears that Symon of Bermersheim is also a key player in Brother Gerard's secret society. Volmar's father went to the Holy Land in 1098 and never returned."

Wolfe heaved a deep sigh. "What else do you know of this young monk's family?"

"Not much, really. Ten years ago, he showed up at our gates carrying his little sister Anya's dead body in his arms. As far as he knew, he had no other relations. For months I inquired of Volmar's family and all I found out was that Volmar's father's name was Symon and he had left to fight in the Holy War for Jerusalem. His mother died of the

[93] Capon: Roasted rooster, considered a delicacy at the time.

same fever as her daughter. I did not know until yesterday that Symon fought as a fellow brother in the Knights Hospitaller of Saint John in Jerusalem. Volmar knew this and never shared it with me."

"Symon was a fool to leave his wife with two small children. Anya was still an infant and Volmar was only three years of age. It was just like Symon to be so cavalier with Katherina's welfare and the lives of his children. It does not surprise me that he would serve as an influential leader in a brotherhood that is after this Holy Relic and the power it possesses."

"You speak as if you know this man well."

The Magistrate looked visibly ill at ease. "Let's just say, Father, that I once knew Symon; and yes, I agree with Matthias's assessment that he is the devil incarnate. He could very likely be a part of this evil scheme to retrieve the Holy Relic."

The Abbot served a portion of the roasted fowl onto the Magistrate's plate. "Volmar has a gentler soul. I have a hard time detecting any vice in him such as what you and Matthias attribute to his father. Oh, don't get me wrong, there is a fire that burns in him which might consume a lesser mind. He is methodical and detailed. He rules with his mind, yet acknowledges his heart and keeps it there as a scale to measure the degree of right and wrong in everything he experiences. In this way, he exercises so much more control over his emotions than most and certainly more than what has been ascribed to Brother Symon. For him to have the seed of greed and power planted in him is hard to believe. If anything, my Lord, he has your sense of order and justice, and your desire to right terrible wrongs."

"Am I that obvious?"

"Wolfe, you two share the same walk, the same square shoulders, and look at your eyes—can't you see? They're the same vibrant blue. The older Volmar gets, the more he looks like you."

"Forgive me, Father. I am no longer hungry." The Magistrate pushed his plate away.

The Abbot stared down at his plate, his fingers laced, waiting patiently for the rest of the story to be told.

The Magistrate got up and stoked the fire. Slowly it came to life, as his memories were also stirring. "Symon and I grew up together and were close friends a long time ago. When we came of age, we both shared affections for Katherina, Volmar and Anya's mother." In the rising flames he could almost make out Katherina's youthful face; it had been so long ago, he'd almost forgotten how beautiful she had been. In every aspect of his business and other affairs, he ran things with a cool, ruthless efficiency. Discipline and obedience were paramount in his world and, until now, he had kept at bay the ordeal he faced nearly eighteen years ago. He kept his voice low, as if by speaking louder her image would become unbearably real and overpower what he knew he must now confess.

"Katherina had told Symon that she did not love him and wanted to marry me instead. However, he deceived her and went to her father, convincing him that she should not marry beneath her status. So her family conspired with Symon and forced Katherina to marry him, even though she loved and wanted me."

Wolfe leaned back in his chair and wiped his forehead with his handkerchief. This was a secret no one else knew anything about. It was amazing how secrets could be infused with so much more than simply the truth. Now, as he stretched across great spans of time to try to turn his feelings into words, he realized that the old wounds were still as raw and painful as they had been all those many years ago. "You see, my family was not of the noble class. Our fortunes, which are considerable, were made through trade and business dealings, not through birth." Flames licked and spitted, illuminating his features. "All of this happened a lifetime ago. The night before the wedding Katherina came to me. She was a great beauty. That night I held her, unwilling to let her go. I have since realized that it was an act of love and revenge; the son she had in due time was mine, not Symon's."

"I see," the Abbot said, thinking back to the day Volmar came to the monastery. "I suspected as much, for over the past ten years you have often inquired about Volmar's health and how he was getting on here at the monastery. I took such interest to be more than idle curiosity. I've often wondered how Volmar's mother managed without her husband for four years until her death. You supported them, did you not?"

"Symon left for the war after a terrible argument with Katherina. He was a man ruled by his insane jealousy," Wolfe continued darkly. "She was abandoned, yet she wasn't free to remarry, nor was there any security left in her marriage to him. It was a trap he'd set for her out of spite. Katherina became like an island unto herself, completely surrounded by water. My financial help was but a foot bridge."

The Abbot shook his head in resignation. "How about her own family, surely they would take her in and care for her in her time of trial."

"Katherina told them the truth and instead of forgiveness she found condescension. They did not want their kinsmen to know of her transgression. Her family essentially disowned her. I suppose, the health of a heart has much to do with the body's defenses against fevers. By the time I found out about her fever it was already too late." He paused and cleared his throat, remembering how with a soft pass of his hand, he had closed her eyes forever. "Anya was infected and I knew her only hope was to come to you and Brother Paulus here at the monastery for treatment. I was the stranger who found the two still clinging to their mother's corpse hoping she would awaken. Anya would not let go of her brother, so I dropped both of them off at your gates on that bitter November night ten years ago. I knew you would find in Volmar an able and willing mind. At the time it was important that his illegitimacy and how it ruined his mother's life not sour his impressionable spirit. He has flourished under your tutelage. I owe to you a great debt. Thank you."

"I believe it is I who should thank you; for I see now, you've been our faithful, anonymous donor here at Disibodenberg for these past ten years."

"And I will continue to give to those who value and cherish my only son. Volmar has found a home here at the monastery and you, more than I, have been his real father."

Abbot Burchard glowed with astonished pleasure. The words gave him an unbelievable sense of pride and accomplishment. "He is your son, my friend, and as you can see from the investigation, he possesses your passion for justice."

The Magistrate stared down at his plate. "I feel that perhaps my appetite is returning, how about yours?"

"Mine too, my friend," the Abbot answered, tucking a napkin under his chin. "Shall we bless our food and enjoy what little time we have left until the bells of Prime?"

Chapter 7: The Devil Prowls

Abbot's Personal Quarters at Disibodenberg Monastery

6th of November, Before Prime

There was a knock at the door. The Abbot frowned. "Wolfe, I believe Rudegerus has received our message. Enter," he announced louder still, drawing his napkin to his lap.

Brother Andres entered the private quarters of the Abbot. The two men were seated by the blazing fire, two silhouettes of black, with halos of golden light touching their outlines.

The Abbot rose. "Were you able to find Brother Rudegerus?"

Brother Andres shook his head as he approached the Abbot. "May I speak with you in private for a moment, Father?"

"Of course, please excuse us," the Abbot said, placing his napkin by his plate.

"Rudegerus is talking out of his mind, Father. He says that I should call him Balaam and told me he would pay for the donkey so that he may leave the monastery. I don't know what to make of it all."

"Where is he now?" the Abbot asked, glancing at the water clock which indicated that Prime would follow in less than three quarters of an hour.

"He's right outside, Father."

"Good. Please show him in, Brother Andres, and thank you for your concern."

The Abbot reached for another chair and pulled it to the table. This chair matched the others, with a heavily carved back and lion heads sleeping on the arm rests. "We have plenty to share with you, Rudegerus. Come join us in our modest meal and conversation."

"Father, I have sinned and am unworthy to be in your company." Brother Rudegerus hung back, his eyes wild and wide.

"I understand that your life has been threatened by an elderly man in the Sanctuary." The Abbot decided to take a direct approach. It would serve the investigation better, and time was of essence. There had already been too many words spoken around the issue of Matthias's death. Now they needed to speak frankly and to the point.

"Father, I have sinned. The Lord made it clear to Balaam when he spoke through a donkey of the seduction of greed. He who loved the wages of wickedness would be rebuked for his wrongdoing. God help me," Rudegerus pleaded, thumping his chest over and over.

The Magistrate interrupted, saying, "Brother Rudegerus, this greed you speak of, is it for a Holy Relic?"

"Father," the monk said, turning to his Abbot, "it is more sinister than that." Brother Rudegerus fidgeted, rubbing his hands together as if they were very cold and needed the warmth of contact.

The Abbot waited patiently, cutting from the platter the rooster's claw. In all his years as an Abbot, he'd learned it is better to listen more than talk. In silence, he served what he thought would be an indulgence to Brother Rudegerus.

The monk stared down at the claw on his plate. His face went deathly white. The Abbot sensed something had gone amiss. "Brother Rudegerus," the Abbot said, reaching for his arm. He looked across at the Magistrate, who shared his worried expression. "You do not look well."

Rudegerus finally spoke but in a voice barely audible. In his eyes the rooster's claw became animated and lunged forward at his throat. "Satan and his dominions have all been released from prison! I will not be poisoned as Matthias was! Leave me alone, you fiend!"

Rudegerus stood up. He stood menacingly over the table, lifted the platter and flung it into the burning flames. The sizzle of burning fowl sickened the air. In a mad fit he snatched the Magistrate's plate and the Abbot's plate and shattered them both across the iron grate. His eyes were blazing, his voice shrill. "In death how can a rooster still kill?" Suddenly he turned to the carved wooden chair he had been seated in. In his mind's eye he saw the lions' heads on the chair rear up and roar. Brother Rudegerus backed away, quoting Scripture. "Be self-controlled and alert. Your enemy the Devil prowls around like a roaring lion looking for someone to devour . . . "

The Abbot took hold of Brother Rudegerus's shoulders and hugged him fiercely, finishing the passage of Scripture in I Peter. "Resist him, standing firm in the faith. The God of all Grace will Himself restore you and make you strong."

Brother Rudegerus collapsed, sobbing. He crawled to the far corner where the shadows were the darkest, and curled into a ball. There, he rocked back and forth, in a state unreachable by human touch or voice.

Chapter 8: A Ghastly Revelation

Anchorage at Disibodenberg Monastery

6th of November, Before Prime

Hildegard bent over Jutta, humming a pleasant melody, hoping it would help lift her Anchoress' spirits as well as her own. She couldn't seem to get out of her mind an image of Volmar in the Infirmary, with Death sitting patiently at his feet. She'd seen Death's gaunt face a couple of times before, at Jutta's mother's and Uda's bedside, and now standing between earth and Heaven with a drawn sword in his hand, at Volmar's bedside. It was more alarming now, for it was not in keeping with the other glimpses of the future she had had of this young Scribe growing old beside her.

Jutta seemed to be responding to her ministrations. Her fever finally broke. Gently, she dabbed the sweat from Jutta's body. The fire Hiltrud had made warmed the common room. It had been wise for her and Hiltrud to move Jutta's bed beside the hearth that first night to take full advantage of its life-giving properties. Jutta had gone far too long without eating. Hildegard knew her despondency had something to do with the physiological effects of lack of nourishment, and wasn't only due to her long exposure to the cold. When she awoke, she would certainly be delirious and impossible to force-feed.

Try as she might to avoid it, Hildegard's mind kept coming back to Volmar. If her vision were true, a sudden death for Volmar would mean he was bound to die traumatically, before his time. She was overcome with guilt and anger. Was she the mistake, the reason, his timing was not in keeping with his true destiny? These fears plagued her as she prayed, "Enough, my Lord! Withdraw your hand. I beg of you, show mercy." She repeated this simple prayer in her mind over and over as the melody she hummed turn sad.

The melancholy tune brought tears to Hiltrud's eyes. The servant girl sat across the room, mending a monk's cassock. She was too distraught and was unable to return to bed, especially after Hildegard confirmed the fact that there had been two unexplained murders in the monastery. Hiltrud knew the only way to deal with it was to stay focused and busy.

Suddenly a man appeared in the doorway to the sleeping chamber. His silhouette cast a chilling shadow across the common room, and the air filled with the smell of evil. He was dressed in rags and wore a snow hood pulled down over his head, obscuring his face. Through the cutaway eye holes he glared into the room, taking in the presence of the three women.

Hiltrud saw him first. She looked up and screamed, pricking her finger on the needle. The sudden pain and the terror of seeing a stranger lurking in the Anchorage was too much. Overcome by fear, she slumped forward in her chair.

"Where is he?" the hooded man said, raising his cane menacingly. "I saw him come through the window and have waited long enough in the bitter cold for him to come out."

Hildegard shivered—ice entered her veins. She rose slowly and reached for the poker resting by the hearth behind her. She could wield it as a weapon if she had to. It was long and made of heavy iron, the tip definitely sharp.

A shape moved behind Hildegard, its voice familiar and warm. The Voice of the Living Light cautioned her. "Put it down," the Voice said gently. "Take instead the basin of water mingled with Jutta's sacrificial sweat over to the intruder."

Hildegard released her grip around the poker and instead took the basin and approached the man in the doorway. Although her eyes were open, she saw neither the stranger nor the common room she was in. She was having a vision, a waking dream, and if she could continue to concentrate on the Voice, she knew she would feel no fear.

"So the coward sends a mere girl to protect him?" the hooded man said, clearly amused. He drew off his face hood and tossed it over his shoulder. He would have been considered a handsome man had not his sins marred his face and turned his eyes into more those of an animal than a human. Deliberately, he withdrew his sword from his cane and leveled it at Hildegard. "Where is the Holy Relic, Sister? Show me and you will live."

Hildegard did not hear what he said. All she heard was the Voice telling her to repeat certain names. She did so dutifully, one after the other, in unison with the Voice: "Bayard of Bermersheim; Godfrey of Trier . . . "

The man froze. Fear suddenly crept into his eyes. "How do you know those people? They've been dead for years!"

Hildegard went on undeterred. "Sumner of Brauweiler; Amelia of Mainz; Letitia of Koblenz; Abul-Khayr; Khashram; Ishandiyar; Shadhan; Nafi'; Bashir; Yazid; Abu Idris; Hisham; Salih; Hamdun; Farqad; 'Umar; Kathir; Abul-Qasim; Rashid; Anas; Makhid . . . " The names went on and on, terrifying in their implication, for these were the names of all the innocent lives wronged or murdered by this one man.

The man tightened his grip on his sword and his own sensibilities. "One more word," he charged, vehemently, "and I will sever your tongue!"

Hildegard went on unrelentingly, " . . . Safwan son of 'Uthman; Dawud son of Masruq; Abu Yazid; Abul-Fath . . . "

Just as the man lunged forward, the sword's tip clearly aimed for Hildegard's mouth, the sword became so hot in his hand that it scalded his palm. The man threw down his sword, stunned.

Thankfully, Hildegard did not hear nor see what was happening to the man. She was submissive only to the words spoken to her from the Voice of the Living Light.

"Throw the water from the basin at his feet," the Voice continued softly, "and tell him thus: *Look evil in the eye, stare down the jaws of iniquity, swiftly burning at your feet. Fall on your knees and repent of your wickedness as Hell welcomes its own.*"

The water splashed from the basin onto the flagstone floor. In its puddle the man was given a vision. In it he saw a chasm beginning to form, a chasm with sharp pointed teeth and a tongue, rough and oozing blood, a monstrous yawning mouth opening into Hell. Mercifully, Hildegard was seeing with the Spirit's eyes and was standing in a blinding light that had taken root below her feet. Its radiance spread its warmth as a protective shield around her, so none of this hideous transformation was visible to her. She continued obediently to recite the names of the man's victims. " . . . Sulayman son of 'Umar; Thawr; Mahistî daughter of Suwayd; Jahân Khâtun daughter of Hamdun; Pâdshâh Khâtun daughter of Abu Idris . . . ."

The man alone witnessed this living, breathing nightmare. In it were the emotions of all he tortured. Although muted by time, they were still palpable, the pain and misery of far too many deaths. The horrors surrounded him.

A heavily cloaked companion rose up from the gaping mouth. Its misty tendrils reached upward, taking the shape of a long flowing cape. The cape of this netherworld creature fluttered, turning into black ravens with their bellies bearing the recognizable faces, not fully formed, looking diabolical, yet unmistakably of all those people the man had wronged or murdered. Now the names Hildegard had patiently recited had faces, grisly and gruesome, distorted by their own rage at the time of their injury or death. These human-faced birds swarmed around the man, pricking him with their sharp claws, taunting him with their moaning and bitter accusations.

"Leave me alone," the old man cried, his arms bleeding, his face filled with terror. He bent and retrieved his sword and with several clean swings, beheaded a few of these feathered tormentors. Their heads fell to the floor and rolled like dice into the stone crevices. To the man's horror these human-like birds grew new heads and mocked him more than before.

The dark, black-faced creature wrapped his winged cloak around the man, carrying him aloft into the flaming tongue of the netherworld. In its cavernous mouth the man witnessed many souls, not just the ones he'd sent to an early death, like black birds hovering over steaming waters, wailing and calling to him by name. All had black souls like his and were cut off from eternal light, consumed in the depths of their despair in this abyss for eternity.

"I am a gentleman and a monk!" the man screamed in protest, his face illuminated as if lit up from the inside by flashes of lightning.

The unearthly, golden-eyed companion seemed to find it all very amusing. *"You flatter yourself."*

"I've killed in the name of war. Why am I being persecuted?"

The cape of this netherworld creature fluttered, turning into black ravens with their bellies bearing the recognizable faces, not fully formed, looking diabolical, yet unmistakably of all those people the man had wronged or murdered.
GMD

The companion acknowledged the man's question, without speaking. *"This is the seat of Eternal Hatred, built from the stones of your disobedience, covetousness, greed, and anger. In your quest for power and fame, you've neglected and destroyed your family and even your friends."*

"Are you talking about Donato?" the man said, choking on the name. "Donato was weak. He wasn't up to the challenge before us. How could I be expected to share all the powers of the Holy Relic with him? The Holy Spear is my destiny, not his."

The companion nodded and continued to communicate without words, explaining to the man that there was more to see and that here for eternity one must suffer according to their crimes. It was to be a ghastly revelation.

"Come," the companion said, *"you cannot hide from the truth through arrogance."*

The man could not resist, though he longed to, the companion's invitation to accompany him on a tour of Hell.

"Enter the dismal chambers you've been building. As you see, there are many who share these chambers with you," the companion said, leading the man to the depths of his own stone fortress. In one, the cheaters were being gnawed on by a beast with no eyes; in another, the thieves were hung suspended by their feet, their bones broken and separated; and in the third, the wrathful were suffering from possession by demonic creatures, forcing them to commit humiliating and horrible acts.

At long last they came to the final chamber. The companion said, *"This one will be your residence."* In it, the man saw murderers being wounded by knives that moved about of their own will. *"Harken unto my words,"* the companion said this time without emotion. *"All were condemned by the judgment of God and hurled from the heights of his authority, forever."*

The man screamed in terror and forced open his own eyes. He saw before him the young nun he had threatened. She had collapsed to the floor, entirely spent.

"I will leave this place, before I am forced to surrender to its living Hell!" he said aloud, his voice shrill with indescribable fear.

Hildegard heard his movements but though her eyes were open, she could only see a screen of fog, blurring the intruder and his living nightmare.

"I am a gentleman and a monk!" the man screamed in protest, his face illuminated as if lit up from the inside by flashes of lightning.
GMD

Chapter 9: Hooded Inquisitors

Infirmary at Disibodenberg Monastery

6th of November, Before Prime

Volmar sat up in the bed, sipping a strengthening tonic of woundwort and Saint John's wort in wine, with a hint of poppy syrup added. He still felt dizzy and nauseous, but very much alive, to his own astonishment and relief.

"Come on, little brother, you must drink it all if you want to feel better," Brother Johannes said, tipping the cup until Volmar had finished every drop.

"You will live, my son. But don't you ever tempt Death like that again, do you understand?" Paulus took the cup from Johannes and sat it on the table nearby. His careful and sober judgment, though harsh, was reassuring. "With cyanide poisoning, as in all poisons, there is a considerable range of sensitivity among human individuals. Thankfully, you've been blessed with a strong constitution, or perhaps as I suspect it's your sheer stubbornness which has kept you alive. The dosage appears to have been insufficient to cause loss of consciousness, which surely would have led to your death, just as it did for Matthias."

Volmar lay back in bed and stared up at the high beam ceiling. "Sister Hildegard was right after all."

"What do you mean?" Johannes asked, sitting on the bed across from him. "Right, about what?"

"She told me this morning after Matins how Matthias's murderer was not human."

Johannes turned to Paulus. "Did you give him something to make him talk out of his mind?"

"He is as lucid as he normally is," Paulus said, smiling.

"What time is it?" Volmar said, slowly recalling the events following his meeting with Sister Hildegard. "Have I missed the bells for Prime?"

"Come now, surely the Abbot will understand you missing one of the offices," Paulus said. "After all, you have confirmed my suspicions about how Matthias died. I suspected poison only after finding Isabella distraught over her dead worms. If she hadn't awoken during the hours before daybreak and went looking for a new home for her worms, I would have been poisoned by Matthias's would when I went to clean it and prepare his body for burial. Thankfully, she saw the gaping wound on Matthias's calf and thought it a suitable home for her worms. Her actions kept me from experiencing what nearly killed you!"

Volmar stared at the candle on his bedside table, trying to focus his mind. "Will Isabella recover?"

"She is as well as can be expected; Isabella and Sophie are a great comfort to one another. Sophie is there with her now in the women's quarters. Our murderer is learned in the healing and deadly arts. Not many are aware of cyanide poison in peach pits, but the incident clarified in my mind that whatever weapon the murderer used was tainted with poison—cyanide poison."

The early morning's activities continued to come back to Volmar. "It was a claw spur. The weapon was a rooster's claw spur, dipped in cyanide; a fighting cock was brought in by the murderers and it is this inhuman creature which murdered Matthias."

Suddenly Johannes's face contorted in fear. "A rooster? Little brother, a rooster killed Matthias?"

"Yes. So confident in their scheme, the murderers were careless and left behind proof of their deed. I unearthed the silver claw spur in the compost pile behind the stables. It poisoned me and killed my cat Samson."

"We must hurry," Johannes said, standing and gripping Paulus's arm. "The Abbot and the Magistrate are to be served a special meal this morning of roasted capon. I'm afraid it is the same rooster; it was left at the cook's door during the night. It could still be poisonous!"

Brother Paulus reached for his medical bag and was at the door as Johannes helped Volmar back to his feet. "Go on, we'll catch up," Johannes said, helping Volmar slip on his boots. The only thing Volmar could think about was that his Abbot's life was in danger.

Brother Andres was napping on a small stool outside the Abbot's chambers when the three monks arrived. The change in everyone's schedule at the monastery was certainly being felt. "The Abbot asked me to sit here until he returns," he told them, stretching and yawning. "Rudegerus is acting strangely and apparently cannot be trusted. Brother Paulus, maybe you'll be able to help him."

"This is important, Brother Andres; did the Abbot say anything else?" Volmar asked.

"No. Nothing that I can recall. Oh wait, he did say that he and the Magistrate had to meet someone by the old well. That's right. When the bells chimed for Prime," he smiled as he stepped aside, content to have been of service. The three monks entered, their hearts beating wildly. The wood-paneled room was dark, lit only by the glow of embers still burning in the grate. Slowly their eyes began to adjust.

"What has happened in here?" Paulus said, resting his bag on the Abbot's desk, surveying the shattered plates and platter.

From the dismal recesses of the darkest corner, Rudegerus rose. His features were drawn and tired and aged him so much that he was barely recognizable.

"Brother Rudegerus—the Abbot and the Magistrate, what happened in here?" Volmar asked.

"I tried to confess to the Abbot," Rudegerus sputtered, making a real effort to speak coherently. "You see, I knew about the two knights," he said, catching Volmar's sleeve. "I recognized them that day you sparred with them outside the Infirmary. You must understand," he pleaded, holding his head as if it might leave him. "I overheard them planning, planning to kill a traveler in our care here at the monastery!" he blurted out. Still, Rudegerus was not above trying to rationalize his horrific actions. "But if I spoke to anyone about what I knew, then I would also have had to explain why I was in the village and worse, why I was at a cock fight."

"You overheard a plan to kill Matthias and did nothing?" Volmar said, incredulously.

"I did nothing." Brother Rudegerus shuddered, turning to each of his three brothers, who in his mind's eye had been transfigured into stern, hooded inquisitors of the Church's High Court. "I admit, I'm possessed by a demon of greed that thrives in the filthy alleyways of human waste and rot."

Volmar turned to face the fire, resting his arm on the mantel. "You overheard two men plotting to murder a returning knight from the Holy Land, a fellow brother, and did nothing?" All he could think about was how a man could knowingly allow another man to suffer a horrible death. Was such knowledge reason enough to make Rudegerus an accomplice to this murder?

"I spoke not a word, and now a man has died because of my silence." Rudegerus staggered and fell to his knees, thumping his chest.

Johannes took hold of the monk's trembling fists and held them still. His voice was calm and steady as he spoke. "Paulus, did you bring anything in that bag of yours that will help Rudegerus?"

Paulus retrieved from his medical bag a small flask of concentrated oils from the lemon balm leaves and showed Johannes how a few drops in a small handkerchief could be held under Rudegerus's nose; this would help calm him and bolster his depleted spirits.

The bells announcing Prime began to chime. Their clear resounding chorus reminded Volmar of his trap and urged him into action. "It's time."

"Go, you two," Johannes motioned, understanding the significance of the meeting at the well. "I will stay with our brother and see that he returns to his cell safely."

Paulus reached for his bag and then, taking Volmar's arm, the two hurried off towards the stables.

Chapter 10: Rising Light of Dawn

Clearing by the Well at Disibodenberg Monastery

6th of November, Prime

The thicket of trees was dark and foreboding, black against the surrounding whiteness of snow. For a fleeting moment, Volmar thought they resembled the upturned hairy tentacles of a dead spider. Thankfully, it had finally stopped snowing. The sky was tinged with the awakening sunlight. Volmar welcomed its warmth against the numbing cold.

By the time the two monks reached the stone path leading from the compost pile to the well, they could feel something had gone terribly wrong.

A voice cut clean through the cold like a steel knife. "Stand back or the Abbot dies!"

"There's trouble," Paulus murmured, tightening his grip on Volmar's arm. The two hurriedly left the path, circling wide around the clearing to get a better view of what was happening. Their lumbering steps sunk deep into the untouched snow and their breath rose like smoke. Volmar wondered, how could Hell be so close?

In the clearing, Wolfe took a step forward, his hands open, in a gesture of supplication. "Let him go, Ulrich, for God's sake, let him go!"

Ulrich laughed. "There's no use appealing to God, for He never listens. Why should He? Are we not to Him mere sheep, bleating in this snowy wilderness?"

"Good, very good. See how they tremble at the truth?" the golden-eyed companion wrapped in his winged cloak leaned into Ulrich's ear and muttered.

Ulrich turned with fury to the voice whispering in his ear. "This is my bargain, not yours, evil spirit! I alone will take the Abbot's life, if I deem it necessary. You will have nothing of it, understand?"

Wolfe moved another step towards him. "Ulrich, what do you mean? Who are you talking to?"

"Go on," the dark companion said mockingly. *"Tell Wolfe that we know of his role in this conspiracy. His innocent posturing is hypocritical. Ask him if he would be as popular with these people if they knew of his adulterous affair with your wife? Go on, ask him."*

Ulrich turned to the demon clinging to him from the depths of Hell. "I will not argue my past with the likes of you," he barked.

The silence that followed was deafening. Volmar held his back stiff against the rough bark of the tree and listened, sensing the rising fear and stark madness. The Magistrate's soldiers were in a circle, their swords drawn, yet powerless against the hooded assailant who held a sword hovering menacingly against the Abbot's bare throat.

Volmar knew the assailant burned with a rage incited by this unexpected trap. He'd come for the Holy Relic but did not expect company. Now, it seemed he was haunted as well. Volmar tensed with icy dread and silently said five *Pater Nosters.*[94]

The Magistrate stood in front of the old soldier, his voice calm amid the terror. "Ulrich, do you really want to have more blood on your hands? Put the sword down and let the Abbot go."

---

[94] *Pater Nosters*: Latin for "Our Father" used in liturgical daily prayers.

"Call your men off first!" Ulrich shouted, nodding to the group of soldiers with their swords already drawn. He backed away slowly, stumbling on one of the upraised roots of a tree hidden by the snow. This was enough for the sword's blade to graze the Abbot's throat. Blood oozed from the wound.

The Abbot raised his hand to stop the Magistrate from rushing forward. "I'm fine, Wolfe," he said, his voice unwavering. "Please, don't risk your own life for mine."

Ulrich steadied his grip on the Abbot, jerking the Abbot's head even further back by grabbing his thinning hair. "You heard him. Let me leave in peace with the Holy Relic and the Abbot's life will be spared." Then, once again, Ulrich turned his head to talk to his deathly companion. "You think you can trick me into giving you the relic? By God's blood, I will fight even you!"

Volmar risked peering out from behind his tree. Ulrich was still wearing his snow mask, which hampered his peripheral vision. Maybe, Volmar reasoned, there is a way out of this stalemate. He studied the tree's branches overhead, noting the ones which leaned out over the clearing. The young scribe then met Brother Paulus's gaze and communicated to him a plan. All those years of hand signaling now proved invaluable. The two communicated wordlessly, each fully aware of the grim consequences should their plan fail.

Paulus made a wide circle around to the stump where Ulrich's warhorse was tethered and snorting impatiently, waiting for his master's escape. The Infirmarian loosened the horse's reins and watched with increasing confidence as Volmar shimmied his way up into the canopy of the slumbering apple tree.

Instinctively, Volmar was confident of his ability to move through the branches, yet wary of his prey below. When he brushed back the snow to move into position, he realized too late his misjudgment.

Abbot Burchard's head was tilted upward. He also saw at that moment that the snowstorm had damaged the branch his young Scribe was inching silently across. Horror knotted up in his throat as the branch released a loud groan before splitting and cracking. At that same instant, Paulus let out a piercing yell, which frightened Ulrich's horse and sent it galloping down the hillside.

In the confusion that followed, Ulrich swung around like a scorpion with his sword ready to fight, just as both the branch and Volmar fell, smashing the old soldier on his shoulder and causing his hand to release his sword. Volmar flung himself directly from the falling tree branch onto Ulrich's back and wrestled him to the ground. The sword was kicked from Ulrich's lunging hand in the last instant by the Magistrate himself, who leaped upon the two of them in their struggle.

Paulus rushed over to the Abbot, whom he led aside, drawing a clean linen cloth from his bag to bandage the nasty cut on his neck. Fortunately, it had missed Burchard's major artery by no more than the width of a single hair.

In no time, the soldiers wrapped heavy chains around Ulrich's neck and ankles. The Magistrate leaned forward and at last pulled off the mask. He gasped at the face sneering up at him. "Symon?"

Volmar turned to the Magistrate, then to Ulrich. "This man is Symon of Bermersheim?" he asked, his heart sinking.

"I am mistaken, son," the Magistrate muttered, turning away. "This is not the man I once knew." The same wooden cart which only a few hours earlier had held the wrapped corpses of Matthias and Donato was rolled out of the woods and into the clearing. "Load him up," the Magistrate called to his men. "We've found our murderer."

A few moments later, Volmar walked around the cart to the side where the assailant sat motionless, staring straight ahead, a sense of strength still emanating from him, despite his defeat. Volmar spoke aloud, emotion giving his voice a sense of unexpected harshness. "Show me your ring!"

The man smiled; his teeth were heavily stained from the exotic teas of the Middle East. "What is it to you?" he barked.

Volmar steeled himself before repeating, "Show me your ring!"

Something in the young monk's penetrating gaze made the prisoner uncomfortable. "My family's crest is of no consequence to a man of God."

"It is of considerable consequence to this young monk. This is Volmar, Katherina's son," the Magistrate said, standing beside the young Scribe.

"So it is true, I was not dreaming you up."

"Brother Volmar set this trap, Symon. Show him your ring or I will cut it off of your finger and show him myself." To make clear his threat, the Magistrate pulled a knife from a sheath on his belt and held it in the rising light of dawn.

Symon finally relented. He lifted his hand and flashed his signet ring so all who had grown silent around them could see and bear witness to the shame of the once powerful crest of the family Bermersheim and how it had been brought to its knees. By now, the crowd of onlookers had grown. Wolfe's men and the villagers watched in stunned silence, shoulder to shoulder.

"Ah, he'll be a free man by night's end," one of the villagers said to another. "Murderer or not, there's money, influence and family history behind that name."

An older man answered knowingly, "Could have told ya, when one forgets yer heritage, the lives of others become meaningless."

The Magistrate took a moment to marshal his own thoughts before turning to address everyone present in a clear, authoritative voice. "Symon of Bermersheim has willfully killed three men in my jurisdiction and threatened the life of our beloved Abbot. My friends, there will be no buying of immunities or privileges from this Magistrate."

"Then, it is true. You are my father," Volmar said in quiet disbelief.

Symon's rueful smile dissolved into a grimace. There was a long moment of silence.

"It is a simple question and I deserve an honest answer. Are you not my father?" Volmar was sickened by this man and all he stood for.

Symon stared straight ahead, the neck iron biting into his throat. "You want honesty? Then I will give you the God-forsaken truth. You, Scribe, are not kin to me."

"Why do you persist with these lies? You are a man of God, a Knight of Jerusalem, of the order of the Hospitaller of Saint John, are you not?"

Symon turned to the Magistrate. Their eyes met, and what passed between them was left unspoken but deeply felt. Symon continued, with less audacity, less arrogance, as he returned his gaze to Volmar. "I am a man who, like so many before me, mislaid my trust in a woman. Your mother, however, did not love me; so I forced her to."

Volmar turned to the Magistrate, then back to Symon. "How can that be?" he said in a low voice. "You were married to my mother and left her when you went to fight in the Holy Land. All of these years, I have waited for your return. Waited to tell you that I am your son, I did not die of the fever, I still lived."

"Look, I was her husband, not her lover." Symon laughed out loud—a harsh, cruel laughter that held no mirth. He stood, grasping the edge of the wooden cart with much difficulty. The cuts from the tree branch were bleeding freely and staining the rags he wore. "I, Symon of Bermersheim, have no family, no heirs, and likely no heavenly chance at eternity." He glared down at Volmar. "Fear not, holy brother, your seed is not poisoned by my evil deeds. Remember this . . . you cannot forcibly take what is not yours, not a thousand-year-old Holy Relic and certainly not the love of a woman. Your mother betrayed me, for I gave her no other choice. She refused to love a man unworthy of her affection or respect. I know now you cannot change a person by simply forcing your will upon them."

No one saw under the folds of his ragged cloak the small vial Symon held in his hand. He spat at the ground and in a gesture to wipe clean his lips, he instead raised the vial and drank from it. Still in his hand, he made a cynical gesture, toasting sarcastically the demonic companion staring at him from the end of the cart. "To Death," he said, nodding to his ghastly companion, "and all of its lost, embittered souls," he added with a sweeping motion, acknowledging the beady black eyes of his accusers, ravens of untold numbers which had suddenly gathered and perched on the gnarled trees surrounding him. "At least," he added, "I'll be amongst my own kind."

"Stop him!" Wolfe shouted, but his warning had come too late.

Symon sputtered, coughing up phlegm and wheezing painfully. "Rest assured," he croaked defiantly, "I'm prepared to kill my enemies all over again, this time in the legions of Hell." He collapsed. The vial he had stealthily put to his lips fell from his hand and rolled to the front of the cart. The scent of almonds filled the air, as it suddenly got colder.

A dark heavy mist passed before them like a veil. The Magistrate squeezed Volmar's weary shoulder.

"Justice has finally been served."

Chapter II: A Violent Wind

Clearing Outside of Disibodenberg Monastery

6th of November, After Terce

As the comforting bells announced the end of prayers of Terce that same day, Volmar came upon Brother Rudegerus packing up a donkey in the clearing not far from the underground tunnel's entrance. He had been searching all over the monastery for Rudegerus after Brother Paulus informed him that he had disappeared from the Infirmary.

"Remember the proverb, Brother Volmar? 'A man tormented by the guilt of murder will be a fugitive till death; let no one support him.'"

"Where will you go?"

"I will manage," Rudegerus said, shedding his monk's cassock and revealing the more humble clothes of a poor peasant underneath. It was the same disguise Sophie had seen, mistaking him for Saint Peter over a year ago. He removed his crucifix and kissed it before handing it over to Volmar. A simple wool cap disguised his tonsure and a wrap of animal skins for warmth completed the transformation. A heavy chest, the one Volmar had come across in the underground chamber, weighed upon the back of his donkey.

"Coins won from cock fights, Brother Rudegerus?" Volmar asked.

"I am no longer Brother Rudegerus. My name is Balaam."

Brother Volmar frowned. "History repeats itself, does it not, Brother? From Judas to Rudegerus and now to Balaam. Changing your name does not remove you from the crime. Many young novitiates change their name when they take their vows, such as Symon to Ulrich and Judas to Rudegerus."

"Such arcane traditions do serve a purpose."

"Your name may be different, but you are still guilty of two brothers' murders, those of Brother Arnoul and Brother Matthias."

Balaam answered defensively, his voice suddenly shaking. "You have no proof, no proof whatsoever. Brother Arnoul attacked me for no reason. He was the thief, not me. He's the one who gave me this crooked nose and stole that priceless book from the library."

"I would be more careful with your tongue, if I were you. Your accuser is here." A heavy fog had gathered, twisting and writhing in a violent wind around the snow-laden branches of the formidable yew tree. A moaning came from its emptiness.

"Surely you jest," Balaam sneered.

The cold pale sun of the winter morning peeked through the branches, illuminating the clearing with its eerie light. From the thickening fog, a fine white mist arose and embodied a shape seen only by Balaam—a man he recognized as Brother Arnoul.

"Brother Arnoul's spirit is watching our exchange. You will have no peace on Earth until you have peace with God." Volmar hung back, as the distinctive odor of death rose from the mist. This time it not only smelled of decay, but of a long-nursed resentment.

Balaam reached for his knife and held it out, twisting and turning in every direction, anxiously attempting to defend himself against the approach of this vengeful spirit. Arnoul's face was veined and pale. Balaam addressed him frantically. "Leave me in peace, you shadow of the Devil!"

Volmar could've sworn he heard a voice answer Balaam back; of course, unbelievers would say it was only the wind.

Balaam suddenly clutched his throat, feeling cold, icy hands wrap around it. He was then forced to his knees by an unseen force. He struggled; someone or something was strangling him. He stabbed at the space where the spirit was, to no avail. A fearless voice whispered in Balaam's ears, a voice recognizable from his distant past and one he'd been trying to forget all these years. "You lie. It was you who stole the book, not I. Give it back!"

Volmar watched from the protruding roots of the old yew tree, knowing full well the boundaries of this spirit's revenge and wanting to be sure Balaam did not escape this time.

Suddenly Balaam was on his knees, gasping for air, his own knife turned and held against his own throat. His knees were covered in blood, as the sharp rocks ripped through his trousers and his skin. Balaam began to sob—a pitiful, ugly sound. He rose and staggered towards his donkey, as freezing fingers threw his knife to the ground. With much effort, Balaam took a wrapped parcel from his leather pack, tore away its humble wrapping, and revealed the priceless stolen book. He then lifted the trunk of gold coins from his donkey and set it in front of the young Scribe along with the book. In that instant, Arnoul's grim features began to dissolve. The flesh around his shadowy eyes drooped, the bones of his cheeks fell as his expression revealed a glimpse of satisfaction.

Slowly, Balaam's breathing returned to normal. Volmar caught the weight of his body and helped him up onto his donkey. Dispirited, Balaam sat upright, rubbing his neck and wiping the tears from his cheeks before whispering, "Pray for me, Brother Volmar."

Volmar nodded and remained for a long time watching as Balaam and his donkey faded into a distant speck on the snow-covered road below.

Abbot Burchard crested the hill, still breathing hard. He approached Volmar, shielding his eyes from the snowy whiteness of the fields beyond. There, with his young scribe, he watched the small black figure of their disgraced brother disappear into the distance.

"Father, I believe you'll find that this book was stolen from the Library over ten years ago by Brother Rudegerus. Another monk, Brother Arnoul, was accused of thievery and died tragically trying to protect his good name. Cormac will be pleased to see it."

"I see," the Abbot said, patting the book with a look of satisfaction. "Rudegerus stole the fake relic, too, you know."

"I know. I saw it tucked under his belt." Volmar paused. "Isn't it ironic, Father, how one so devious has, himself, been deceived?"

Afterword

Volmar scooted the milking stool up to the leather flap over the window opening outside the Anchorage and sat down on it. He listened quietly so as not to disturb the musician, nor her music drifting out into the cold late afternoon. He had much to ponder. In the end, the Spear of Destiny had brought Symon of Bermersheim back to face the past he had loathed and run from all those years ago, and had given Volmar a glimpse into his own murky past. He might never know who his real father is, he thought, in the aftermath of the shocking revelations of the morning. But, he'd lived this long without knowing—at least, he thought with an air of cynicism, his illegitimacy assured him that he was not contaminated by Symon's wicked nature.

In a little while, Volmar reminded himself, he would give Sister Hildegard a letter he'd written using her secret alphabet. In it, he apologized to her for his unseemly behavior. He winced over the memory of his pathetic attempts to convince Hildegard to renounce her vows. Symon had been right about one thing. Love cannot be forced. Life was certainly more complicated since she had danced her way into his heart. He also wrote to her all about Symon of Bermersheim's arrest, Katherina's disdain, and the knight's relentless quest for the Holy Spear of Longinus.

For the moment, the monastery rested, understandably exhausted from the ordeal of the past few hours. Fresh snow gave it a serene atmosphere. The world around him seemed crisper and whiter than ever. There was no other sound save the melodic notes of Hildegard's lyrical music.

The Magistrate had already left with his entourage, obligated by law to return Symon's body to his family's estate in Bermersheim. Rumor had it that he and his men would be back in a few days for Donato's remains, which were to be returned to the knight's home village outside of Florence, accompanied by an official letter to the Pope concerning their crimes. They might never know for certain if the two knights had been acting entirely on their own or if they had been a part of a larger conspiracy and were simply following orders from their powerful leader, Brother Gerard.

As was customary, two of the three bodies remaining, Atif and Matthias, were to be laid in state in the church for three days. Their coffins were surrounded by a blaze of candles. One by one, the holy brothers were to take turns sitting in watch, keeping a holy vigil and praying for their souls. Curious townspeople and peasants from the surrounding villages were already filing into the nave, despite the wretched cold. Whispers of beleaguered fallen knights, a foreigner, and their deadly quest for the Holiest of Relics, the Spear of Destiny could not be silenced. There had been too many witnesses. Volmar sighed. Whether or not they were prepared, rumors would spread . . . of how the monastery of Disibodenberg possessed the most elusive and arguably one of the most valued of all Holy Relics . . . the Spear of Destiny. Yet, over time, even these rumors would subside.

Volmar recalled the time he had spent the rest of the morning taking dictation for the letter to the High Court in the Church, Pope Paschal II. Given the complexities of the current political climate and the allegations Matthias had made of the Holy See's corruption, this letter had to be carefully edited. As the monastery's chronicler, he was beginning to understand that recording history, like most things in life, was a subjective, compromising affair.

In this letter, the Abbot requested the Pope's permission to exhume the body of one French traveling monk to re-inter his remains in the monks' consecrated cemetery. Volmar heaved a sigh. At least, justice had prevailed here. Brother Arnoul's spirit would at last find peace. The Abbot had also informed the Pope that Matthias, a travelling knight, would be buried in consecrated ground in the monks' cemetery, his death having been sufficiently cleared of any suspicions of suicide. He would be the first Knight of the Hospitaller of Saint John to be buried in Disibodenberg's cemetery, and his headstone would glorify his sacrifice for Christendom. Atif's remains, too, were mentioned in the letter. He was to be buried next to his old friend and mentor. Sophie, on hearing the full story from Brother Paulus, insisted on a suitable epitaph for Atif's headstone: "A Good Samaritan." The Abbot had given her his approval.

"Father," Volmar had asked. "Do you doubt the relic's authenticity?"

"My son, I have prayed all morning for guidance. It is such an unpredictable, frightening world. I can understand how having a tangible, powerful relic to protect you in such volatile times could serve an important purpose."

"You still haven't answered my question."

"I know. Because I do not have all the answers. Perhaps one of our biggest obstacles in this life is how we cling to our perceptions and believe they are the truth. Faith and the truth about this relic's power lie beyond our human intellect, our senses and sensibilities. Spirituality is an active journey full of mystery, and certainty has little to do with it." It was a deep conversation with talk about divine purpose taking precedence over spectacle and greed. In the end, the Abbot decided that not a word of the relic was to be mentioned in the letter to the Pope.

Thinking back on the Abbot's decision, Volmar realized it was equally important to Burchard that he keep his word. Matthias had entrusted *him* with the relic, not the Pope. The knight had made the ultimate sacrifice to bring the relic to Disibodenberg. Ultimately, the Abbot had reasoned to his young scribe, the church was to offer a spiritual sanctuary to all those who entered its high walls, not promises of earthly rewards. It was then the Abbot made clear his plan. He had quietly retrieved Matthias's Holy Relic from the Anchorage and now wanted Volmar to help him tie it onto the handle of Brother Hugo's spade. While everyone was sleeping the two had solemnly made their way through the deep snow, over to the stables, and there, in the adjoining tack room, fixed together with leather twine one symbol of God's omnipotence to another symbol of Adam's curse, as foretold in the book of Genesis. [95]

"In this way, the relic will be in humble service to all," the Abbot had concluded. "No longer will its powers be used by a few men to selfishly assert control over others; rather, it will modestly till the soil,

---

[95] Adam's Curse: "And to the man He said, 'Because you have listened to the voice of your wife you have eaten of the tree about which I commanded you, saying, you shall not eat from it, cursed shall be the ground because of you; in sorrow you shall eat of it all the days of your life. And thorns and thistles it shall bring forth for you, and you shall eat the plant of the field. By the sweat of your face you shall eat bread until you return to the ground; for out of it you have been taken; for dust you are, and to dust you shall return.'" (Genesis 3:17-19)

planting seeds of life and hope for the community of Disibodenberg. A higher purpose of work and prayer, the true dictates of the Benedictine Rule."

Perhaps they were living out a pre-ordained script, as that old crone had prophesized to him last week. Could Disibodenberg, a modest, backwoods monastery, be on the cusp of tremendous changes? Abbot Burchard had certainly been wrong about one thing, Volmar mused, all those years ago. All the mystery, intrigue, and romance he could ever yearn for was here, within the porous walls of Disibodenberg.

The young Scribe leaned back against the jagged stone wall. He shut his eyes, enjoying the comfort of Sister Hildegard's music. It was a rare moment when he could truly feel the breathlessness of eternity.

Historical Note

History is full of prejudices, for it is told and retold from the eyes of the victors and the powerful. One cannot read it without being aware that it is riddled with interpretations from those who are determined to "set the record straight." So, from our viewpoint here in the 21st century, writing convincingly about a 12th century monastery and what people of that time actually thought and did cannot be done in a totally objective manner. Nevertheless, I have sought to remain as close as possible to the primary source material in framing this tale.

The First Crusade of 1098 A.D. was like most wars. It was fought for a variety of reasons, not just for Christians to take back Jerusalem from the Muslims. Lesser nobles who volunteered for the Pope's call to arms did so with their own personal agendas, which included bloody raids on holy shrines for priceless relics and treasures.

Even the respectable Knights of Saint John, the Crusading Order of Hospitaller in Jerusalem, had their own dual intentions. On the one hand, they were holy men who ministered to the sick and wounded in hospitals for the pilgrims and military orders fighting in the Holy Land. And they also took up the sword, participating fully in the mass slaughter and enslavement of Muslims and Christian Arabs. For them, a religiously motivated war held no contradictions. It was interpreted as being lawful and righteous, an act of love. For to defend the Holy Land was in their eyes a form of Christian charity.

It is true that Brother Gerard is credited with being the founding father of the Knights Hospitaller, the military order's first master. It was his ambition to spread the crusading order's wealth and influence throughout the Mediterranean region. Whether he saw the potential to accumulate all of the powerful relics, holy writings, and treasures to establish his own authority over the church, as did the Knights Templar formed later in 1118 A.D., is purely a fictional construct for this novel, as are all the murders.

The story of Matthias finding the Spear of Destiny in the church in Antioch on the 10th day of June in 1098 A.D. does in fact follow the legend associated with the Holy Relic revered today in Echmiadzin, Armenia. In this story, Matthias recounts how the relic had turned him from a mediocre knight into an impressive leader. This too follows the legend. Throughout the centuries, Longinus's Spear has been revered as a potent relic believed to grant whomever possesses it the power to control the world—and losing it is said to bring immediate death.

In the 20th century, Hitler sought this relic during his reign of terror and committed suicide the day the Americans seized it from Nuremberg, thus fulfilling the legend. Today, three other spears claim to be this cursed relic. One is at the Vatican, in Rome; another is in Krakow, Poland; and the third resides at the Hofburg Treasury House in Vienna, Austria, where I have seen it on display.

The scenes in *Spear of Destiny* that describe political turmoil between the church and the Emperor are accurate as well. Not only did King Henry the Fifth arrest the Archbishop of Mainz in October of 1112 AD, he also publicly went back on his promises to the Pope in an attempt to assert his power over the Church.

All of this turmoil shaped the world Hildegard and Volmar lived in and puzzled over. Subject to the Benedictine Rule, the two promised to live out their lives in observance of poverty, chastity, and obedience. Such radical devotion seems alien to many of us today who are accustomed to services held once a week on the Sabbath. The Rule of St. Benedict was followed faithfully by the monks and nuns of Disibodenberg. They went to bed after the service of Compline and rose for the early morning service of Matins, sleeping, working, and eating in strict adherence to the structure and rituals signaled by the ringing of the monastery's bells.

History records Jutta's enclosure with Hildegard on the eve of All Saints' Day in 1112. As the Anchoress at Disibodenberg, chroniclers report that Jutta had a great following and was an extreme ascetic, adhering to a regime of fasting and self-mutilation to strengthen her faith.

The chronicler Guibert gives us only a brief description of the personality of Volmar, Hildegard's monk collaborator. Volmar, he writes, was sober, chaste, and learned, concluding that he had the temperament of a typical monk. Upon reflection, I disagreed with this footnote in history, finding in Volmar's devotion to Hildegard an altogether different character, extraordinary for his time, for women were held almost in contempt by the church due to the doctrine of Eve's temptation of Adam in the Garden of Eden. For Volmar to courageously teach and nurture one woman's mind signifies to me a progressive free-thinker.

Of course, if Hildegard had chosen a more traditional calling, marrying and bearing children, she would not have had the opportunities or the time to develop her gifts. So, as cruel as her early life may seem to our modern sensibilities, it afforded Hildegard the means to write several major works in theology, which she completed later in her life.

Her accomplishments do not end there. She is credited with many firsts, having composed a musical play and more than seventy songs. She consulted and advised bishops, popes, and kings, and she openly denounced the corruption in the church and preached publicly well into her seventies. She went on to establish two abbeys and used her curative powers for healing, writing books on natural history and the medicinal uses of various plants, animals, trees, and stones.

Spear of Destiny attempts to fill the gaps where history is silent. To me, Providence had a hand in the story from the beginning, bringing together these two wards of the church, creating a rare moment of light and hope in an era renowned for its darkness and quiet desperation, a legacy far greater than either of their individual voices—one we need to remember.

Monastery of
Disibodenberg
Kingdom of
France
Macedonia
Rome
Athens
Sicily
Mediterranean Sea
Malta
Libya
Alexandria

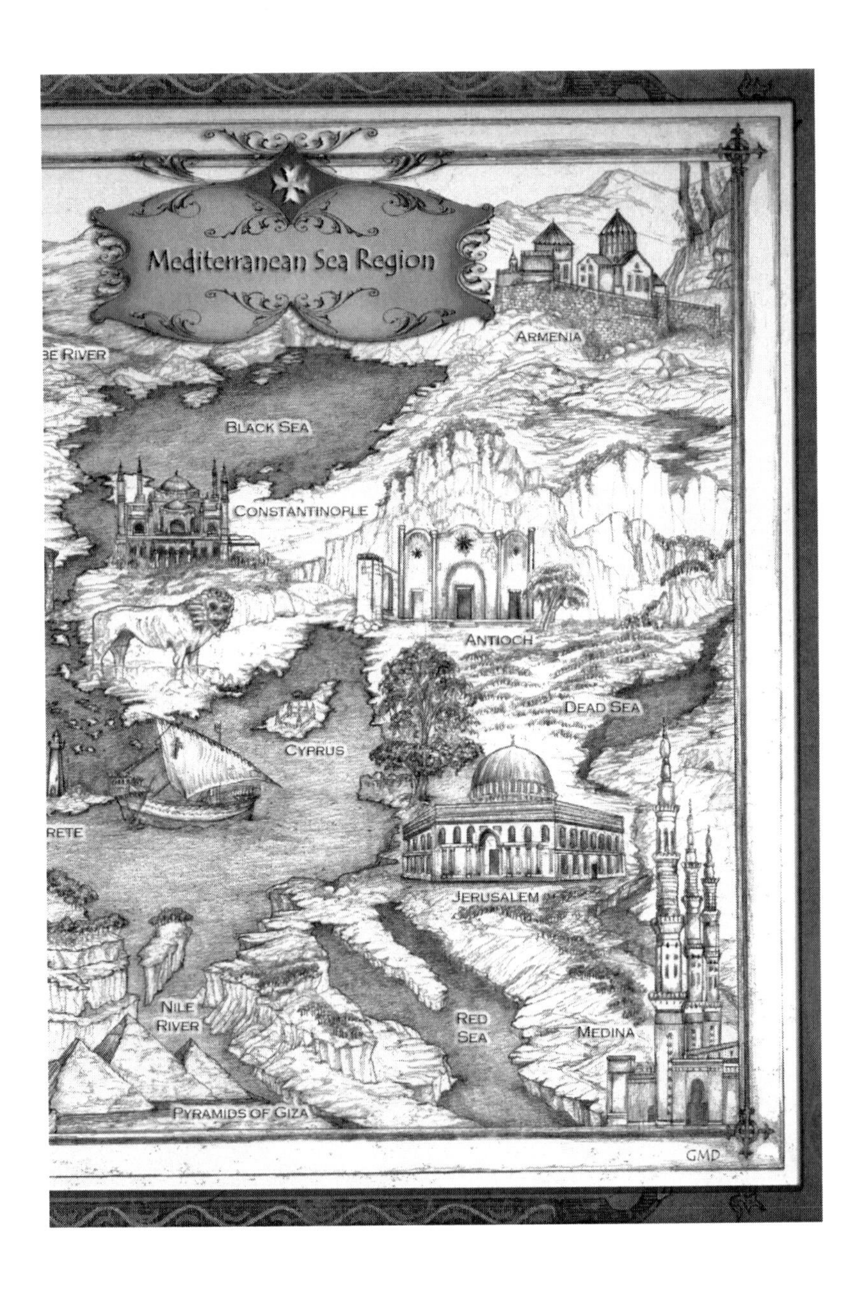
Mediterranean Sea Region
ARMENIA
BE RIVER
BLACK SEA
CONSTANTINOPLE
ANTIOCH
DEAD SEA
CYPRUS
RETE
JERUSALEM
NILE
RIVER
RED
SEA
MEDINA
PYRAMIDS OF GIZA
GMD

About the Author

G.M. Dyrek was born in New Orleans, Louisiana and has lived in over 30 addresses. Her father was a preacher then an Air Force chaplain. Along with her four brothers and mother, who was a missionary's daughter from Southern Rhodesia, she spent most of her growing up years traveling, adjusting to new schools, different cultures, and the usual chaos at home, while dreaming of living in a castle or aboard the Starship Enterprise.

She holds a degree in psychology and two masters degrees, one in psychology and one in library media education. As an adult, with each move, she declared a new career, ranging from an emergency room counselor to a graphic illustrator for the CIA. Her current position as the librarian at a middle school for 1,200 students allows her to indulge her love of children's literature and provides her with the perfect audience for her novels.

G.M. Dyrek's son was born in Asia, spent his youth in Central America, came of age in Europe and now attends college. She lives contentedly with her husband, her son, and a fat grey kitty named Hildegard ("Hildy") on three wooded acres in Tennessee, in a home fondly christened, "Traveller's Rest," where she is currently working on Book Two of *The Seer and the Scribe* series, titled *Methuselah's Secret.*

Visit G.M. Dyrek online at www.gmdyrek.com. Discussion questions for *Spear of Destiny* are available online at www.luminisbooks.com.